NEW DAY

T0388892

ALSO BY V.S. REID

The Leopard
Sixty-Five
The Young Warriors
Peter of Mount Ephraim
The Jamaicans
Nanny-Town
The Horses of the Morning: A Life of Norman Washington Manley

NEW DAY

V.S. REID

INTRODUCTION BY

JEREMY POYNTING

PEEPAL TREE

First published in the USA in 1949
by Alfred A. Knopf
This new edition published in 2016
Peepal Tree Press Ltd
17 King's Avenue
Leeds LS6 1QS
England

Copyright © 1949, 2016 Mr Peter Reid
for the estate of V.S. Reid
Introduction © 2016 Jeremy Poynting

ISBN13: 9781845230906

All rights reserved
No part of this publication may be
reproduced or transmitted in any form
without permission

Supported by
ARTS COUNCIL
ENGLAND

CONTENTS

Introduction   7

Author's Note   47

Part One   49

Part Two   199

Part Three   257

Glossary   357

To Robert Herring, Bryher, Frederic Wakeman, Bob Lightbourne, Norman Manley, Phyllis Bottome, and all those others who helped, I offer a hearty *thankie*.

And to all these and

TO MY WIFE

I dedicate this book.

JEREMY POYNTING

NEW DAY, EPIC OF JAMAICA

1. Reputation: New Day Over 67 Years

This is the third appearance of *New Day* since 1949. At its first publication, Philip Sherlock found "Beauty and inspiration".[1] Two decades later, Kenneth Ramchand's The *West Indian Novel and its Background* (1970) established its status as a pioneering text in the West Indian canon as a novel that forged a language of narration that was significantly Caribbean in tone.[2] It was reissued in the Heinemann Caribbean Writers series in 1973, with an introduction by Mervyn Morris that reminds us that it is Reid's character, Johnny Campbell, and not Reid who narrates the events of the novel, and that Campbell has a point of view related to his colour, class and age.[3] A decade later Neville Dawes offered the best case for *New Day* as a Jamaican epic, despite its ideological flaws, about which, from a Marxist perspective, he is sharply and wittily disparaging. He regarded *New Day* as self-deceiving in treating 1944 as a real break with the past,[4] a view also expressed in Sylvia Wynter's "Novel and History, Plot and Planta-tion".[5] Dawes locates *New Day*'s claim to be a national epic in its sensual celebration of the Jamaican natural world, and of ways of seeing embedded in Jamaica's language. As George Lamming's char-acter Mark Kennedy declares, nation is about "the private feeling you experience *of possessing and being possessed by* the whole landscape of the place where you were born",[6] and Reid, Dawes suggests, creates that "whole landscape" and celebrates it as a resource for all races, all classes – however unequal their access. More recently, though, Victor Chang wants to sweep *New Day* from its position of respect in the Caribbean canon, on the grounds that "it was a novel of its time, filled with idealism and dream but now it seems antiquarian and dated".[7]

New Day is a flawed novel, and in some respects a novel of its time, limited by its masculinism, its social conservatism and failure to reflect the political and cultural existence of the black majority, but it is also an ambitious novel with a living core. It has been read primarily as a work of historical and political fiction – inevitably since this was how it was presented – but this has diverted attention from what is most achieved in the novel. Rather than as a narrative primarily *about* the Morant Bay rebellion, *about* Davie Campbell's commune and Garth

Campbell's performance as a politician, what is most enduring in *New Day* is found by a reading that adjusts the focus: this is not just the story *told* by John Campbell, but the story the book tells *about* John Campbell and his changing ways of seeing the world. This narrative tracks a tragic loss of vision, whose trajectory cannot be other than downhill, as the intensity of Campbell's childhood experience fades into a dull and comfortable middle age and an old age lived vicariously. This is more than an echo of Wordsworth's perception that with childhood "hath passed away a glory from the earth". There is a coarsening of his sensibilities – most manifest in his treatment of Lucille – that runs parallel to his increasing reluctance to question his perspective as a near-white man of wealth. This narrative runs counter to the novel's overt upward trajectory from defeat in 1865 to victory in 1944, and it raises doubts about Reid's reputed acquiescence in the bourgeois nationalist agenda.

The intensity of Campbell's childhood comes from the novel's concentration on the human body and its connections with the animate and inanimate worlds of nature. The young Campbell not only feels *in* his body but thinks *with* his body and deduces the thoughts and feelings of others in that way. In this focus, *New Day* expresses a vision of ecological possibility for the human place in the natural world and how it may be lost. It anticipates recent work in embodied naturalist philosophy and cognitive science,[8] and the turn towards the body in contemporary literary and cultural criticism.[9]

New Day is also ambitious in a hitherto unrecognised way as being almost certainly the first Anglophone Caribbean novel to engage intertextually with the legacy of the ancient and established classics – Virgil's *Aeneid* and Milton's *Paradise Lost* – relationships seeking epic resonances that have mixed consequences for the novel.

2. What Happens in New Day

John Campbell's narrative begins in 1944 when, as an old man, on the eve of a new Jamaican constitution, he reflects on his life.

Part One, when he is eight, focuses on the consequences of the 1865 Morant Bay rebellion for his near-white family, whose relative prosperity keeps them from the sufferings of the people of Stoney Gut. It deals with the conflict between his father, Pa John, a pious Anglican who disapproves strongly of Paul Bogle as a Native Baptist and challenger of the colonial status quo, and his second son, Davie, who supports Bogle's campaign. When Davie is arrested, Pa John is about to disown him until he learns that his son will be flogged like a black "yam thief". He is so outraged that he signs the Stoney Gut petition, and then as a signatory is forced to flee to the mountains with his wife and children, to escape from the state pogrom that follows the violence outside the Morant Bay Courthouse. A mixture of piety and a misplaced faith in British justice leads to his death when he is shot by the redcoats. In Part One, Johnny plays the role of messenger between Davie and the people of Stoney Gut and witness to events at home, at Stoney Gut and outside the court house. Part One also establishes his friendship with Timothy M'Laren, and ends with the flight of Davie, Lucille Dubois (a white creole who is also a supporter of Bogle) and Johnny to one of the cays off Morant Bay.

The second part covers the years from 1865 to 1882 in some detail, and then very briefly until 1907. On the cay where Johnny, Davie and Lucille have escaped, they are joined by other Morant Bay survivors. Davie sets up a religious commune, "Zion", and changes from being a life-loving fighter for social justice to a pleasure-denying sectarian zealot. Zion ends with Davie's death and Lucille's disappearance in a hurricane in 1882. Later, Johnny, now in his mid-twenties, ignores a letter from Lucille begging for help because he thinks she has betrayed his brother. Belatedly, he goes to Jamaica to find that she has been driven into prostitution. When he goes back to look for her on his second day in Kingston, she has died in the fire that sweeps the city.

The years between 1882 and 1907 see the commune becoming a conventional capitalist enterprise. Following the earthquake of 1907, the survivors return to Jamaica.

By Part Three, John Campbell is a prosperous business man. The years before 1925 are compressed into an account of the rise of Davie's and Lucille's son, John Creary, an entrepreneurial capitalist who develops the business, marries a white woman and becomes part of the Europhile elite. The years between 1925 and 1944 focus on the relationship between John Campbell and his nephew, Garth, whom he and Timothy rescue when cholera kills his mother and father. John sees the spirit of Davie in Garth, and invests in his education, sending him to England to study law, encouraging his nationalist spirit with stories of 1865, but cautioning him not to repeat Bogle's mistakes. When Garth returns from England, he becomes a successful barrister who discovers "his people", the leader of an ill-organised trade union action, and then a reformist politician. Part Three mixes a mythic narrative in which a scion of the Campbell family is destined to become the national leader, and a fictive version of the actual events of the immediate pre-war years, in particular the workers' uprising of 1938.

3. John Campbell's Voices and Those of Others

It is with John Campbell's voice and story that the reader should start – or rather voices, since *New Day* is a *multi-vocal* work. There is the child witness of Morant Bay; the youth who sees the decline of Davie; the prosperous man who lives through his nephew Garth; and the old man looking back on his life. Each sees differently, and Reid is at pains to distinguish between the remembering old man and the narrating boy who relives his experience, a shift usually signalled by the movement from the historic to the present tense. Occasionally those voices collide: "I <u>am</u> no' the only one <u>shrieking</u>. How could it be me one a-shriek? You ha' not <u>heard</u> say that forty o' we people <u>fell</u> when militiamen muskets talked the first time?" (153, refs. this edition).

There is also an authorial voice that carries a level of understanding beyond the young narrator's years. Sometimes it intrudes as a slip in plausibility – for instance Johnny's over-sophisticated response to Gourzong's inane question "What exactly are they petitioning for?": "But what a fool-fool mulatto-man, that! […] Then people are not starving? And don't they must pay tax…?" (125). Mostly, though, the authorial voice emerges at those points where the novel draws attention to the limitations of John Campbell's perspectives.

There is also a collective, commenting voice of "epic apostrophe" that steps out of time to connect present and past, which is discussed below in the context of *New Day*'s relationship to Virgil's *Aeneid*.

In Part One, Reid emphasises Johnny's childishness. He smirks during prayers, pinches his sister's backside and plays with a captured crab in church. He is prone to schadenfreude, pleased that someone else is getting a paternal whipping (58). He admits: "though I am tall for my years, eight-year-old can no' be long without sleep" and recalls how he has to be picked up sleeping from the road (168).

His life is framed by paternal violence and maternal tenderness; the images of the whip and the breast form key constructs in his perceptions of adult behaviour. He sees Pa John lashing Davie (twice) and Moses and Aaron Dacre, and even knocking his mother down. The breast, maternal, sexualised, and sometimes both, is the counter construct. Johnny speaks of how when he wakes from a nightmare, "Mother hugs you […] and her breasts are a-kiss your face and there is peace on you" (67). Later, these feelings are transferred to Lucille, when "all of a sudden I am in her arms, and soft are her breasts on my face" (195). Breasts are also signs of the munificence of nature ("you must open your arms wide and feed on the breast o' the new day), a feeling Johnny associates with the moment "when I first saw Lucille". He is well aware of the sexual role of breasts, noting how "Every time Ruthie sees Moses smiling his white-teeth smile at her, her hands must go to her breast" (108). Reid's treatment of John Campbell's evanescent sexuality (with its roots in his childhood relationship to Lucille) is a curious element in the novel that hints at themes Reid drew back from developing.[10] Johnny's feelings for Davie veer between these two poles. There are the maternal images of being in Davie's arms ("There is everything settling in its right place and quietness there inside of you" (135)), but when he witnesses Davie's anger over the suffering at Stoney Gut, it is the whip he hears: "You ever take a bull-whip and throw the lash forward and bring it back quick so the cowskin fringe curls up and talks sharp to you? Is so Davie's voice" (70).

Reid also locates Johnny's attitudes in his family's near-white-ness, as people who are looked up to by their black neighbours, and on social – though not equal – terms with the real "buckra" whites. When he walks out with Davie, he neither wants to talk to the barrack people (71), nor understands Davie's reproof:

"They will say we are playing like buckra," says Davie.
Is not bad, that? Then why Davie serious so? I am a-think that buckra are great people; for ride, they ride horses all the time and do not walk like negroes and poor whites. [...] (75)

His alarm over Davie's vehemence in support of Bogle is aestheti-cized between images of white beauty and gentleness, and black (and Jewish) ugliness and terror:

Is not the beauty of Davie this I see. I can no' see his broad forehead brown under the hair o' sea-flax. I do no' see the west sky before sun-up that is the colour of his eyes. [...]
Like Paul Bogle's and herring-Jew's was Davie's face when he said: *Who it runs over, it runs over!* (37)

And when he's at Stoney Gut, Johnny's images of Bogle are those of a child who has heard the scaremongering talk. His fear, when he is on Mr Abram's back, that "if I fall, down I will be on Deacon's big teeth" (159) make the analysis of *New Day* as an historical novel *about* the Morant Bay rebellion rather beside the point.

But Johnny is also open to learning of a bodily kind. Buffeted by the crowds on the street, he resents that his whiteness is not acknowledged, but then realises that this is how black children are treated, "No softness is on the stones for street Arab" (96). When the militia men charge, he is initially pleased, because he sees the black crowd as the enemy: "Ride them down, soldier men! Ride them down!" (97). Only when he realises that they will ride him down too does his attitude change.

At one level, this is a boy's adventure story, with echoes of *Treasure Island* and the apple barrel, when for instance he listens "to big people talk" from under the barbecue (119), about the danger brewing in Stoney Gut. But as Reid acutely observes, Johnny is soon bored by this talk, and diverts his attention to watching a mule walk by, observing how the "hind-legs glide and roll behind like sugar-boat men who have just come ashore" (122). His role as messenger is a Tom Sawyerish game. He enjoys being "Bro' John" (99), or "Johnny Newsmonger" as Ruthie calls him, because of the attention he gets – and the chance to irritate his sister ("Poor Naomi, nobody has ever called her *Sis* Naomi" (99)). Johnny's juvenile sexism persists throughout the novel, and it has to be said that *New Day*'s gender politics scarcely goes beyond the observation that this is a man's world.

Reid does observe the authoritarian patriarchy of Pa Campbell's household, including his violence towards his wife. He shows how such gendered roles are learnt early in Johnny's desire for "man-talk" with his brothers, and his contempt for his sickly brother Zekiel, whose weakness is a coded euphemism for effeminacy, who helps with "women work" in the house. At best, Reid's portrayal of Naomi in Part Three suggests that he recognises this is not the natural order of things. Naomi is now a determined woman who speaks her mind very forcibly, dismissing John's cautiousness and his tedious old world metaphors as "man-foolishness", a nice inversion of the "man-talk" that used to exclude her. Later, when Naomi refuses to leave a demonstration despite the danger, John asks her if she wants "To play street-Arab woman and pass up bricks for men when fighting starts?" She riposts: "If I was no respectable, help, I would help toss rockstone... (294)"[11] But though John admits his sister to honorary manhood, he still reflects "Funny how when time comes like this, Zekiel does no' seem a Campbell" (294). Naomi's ire over Garth's defeatism after the debacle of the strike is one of the points where an forceful alternative to the dominant narrative is expressed.

Where Reid excels is in providing Johnny with vivid and psychologically plausible accounts of his inner feelings, which draw on his previous experiences. When Johnny is brought face-to-face with death at Morant Bay, his account catches his relief, his emptiness:

I am sitting on the ground inside Humphrey's church, not thinking of anything at all.

12

I call to mind that one time at Salt Savannah, Timothy and Quackoo and me were sporting in a morning sea, riding on a bamboo raft. We did no' notice that the sea was coming up till we were 'way beyond the blue-water mark. [...] But race as we could race, a heavy sea caught up with us, and up we are gone and down again, down to sea-bottom. And then there was a struggle at sea-bottom, with sand a-fill our ears and nostrils, and water pounding out our breaths. When well bruised and full o' aches we crawled out on to the shore, gasping like groupers in net, we just lay flat on the sand, a-think on nothing at all, at all.

So, is how I stay now, my back leaning on Humphrey's wall. (154)

5. An Embodied Narrative

But what Reid achieves in this first part of the novel is much more than vivid imagery and intimacy of observation. The *more* lies in the foregrounding of the body-focusedness of Johnny's narration, the embodiment of his mental processes and the use of metaphors drawn from the natural world in which he leads his life. This is what is most original and achieved in *New Day*. From the focus on eyes (as one would expect in a narrative of witness), on ears, mouths, throats, noses, hearts, feet and so on, Reid provides Johnny with a rich psychology of perception. For instance, observing his father's response to Dr Creary's advice to quit their home, Johnny records:

> Father looks around on we, *his eyes walks away and goes to long distance.* Still Doctor Creary talks to him, but his eyes are *gone away to think.* They come back to look at us to see if he is thinking right; he looks away again, and when he comes back to Doctor Creary his eyes say the doctor is right. *But aloes thick at his throat.* (176, my italics)

This is prose that is alive, where the reader is placed in the active, interpreting position of the child.

To see just how committed Reid is to networks of embodiment, particularly in Part One, consider a few statistics. *New Day* has over 322 iterations of *heads*, 300 of *eyes*, 99 of *throats*, 89 of *shoulders*, 81 of *feet*, 75 of *bellies* and *stomachs*; 62 references to *blood*, 47 to *hearts*, 36 to *noses* and *nostrils*, 30 to *ears*, 16 to *lips*, 14 to *mouths*, 12 to *sweat*. There is only one reference to *brain*, and whilst there are 47 references to *mind*, these treat mental operations in thoroughly embodied ways. To give one example of the distribution of bodily reference in the novel: of the 89 iterations of *shoulders*, 68 are in Part One. By contrast, Roger Mais's *The Hills Were Joyful Together* (1953), a novel of similar length, with a close focus on the physical existence of Kingston yard-dwellers, has roughly half the iterations of body parts (152 heads, 127 eyes, 37 throats, 50 shoulders, 45 bellies, 15 ears). The only reference that exceeds *New Day* in frequency is to feet (88 references), which is not surprising in a novel that has a thematic focus on pursuit and flight.

It is not just the frequency of reference (some simply point to body parts in naturalistic ways – as do almost all the references in Mais's novel), but how the body is given agency. Eyes, for instance, don't just see, they make four or don't make four; deep thinking goes on back o' them; they watch thoughts inside, walk over, roll, stumble, laugh, go to bed, a-hide, a-dance. Reid's location of Johnny's perceptions *in* the natural world is discussed below, but there are also ackee pod eyes, young moon eyes, eyes like glass marbles, fish-eyes, yellow-snake eyes, mouse eyes. Johnny describes Davie's hate-filled eyes as being like a yellow snake's, whilst Davie accuses Johnny of being like "a two-day tweet-to-whit with two eyes that are no' opened yet" (72). Within this network of reference, Johnny's personification of "Day is just rubbing sleep out o' his eyes" (174) hardly seems fanciful.

Other organs of sense are either active or beset by action. Ears cock, are deaf, ring, and are torn at by loud sounds. Noses are looked down, spoken down, picked, have Saturday night put on them (i.e. go red with drink), and body scent is rank in nostrils.

Organs associated with feelings are brought into vivid play. Hearts pump and pump, beat strong, go bump, bump, bump; a-leap, come up to the mouth, jump; be a-swelled by pain; feel like trace leather has been fastened around them; batter against the walls of the chest. The physicality of these descriptions reanimate such dead metaphors as *know it by heart*, *singleness of heart*, *hardness of heart*, with *heartiness* and being *hearty*. Similarly, bellies are heavy, fattened, filled with air, kiss ribs, feel pain, fear; cymbals crash inside them; they are the source of laughter, hiccups; they creak up and down, can be deep in thought ("talking away the full of his belly"), and can be lost – as in Ruthie's "lost belly" when she loses her baby.

Perhaps even richer in descriptive variety are the organs of communication – though in Johnny's narration no part of the body does not speak. So, heads toss leader-bull fashion, shake, are raised, lowered, turn, are held high, look over, bob, jerk, twist, nod, beat in time to tunes; are like a wild boar's, are flatheads, long-heads, hot-heads, scratched, rubbed, held proud, can make head nor tail o', are thrust forward, bent, scattered (confused), are young, bald, old, grey.

Mouths open like macca-back fish, like rat-trap, like a shored mullet; are pot-mouths, blabber-mouths, heavy mouths; Davie is "two-mouthed" (deceitful); gourd-mouth Johnny is told not to blab; Lucille's mouth is like a two-day kling-kling a-beg for air; a woman is blah-blah mouthed; hearts jump through mouths; one character is a "water-mouth man who must flow and flow", another's mouth went too far before him, whilst Naomi "tucks in her mouth", but also utters crudely proverbial saying when she tells her nephew, Garth, "*Cover your mouth!* You blabbing like the bottom o' sick barrack people who ha' taken castor oil!" (303).[12] There are *lips* o' stiffness, lips that suck at a blood-plum (Lucille has red lips); someone has no fullness to his lips, another has no lips to his mouth, whilst Mr. Abram has lips to his mouth – he is talking enough-plenty! Before words reach the mouth and lips, *throats* and the sounds coming from them are often the most reliable sign of meaning. Throats have molasses in, treacle in, iron in, aloes in (frequently); thunder rolls in them; Davie talks with teeth in his throat; throats have croaks in, spittle in, dryness in, music in; they a-tremble like humming bird, fear whistles in them, john-to-whit [sounds] bubble in them, happiness is thick in, eye water is in them; they are filled with slime, thirsty men suck at their throats; a shriek is a bubble in John's throat, whilst sorrow a-tear through it. When Davie is dying: he "whispered with his throat like how the dying do when their lips die first" and on the last morning of the novel: "deep-running water is the song that pours from their throats to greet this new day" (355).

Much the same can be shown in Reid's treatment of the limbs of action – feet, arms, hands – but the role of shoulders will suffice. In earlier chapters, they are the passive recipients of the beatings (and are proverbially the bearers of burdens), but in *New Day* they become the principal metonym for the militant actions of the Stoney Gut men:

> "Shoulders, shoulders are all I see; but ha' shoulders ever talked to you like how they talk to me this day? Men are ploughing there up courthouse way, and their shoulders talk back to me [...]
> "They plough and plough and plough. Presently they have stopped working, and the shoulders move away. I can see they had been ploughing at death." (154)

The conjunction of shoulders and ploughing is one of the places where *New Day* echoes the *Aeneid*, which reiterates references to shoulders 74 times, mostly in scenes of war. Robert Fagles' translation has the lines (2/448-450): "so through spears, through enemy ranks we plow/ to certain death".[13] Bogle was also recorded in the Royal

Commission (which Reid studied and used) as saying his people would be "compelled to put shoulders to the wheel" if matters got any worse.[14] But if shoulders signify the actions of the hitherto powerless entering history with their bodies, the image also suggests, more ambivalently, that it is the shoulders that act rather than conscious minds. "Morant Bay men are coming with their shoulders ready to talk":

> [...] Then I do no' see Custos any more, for he is gone to his knees. Men say he prayed then to Deacon; but from where I am, *Deacon shoulders worked in conversation.* When they stopped talking, redder was his cutlass.
> Then all the *shoulders* are standing straight now and turning back to us, finished. (164)

If the body thinks, feels and perceives, *mind* is also embodied. For instance, *mind* turns back, walks back, jumps, has gone on, has gone long distance, is working hard, is *carried* by perceptions, is looking on, talks of secret things; Johnny speaks *from* his mind (ie inadvertently); mind goes from them; memory is pricking, knocks at minds; minds are sealed; things ... ha' lately grown in my mind; mind reads of things not written, says right, has stood up, and many more.

What Reid achieves in Part One, is a reliteralisation of the dead metaphors of embodiment buried in language. He does this through foregrounding their literal physicality, by revisiting the proverbial speech of older, rural Jamaican patwa, and by using more consciously modernist defamiliarisation strategies – actually traditional rhetorical devices such as *anthimeria* (using one part of speech as if it was another) as in Davie's question "Is that what will bacon we, wine we?" (64); or *anastrophe* (a reversal of the usual syntactic order) such as "Buttoned is his coat" (127), or *prosopopoeia* (personification) such as "Quill has finished scratching on paper now" (126).

6. Nature Within and Without

Embodiment is frequently associated with external nature – with Jamaica's flora and fauna, weather and food. The associations identify particular characters and their similarities to or differences from others. In its totality, the network of human-animal linkages presents the young John Campbell's way of seeing the world and, by implication, Reid's vision of nation that exists in all its physicality, if not yet in its political and social arrangements. And as Paul Gilroy argues, "a sense of the body's place in the natural world can provide [...] a social ecology and an alternative rationality that articulate a cultural and moral challenge to the exploitation and domination of "the nature within us and without us".[15]

Animal images constitute the most numerous and significant elements of connection. Again, there are significant differences of frequency and mode of use between Part One and Parts Two and Three, and whilst the change diminishes the novel's textual richness, it does indicate Reid's creative realisation that his adult narrator has lost the heightened vision he had as a child.

The most striking presence is the horse – an iconic image for Reid. It references Edna Manley's epochal sculpture, *Horse of the Morning* (1943), which Reid also uses in the title of his biography of Norman Manley, *Horses of the Morning* (1985), and the fact that the Manleys rode and bred horses at Drumblair.[16] In *New Day,* the horse is an Homeric epithet for Davie who is seen "railing and prancing like colt-horse" and "goes to his feet like a yearling" (68). Whilst Pa John's shoulders are "like stallions", and though "colt horse can no' have shoulders like stallions", when Davie carries Johnny, "Stallion eagerness is a-ripple against me shoulder" (84) and he is "a young stallion a-stride without fear" (116). By contrast, "Red is the Inspector's face as he champs his moustache like pasture horse mouthing dry grass" (143); Martha, the innkeeper, is described by Davie as "a payable mare" and later in the novel, John Campbell disparages his nephew John Creary, son of Davie and Lucille, when he says, "Two high-bred colts ha' mated and brought a good cart-horse" (262). Horses and carts also provide proverbial sayings such as "young men must be strong like boar and quick like goat and with breath like racehorse of St Dorothy's parish" (130). By Part Three, though, the sayings have become markedly "old-school" and sententious: "You teach young colt to haul a log so he knows how to brace to the pull" (277), or "young colt that does no' frisk will be no good for the long pull ahead" (327).

Bulls/steers and cows provide another source of reference. Pa John's Homeric epithet is "leader bull", though when he is in a bad temper he is "a bad steer coming from the branding pen". When he leads his family to presumed safety after the defeat of the rebellion, "My father has the strength of ten; a leader-bull is he, leading his herd to the high places" (179), and Davie is sure that the rest of his family will be safe after his death, since, "they will no' harm the herd since leader-bull is dead" (190). Steers (castrated bulls) are of course frequently yoked, and when Davie is arrested, "Constables have turned my bro' Davie into a cotter-head plough-steer" (116); chained with Mr Abram, and two Morant Bay men "all are joined together by a long iron bar 'twixt them", an image that also recalls the slave coffle. When the crowd releases the men, they are like plough steers "racing for clear pastures" (117). The metaphor of emasculation is also one that John Campbell attaches to his weakly brother Zekiel, in the rather obvious innuendo that he has been unhappy in marriage "for he was no' born with the cut of a leader-bull" (259). Bovines also provide images for insult as in Johnny's description of the Whites at Dr Creary's dinner party: "You red-faced back-draw bulls and your stringy cows!" (229), whilst leader bulls contrast with biddable "heavy belly pasture bulls" (the other estate owners) whom Garth's persuasion fits "with nose rings" (324).

Mules have a slightly less prominent metaphoric presence, though Pa John is a "stubborn hamper-mule", Mr Abram "is broad in the back like penny-a-ride donkey at Morant Bay Fair" and Naomi curses Garth for his caution/cowardice as a "Dam' mongrel mule".

Dogs feature as images of both aggression and victimhood. The angry Davie's voice "sounds like a butcher-dog... when it can get no scrap meat" (82), and the disappointed Aaron Dacre is like "a strayed dog in a strange town watching the sun set and night come with rainclouds" (80). Whilst Deacon Bogle has the ferocity of a "hunter-dog", other canine images are of vulnerability. When the redcoats are ready to "shoot we down like dogs", when they are "thick around the Bay like fleas on a mangy dog", all Pa John can manage is watchfulness, "his head held like a pointer dog", and when he and Manuel are slain, "we run in little circles like wounded hound-dogs" (189). Later, when Lucille reproves Davie's self-indulgence when he rejects Creary's suggestion that he should give evidence to the Commission, "My bro' is like a house dog what has been slapped" (212). The most extended dog/hound metaphor comes in Davie's explosion of rage over what he sees as the Commission's hypocrisy:

> Down on other people go the hounds o' Britain, running without leash, savaging and mauling the poor ones who have been sinful 'cause they talked for freedom. Then when we bowels ha' been ripped out, Mother England plays like soft and begin to holler that she did no' want it so; that the well-trained hounds she has sent out ha' only gone mad because they scented blood. (212).

Creatures of the small peasantry such as hogs and lambs provide paired comparisons. When Davie unwillingly kneels for family prayers, he looks to Johnny like an "overgrown lambkin", so when he describes his shock over Davie's anger, the images of boar and lamb readily connect. Gone are the "two spring lambs what dance at his mouth every time my bro' laughs" and in their place "teeth are wild boar's tearing down Wareika Mount." (75). Porcine images connect the overfed, parvenu black empire loyalist Zaccy O'Gilvie who "slops his coffee like hog at buttery door" (124) to the fat German Custos who orders the Morant Bay shootings, though, at Bogle's hands, the German boar becomes a sacrificial lamb. Here, the description (whilst metaphorically ingenious in describing Bogle as if he was the shepherd of a myalist cult – which he was not) is quite implausibly complex in Johnny's mouth: "Shepherd Bogle's German lamb comes. Fat he is, fed on young spring grass and running water 'gainst the time when he must come to Bogle" (164). But if this does not sound like Johnny, it shows how determined Reid is to rift the texture of *New Day* with the ore of human-animal reference.

Other images drawn from Jamaica's fauna draw on more conventional constructs of higher and lower orders of nature, with birds as symbols of beauty, fragility, and sometimes warning, whilst snakes, worms, insects and fish represent the furthest point from the divine. The angry Davie's face is like that of a yellow snake with "two eyes like glass marbles" (72), and "Nanka snake hissing from stonehole is Davie" (191). In the crowds pressing in on him in front of the Morant Bay courthouse, Johnny is "a worm in a calaloo field" (140), whilst hiding from the Maroons on Morant Cay he is a "tumblebug in the mud" (197) … "a congo worm in a farmyard thick with moulting hens. I do no' know what I am" (198). And when the hurricane devastates the Cay, the survivors become "a long snake o' humans grovelling along in the dark" (247).

The corrupt Pastor Humphrey is "a tall and pale conger eel" with "fish-eyes a-stare" (85); giving his sermon, his "long neck shot out, then drew back into his cassock like iguana in stonehole"; "pigeon a-coo in his voice, but yellow snake looking out o' his eyes" (89). Johnny both applies such negative images to himself ("oyster at rock-bottom, me, my mouth pouting" (105) and records those turned against him, such as Naomi's put-down for playing force-ripe man: "Johnny Piper turned Kingfish" (114), or Ma Tamah's "Coo here! [...] When since kling-kling turn into hawk-bird? *Heh!*" Johnny reflects: "Good it is to hear her laugh, but when Mother says *heh!* like that, all of your manhood is gone, and smaller than calaloo worm you feel. Is funny it is how your breeches drop off any time Mother says *heh!*" (177). Part One has a good deal of that kind of witty (and suggestive) earthiness.

Birds provide perhaps the most frequent and varied source of metaphor, making *New Day* a rich aviary of Jamaican reference: nightingales, parrots, kling-klings, hawks, ploves, screech owls, man-o-war birds, solitaires, pitcharries, gaulins, hopping dicks; sultanas, bitterns, carrion crows, Johncrows, blackbirds, yellowthroat warbler (whose whistle is Davie's signal when the family is on the mountain), green-back mallards, pelicans, noddies, sooty terns. Birds are Lucille's epithet: nightingale, hummingbird, and after her dissension with Davie, "the weep of a lost *kling-kling*" is in her voice (239).

As one would expect, the natural forces of weather – hurricane, drought, earthquake and flood – join with quasi-natural forces such as fire to provide the bedrock of human existence in *New Day*. They provide crucial triggers to plot action – the Stoney Gut rebellion, Davie's death and the end of the Salt Savannah Cay experiment – as well as reminding that nature is not to be sentimentalised. There are moments of a naturalistic pantheism as when "Down in the Bay the sea kneels on the shore" (177); or of the "twisty lignum-vitae shaking hands over our heads. Pitcharries whistle howdy-do to we…" (178) – though both images are ironic since they precede Pa John's and Manuel's deaths – but in general *New Day* is clear that nature both gives and takes. After the drought, floods come:

> Yallahs and Morant and Plantain Garden rivers heavy so, until you do not know where rivers end and land begins. That was the time when an alligator swam clear up to the barrack and took away my friend Timothy's baby bro'. (83)

As well as being direct forces in the novel, thunder, hurricane and fire are frequent sources of metaphorical comparison – and another connection between the Jamaican natural world and the epic world of the *Aeneid*. For instance, there are 40 references to thunder/thunderheads in the *Aeneid*, 41 instances in *New Day*, and though Reid's novel does not have quite the ubiquity of fire as the *Aeneid* (75 against 160 instances), fire is central to *New Day*, when "not until men's habitations from the Bay to the foot of the great mountain ha' been put to fire did Governor Eyre stay his hand" (208). And there is, of course, Lucille's Didoesque death by fire. Elsewhere there are multiple references to fire in eyes, and to hell, fire and brimstone.

Reid is doing several things with these networks that locate the human body both *in* and *of* nature. In the first place, they provide Reid with psychologically plausible sources of moral analogy for the boy's descriptions of the human behaviour he witnesses. In this,

Reid utilises all the concrete physicality of the lexicon of Jamaican patwa, and adds to it inventively. Very few of Reid's coinages are, for instance, referred to in F.G. Cassidy's *Jamaica Talk* (1961), but they are created by the same linguistic processes that Cassidy describes.

The body in nature is also central to the novel's political vision. Images (particularly those of horses) signify an inherent desire for freedom, whilst the images of yoked-steers point to the fact that freedom denied is, in the first place, felt through the body. Davie's argument to the Commissioners about the origins of the rebellion makes a theological, Blakean connection between the divine body and the dignity located in the human body made in God's image:

> "Man was no' built for slavery [...]. In him are the Image and Likeness, and it is no' of the skin. Inside o' him there is the dignity of God, whether he was birthed in a hut or in a buckra's mansion. [...] the dignity inside every born man would 'low no rest to these slaves [...] [and] the shaming of man's highest calling – the calling o' labour with the hands, the sweat by which the Big Master said we should eat our bread." (220)

Whilst this character-driven reflection is not necessarily central to the novel's meaning, a reading of Thomas Staubli's and Silvia Schroer's *Body Symbolism in the Bible* (1998, 2001)[17] suggests that in part at least Reid's body-focus and analogies drawn from the animal/natural world are either inspired by the Bible or arrive at the same place. Staubli and Schroer suggest, for instance, that Biblical imagery is less concerned with offering static visual descriptions, than with describing what the embodied person is doing – such as Reid's "eyes going for a walk". Their reading of the Bible may be oriented to the Old Testament, but their case for the embodiment of God in man, their examples of the body as the site of spirituality and argument that the Old Testament, at least, refuses body/mind Cartesian dualities, has many resonances with *New Day*. Reid is undoubtedly mindful that his characters exist in a Bible-infused world, and whilst *New Day* cannot be described as a Christian novel (in the sense that it has no concern with individual salvation) it takes place in a world that has a space for transcendence. This, though, to use the distinction made by Mark Johnson in *The Meaning of the Body*, is perhaps of a horizontal rather than a vertical kind,[18] of moving beyond the individual body into relationships with other bodies, minds and the natural world, rather than seeing life as a preparation for a bodiless transcendence into pure spirit. Reid's narrative is, for instance, very concrete in its focus on what death means, whether natural or brought about by chance or human malignity. What Reid signals in the account of Pa John's death is waste, of a death that did not have to be. Pa John might see himself as a martyr, but his death has no inspirational impact on other lives, other than trapping Davie into becoming his dour, life-denying clone. Though characters make conventional references to the after-life, the descriptions of the very physical moments of death, or those moments of heightened life such as the boarhunt, suggest that Reid's vision is in essence a richly material one.

7. *Capitalism and the Estrangement from Nature*

Whilst a network of reference to the natural world continues to link *New Day* as a whole, its density and vividness unquestionably dissipates in the novel's latter parts. But though the prose is less alive, close reading convinces me that Reid is wholly conscious of what he is doing in ways that have been insufficiently recognised.

Most pertinently, Part Two charts the conversion of the religious commune of Zion into a capitalist farm and the emergence of the Campbell family as capitalist owners of land and businesses. Davie has tried to create Zion as a replacement for the helotry of slavery, but his utopia replicates the organisation of the old sugar estate, except that the whip has been replaced by the Bible. There are compensations in the free schooling and collective feasts, but Davie's authority is the sole guide to behaviour. What is actually going on under the religious surface of Zion is the primitive accumulation that will seed full-scale capitalist production, based on the cays as a source of guano, and on the eggs the boobies (the sooty tern – *sterna fuscata*) lay there, a delicacy later sold on the mainland. For the utopians, the arrival of the boobies is a gift from god: "Wings beating on wings. [...] Ten thousand greywhite messengers are coming down from heaven heavy with speckled manna in their wombs... leaving their gifts in the sand" (235). When Reid wrote *New Day*, booby eggs were still to be had, but by 1980, according to B.W. Higman's *Jamaican Food* (2008), the supply was exhausted by overharvesting.[19] The presence of guano is also seen as another sign of God's blessing, but the need to bring more labourers to dig the manure for sale to American ships begins the conversion of Davie from equality with his fellows to becoming "Mr Davie". What Reid doesn't say is that the frantic search for guano (what John Bellamy Foster calls "guano imperialism" – the planting of national flags on any piece of bird-beshitten rock) was a response to the crisis in capitalist agriculture over the impoverishing of soil fertility.[20]

The transformation of Zion to capitalist farm occurs after Davie's death, when his son James Creary concludes that people will work harder and profits will be greater if the workers become wage labourers. Both predictions prove true, though James Creary fails to see that, alienated from both their own labour and the land they work on, wage labourers will look for their satisfactions in consumption. Reid conveys this in a couple of neatly condensed paragraphs:

> Year after year our people got their coins for their labour, and much of it they have saved, for there was nothing to spend it on. James opened a shop on the Cay, and for a while things went level. [...]
> First times, Sunday afternoons [...] had our young ones full in their finery, walking up and down the sands. But after times they would no' walk much again, but stood in their finery looking lost and pitching flat stones out to sea and laughing a little when the stones skipped four times before sinking. After more times they do no' laugh again. (263)

Many of the workers have drifted back to the mainland long before the earthquake and tidal wave destroy the cay's agricultural land.

By Part Three, John Campbell lives in urban Kingston, his habitat the counting house. In the process, the metaphors he uses shift away from lived experience and become self-consciously folksy comparisons between what are now discrete worlds: man as producer and rentier under capitalism and the world of nature. Now he engages in the laboured metaphors of steam-valve mechanics:

> "I am a-think that steam train would soon blow up and destroy all if men had no' made pipes to lead the steam into ways which will drive the wheels. But still, if the engine stands quiet in the yard without ever moving, then the fires must be banked; and fires banked overlong will die. [...] You understand?"
> Laugh from Garth. "Now, let's see. You say we should remain in the Empire, but our energy for life should be guided into ways that would spell progress for our people – and not just to let the engine stand still in the yard of Crown government, for soon our fires will be out. Right, Uncle?" [...]
> "Good," says Garth. "Conceded. But how can we get Whitehall to see our way?"
> "By rumbling in our boilers, Son." (279)

Garth is to "Mount to the footplates [...] and drive off from where your grandfer left", but as he reassures his uncle, "I won't lose the safety valve you made them weld on to me in England" (283). What is not admitted is that this strategy is about preserving the wealth and privilege the Campbells possess, by funnelling popular discontents through the safety valve of very modest reform. Now the metaphors are of roads, paths, running races, milestones, being "mortgaged to a dream" – the dreary metaphors of political cliché. Now the metaphors John draws from nature have a forced, sententious air, as when John counsels caution ("In dry weather a horse can stand beside the stream, but the stream is no' bound to give him water" (288)), pompous sayings that locate him in the past, as Garth's friend Chris teases: "There you go again with your nineteenth century quotes". Metaphors that once signalled an organic relationship between people and the natural world, now convey the snobbery of class. When Greg and Chris accuse Garth of over-caution in his strategy for the union, John explodes: "Bred horse should no' team with scrub, Garth Campbell..." (289), though Chris and Greg's strategy for the strike is unquestionably more realistic than Garth's – one of those points where the action critiques John Campbell's point of view.

The clue that Reid knew exactly what he was doing here comes when the Campbells are trying to persuade a group of reactionary planters to behave with paternalistic foresight. "Don't give me any dam' metaphors" one bawls out – a witty metafictional comment on a book built around metaphors. What glares is the inaptness of the metaphors John Campbell uses to describe the modern world: the war becomes the time when "King George was a-shape his arrows" (348); Garth is "the leader-bull and the brake-iron o' both the party and the union" (349). In contrast to the literal physicality of the descriptions of the heart in Part One, in Part Three, the heart becomes the conventional vehicle of abstractions such as: needing the daily bread o' charity to sustenance my heart; memories locked in the upper closet o'me heart; if eyes do no' see; hearts can no speak o' share; my heart is with you. These metaphors suggest the continuity of John Campbell's verbal habits, but they also hint that, for all his folksy wisdom, he is not a reliable interpreter of these changed times.

8. A Novel of Mixed Genres

But of course, New Day is also about the Morant Bay Rebellion and Jamaica's emergence towards modernity and nationhood, and it would be wrong to evade the novel's flaws in its treatment of this subject matter – though I think the flaws are interesting and part of what makes New Day a much richer and less monolithic work than the "idealism and dream" evaluation suggests.

To begin with, *New Day* is *multi-generic* in that it invites various kinds of reading. It can *best* be read as a narrative *about* John Campbell and his changing perceptions of the world, but it has mostly been critiqued as a pioneering Caribbean historical novel and, as others have done, one can note how it diverges from the historical record for both fictive and ideological reasons. Nana Wilson-Tagoe's discussion in *Historical Thought and Literary Representation in West Indian Fiction*[21] provides a useful survey. There is, for instance, no historical evidence that Bogle killed the Custos, as he does in the novel, and his portrayal as a premature nationalist demanding secession relates more to Reid's desire to create linkages between Davie in Part One and Garth in Part Three than to any historical evidence. Again, Reid's portrayal of G.W. Gordon as a moderate at odds with Bogle has no historical reality. Readers who wish to compare Reid's novel with professional historiographical treatments should consult Gad Heuman's *The Killing Time: The Morant Bay Rebellion in Jamaica* (1994),[22] and whilst Devon Dick's *The Cross and the Machete* (2009), is less than persuasive in arguing that Paul Bogle and his followers were not engaged in armed rebellion, his book nevertheless helpfully locates the Native Baptists as an articulate Bible-centred group very different from the primitive cult implied in *New Day*.[23]

What has been less noted is *New Day*'s focus on the meaning and uses of history. Here it should be credited with being the first Caribbean novel to go beyond historical recreation – H.G. De Lisser's fiction can claim that achievement[24] – to setting out the parameters of a philosophical debate that persisted for many decades in Caribbean discourse. In Part One, Davie gives Johnny a history lesson on slavery, the maroon wars, Tackey's insurrection and Bro' L'Ouverture (100), making it clear that it is this knowledge that animates his desire to overthrow the inequalities of race and class inherited from slave society. Davie also complains about the imperialist history that Johnny is taught in school by Mr M'Donald, who "the buckra government pays […] to fool poor people's children" with romanticised stories of British kings and queens (115-116).

However, in Part Three, John Campbell concludes:

> Books what Davie had read at the Gut did no' settle down in him as books should settle. Much o' the good did no' go in at all, and the bad only floated on top like scum in molasses tank. When he wanted to reach for the knowledge that could make him tell o' his country's history, oftentimes only the scum could my bro' Davie see. (316).

Now it is in the Campbell family's interest to oppose the radical social changes that Davie once sought. Indeed, Garth evidently thinks that it is imperial history that should inspire, and he proposes setting up a few scholarships to England and America. John agrees, because Davie "had but the little knowledge that makes men dangerous". What is needed, evidently, is a good colonial, Europhile education. I find it hard to believe that this is what Reid himself thought, though one might question why he is not more explicit on this point.

9. A Poetic Epic and Its Intertexts

Both the readings of *New Day* so far discussed – as a bildungsroman focusing on John Campbell, and as historical fiction – locate *New Day* as a realist novel that, *in the main*, develops plausibly-motivated and psychologically-coherent characters. I say *in the main*, because *New Day* also invites reading as a poetic epic that strains away from realism to the myth of a family destined to found the nation. Reid's ambitions here are both textual and structural. He spoke explicitly of his intention to create a "poetic dialect".[25] Look, for a start, at this paragraph marked up as blank verse:

> Hear the shells how they blow! First a-moan/ with sadness and loneliness, of earth/ heavy with sorrow; then there is the swift / ascension and no longer near the earth/ but is leaping from treetop to treetop,/ a-leap to the wild stones high on one another,/ and your head is twisting all about,/ sending your eyes up after the sound of it./ So till reached, your eyes have reached the highest crag/ and there against the sky is the shell-blower... (133)

Somewhere in his memory, I suspect Reid heard echoes of Wordsworth's *The Prelude* (1/334-338), as in:

> "...Suspended by the blast that blew amain,
> Shouldering the naked crag, oh, at that time
> While on the perilous ridge I hung alone,
> With what strange utterance did the loud dry wind
> Blow through my ear!

Similar points could be made about other passages, such as the paragraph at the beginning of Chapter 33:

> I ha' heard the flute o' the solitaire piping through the silence of the secret mountains as he floats through the valleys at dawnlight. I ha' watched the sun which comes in far morning thundering over the peaks to beat back the heavy mountain mists. I ha' seen holes whose

bottoms no man knows of. I ha' wondered if on top of a tall grevillea
growing up into heaven I could no' touch the stars. (180)

In this you can hear the two-part parallelisms of the psalms, something also found in George Campbell's work, whose *First Poems*
(1945) Reid would certainly have known. There are a good many
sentences where one hears Reid filtering Campbell, such as "...
there are tears all over the land and only the rich laugh deep." (56).[26]

The poetic ambition of Reid's prose has displeased those who saw
in its rhythms inauthentic versions of Jamaican creole syntax.[27] It is
not hard to mount such as case, but perhaps Reid should not be
criticised for failing something he was not trying to do. Whether he
wholly succeeds at what he was attempting is another matter.

Compared to the language of *New Day*, Reid's intertextual ambitions have received little if any attention, but the clues are unmistakeable: that he looked to existing models of epic structure and language,
in particular Milton's *Paradise Lost* and Virgil's *Aeneid*, as means of
giving his narrative heroic resonances. Whether these relationships
are wholly successful, readers will have to decide. My view is that
Reid's ambition should be acknowledged, even though it results in
issues of coherence and plausibility. But what he attempts goes far
beyond what a host of earlier, distinctly colonial Caribbean poets were
doing in their Miltonic or Shelleyan imitations – poetry designed to
prove mastery of colonial culture, with little investment in what is
Caribbean in language or reference.[28] Reid's treatment of the body in
nature shows he was hugely invested in the Jamaican world. Whilst
Reid can't be said to "write back" to the classics in the way that Jean
Rhys does in *Wide Sargasso Sea* (1966) or Derek Walcott does in *Omeros*
(1990),[29] no previous Caribbean novelist had attempted to forge any
kind of intertextual relationship with the literature of the past that
was more than imitative, though two contemporary Jamaican plays,
M.G. Smith's "The Leader" (1943),[30] and Roger Mais's "George
William Gordon" (1949),[31] both employ the choric device of classic
Greek drama translated to Jamaican settings.

What I think Reid is saying through these intertextual resonances
is that the lives of his Jamaican characters and the mission of
founding a new nation on a small island in a decaying empire should
be afforded the same dignity of regard accorded to the characters of
the ancient classics, and there are certainly episodes in *New Day* that
achieve this, such as the flight of the Campbells from Salt Savannah.
But I also think that the classical resonances connect to the most
flawed element in *New Day*: the attempt to make the mythic destiny

27

of the Campbell family stand for the destiny of the nation. There are points, too, where realist and mythic forms overlap in uncomfortable ways. The connections Reid makes between Milton's Satan and the historical figure of Paul Bogle is troubling. What is gained in striking language is lost by making Bogle a figure of evil – the references to Satan draw on Milton's least heroic images – and though Reid may not have intended it, the parallels locate the Stoney Gut rebellion just as Governor Eyre saw it: as a rebellion against a divinely ordained legitimate authority.

10. New Day and Paradise Lost

The echoes of Milton's Satan and his rebellious angels in the imagery and language of the portrayal of Paul Bogle and the rebels of Stoney Gut are unmistakeable. Milton's Satan has "eyes/That sparkling blazed" (1/193), whilst Bogle's "eyes are blind with a red shine." When Bogle says "Some of we now are in durance vile", this surely echoes Satan's "…Let him surer bar/His iron gates if he intends our stay in that dark durance" (3/898-99); whilst the question posed by the council of war in Stoney Gut chapel: "Is war it or peace buckra is looking for?" echoes the council of the fallen angels in Book 1 of *Paradise Lost*. Compare *New Day*'s "In his long, black coat, Deacon is a John Crow a-hover over Cuna Cuna Pass" (109) with *Paradise Lost*'s "Then with expanded wings he steers his flight/Aloft incumbent on the dusky air" (1/225-226) and "weighs his spread wings at leisure to behold/Far off the empyreal heaven" (2/1046-47). When Bogle grasps Johnny's shoulder, the boy thinks "this is how small chicks feel inside when hunting-hawks swoop down from the banyan tree" (111). The imagery of Bogle as vulture (the "quartering john crow") is repeated more than once, and the echoed image of preying on the sacrificial lamb is surely not coincidental. Compare the following:

> Deacon is a hunter-dog quartering the hole o' the German boar. Deacon is a cult shepherd in Yallahs Valley waiting for the sacrificial lamb. If after the shoulders cease talking anybody should see Deacon there, then he will be a quartering John Crow, working up his appetite before he swoops for carrion meat… (163)

Here is Satan in flight as a vulture: (Bk 2/ 431-435)

> As when a vulture on Imaus bred,
> Whose snowy ridge the roving Tartar bounds,

> Dislodging from a region scarce of prey
> To gorge the flesh of lambs or yeanling kids [...]
> So on this windy sea of land, the fiend
> Walked up and down alone bent on his prey...

Milton's last line finds its echo in Reid's "Watch how Deacon runs his little race! (164) and the curious detail of Bogle's movements: "He runs about in little quick steps, a few steps to his right, a few steps to his left, his cutlass a-flame in his hand" (163) resonates with *Paradise Lost* Bk. 2/ 630ff where Satan:

> Explores his solitary flight sometimes
> He scours the right hand coast, sometimes the left...

11. New Day and The Aeneid

The dialogue with *The Aeneid* exists at several levels: in specific episodes and echoes of narrative trajectory; in the use of certain epical devices, such as apostrophe, extended metaphor and identifying epithets; and in shared thematic and ideological concerns.

New Day shares, as Louise Cowan describes it, the *Aeneid*'s concern with: "*Fatum*, a sense of mission; *pietas*, duty towards family, country and the land; *memoria* and the preservation of the sacred"[32] Whilst I'm sure Reid didn't share the *Aeneid*'s "belief in a divine order expressing itself obscurely in history", John Campbell certainly sees "Mas'r God's hand hammering a mould together" in the connection between Davie and Garth; and if there is no supernatural machinery of manipulative goddesses, there is the hurricane in Part Two, and the machinations of the absent gods of the colonial office. *Fatum* describes very well the roles of Davie and Garth in pursuing a mission that is uniquely theirs, and if anyone exhibits *Pietas* as duty to family it is John Campbell. *Memoria* – the need to remember and pay respects to the past – is very clearly John Campbell's *fatum*, and where the values of character and novel are most closely aligned.

The *Aeneid* emphasises the need to tame the crowd as slaves to passion (*Aeneid* 1/174-181) and subject warring peoples to the order of the new nation. This is Garth's mission; he, too, "rules their furor with his words and calms their passion". And whilst Reid ignores the imperial echoes of the *Aeneid*, Garth's mission is to create the Jamaican nation out of the diversity of Africans, Europeans and Mulattos (East Indians and Chinese are mentioned as labourers in *New Day*, but not as potential citizens of the new nation).

Beyond ideology, *New Day* shares structural echoes with the

Aeneid, in the pattern of *failure/ regression* (the sack of Troy and Aeneas' flight, which is paralleled by Eyre's pogrom and the Campbells' flight from Salt Savannah in Part One), *stasis* (Aeneas's long voyages and delay in Carthage which is paralleled by the sojourn on Salt Savannah Cay in Part Two) and *moving forward* (Aeneas' arrival in Italy paralleled by the Campbells' return to Jamaica in Part Three). Like the *Aeneid*, *New Day* does not foreground the fact that it is a narrative that looks backwards, because it either returns the narration to a still unrolling present, or embeds the future in the past through prophecy, predicting the new day.

Thus Creusa's prophecy to Aeneas, "There great joy and a kingdom are yours to claim, and a queen to make your wife..." (2/ 967-980), not only fits Garth, but is echoed in Davie's enigmatic augury as they lie by Maroon Hole : "Eight, Johnny? Well you will live to see it?" and Johnny thinks "Live to see what? But I do no' ask, for that is how Davie says funny things sometimes with his eyes gone to bed deep in his head" (68). Davie is playing the vatic role of a Sybil.

After the burning down of Morant Bay, Dr Creasy, the Campbells' guardian angel, plays the part of Venus in telling Aeneas to flee Troy. The scene where Pa John leads his family away from Salt Savannah with his wife at the rear echoes the journey Aeneas makes on foot to the coast with Creusa at the rear (*Aeneid* bk 2 lines 650 onwards and 2/967-980). Like Creusa, Ma Tamah dies, though not during the flight. Pa John's epic promise echoes Aeneas's destiny for his son, Ascanius/Iulus: "I do no' die if my boys live" (186).

In Book Two of the *Aeneid*, Aeneas arrives in Carthage, falls in love with Dido and is tempted to help build her new city. But this is not his mission, as his goddess mother reminds him. This is echoed in Davie's diversion into building his Zion on the Cay (which does not become Jamaican territory until after his death). The Campbell duty is to create the new Jamaica, as Zion's and Davie's fate makes clear. Aeneas has to discover that *his* mission is not to rebuild Troy, but to start the journey towards founding Rome, a recognition underpinned by the episode (Book 3: 349-350) when he visits the exiles Helenus and Andromache whose attempt to build a little Troy is merely a sad mimicry of the original city. Davie's renaming of the Morant Cays as "the new Salt Savannah" (194) is a similar act of nostalgic imitation. It can neither recreate the old Salt Savannah homestead, nor be part of the creation of the new Jamaica. John Campbell's later effort to rebuild a new Salt Savannah in the hills of St Thomas echoes Book 5 of the *Aeneid*, where Aeneas does leave behind a contingent of Trojans to support a little Troy, so that the buried Anchises can be tended with the appropriate rites. Here, perhaps, the novel reflects critically on John Campbell's family obsessions. The new Salt Savannah is little more than a rich man's self-indulgence (315), though Garth understands John's family pieties enough to talk of bringing his siblings Naomi and Zekiel there, though both die before the house is completed.

Reid's least happy echoing of the *Aeneid* is in the role of Lucille Dubois. There is a realist psychological perceptiveness in the treatment of Lucille's response to Davie's repressive spirit on the Cay (though there is a sad failure of male imagination in limiting her discontents to access to fashionable clothes – particularly since Reid has used her as his politically engaged mouthpiece for the message of Fabian gradualism in Part 1), but her fate is melodramatic. As a Virgilian echo it makes much better sense. Like Dido, Lucille has been driven from her native land (Haiti/Tyre) to Jamaica, and then to the Carthage of the Cays. When she and Davie arrive on the cay they are not yet married (though they intend to be), an echo of the night in the cave (*Aeneid* Book 4, ll. 170-173) when Dido can only pretend to herself that she is married to Aeneas. Reid disposes of Lucille melodramatically when she is accidentally carried away in Captain Grantley's ship after the hurricane, shipwrecked on Cuba, raped by drunken seamen and forced to work as a prostitute when Johnny refuses to help her. Part Two ends with a reprise of references to the sack of Troy when, on the night of the Kingston fire of 1882, Johnny/Aeneas must save his last surviving kin. Like Aeneas with Iulus, he must "a run with James Creary in my arms" (254). When he goes back to look for Lucille, she has met her fate like Dido on her funeral pyre: The brothel madam tells him:

> "Cuba Lucille got drunk after you left 'cause you would no' cover her! Drunk all day, drunk all night – There she is, still drunk, eunuch boy!"
> I saw her dirty fingers point at the rubble. (255)

Beyond echoes of character and episode, Reid makes use of several poetic devices found in the *Aeneid*. For instance, Virgil makes use of several symbolic objects – such as the shield that Venus has Vulcan make so her son will be invincible in battle (*Aeneid* 8, ll. 612-625) – that change the outcome of events. In *New Day*, Pa John's coat plays just such a magical role. Given to Davie after Pa's death, the bullet holes carefully sewn up by his mother, just putting on the coat transforms Davie into the worst aspects of his father.[33]

The Virgilian device used most extensively in *New Day* is the epic apostrophe. In his prelude to the narrative, John Campbell apostrophises several times, such as when he declaims, "Then, now! All o' you Dead Hundreds who looked at the sun without blink in your eyes, […] tell me, you Dead Hundreds o' Morant Bay, are you hearing that tomorrow is the day?" (5). As P. Hardie and others have argued, the function of the apostrophe is atemporal, to take the narrative out of time, or, as in the *Aeneid* "to forge a continuity […] between the times of narrated events and narrating"[34] – which is of course the function of Campbell's apostrophe to the singers coming up the hill: "Edge up yourself sharp, Coney Mount tenor-man!" (54) The singing also reminds us of the oral conventions of the epic, where even that most literary of poets, Virgil, begins "Of arms and the man I sing".

Reid's most powerful use of apostrophe directly references the *Aeneid* when he personifies the bullhorn, the abeng, as the merciless self-interest of War. It echoes Virgil's references to the "iron fist of Mars", "Ruthless Mars … drawing the battle out". In *Aeneid* Bk 8, lines 700ff., Virgil lists the countrymen who march towards slaughter, accompanied by the "sound of the trumpets' rasps". Reid echoes this in the apostrophe to the bullhorn ("Come O, hunting-bees! Come in anger and hate from two scores o' curving bullhorns"). Then the apostrophe lists the bullhorn's promiscuous loyalties, beginning: "Did no' the English redcoats and traitor Juan de Bolas sweat in terror as you spoke o' death in the bush? (156), and after giving many examples concludes: "Wartime, hunting-time, hear the shells talk! Much glory and much shame ha' you seen. Sometimes against one, sometimes against t'other – *human you are, Bullhorn?*" (158).

The other device that Reid borrows from the *Aeneid* is the extended metaphor – most frequently attached to Davie in his heroic phase. As John Campbell recalls, "There have a fall in the Plantain Garden River, where water tumbles down in deep-voice quickness; so Davie's words are a-tumble" (63), whilst Davie's fierce anger is also metamorphosed into a force of nature:

> Then is time it to batten barrack windows. Kirk-bells start a-ring and we are leaving seaside for hill; for soon the wind will be coming, roaring down from the lost morning. […]
> Trees and houses and men and beasts are a-whirl through the mad night of lost morning. […] and you, a-run, a-run, for frighten has come to you –

Davie O! Davie O! (75-76)

At other times it is hard not to hear Virgil's famous image of the statesman and the unruly crowd in the several occasions when Reid portrays Garth in this role (296-297):

As often in a crowded gathering
Crude commoners in rage begin to riot,
Torches and stones fly, frenzy finds its weapons –
But if they see a stern and blameless statesman,
They all fall silent, keen for him to speak... (Aeneid: 1. 148 ff)[35]

12. New Day and the Bible

The most extensive intertext of New Day is the Bible. Many of these references are given only in vestigial form – a pointer to the kind of contemporary readership that Reid thought he had – but they often say more than is on the surface. Since the introduction can discuss only a few of these allusions, I hope readers will think it worthwhile to pursue the significance of others.

For instance, when Pa John is reading from the Book of Isaiah (40: 31) at family prayers, Johnny admits "I do no hear much though, for I am watching Davie" (59). What he does not hear is the verse that precedes the one quoted, and verse 30 carries the ironic message: "Even the youths shall faint, and the young men shall utterly fail" – the message Pa John wants to convey to his errant son.

Another compressed reference is Ma Tamah's criticism of Bogle as "just like the Apostle what Father reads of who believes that Mas'r Jesus meant a fight with the sword when he meant a fight with the spirit like Jacob in the dream" (74). The reference is firstly to Matthew 26: 52, to Simon Peter who cuts off the high priest's servant's ear, and then to the angel that Jacob wrestles with in Genesis 32: 22-32. What is implied is Jesus's command: "Put up again thy sword into his place: for all they that take the sword shall perish with the sword" – one of the novel's core themes. Another example comes when Pa John is telling Zaccy O' Gilvie that Davie must "lay in the bed he has laid", and Zaccy says: "Jehovah-Jireh" and slaps his knee (119-120). The words (God will provide) are from Genesis 22:14 and refer to the moment when God tells Abraham to offer Isaac as a sacrifice. This is really what Zaccy is telling Pa John: that he must sacrifice Davie.

Sometimes, the intertext is just comic, as when the pale, frightened Custos comes out of the court house and Johnny comments: "is like the story in the Book about Saul and the duppy-ghost" (149) – a reference to the First Book of Saul (28: 3-25) when Saul disobediently seeks out the witch of Endor and hears his downfall prophesied.

Reid also expects a knowledge that deepens the references to Deacon Bogle's Old Testament morality. When Bogle preaches: "We will do it like the Children o' Israel. Put to the sword our enemies and their household. Forty for forty" (159), he references Leviticus 26:7 "You shall chase your enemies, and they shall fall before you by the sword". The significance of restricting the number of eye-for-an-eye killings to forty ("a good Bible number that" says Mr Abram) is the fact that forty is apparently mentioned 146 times in the Bible, generally as a time of testing – from Moses' 40 years in Egypt and slavery to Jesus fasting for 40 days and 40 nights.

What these references point to is how all sides use the Bible to justify their positions. Pastor Humphries preaches (Ephesians 6:5): "Servants, be obedient to them that are your masters" (85) and Pa John challenges Davie: "Change, you want to change God's order?" (63), whilst Davie quotes George William Gordon's preaching on the text of "By the waters of Babylon we sat down and wept" when he proclaims that "the voice o' the people is the voice of God, that the heathen would hear and shake with fright" (74) – a Native Baptist sermon. For Bogle, the people's voice *is* the voice of God and the people's blood *is* the blood of Christ (142).

Reid juxtaposes such contrary Biblical justifications without comment, but his account of Pa John's response to the state's pogrom after Morant Bay points to the danger that interpreting the world through the Bible can become a form of false consciousness, more compelling than what is actually happening. As the revolt unfolds, he reads Psalm 78 to his family ("Give ear, O my people, to my law" (170)) – the gist of which is that fathers must teach their children obedience to God's law, and warns what will happen to "a stubborn and rebellious generation" who will be smote down by a vengeful God in rivers of blood. Then Dr Creary brings the news of Eyre's slaughter, including that Moses Dacre, before being hung, has "the cat-o'-nine on [his] behind" (172) (this echoes verse 66, telling that God "smote his enemies in the hinder parts: he put them to perpetual reproach"). Pa John cannot believe what Creary tells him about the state's sadistic revenge: "I feel sure the officers will permit no cruelty, martial law or no martial law" (173), and "God's will be done… Since is martial law it, all rebels must prepare for such" (1174). When Creary tells Pa John he must leave Salt Savannah, Pa John's rebuttal ("The wicked fleeth when no man pursue" [Proverbs 28] and the unspoken remainder of the proverb, "but the righteous are bold as the lion" (175)), points to his family endangering self-righteousness. Reluctantly persuaded, he says: "Go, I will go, Doctor Creary. I will hide in caves like mountain boar. I will flee from the mighty King Saul so till his wrath subsides" (176) – seeing himself as David fleeing to Gath (Samuel 21 and Isaiah 2: 19), and living out the verse: "And they shall go into the holes of rocks, and into the caves of the earth, for fear of the Lord…"

On their march to the hills, Pa John recites "that Psalm for the sons of Korah" (179) – Psalm 88, a complaint to God by one who feels abandoned. The sons of Korah (Numbers 16:28-35) are the sons of those who challenged Moses for the priesthood. The sons were spared, whilst the Korahites were swallowed up by the earth – as Pa John is, whilst all but Manuel of his sons survive. The verse he quotes ("Shall they loving-kindness be declared in the grave?") is dramatically ironic since it precedes his discovery of Ruthie's pregnancy. Here the limits of his biblical mind are tellingly exposed. He strikes down Ma Tamah as the innocent bearer of the news and sees the event as some hidden offence *he* must have committed against God: "Search me life, Tamah. Search me life. […]What ha' I done to God? Why filth must drag at me loins?" (181). And, of course, his belief that only Ruthie's marriage to the already dead Moses Dacre can save their souls leads them down from the hills to his and Manuel's deaths. Pa John marches on, thinking "The English will no' make war on Christians", commanding his family, "Sing, all! Sing the devil away!", until he is shot down like a dog (188-189). Reid surely speaks through Davie's accusation: "You think say your head is big enough to carry all the blood? God strike you for a stubborn fool!" (188).

Perhaps the clash of Bible intertexts most pertinent to Reid's vision comes in Lucille's response to Johnny's defence of Davie's authoritarianism on the Cay. When he says that Davie is "building an Ark and must hold himself to put in so many nails a day", Lucille responds: "Johnny, your brother is building a Tower of Babel. By the time he is finished we might not speak the same tongue!" (240). What she refers to is, of course, the story in Genesis 11, 1-9, when "the sons of men" build a tower "whose top is the heavens", lest [they] be scattered abroad over the face of the whole earth." However, God sees the arrogance of this effort, confuses their languages and scatters them "abroad over the face of the earth". It is amongst other things a story against hubris, though as Thomas Staubli and Silvia Schroer argue in their gendered reading, this is one of the stories that must "be read anew as texts about the sin and hubris of *male* human beings".[36] As Lucille says: "He is not my husband. He is my overseer" (238).

Davie reinforces the connection between the Babel story and gender oppression when he insists that Lucille is "no' unhappy", but adds: "but a woman she is, and women sometimes do not think straight. Soon she will come out of the dark passage and see the light." This is one of the rare occasions when Johnny challenges his brother:

> I do no' know why I said it, but I remember it just came from my mouth:
> "But suppose she does no' see *your* light, bro'?"
> His hand left my shoulder, and his eyes went to long distance. When he spoke, it was Davie talking to Davie:
> "What then? And if thine eye offend thee, pluck it out and cast it from thee."

Significantly, what Johnny thinks, but does not say, in response does not draw from any Biblical text, but from the text of Jamaican nature:

> I could ha' told my bro' that nightingale will no' sing as sweet if bamboo springe has caught her feet. Say that night jasmine will no' scent as sweet in a vase as growing on a rock in the moonshine. (243-244).

13. New Day in Its Own Time: Race and Class and the Nationalist Agenda

Finally, it is difficult *not* to read *New Day* as a work written within the ambit of the Manleys and deeply inscribed in the ideology of the PNP's bourgeois nationalism of the 1940s. Reid records that:

> in 1945/46 when I was writing the novel NEW DAY [...] we [Reid and N.W. Manley] developed an understanding that at least once a week we talked about the book in the dingy but quiet barristers' robing room at the Supreme Court. [...] He read the rough mss., offered suggestions, praised and envied my "patience", and ended up on the dedicatory page...[37]

That connection begins to explain why Reid tells his story of Jamaica's national awakening through the lives of a near-white family, part of the capitalist bourgeoisie, who are committed to the PNP's ideology of a nationhood that "ignored" differences of race, class and gender. Reid himself was from a propertied family; his father became an employer, and Reid's own earlier occupations locate him in the lower professional middle classes. He was a "brown" Jamaican (who could not have been taken for white), though he recorded that aspects of the Campbells were based on members of his own family.[38] An extract from Reid's unpublished autobiographical poem "Kingston Chronicles" and family photographs shows his family as being from brown to fair, and middle class.[39] It would not be improper to suggest that the Reid who wrote *The Leopard* (1958) became ideologically "blacker" in the years after writing *New Day*. Whilst Reid's later biography of Norman Manley, *The Horses of the Morning* (1985) shows an awareness of the nuances of race and class in Manley's public and political career (including the role of Marcus Garvey in Jamaican politics), at the time of writing *New Day*, it is probably safe to say that Reid wrote as part of the near-white/brown elite who thought it was their destiny to provide political leadership to black Jamaicans.

It is not just that the Campbell family is near white, but that, apart from those sections of the first part of the novel that focus on the people of Stoney Gut, black Jamaicans largely disappear from the narrative, with the exception of Timothy M'Laren. This has to be a significant flaw in a national epic.

Reid does not hide how the Campbells' identity is constructed around colour and class. Whilst Pa John asserts that Stoney Gut people "are my people all the same", his horror at finding Ruthie in Moses Dacre's arms is not least because the Dacres are several shades blacker (64), and his outrage over Davie's threatened flogging is not extended to the black men who will also be flogged.

But Reid also wants to establish that there is no necessary connection between race and political attitudes. So, flaxen-haired Davie's anti-colonial radicalism contrasts with the conservative loyalism of the black butcher, Zaccy O'Gilvie, "a hurry-come-up man" as Ma Tamah calls him (163), who Davie describes as a black imperialist, "more English than Lord Derby" (90). All this is fine. The glaring absence is that Abram M'laren is the only black Stoney Gut character who is in any way individualised. He is "a nice man", a resolute and fierce man, "a Wareika boar bellowing down on them" (117), but also a man of sharp wit in his observations on the avaricious white clergyman ("Bring out Parson Contractor Humphrey! Come preach and tell us the price o' cement in heaven" (148)), and the lecherous Custos ("Try and drop a ball under Custos's tool so he will no' chisel stray gals in his buttery-room longer!" (155)). He is a drummer, a dresser of wounds, a hearty, blaspheming man, committed to an eye for an eye, ("40 for 40"), but also Johnny's protector who meets his fate with exemplary honour and courage (185). He offers us a glimpse of a black Jamaica whose humanity is mixed with a thirst for justice.

37

Thereafter, only in his son Timothy's occasional appearances in the text does the presence of black Jamaica offers a small counter-voice to the ideology of reformist gradualism and "all of we are one", such as when Garth says, "They are my people, all of them, regardless of the colour of the skin. We are all Jamaicans – in the sun on high places or in the deep valleys heavy with life!" (282). But when John claims that Garth is "on the march already-already", Timothy demurs:

> "Eh, no, Bro' John. Son-Son will no' march so. When he is ready, shells will sound and you will hear feet a-move on the road."
> I must smile and put my hand to his shoulder. "Time has gone by, friend. Men do no' seek right with the sword longer."
> "Eh? So, Bro' John?" says Timothy. "Then how is it that right comes, *Johnny Piper*? Those who ha' taken your right by their blood will give it back to you without taking some o' your own blood? Eh? Do no' talk without sense!"
> I did no' know Timothy was thinking this way. (284-285)

And though John Campbell's narrative does not acknowledge it, the novel's references to the strikes and demonstrations of 1938 make it clear that the shells *did* have to sound, and people *did* have to march before there was any response to their discontents. This is a truth that Reid leaves several clues to in the novel. When, for instance, Timothy tells Garth's two white radical friends about Stoney Gut and is lauded by Greg, one of the friends, as "a good red", Garth tells Greg to shut up and John sends Timothy to bed like a naughty child. The scene has a further subtlety because we know that Timothy's statement ("Black like me, white like you, everybody who were no' buckra planterman got the cat that day, for cat and the rope are made for the poor whether they be black or white..." (286)) is not true – only blacks were catted – and the reference to "black or white" is said out of consideration for the others present. Timothy's real feelings are signalled by his action in placing his trash hat on his head, and his curt "God be" after he is dismissed.

Some months later, Timothy returns to ask Garth if he will march with the men on Garfield's property in their search for higher wages, Timothy is silenced yet again, ("I sent old Timothy to bed" (332)) and later, when John tells Timothy how Garth has persuaded the strikers to go back to work, he records, "Sorry I am to see that Timothy is no pleased. A man of war he is" (340), and patronisingly dismisses Timothy's reasoning as an old man's return to childishness. John's reflection on Timothy's next absence – that he "goes off sometimes to listen to barrack talk" – signals the divide of race and class between them. When Timothy reappears for the last time, he has walked to Kingston to tell Garth "he came to march with me. He said the shells were blowing but I couldn't seem to hear them" (343). In a death scene of Dickensian heart-tugging, we cannot doubt John's grief for his old friend "one of the family for true", but though they may well lie side by side in death, John never recognises that for Timothy the social justice that Stoney Gut sought remains unachieved. And when Garth's sculptor wife, Mary, carves a memorial bust of Timothy (of "mahogany, rich old mahogany"), isn't Reid inviting us to see this as an act of substitution – an aestheticising of blackness in place of a politics of decolonisation that put working-class black Jamaicans and their culture at its heart?[40]

But *New Day* makes no reference to the culture of resistance amongst black workers and peasants to Eurocentric cultural hegemony – in religion, family life, cosmology and expressive culture, such as Brian L. Moore and Michelle A. Johnson record in their two important books, *Neither Led nor Driven: Contesting British Cultural Imperialism in Jamaica 1865-1920*, and *"They Do As They Please": The Jamaican Struggle for Cultural Freedom after Morant Bay*.[41] In Part One of *New Day*, blackness is inscribed in the religious sectarianism of the Native Baptists, but we see little of other aspects of African Jamaican culture. Again, in Part Three there is no reflection of the independent action of elements of the black working class in 1938, such as is recorded in Patrick Bryan and Karl Watson (Eds.) *Not For Wages Alone. Eyewitness Summaries of the 1938 Labour Rebellion in Jamaica* (2003)[42] or in the studies of Ken Post and Richard Hart.[43] This was literary choice, not ignorance, as Reid's later biography of Norman Manley shows.[44]

Yet, on the matter of class privilege, Reid is at pains to show how far Garth has to travel towards potential leadership. He returns "wearing English tweeds" and speaking like an upper-class Englishman ("It's this awful poverty that gets one…"), announces he will practice in criminal law so "I will get to know my people better" – an admission that shocks his uncle. But as Garth says, "I grew up a buckra boy who wore shoes and had his daily quart of milk as a matter of course. […] Really I grew up *among* my poor friends, but not *with* them" (278). Yet far from being an admission of anything problematic, John seizes on this as the fulfilment of Davie's promise, of "Mas'r God's hand hammering a mould together" (278). But if Garth is Davie returned, he is also a figure whom privilege has taught that he "must not make the mistakes he [Davie] made" of forceful confrontation with colonialism. Uncle and nephew share the view that the real failure of 1865 was the loss of the very limited constitutional representation enjoyed by the middle class: "Secession was what Bogle asked for – and what he got? Constitution taken away and the Crown a-rule from Whitehall." (279). Secession was never part of the historical Bogle's demands, and the old constitution had no more space for the representation of the black majority than Crown Colony government.

Yet there are threads within the narrative that question John Campbell's perspective. When John berates Garth's radical white friends as "Idle sons o' idle wealth who are a-seek for shell-blowing" and wonders why they should "a-seek to fight wealth now", Garth claims (not wholly truthfully), "Am I not fighting capital? And am I not a son of capital? Eh? You old Croesus, you!" (290). John has to admit that he has prospered, "but no' on poor people's eye-water. So must be in one o' the mysterious ways, this, what the Book says God moves in" (290) – as if the family fortunes are divinely come by and not through the surplus value of their labourers' work. He claims that "my measure has been pressed down and running over 'cause I do no' fail to give to men who ask" (290). But this is not a claim about being a fair employer, because the verse he quotes (Luke 6: 38) is about the giving of charity: "Give, and it shall be given unto you; [...] For with the same measure that ye mete withal it shall be measured to you again". The men who ask are not his workers, but beggars.

Again, can one think that Reid was not aware of how elitist and arrogant he makes Garth sound when, though admitting his inexperience, he asserts that it is not his naivety that is to blame when things go wrong, but that "our people are not ready for the things I would bring them", that "the union is scotched [...] because they couldn't think far enough ahead" (312)? Yet the novel does not acknowledge that in the period it covers, trade unionism, even under Bustamante's idiosyncratic and egotistical leadership, was growing strongly.

Again, did Reid intend that Garth's strategy for encouraging the workers on the Campbell estate to form a union be seen as admirable, or as a patronisingly devious way of creating a company union? The scene when the deputation of workers comes into the new great house and stand blinking in the bright electric lights, and leave saying "Thank you very much, sir" suggests the latter. All this takes John back to Davie's prophecy before the Commissioners "that in years to come there will be no buckras leading his people, but the said poor like whom they had killed" (318). It is a conclusion that is hard to reconcile with the scene just shown.

Garth's turn to politics is similarly located in middle-class neo-colonial self-interest. They will be getting wings to fly as part of the Colonial Empire – "each of us with our own pair of wings, but flying together [...] We had them [wings] once... We lost them. We flapped too heavily, so mother bird clipped them. For our own good, she said. She was probably right. They would have flapped us into trouble" (330). Is Garth actually saying that Britain was right to slaughter the black Jamaicans of Stoney Gut who demanded their rights? Can Reid have thought this? Behind Garth's words one guesses the spectre of Haiti in the brown middle-class consciousness. If the new constitution offers "The climb back to where we fell from" (330), the implication is that whilst all Jamaicans have the vote, the brown middle classes will be in charge. The irony that Reid struggles to deal with is that his Garth/Manley figure was decisively beaten in the *actual* first adult suffrage elections by the Fernandez/Bustamente figure, the latter garnering the vote of black working-class Jamaicans.

When a strike breaks out on the property of Garfield, a reactionary Englishman, Garth contextualises his efforts to bring peace there within a classic bourgeois nationalist view:

> "Garfield is a just-come Englishman who has no' been on our island many years yet. He does no' know that here men are no' measured by the quantity o' daylight under their skins. Or say that black foreman Bogle and near-white John Campbell and full-white Reeves are hoeing the said row without a-shoulder of each other. Say that, march, we are marching together." (335)

In reality, this statement was profoundly untrue. It has been taken as one of the novel's key ideological framings, but one must wonder if Reid was wholly aligned with such a perspective. Garth says his task is "to obtain the confidence of these poor devils. I must have their faith in me" (283). Again, is Reid to be taken at face value, or is he critiquing the rise of charismatic hero politicians who dominated West Indian politics to such damaging effect?

What the novel does not explore is how circumstances have changed since Davie resisted with "helpless bitterness", whilst Garth can run "his race with confidence" (283). The problem is Reid's investment in the epic myth of family destiny (and, one suspects, his actual glamouring by the Manley family). Even when Garth finds that the "soil he is ploughing is not altogether rock-stone and cactus. On all the estates he has found men whose eyes were no' blinded by years o' suffering, and these ha' rallied to his call" (284), such interactions play no part in the narrative. What is missing is both the kind of attention that a more consistently realist novel would have given to social change in Jamaica – the rise of an urban working class, and the diversification of the economy[45] – and the vision of how radically Jamaica needed to change that one finds in Roger Mais's almost contemporary novels.

But *New Day* is not consistently realist, and what I hope I've shown is that what is most interesting and rewarding is the conflict at its heart: between the contrary trajectories of its overt historical and political narrative, and the vision of loss embedded in John Campbell's telling of that narrative. I have argued that Reid's portrayal of John Campbell's "fade into the light of common day" touches both on what Wordsworth saw as the inevitable loss of the child's visionary gleam, and his own sense that Campbell's particular loss is a consequence of his passage from the peasant world of his childhood to a manhood in the counting house, managing and profiting from capitalist agriculture. The one preserves the possibility of an intimacy with nature; the other involves an inevitable alienation, a separation between man and the natural world in the process of its commodification. It is a perception that is, of course, at odds with the apparent direction of the historical context of his life: from the horrors that he witnesses outside the courthouse, the slaying of his father and brother Manuel, and what he hears about the state pogrom of Bogle's black supporters in 1865, to his belief in the new day that is coming through Garth's leadership and the modest constitutional reform of 1944.

But then, like Wordsworth, Reid comforts himself with the thought that something of the gleam survives: that for the adult who has been the child immersed in nature "in our embers/ Is something that doth live/ That Nature yet remembers/ What was so fugitive!".[46] In *New Day*, this is manifest in the very act of remembering, the fact that John Campbell is still able to inhabit the sensibility of the child he once was. The significance of these embers is suggested in the reflection he makes as an old man when, in talking about the "song" of the inward man ("the secret o' his thoughts"), he implies a difference from the more public, outward man (and perhaps the novel's overt historical narrative). It is also a reflection that points to the privileged, perhaps even subversive role of metaphor ("song") in the meaning of the novel as a whole:

> If a man would keep well the secrets o' his thoughts, then he must no' sing his songs. For hear me now. I tell you that try howsoever he may try, his thoughts will fly out on the wings o' his song, and

see, you will see their colours; sable like carrion crow going to death, or gold o' the solitaire a-wing towards the morning star. (144)

It is a lovely sequence of images building on the opposites of colour (black/gold), birdsong (carrion crow/solitaire) and between death and the morning star of new day. It is also an ambivalent sequence since it contrasts the vivid world of the narrating boy (his is the world of the solitaire) with that of the old man, listening in the blackness of night to the singing crowd outside Garth's house.

So, despite its flaws in the treatment of race and gender, for the poetry of its linguistic innovations; for its celebration of the Jamaican nation in its landscapes, flora and fauna; for the honesty of its portrayal of the falling trajectory of an individual life; and above all for the livity of its treatment of human embodiment and the network of connections between the human and natural worlds – a record of the possibility of an ecology that includes humankind as a partner, not as an exploiting master – I hope this introduction presents Victor Stafford Reid's *New Day* as more than deserving of our respect and renewed attention.

End Notes

1. Philip Sherlock, "Victor Reid's Novel a Memorable Experience", *The Daily Gleaner*, 26 February 1949, 5.
2. See *The West Indian Novel and Its Background* (London: Faber, 1970), 100-101.
3. Introduction, *New Day* (London: Heinemann Caribbean, 1973); introduction not paginated.
4. Neville Dawes, "The Novels of V.S. Reid", in *Fugue and Other Writings* (Leeds: Peepal Tree Press, 2012), 250-261. Originally given as a lecture c.1980, some extracts published in *The Star*, Jan. 1982.
5. "Novel and History: Plot and Plantation", *Savacou*, 5, 1971.
6. *Of Age and Innocence* (Leeds, Peepal Tree Press, 2011[1958]), 198.
7. *Routledge Companion to Anglophone Caribbean Literature*, Ed. Michael A Bucknor and Alison Donnell (Abingdon: Routledge, 2011), 168.
8. See Mark Johnson, *The Meaning of the Body* (Chicago: University of Chicago Press, 2007).
9. See *The Cambridge Companion to the Body in Literature*, Ed. David Hillman and Ulrika Maude (Cambridge: CUP, 2015).
10. Look at this scene of virtual seduction:

"...Now, listen, if you love Davie and I love Davie and Davie loves both of us, shouldn't we love each other too?"
I am quiet while love for Miss Lucille [...] is a-push anger out of me. Quiet, me, while the beauty of her holds hands with my eyes and will not let go. I will no' be untruthful, but I do no' remember when I said: "Love, I love you too, Miss Lucille."
But all of a sudden I am in her arms, and soft are her breasts on my face...(195).

Later, as a youth, he becomes Lucille's confidant in the war between herself and Davie, and the intensity of his image of how the "Late sun was a-play at hide-and-seek in the dark-night o' her hair. Beautiful, she was..." (206) points to why he responds in such crudely sexual terms to her supposed defection as "Captain Grantley's whore" (250), and goes to "see with my own eyes if hogs are a-root in my dead bro's garden" (251). When he finds Lucille and hears the story of her fall into prostitution, he goes off to find a whore and, for what appears the only time in his life, has sex. He recalls, "my mind says right, I should go with the stranger. I put my body on a grindstone o' sorrow while she thought there was pleasure in it for me" (253). The following day, after Lucille's death, the brothel madam insults him as a eunuch (255), an insult that appears prophetic, since the Johnny of Part Three is an actor without sexual being.

11. Here, Reid perhaps alludes to the fact that though NWM kept his distance from the strikes, Edna Manley brought food and gave other acts of support. See Colin Palmer, *Freedom's Children*, 127.

12. Note Mrs Grandlieu's version in *Guerillas* (Penguin ed. 1975), 52: "his mouth ran 'like a sick nigger's arse'."

13. *The Aeneid. Translated by Robert Fagles* (NY, Viking, 2006).

14. See Devon Dick, *The Cross and the Machete: Native Baptists of Jamaica, Identity, Ministry and Legacy* (Kingston: Ian Randle Publishers, 2009), 185.

15. *There Ain't No Black in the Union Jack* (London: Hutchinson, 1987), 309.

16. See David Boxer, *Edna Manley: Sculptor* (Kingston: The National Gallery of Jamaica, 1990), fp, 120, 121, for a reproduction of *Horse of the Morning*; V. S. Reid's *The Horses of the Morning: About the Rt Excellent N.W. Manley: An Understanding* (Kingston: Caribbean Authors Publishing Co. Ltd, 1985); and see Rachel Manley *Horses in Her Hair: A Granddaughter's Story* (Toronto: Key Porter Books, 2008), 16-18, for the importance of horses and riding at Drumblair.

17. Thomas Staubli and Silvia Schroer, *Body Symbolism in the Bible* (Minnesota: The Liturgical Press, 1998, 2001).

18. Mark Johnson, *The Meaning of the Body*, 281.
19. B.W. Higman, *Jamaican Food: History, Biology, Culture* (Kingston: UWI Press, 2008), 338.
20. See John Bellamy Foster, *Marx's Ecology: Materialism and Nature* (New York: Monthly Review Press, 2000), 149-158.
21. *Historical Thought and Literary Representation in West Indian Literature* (Gainsville: University Press of Florida, 1998), 43-50.
22. 'The Killing Time': The Morant Bay Rebellion in Jamaica* (Knoxville: University of Tennessee Press, 1994, 2000).
23. See Devon Dick, *The Cross and the Machete*.
24. For instance, *Revenge: A Tale of Old Jamaica* (1919) and *The White Witch of Rosehall* (1929). The former deals with the Morant Bay Rebellion.
25. *New World Adams* (Leeds: Peepal Tree Press, 1992, 2008), 222-223.
26. George Campbell, *First Poems* (Leeds: Peepal Tree Press, 2012, first published 1945). See: "Litany", "Last Queries", "Mother", "Dawn".
27. See R.B. Le Page, "Dialect in West Indian Literature", JCL, 7, 1969, 1-7
28. See for instance, *Voices from Summerland: An Anthology of Jamaican Poetry* (Kingston, 1929)
29. See Emily Greenwood, *Afro-Greeks: Dialogues Between Anglophone Caribbean Literature and Classics in the Twentieth Century* (Oxford: OUP, 2010).
30. M.G. Smith, "The Leader: A Play", *Focus*, Jamaica 1943, Ed. Edna Manley, 104-118.
31. Roger Mais, "George William Gordon: A Historical Play in 14 Scenes", in *A Time and a Season: 8 Caribbean Plays*, Ed. Errol Hill (Trinidad, UWI Extramural Studies Unit, 1976), 1-92.
32. Louise Cowan, "The Pietas of Southern Poetry" quoted in Theodore Ziolkowski, *Virgil and the Moderns* (New Jersey: Princeton University Press, 1993), 173.
33. For other references to the coat see 77, 93, 96, 144, 169,213.
34. Quoted in Aaron Seider, *Memory in Vergil's Aeneid: Creating the Past* (Cambridge: CUP, 2013), 38.
35. Quotation from *The Aeneid*. Translated by Sarah Ruden (New Haven: Yale University Press, 2008), 5.
36. *Body Symbolism in the Bible*, 22, 122
37. *Horses of the Morning*, 59
38. *New World Adams*, 224.
39. "Some Extracts from Kingston Chronicles", *Jamaica Journal*, Vol. 19 No. 1, Feb-April, 1986, 32-38.

40. In "No Place for Race: The Bleaching of the Nation in Postcolonial Jamaica", in *The African-Caribbean Worldview and the Making of Caribbean Society*, Ed. Horace Levy (Kingston: UWI Press, 2009), 94-113, Annie Paul charges the early PNP of denying the majority presence of African Jamaicans and restricting cultural "blackness" to an iconic presence in art.

41. Both Kingston: University of the West Indies Press.

42. Mona, Jamaica, UWI, Social History Project, 2003.

43. Ken Post's two studies of worker consciousness in pre-independence Jamaica are *Arise Ye Starvelings: The Jamaica Labour Rebellion of 1938 and Its Aftermath* (The Hague: Martinus Nijhoff, 1978) and *Strike the Iron: A Colony at War. Vol 1, Jamaica 1939-1945* (New Jersey: Humanities Press, 1981); Richard Hart's participant account is *Rise and Organise: The Birth of the Workers and National Movements in Jamaica* (London: Karia Press, 1989); his more analytical study is *Towards Decolonisation: Political, Labour and Economic Developments in Jamaica 1938-1945* (Kingston, Canoe Press, 1999). A good general introduction to 1938 is Colin Palmer's *Freedom's Children: The 1938 Labor Rebellion and the Birth of Modern Jamaica* (Chapel Hill: University of North Carolina Press, 2014).

44. *The Horses of the Morning*, on Garvey, 65-68; on A.G.S. Coombes and St William Grant, 115-116.

45. See for instance Gisela Eisner, *Jamaica 1830-1930: A Study in Economic Growth* (Manchester, Manchester University Press, 1961)

46. William Wordsworth, "Ode", *William Wordsworth: The Oxford Authors* (Oxford: OUP, 1984), 300

AUTHOR'S NOTE

In 1785 the population of Jamaica approximated 300,000 – 30,000 whites, 10,000 free Negroes, and upwards of 250,000 Maroon and Negro slaves. (Maroons are descendants of Spanish-owned slaves who escaped into the hinterland at the time of the 1655 British invasion; Negroes, in Jamaican terminology, are descendants of Africans who arrived under British rule.) Slavery was abolished in 1838. In 1842 the Maroons were granted the full rights of British subjects.

In 1865, when my story opens, Jamaica was ruled by a governor appointed by the Crown. There was an advisory assembly elected by the wealthier landholders. The emancipation of the slaves had financially crippled most of the planters. Many of the large estates had ceased to function. Labour had become scarce because many of the Maroons and Negroes preferred subsistence living on small plots of land to work on a plantation. In 1863, 1864, and 1865 a severe drought worsened conditions throughout the island. Resentment grew against the local government and the Crown, both of which turned deaf ears to the clamour of the unenfranchised for universal adult suffrage and an administration that would be more fully representative.

In October 1865 this resentment led to the Morant Bay Rebellion in the parish of St. Thomas. The chief magistrate of the parish, members of the parish vestry, and hundreds of rebels were killed. The Crown governor, Eyre, hanged the leader of the rebellion and a member of the assembly who had favoured it. The assembly proclaimed martial law and abrogated the constitution. In England, indignation against Governor Eyre's excessive actions arose. He was recalled, and a new governor was sent to the island, which was reverted to Crown colony government, amounting to rule by edict from London.

47

From 1886 on, there was continuing agitation in Jamaica for restitution of the representative government. In 1883, for example, it was ruled that nine members of the legislative council, previously appointed by the governor, should be elective. It was only in November 1944, however, that Jamaica was granted a constitution guaranteeing what amounts to self-rule under Crown supervision. It is this constitution that inaugurated the "new day".

I have not by any means attempted a history of the period from 1865 to 1944. The entire Campbell family of my narrative is fictional. What I have attempted is to transfer to paper some of the beauty, kindliness, and humour of my people, weaving characters into the wider framework of these eighty years and creating a tale that will offer as true an impression as fiction can of the way by which Jamaica and its people came to today.

V. S. REID

PART ONE

THE EVENING

TOMORROW I will go with Garth to the city to hear King George's man proclaim from the square that now Jamaica-men will begin to govern themselves. Garth will stand on the high platform near the Governor and the Bishop and the Chief Justice, and many eyes will make four with his. Garth will stand proud and strong, for mighty things ha' gone into his conception.

Eh, but now I am restless tonight. Through the half-opened window near where I sit, night winds come down the Blue Mountains to me. Many scents come down on the wind, and I know them all. I know all the scents o' the shrubs up on the mountains. There are *cerosee*, mint, mountain jasmine, *ma raqui*, there are *peahba* and sweet cedars. I know that the bitter *cerosee* will drive away fever, that *ma raqui* will heal any wounds – even wounds from musket balls.

I am restless tonight. There is a blue velvet case on the table side o' me, and my fingers caress this case. My fingers find the catch and press inwards, and six little gold studs wink at the light – the studs which Son-Son gave me.

Sundown this evening, Garth, who is Son-Son, came in from Morant Bay. Handing me the velvet case, he told me:

"In memory of the great-grand whom I didn't know. These will make a dandy granddaddy tomorrow."

Aie – Garth remembers all the old things I ha' told him.

This restlessness will no' make me find my bed. You know how long I have sat here? Nine o'clock come, and gone, and first rooster crowed, and here I am sitting down.

I move my feet to find firmness on the polished *yacca* floor. Find, I find it and get up without touching the chair arm. If Son-

Son was here with me, he would laugh and say I grow younger every day. I step to the window and open it wide. But how good are the scents!

Clock is talking of the hour. Is what it the clock say now? Ten o'clock? Eh, you mean I ha' sat here till now?

I can no' go to my bed now. I must wait until the Morant people come, for I ha' heard that they will come and sing mighty hymns under our window tonight. They will sing away the old time and sing in the new, for tomorrow the English Governor o' our island will proclaim that Jamaica has got a new constitution. Garth will be up there on the platform near the Governor and the Bishop and the Colonial Secretary and the Chief Justice, for all o' these know he will be leader of the new government after the General Elections...

But God O! Look what my eyes ha' lived to see!

Then, now! Pa John and Ma Tamah, father and mother o' sorrow – are you hearing? And my brethren, Emmanuel, David, Samuel, Ezekiel, Ruth, Naomi, are you hearing?

Are you a-hear, George William Gordon? And Paul Bogle, Abram M'Laren, and the good Doctor Creary?

And you too, bloody Governor Eyre and your crow Provost-Marshal Ramsey, are you hearing wherever you are? Tell me, Bro' Zaccy O'Gilvie, are you a-listen of me tonight?

Then, now! All o' you Dead Hundreds who looked at the sun without blink in your eyes, you Dead Hundreds who fell to British redcoats' bullets and the swords o' the wild Maroons, the wild men o' the mountains; tell me, you Dead Hundreds o' Morant Bay, are you hearing that tomorrow is the day? And that sorrow and restlessness are here with my joy, for I am standing here alone?

Aie – me, John Campbell, youngest o' Pa John Campbell.

I turn back and look in at the room. Younder in another room Garth is asleep. Hard day it has been for him today, and the long, long tomorrow only hours away. Rest, he will rest now.

A good house, this. Well has my grand looked after me. There is thick mahogany in this room, much silver and glass talk to me o' prosperity, tells we ha' come a far way since 'Sixty-five.

I hear the singing now. Our Party people are coming to our house at Salt Savannah, marching with torchlight and mighty hymns. Make them come.

Bring your torchlights and your voices and put fire and music in the soul of an old man tonight!

For many years now bank the flame that was young John Campbell. If the Master plans that I turn this year my face to the wall and sleep, then Son-Son must make a head-cut to say:

BORN 1857, DIED 1944

Music is swelling in my ears as I go over to the east window. Our people are marching from the Bay, and now I can glimpse the torches carried by those taller ones. I listen good, and can hear the words...

Onward, Christian Soldiers...

Funny how my mind turns back and I can remember it well.

'Sixty-five, it was. October morning; sun-up is fire and blood, and fear walks with my family. Remember, I remember, that this was the tune Pa John told us to sing that time when we came down out of the mountains.

Hear my father: *Sing, family O! British redcoats do no' make war on Christians.*

But just the same time was when Davie came out of the bush so sudden that Zekiel and Naomi must cry out. Davie was nineteen years old that time, and tall nearly like my father. He has taken up Maroon war style, with shrubs tied on all over his body, to fool the English redcoats. So, when we looked at him, we did no' know where Davie ended and the shrubs began.

Hear my bro' Davie to Father: *Do no' go down, Father. Stay up here in the mountains. Mr. Gordon and Deacon Bogle are hanging by their necks from the courthouse steps.*

But how my father was stubborn! His head was tossing leader-bull fashion as he walked out in front of us.

Come behind me, Tamah, he said. *Sing after your mother, you pickneys.*

So, we went out of the mountains down into Baptism Valley, a-sing...

Now they round the foot of the hill and come up to our house. Candlewood torches make our road, as bright as day.

You know how you make candlewood shine? Go into the woodland and find a limb as big as your wrist and a half. Strip the bark partways down, and leave it hanging over your hand to keep off the sparks. Sharpen the point, then light it with a lucifer-match. And then how it will burn bright!

Under our windows they are now, many, many o' them. The song has changed and softer it is now. From their throat the song sobs, but with no sorrow in it. A plaintiveness like a January nightingale winging through the Cuna Cuna Pass, and yet with deepness and richness like cloud robes wrapping an evening sun.

There are children and full women and full men. There is me there, at the window, singing too; for good it is that a ripe man should have music in his soul. So soon they sing a hymn to the finish, so soon do they change. No time this is for quiet.

Edge up yourself sharp, Coney Mount tenor-man! Roll it out, big-bone bass-man from Cedar Valley! Roll it out, for the girls from Morant fishing beach must ha' something solid to pour molasses from their throats on. Sing, my people, for good this is.

And then the hymn is finished, and there is:

Hooray! Hooray! Bring out Garth Campbell! Bring out our Son-Son!

But tired Son-Son is, and there is tomorrow soon to come. So I shake my head and put finger to my lips and form like I am asleep. They know what I mean, and there is a long *sshh* to one another; so, although they meant it for quiet, the hush is loud as the *hooray*.

That time, then, they all laugh and nod at me so I must laugh too. Then, humming of the tune, there is *Abide with Me*.

God o' me! Hear my people sing! Is no' the Image and the Likeness this?

No sleep will come to me. Restless memories are rising inside me, bringing wetness to my eyes. But old men must no' cry. Cry, and is the end of the purpose, that, leaving just a waiting. But ripe men can no' forget their memories. Most of everything is behind, so little is in front; unless there is a son-son.

Then behind and in front will be the same distance, for a man can live in the son of a son.

Tomorrow after I ha' put on my shirt with the gold studs, Son-Son will knot my tie. Then I know down in the garden where a pretty rosebud is. I will fasten it in my buttonhole, and he will laugh and say: *Sheik*.

We must eat a good breakfast tomorrow. Newspapers say the ceremony to proclaim the new constitution will be short; but the city sun is much hotter than Morant sun, so a man must have heavy provender back o' his waistband. Tomorrow we must have *renta* baked in coconut milk and new butter. We will eat i' with *ackee* and codfish mince. We will wash down our *bammie* with Blue Mountain coffee. Good I will feel when Garth leaves the table with heavy provender packing his insides.

Newspapers say Morant and Pedro Cays will be in the declaration o' the new constitution. I read o' Morant Cays, and memories shake at me.

Memories are a-shake me tonight. Memories o' hot sand and mangrove bush and hunting-Maroons with naked swords. Of the boom of redcoats' muskets, the whistle o' whips, and the crack o' lashes; of a dozen men twitching on Provost Ramsey's gallows.

Memories o' Colonel Judas Hobbs of the Sixth Regiment o' Foot. Memories of Mr. Abram and his forty for forty. Memories of a high wind, and weakness coming to my bro's loins when his woman was no' with him. Memories o' two old men stumbling through dark-night to bring Davie's seed from a plague house.

Aie – I must no' be restless longer. Quiet, I will sit quiet, while they sing and make my mind walk back. I will talk a talk o' the years what ha' passed.

CHAPTER 1

For three years now, no rain has come. Grass-piece and yam-vines are brown with dryness, cane leaves have not got much green to them. Thirst and hunger walk through our land, four hundred thousand people have no osnaburgs to their backs.

For three years now, no rain has come and only the rich laugh deep.

It is the year 1865. For three years, there have been no crop-times in our fields. In America, brothers o' the North have just done warred with brothers o' the South, and so no clipper ships are riding the ocean to bring flour and codfish for our empty bellies.

No growth on the land, no ship on the sea – Lord O! But there is suffering!

For three years, Edward John Eyre has been a-sit in the Queen's House at St. Jago de la Vega parish as Governor of our island. With dryness on the land and a shipless ocean we turn to the man who stands for Missis Queen Victoria. Men ha' lost skin off their feet tramping with Petitions on the rocky roads to St. Jago. But always they are met with muskets and bayonets, and always they come home with foodless bellies but vexation curdling their bowels.

But now, badness is coming. From Westmoreland parish in the west to St. Thomas parish in the east, men are talking in secret under heavy cotton-tree roots.

Mr. George William Gordon and his friends in the House of Assembly ask for the recall o' John Eyre. Good pastors from their pulpits plead say we must be calm. Buckra planters on great estates and pastors o' the Established Church say hooray for Governor Eyre, curse the Baptist pastors and laugh at the hunger of our people. For soon then, by-and-by, labour will be cheap. But at length and at last Westminster is hearing.

Rage and bitterness walk with Eyre's voice as he tells his Council of Doctor Underhill. Underhill is o' the Baptist faith and he has penned a letter to the Secretary of States for the Colonies telling him of our sufferings. Rage and bitterness walk with the voices of Eyre's Church of England clergymen as they deny that men are very hungry. And same time, now, they are calling with heavy voices for more and more tithes from the poor. And same time, now, the Established Church sends a note to the Queen; but still we wait in hope on Westminster.

Is the year it 1865, and pastors o' the Baptist faith stir again to help the poor. A Petition has gone by packet to the Queen, praying that starvation should no' take us. We wait in hope on Missis Queen.

But when the packet returns, and the *Queen's Advice* is taken to every village church and nailed to every constabulary station, and on market-day we gather around and read it with lips o' stiffness – *aie*, bro'!

Then we know the Church of England has won the fight, the Baptist letter has no' been credited.

Hear the QUEEN'S ADVICE:

THE MEANS OF SUPPORT OF THE LABOURING CLASSES DEPEND ON THEIR LABOUR. HER MAJESTY WILL REGARD WITH INTEREST AND SATISFACTION THEIR ADVANCE-MENT THROUGH THEIR OWN MERITS AND EFFORTS.

Wait! plead good pastors from their pulpits, *Her Majesty has been wrongly advised!*

Wait, says Mr. Gordon at his Underhill meetings, *we will take the case to Whitehall ourselves.*

Wait? Paul Bogle asks at Stoney Gut, *Is war it, or peace, they want?*

It is the year 1865. June and July and August gone, and no rain comes with October. Brown on our yam-vines, the earth a-crack with dryness, there is no *osnaburg* to make clothing for our backs, four hundred thousand are a-moan.

God O! – there are tears all over the land and only the rich laugh deep.

CHAPTER 2

This Sunday morning, day-cloud has no' peeped, but my father is calling:

"Manuel O! Davie! Ruthie! Get up and come all o' you, prayer-meeting time."

There is straw a-rustle and yawns from the other rooms. From my kitty-up in the same room as Father and Mother, I hear when Davie grumbles something. You always know when Davie grumbles something 'cause everybody giggle. Everybody, 'cept Manuel.

Pa John and Ma Tamah heard it too, for in the young light o' dawn, I saw him stiffen and look at Mother.

"You hear that boy, Tamah? Hear him?"

Then me fearful for Davie, for my father is vexed. My father leaps from his bed and rushes to where the trace-leather hangs back of the door, but Mother is quick after him and is holding to his arm. She whispered and whispered to my father until deep breath pushed anger from him.

Some of the worry-marks left my mother's face. She called:

"Hurry, all o' you *pickneys* – your father is a-wait!"

Then me, less fearful but more sorry, for nice it is and yet not nice when someone else is getting the whip. Davie must ha' heard when Father went for the trace-leather, for now he is first into the hall and on his knees looking like overgrown lambkin.

All o' us are in the hall on our knees now, Emmanuel, David, Ruth, Samuel, Ezekiel, Naomi, and me, Johnny. Father struck a lucifer-match for the lantern, raised the shade, and put flame to the wick. Young light swelled quickly to manhood, and Father puffed out the match. All of us watch as light flows down Father's face. Blue eyes which bed deep down in his head look one time on Davie and then on all o' us.

Anger-marks are still on Father's brown forehead. Funny thing, but when Father is vexed he looks more like white man than brown. When he is at peace, there is softness in my father's face.

Ruthie says it is because Scotchmen are always warring and

brown people are always singing, so that when Father is vexed he looks like his Scottish sire, and when at peace like his mother who had brown blood in her. Must be true it.

Father rested the lantern on the table and opened the Book. But no words come from him, and Mother looks on his forehead and see there are still anger-marks there. So then, feel, I feel her arms hug my shoulder and same time she begins *Sweet Hour of Prayer.*

In the long metre she sings the hymn, and all o' us take it up with her, 'cept Davie and my father. But after Father listened a little he raised his head and looked at Davie – eh, quick my bro' Dave commenced a-sing too. By-and-by, Father came in at the second verse. Then we came to the end.

Through a chink over the door which Mother always covers when the Christmas wind is northing, day-cloud is peeping now at me. Down in the Bay, the sea is kneeling for early matins. There is the whisper and the roar of the chant when groundswells creep out and then come in like thunder. I am thinking say the spray must be near up to the barrack this morning and I wish say the prayer meeting was over. Is nice, it, to have spray on your face and you with nothing on, rolling on the sand.

A good light is on the Book now. Father says he is reading from the Book o' Isaiah. I do no' hear much though, for I am watching Davie. I love Davie.

I saw when Sammy touched him with his shoulder. When Davie looked up from under his brow, my bro' Sammy shook his head as if to say: *Do not make Father more vexed.* I know that Sammy loves Davie too, so when Davie's and my eyes make four, I shake my head too.

But I am eight, while Sammy is fifteen and Davie is nineteen, so Davie forms his mouth like saying *Shut up,* and I see Naomi grin. Naomi is ten. I want to rub sea-sand in her hair but Father is reading from the Book.

FOR THOSE THAT WAIT UPON THE LORD SHALL RENEW THEIR STRENGTH. THEY SHALL MOUNT UP WITH WINGS AS EAGLES. THEY SHALL RUN AND NOT BE WEARY, THEY SHALL WALK AND NOT FAINT.

There is iron and heavy wind in my father's throat.

All of us know the Psalm which Mother recites; all, 'cept
Naomi and me, but I know more than Naomi. A good. I go to the
second verse but Naomi stops at the first. I say the second verse
loud and she is vexed. A good. We sing a hymn and prayer meeting
is over.

Outside in daylight, and sea-breeze is putting anger-marks on the
face of the Bay. It is October month, and all over Salt Savannah
silver arrows wave above our cane-field to say that the juice is ripe.
But cane leaves are brown and the earth is dusty, and I know are
bad, these.

Davie says cane leaves should be green and the earth should
be mouldy if hunger, thirst, and nakedness must no' be on the
land.

My friends Timothy M'Laren and Quackoo M'Laren down at
the barrack will be ready to go into the sea. So then, I was running
down the hill to the barrack when Mother called me back. She
said this is the Sabbath morning and she will ha' peace on Salt
Savannah. Naomi grins and says *A good*. I put two fingers to the
fat o' her buttocks and cry, she is crying now. Howsoever, Mother
has got me by the arm and is hauling me inside the house.

She puts on me the *osnaburg* pantaloons which are too short for
Zekiel and too long for me. Mother turns up the bottoms so they
fit. Sunday clothes, these.

Mother and me were inside our room when I heard Father call
Manuel and Davie to the hall-room. I saw her cock her ears, a-
listen to what was in my father's voice. Then she told me to go
outside and keep the pantaloons clean for I will wear them to
Chapel. But me for outside when I ha' just heard what is in my
father's voice and see trace-leather is not hanging back o' the
door?

So I say nothing to Mother but go to the corner near my kitty-
up.

There is a box-kite under my kitty-up which I swopped from
Quackoo M'Laren yesterday-day for a *buntung* mango and a
croaker-lizard skeleton. A good kite, this, with one singer torn; a

good kite, this, but Quackoo is always hungry. *Croaker* skeleton is a *brawta*. Quackoo is a Jew in business, always wanting extra when there is a swop, so now he has my *croaker*. But I know where an iguana died last week, and an iguana is very bigger than a *croaker*. A good.

I am sitting on the floor with my box-kite on my knees and form like I am looking on the torn singer while Mother makes her bed with clean Sunday sheets and pillowcases. Ruthie and Sammy are gone to woodland to look firewood for our breakfast, Zekiel and Naomi are gone to the stream for water, only Mother and me are here.

Soon I hear Pa John's voice: "Manuel, David, I want to see you both."

Father's voice has heaviness like when he recites the Psalm what asks: *How long, O Lord, how long?*

I heard the boys move their feet a little but none made answer to Father. Mother has stopped making her bed, stands with ears a-listen, worry-marks on her face. Why is Mother worrying so when she will no' be getting the whip?

Mother is funny, though. She loves Manuel more than Davie 'cause Manuel reads the Book on Sabbath-day. But my bro' Davie? Eh!

Davie goes to Stoney Gut and listen to Paul Bogle preach secession. When meeting stops for eating-time and after we ha' had the roast pig, Davie jumps the wall at Pastor Humphrey's estate and eats *Number Eleven* mangoes. Know, I know, for one Sabbath-day I went to Stoney Gut with him. How come?

We told Pa John and Ma Tamah that there was a she-goat which had strayed from our compound and say we will go to look for her. But 'stead o' that, we were off for the Gut and the big meeting there.

There, the men sang heavy that *The Year o' Jubilee is Come*, and Deacon Bogle preached say God is right and God is might and if we ha' God we ha' might and right. And everybody shouted *Amen!* and *Alleluia!* and *Jubilee!* Me, too.

Afterwards, Davie and me climbed Pastor Humphrey's wall and fed on his cane and *Number Eleven* mangoes. I love Davie.

★

"Davie, I want to see you. Is what kind o wickedness, this?"

I do no' like the iron in Father's throat. Peep through knot-hole into t'other room and see Father and Manuel and Davie. Father stands in the middle of the room, two fists doubled and resting on the table. Manuel and Davie are on t'other side of the table, a-face my father.

There is the trace-leather on the table 'side of my father's hand. Davie's breath is coming quick-quick; same way his chest leaps when Paul Bogle cries: *Secession! Secession! Total freedom!*

Worry is on Manuel's face, but nothing on Davie's face. Smooth and flat is Davie's face and there is nothing till you look into his eyes. Then you see a watchfulness there, like say in barrack people's eyes when Custos Baron Aldenburg is passing on his way to courthouse.

"Did I no' tell you Stoney Gut is not for you?"

Father is talking again. I see Davie's mouth being stubborn like Custos's mule.

My father took the trace-leather in his hand; coconut tree a-tremble in March wind is my father now. There is a groan back o' me and I know it comes from Mother, but I can no' turn from my knot-hole.

Hear Father with loudness: "Answer me, boy! Answer me!"

Barrack-cart going to market on Saturday-day sometimes has no grease on the axle, and that time, the iron rubs on mahoe wood and so is Father's voice.

My bro' Manuel is a peacemaker; he talks through treacle: "Father, beg, I am begging that you take time, sir."

Now, Manuel has turned twenty-one, and his eye is same height from the ground as is Father's, but there is not anything more of my father in Manuel. For such a way he favours Mother, does my bro' Emmanuel!

But Davie? Now there you see Father a-face his own self across the table, 'cept that one face is smooth, while t'other has seen many mango seasons.

"Answer me now, boy!"

When Davie answered, his teeth were tied together. "Yes, is that what you said."

"But you go all the same and listen to wickedness from that Paul Bogle? Listen to a man preach 'gainst what the Book says?"

"How you know I ha' been to Stoney Gut?" Davie asked.

"Bro' Zaccy O'Gilvie told me o' your wickedness!" Father shouted.

Now, a smart way Davie has fixed for Stoney Gut. He has told Father that with dryness on the land all o' us should no' go to church on Sabbath, for if the animals get into what little cane we ha' on Salt Savannah, who will be there to drive away the animals? So, then, Davie stays; but when the rest o' us are on to Chapel, gone, he is gone to the Gut.

Bro' Zaccy must ha' heard of this, and told it to Father yesterday when we were at Morant Bay market.

Thunderhead for day-cloud and the sun peeping through blackness on grey water in the Bay, so is Davie's eyes. Father in a temper, Davie in a temper, Mother worrying, Manuel worrying. And, me?

When another might get the whip, and you know your conscience has nothing on it, it is nice, and yet no' nice.

Hear my father: "Is what it you want? Change, you want to change God's order? You and those others can no' wait for Jehovah's plan? Paul Bogle's wickedness is better than the ordinance o' St. Paul?"

Temper bursts in my bro' Davie. There have a fall in the Plantain Garden River, where water tumbles down in deep-voice quickness; so Davie's words are a-tumble.

"Wickedness? Wickedness? You call it so? Wickedness to want even rice and flour and *osnaburg* while *buckra* Englishman eats bacon and wears Shantung silk? Why do they no' make us govern ourselves and see if we would no' eat bacon too? Why they will no' give the vote to all o' us and make us choose our own Council?"

I can see worry riding Manuel. I see him look on my father and fright comes to his eyes. I look on Father too, and see there is lightning coming down the Blue Mountains, a-lick all sides o' Yallahs Valley. No worry is worrying Davie. Words are a-hiss and a-foam through his teeth.

"Wickedness? You say Paul Bogle is preaching wickedness? What has Governor Eyre said about our Petition to the Missis

Queen Victoria? What ha' they got on the paper which hangs from Pastor Humphrey's church door? Forgot, you ha' forgotten?"

Nobody has to tell me say it is the *Queen's Advice* Davie means. 'Member, I remember the morning when Bogle read it at Stoney Gut, and all the men they laughed. But frighten takes you and you feel cold when the men o' Stoney Gut laugh that time.

Hear Davie: "Is that what will bacon we? And wine we? And Shantung silk we? And you say wickedness it is to listen to Deacon Bogle? Time now, I tell you, that we should swop Petition for powder – and God strike us if we do no' that!"

Thunderhead opens in my father's eyes. What comes out I can no' look at. I see his hand moves. Up goes the trace-leather and down on Davie's back.

"Davie Campbell! Swearing in my house! Swear God's name in John Campbell's house in front o' his very own face?"

Father is a cane-band shaking in sea-breeze. Trace-leather is a cassava-beater flailing on Davie's shoulder.

"Blaspheme Jehovah's name in my house? Eh, Davie Campbell?"

CHAPTER 3

Only one time before I had ever heard all what I heard in my father's voice that day. Only one time.

'Twas a young moon night after the August Fair at Morant Bay. Father and me were coming through the shortcut what goes through Bro' Aaron Dacre's cane-piece. T'others of our family had left the Bay before sundown, but I had stayed with Father to see the finish of the mule auction.

So then, we are coming through this cane-piece, and as we round a patch o' high cane, what do we see but young Moses Dacre with my sis Ruthie in his arms. There was one piece o' young moon in Ruthie's eyes and t'other in Moses's eyes.

Father stopped quick, his breath going with rush. Surprise there was on him, which made me wonder why; for Naomi and me knew well about Moses and my sis Ruthie. When we reached home, I asked Naomi why surprise should ha' taken Father, but she laughed and said all menfolk were fool-fool. Naomi is a mouse-face with funny ways.

But I am a-tell you of Father's voice that night. When he lifted his coco-macca stick and dropped it on Moses's shoulder, heard I heard in his voice all what I hear now as he shouts at my bro' Davie.

"Take the Lord's name in vain in my house, Davie Campbell? Call on His name without justness?"

Manuel is holding to Davie, who is railing and prancing like colt-horse on merry-go-round at Morant Bay Fair. Trace-leather comes down so fast on Davie's shoulder that poor Manuel gets it on his face one time.

Just then Mother rushed out from our room screaming like *kling-kling* bird homing on evening wind. Fright was there on her face, but she held on to Father's arm and was up and down like kirk bell before he stopped using the trace-leather.

"Pa John!" comes from my mother, "Pa John! Done – you hear? Enough that – ha' done!"

Kling-kling pecking at rain-beat hawk is Mother beside my father. Manuel has got Davie by his arm and is talking fast to him. I can no' hear what Manuel says, but Davie stops railing and prancing and only breathe fast through his mouth. Mother is talking to Father, and I see her take the trace-leather from his hand.

Now Father has got her to one side. Quiet, he talks to Davie now but north wind blows cold in his voice.

"Come out o' my house, Davie Campbell. Leave out o' my house before the Devil takes charge o' me right hand."

Davie's calico shirt is torn where the trace-leather has walked. Davie has no' been licked since two years a-back when he drank rum and coconut water at August Fair. A long time it has been now, and now he is grown to near manhood, for he has drunken his rum after boar-hunt before my father's very face, and moreover is playing with Ma Abigail's Adassa, who lives in Bath Town. Father does no' like Adassa, though, for she walks and hoists her backside too much like sport-girls at Port Morant who crowd the promenade when sugar-boats come in.

Me? Hear everything in our room at night when Father and Mother talk and believe say I am asleep. A good.

Howsoever, the licking has hurt him, and thunderhead has left his eyes to a Christmas moon shining on white clouds.

Hear my bro' Davie, dryness in the Garden River now: "Thankie, Father, this is no' my house. Wrong I am, and will no' say more."

He was leaving the house when my father spoke again.

"You understand, boy? Understand say if you go to Stoney Gut you do no' sleep here any more?"

Mother talks with my father's ear; but why is she a-talk so low so that I can no' hear? Stillness is there on Davie, no answer comes. Then through the door fast, and not a Davie in the house.

Thunder rolls low in my father's throat and he is making for the door, but Mother and Manuel has his arm and is begging him to ha' done. Manuel favours Mother, with the selfsame worry on his face.

I can hear the other *pickneys* coming up the hill. Naomi is hollering, so I believe Timothy must ha' tossed a dead cockroach on her when she passed the barrack. Timothy is my friend. A good.

Hear my mother: "*Pickneys* are coming back now, Pa John."

Father shook his head. Father is a bad steer coming from branding pen.

"Today-day is the Sabbath, Pa John. Is a day o' peace this, yes?"

Father said with heaviness: "A day o' peace, Tamah." Then he has turned and is walking into our room.

Me? Quiet. Creep out softly into t'other room. Manuel is gone. Gone, me too. I want to find Davie, for I love Davie.

CHAPTER 4

I know where to find Davie. There have a place in the mango-walk where the water goes to bed. We call it Maroon Hole. There are trees all around, branches bend low to whisper to it, and you do no' see the water-hole till you come right on it. Davie says it is like the wild Maroons who live in the Blue Mountains.

But it does no' spring on you and cut off your head like the wild Maroons o' the mountains.

Cool and sweet is the water, and you take off your pantaloons and swim from bank to bank and the water hugs you close. Like say when you dream at night that duppy-ghost is a-chase you and you cry out and Mother hugs you and you wake up and her breasts are a-kiss your face and there is peace on you. Is so Maroon Hole.

I creep through the trees and come to the Hole. Davie is laying on the bank, on his back, with his feet in cool water.

I say softly: "Bro' Davie?"

I lay down like him with my feet in the water and say: "Poor Davie."

Davie quiet; then he turned on his face and looked down on me for a long time; looking like I am no' there. But presently his eyes made four with mine and he laughed and said: "Cho, man, nothing."

I turned on my side and looked at him too and said: "Cho, man, nothing."

Laugh comes to Davie's eyes, summer moonshine on Maroon Hole.

"You were peeping?" he asked. I nod me head.

"From where?"

"From in our bedroom," I tell him.

Heavy laugh rolls from my bro's belly. Is good, this.

There is a small quiet, then I ask: "You will go for Stoney Gut?"

Aie – bad, that; for night-clouds cover the moonshine. Wrong, I am wrong and feel to holler; but Davie jumped to his feet and hoisted me too and said: "Come, we will swim."

There is a pull at the string o' my pantaloon. His own comes off too, and over we are gone and are in the water before you can say *Jack Mandora*. When my head comes up, he is there beside me. We swim from bank to bank, then we are out and flat on our backs on the bank. Feel good and quiet now, me.

All of a sudden I hear Davie: "Johnny, you old how?"

"Eight," I say quick, for I heard from Naomi yesterday-day when we were a-row about some tamarinds we got from Ma Katie at Guanaboa Vale. Naomi had said her portion should be bigger, for she was ten and me only eight.

"Eight, Johnny? Well, you will live to see it."

Live to see what? But I do no' ask, for that is how Davie says funny things sometimes with his eyes gone to bed deep in his head. But I do no' like it, for clouds are banking on Maroon Hole again. I do no' want to talk. He makes a pillow with his hands and lay looking through the leaves at the sky, so I do so too. Leaves lace 'gainst the sky like the edging on Mother's Sunday shift with blue petticoat under it.

"You ever hear about slavery, Johnny? You know our parents were born in slavery times?"

Davie down on me for talk, so what must Johnny do?

So I say: "Yes, Ruthie says Pastor Humphrey says –"

Wayah! His feet slap water, and cold sprays my face.

"Humphrey! Pig, that! Do no' call his name!" Teeth are mixed with his voice. "Pig, that! A man who knows how people are hungry and yet tax us for money to build his new church at Morant Bay – and no' only that, but takes the contract himself to do the building! Is a buttery-hog, that man. Machete in the belly for him! You know what, Johnny – ?"

But Davie sees I am no' happy, so he sits up and raises me too. Now he talks with teeth in his throat. "Listen, Johnny, eight you are now, time you should know about things."

There is a naseberry tree hanging far over the water. Davie goes to his feet like a yearling and pulls in a branch with a full ripe fruit at the end. I am wondering how Timothy and I had no' seen it before; but that is how Davie is. Even guinea-fowl can no' lay in deepest mangrove but Davie will find the egg.

Naseberry pulpy and thick, and when you ha' finished with the richness, you roll the seeds around your mouth so they click against your teeth. Fright has gone, contentment is at Maroon Hole.

We lay down again. He placed a dead bamboo root under our heads so we were like how Father cotches up the pillows on his bed night-time when he wants talk with Mother. Cool it is under the trees. A *john-to-whit* is a-dance in a guinep tree and making music with whistles in his throat. To me, it sounds like militia-men making skirl with their fifes at Morant Bay when they drum down the Jack at sunset. If my bro' Sammy was here, there would be shine in his eyes. Funny how my bro' Sammy likes soldiering.

Hear Davie: "When slavery was run out of the country, *buckra* English promised the poor land and wages. They gave the land, but all rocks and swamp, and nothing will grow there. They gave the wages, but man can no' live on sixpence a day."

He is talking quiet now, and there are the naseberry seeds at my teeth and *john-to-whit* a-skirl like mad overhead.

"Is true it, that our family are no' badly off, for near-white we are, even if poor, and ha' been landowners for three generations, and now Father is an estate headman. But no'-the-less, Johnny, and listen well to me, we are all Jamaicans – six o' one and half dozen of t'other to the *buckra* English.

"For three years now, there has been dry weather. For five years now, Americans ha' fought with Americans. Bro' Abraham Lincoln has won his victory, and slavery has gone from his land, but still no clipper ships have come south with flour and codfish. Governor Eyre is there fat at St. Jago with good living, and the Missis Queen says we must prosper on cactus and iguana."

Davie's voice sinks low as if he is a-talk with Davie. I turn my head on the bamboo root and see that his eyes are gone to bed. So, is true it, that perhaps he is talking with himself.

"What happens when hard time comes on us? Some poor people borrow money on their crops from buckra estate owner. Even before payback time comes, estate owner takes them to court. But since poor people ha' not got any money, since dry weather is here and no canes will grow, buckra magistrate tells buckra estate owner that he must take the land, for poor people will no' pay.

"So, then, turn buckra turns his cattle on to the land and have them trample down yam-hills and cane cultivations. The poor take back *buckra* to the court, and another buckra magistrate says the order has been made and the land does no' belong to the poor any longer.

"And if you ever talk o' injustice, is to prison they send you. Some charge without foundation sends you to the crank and the treadmill, or you get the gallows for treason."

There is deep breath from Davie, but it does no' push the anger from him, and Davie is still talking with Davie.

"Look back on last year. You will see a woman in a family way travelling to her cultivation with her hoe on her shoulder. On the Bath Road it is. See, you will see Judge Boltin passing, riding on his horse. Bath Road is narrow, and the hoe touches the nose o' the horse so it shies – *wayah!* Down Judge jumps from his horse and flogs the woman with his *supple-jack* so she must fall like dead! *God o' me!*"

Davie O! Come, quiet again!

Davie came quiet again. "Later, she loses her baby for the beating she gets. Deacon and his Councilmen give her money to fight in court. Custos is there on the Bench, and he puts it off and puts it off and puts it off so that Bogle must send Petition to St. Jago. Eyre does no' want Missis Queen to hear of it, so he has talk with Custos. Month, gone, market-day, Custos meets Deacon and tells him he has fined Boltin five shillings."

Davie laughed and his feet stirred water.

"If it was in slavery days, Boltin would ha' paid a bigger fine for making a woman lose a manchild – *God strike him!*"

You ever take a bull-whip and throw the lash forward and bring it back quick so the cowskin fringe curls up and talks sharp to you? Is so, Davie's voice.

"But, tell, I tell you, Johnny, none o' these would ha' happened if for true we were governing ourselves."

Davie blasphemes a little more. Good it is to hear him blaspheme and Father no' around, so I blaspheme too. Davie grinned on me. Hear him:

"Johnny, you know about William George Gordon?"

I nod me head and say I ha' heard of Mr. Gordon.

CHAPTER 5

Most o' this what Davie is saying I have heard already. I heard it that Sabbath-day when we went to Bogle's chapel.

You know how to go to Stoney Gut? You come from our house at Salt Savannah and turn your face for sun-up. When you go to Morant Bay, you turn a little towards sundown. But you are for Stoney Gut so you turn your face for white road and distance.

A good walk it is. My bro' says it is four miles, but he and me talk plenty on our way and he learns me to whistle while we walk. So, by the time we leave white road and turn into Stoney Gut track, whistle, I am a-whistle:

PASTOR HUMPHREY THIEF, PASTOR HUMPHREY ROBBER, PASTOR HUMPHREY GO TO HELL FASTER THAN MORANT BAY COBBLER.

While you are there on the road, one side is cane and t'other side is coconut trees on the walk. Davie says they are no' walking, but 'cause we go so fast then it looks like say the trees are walking too. Is true, that. You never seen a body walk as fast as my bro' Davie. And me there, on his back, a-bob like Judge Boltin riding the mare which he took from Timothy's father, Mr. Abram.

But I must mind, and cover me mouth, for Mother says I must no' talk o' everything I hear in our room at night-times.

Very well. All the way along the white road we meet barrack people going to river for Sunday-day wash. Davie stops whistling every time to tell howdy, so I tell him not to stop to tell howdy for that will spoil *Pastor Humphrey*. Eh – !

Davie puts me down by a hog-plum root quicker than you can say *Bro' Anancy*! When he turned to face me, a gale-wind was stirring his countenance. Frighten came on me, for I could not tell what had happened to bring anger on him. But the gale-wind soon blew out and my bro' was a-talk to me quiet again.

"Cho, man, you frightened? I am not hurting you, but look on our skin, see how like English plantermen we are."

True, that. All our family have got daylight under their skins and hair like English flax. Ruthie says it is only because my father does no' like fuss, otherwise he would be a big Vestryman.

"Now, then, Johnny, you know how our parish people like to tell howdy to one another. If the two of us pass them and do not say howdy, you know what they will say?"

Tongue-tied, me, and just a-listen for what parish people will say if we do no' tell them howdy.

"They will say we are playing like *buckra*," says Davie.

71

Is not bad, that? Then why Davie serious so? I am a-think that *buckra* are great people; for ride, they ride horses all the time and do not walk like Negroes and poor whites. Live, they live in Great House and stand on courthouse balcony on market-day. Ice water and beverage for *buckra* when hot sun is on the land, but negroes and poor whites must hie to stonehole where water flows from. Then why Davie serious so?

"And Mas'r-No'-Tell-Howdy-Johnny, the day is a-come soon when all *buckra* plantermen will be sorry they ha' passed and not tell howdy-do!"

Mercy O! How Davie's face stay?

Listen to me. One day I was with Father when he was a-plough the piece of fallow land that lies bottomside the cassava half-acre. Hot sun was on me, and strong thirst took me, so I went to a stonehole deep in fallow grass. I stopped with my face near the stonehole – and there was a yellow snake curled in the hole, and both our eyes made four!

Flat and narrow was that face, with two eyes like glass marbles you grab at Morant Bay Fair – and so now was Davie's face.

I am glad when the flatness leaves my bro's face, and a good belly laugh comes up and shakes the whole of him. So, with the laugh, he says I am a two-day *tweet-to-whit* with two eyes that are no' opened yet; says that I ha' not got feathers yet, so I must fly on my big brother's back. Then is off the hog-plum root, me, and up on Davie's back. We are going to Stoney Gut! Whistle, man, whistle!

PASTOR HUMPHREY THIEF, PASTOR HUMPHREY ROBBER...

Howsoever we are there at Maroon Hole and a-talk of Mr. Gordon.

If I have ever heard of Mr. Gordon? *Coo, here, Lord!* Like is not me who night after night hear of Mr. Gordon! When Father and Mother believe I am asleep they sometimes talk of him, and so I know that this Mr. Gordon is our bread and salt.

Listen to me. Father is a headman on Mr. Gordon's property along the Spring Road, and I know that the saying in Morant Bay is that there is no man whom he loves like my father. I know that when I was greener, at times which I can no' remember, often he would stay at our house when he happened at Morant Bay. But of late, he does no' visit our parish much 'cept when he comes for Vestry meetings.

Like us, Mr. Gordon is near-white, the son of a *buckra* Englishman, and I can remember seeing him one time when he came to the Bay for the Vestry meeting. Was a Saturday it, market-day, and Mr. Gordon came a-ride on his high silver stallion – high silver stallion which people say he afterwards sold to Governor Eyre to ride at the Queen's Birthday Review. Timothy says that people at barrack say that the stallion grounded Eyre at the parade, and that is why Eyre hates Mr. Gordon. But this Saturday-day when I saw Mr. Gordon he was riding the high silver stallion.

He cantered into the courthouse yard a little before Custos. There were people cheering when he rode in, but they laughed and meowed when Custos came. Nobody had to tell me why they laughed for such a way Custos looked funny on his heavy-belly old mule.

Davie said it was the first time he had ever seen a mule in a family way. But he said it so Father did no' hear.

Pastor Humphrey and the magistrates were standing on the courthouse steps. Wave hands, they waved to Custos, but they did no' wave to Mr. Gordon. Father said they hated Mr. Gordon 'cause he fought too much for the poor.

Funny to me, I could not understand, for Mr. Gordon was smiling and you felt good when you saw him. But Custos? Eh – you feel like when night-time comes and you must pass Mother Cruikshank's burying-ground. That time, a million memories o' barbecue night-talks make your hair grow straight out o' your head. So how come they hate Mr. Gordon?

But Davie is a-talk to me at Maroon Hole and I nod me head and say I had heard o' this Mr. Gordon.

Hear Davie: "Last month Mr. Gordon came to Stoney Gut and preached to us."

Now hear there! Who is right? For since Mr. Gordon came to Morant Bay last time, I heard my father told my mother one night that he would not be back at Morant Bay any more just now. Say that government people in Kingston and St. Jago are saying he is making trouble for them among the poor in St. Thomas parish.

'Member I remember that Mother even said: *A good, for that Paul Bogle is a wild one and does not understand what Mr. Gordon means when he speaks with him.*

She even said that Deacon Bogle is just like the Apostle what Father reads of who believes that Mas'r Jesus meant a fight with the sword when he meant a fight with the spirit like Jacob in the dream.

Then how come now what Davie has said? Good this will be to tell Naomi.

"Mind you tell nobody, Johnny, for this is secret," said Davie all of a sudden.

But Davie is smart, though! How he knows about Naomi and me?

So, I look over me right shoulder and over me left shoulder and kiss green bush three times. Which is oath that I tell nobody.

Davie said: "Mr. Gordon took his text from the Psalm what says: *By the waters of Babylon we sat down and wept; we hanged our harps in the middle of the valleys thereof* – and what a sermon was there! He said the time was coming when we would take down our harps and the voice o' the people would be heard in the land. Said that no more nakedness would show our backs, nor hunger would ride our mouth corners with white bridles. Said that the voice o' the people is the voice of God, that the heathen would hear and shake with fright.

"Same time, Deacon Bogle called out: 'Amen, the English heathen!' But Mr. Gordon shook his head and said: 'Stand to, there!' and I believed he was no' pleased.

"But after service over and Mr. Gordon had left the Gut, Deacon laughed so I thought he would crack. Then told, he told us that Mr. Gordon did no' mean his rebuke, but he does not want people to know how he hates the buckra English since he is 'most white himself and married to an Englishwoman."

Is true, that. One night in our room I heard my mother said he had married into the English, and asked how was it that Stoney Gut people believed he would fight the English? But Father told her that Stoney Gut people could good and well believe it, for has

Lincoln not just done his fight with Davis? And both o' them of the same race and nation. Father says hell is waging war when brother fights with brother.

★

Maroon Hole water is cool and soft on your feet, and when you move your feet the water holds them and yet flows with them just like sleep creeping up at day-end.

Hear my bro' Davie: "Mr. Gordon is a great man – Assembly-man, Vestryman, Justice o' the Peace, property-owner, even Baron Aldenburg can no' play the fool with him. And if he be there with us, then we can no' lose when we move. And Mas'r God sees and knows that we will ha' to move! We must put our shoulder to the wheel and who it runs over, *it runs over!*"

Davie is on his belly again, looking sideways at me. Fire-coals make his eyes, teeth are wild boar's tearing down Wareika Mount. All of a sudden I see Davie is Deacon Bogle, and frighten comes on me.

Is not the beauty of Davie this I see. I can no' see his broad forehead brown under the hair o' sea-flax. I do no' see the west sky before sun-up that is the colour of his eyes. Where are the two spring lambs what dance at his mouth every time my bro' laughs? It is no' the beauty o' Davie that looks at me today.

There have a picture at the back o' Father's Book where a man in rich robes and a hat like Popish priests' is handing money to somebody what favours herring-Jew at Morant Bay market on Saturday-day. Ruthie says the writing under it says: *The Price of Blood.*

Like Paul Bogle's and herring-Jew's was Davie's face when he said: *Who it runs over, it runs over!*

Sometimes the sun gets sick and does no' come up out of his sea-bed with morning. Bilious, he must be, for heavy clouds spew out from where he rests, and rolls and rolls on Morant Bay town.

Then is time it to batten barrack windows. Kirk-bells start a-ring and we are leaving seaside for hill; for soon the wind will be coming, roaring down from the lost morning. And then there will be whine and shriek and howl and heat and a-run for something that will stand firm.

Trees and houses and men and beasts are a-whirl through the mad night of lost morning. Barrack negroes are a-dirge in the half-world... *Lord O! Ha' mercy! Day o' wrath, O day o' mourning...* but you do no' hear it plain at all, for the wind is whipping it into little bits which come to you in the lulls... and you, a-run, a-run, for frighten has come to you –

Davie O! Davie O!

I jumped up from Maroon Hole and ran, ran leaving my pantaloons same place. Then there was Davie calling to me, but I am still on the run, for today afraid I am o' Davie. And I do no' stop running till I reach home and tumble into my kitty-up. Mother in the kitchen with breakfast does not see me coming naked.

After time, Davie came into our room and stood at the doorway. Looked at me and grinned. Flung my pantaloons on my kitty-up and called me *Johnny Coward*.

Is a nice grin, that; Davie favours Davie again. Me? A little 'shamed.

CHAPTER 6

There have a way to Pastor Humphrey's church along the white carriage road. But we never use the white carriage road for it is three miles with sun hot on your back. There have a way to Pastor Humphrey's church where you walk through green shady. Is that the way we go.

But what a way young ones can remember things! 'Member I remember those Sabbath mornings when Father takes the Book and says: *Come, Tamah.* Father never calls the rest of us, for is Mother there to look after us. Just takes up his tall beaver hat, blows on it, rubs it with his red handkerchief, claps it on the crown of his head.

There are seven brass buttons on his blue frock-coat, which he fastens while his eyes walk 'round. Remember I remember how I used to think say each button was one of us pickneys. For my father fastened them slow one by one, while all the while he looked on us, one by one – top button for Manuel, next button for Davie, next button for Ruthie – and so till his fingers hook the bottom button and he is looking at me.

Then, *Come, Tamah,* and leader-bull is walking proud and strong leading we through the shady.

Up to today-day when I go to the city with Garth, hard it is for me to walk side-and-side with him. For from since I was a green one at Salt Savannah, all of us were taught to walk behind one another. Shady track was narrow, carriage road only little wider, and better for us to walk back a' one another.

Ma Tamah walks behind Father, then me, then Naomi, then t'others with Manuel at the end. Ruthie it was who first times used to walk at the end, but since Father saw Moses Dacre in the cane-piece with his arms around her, she does no' walk at the end any more.

Howsoever, this Sunday morning, breakfast is finished and we are on the shady track going to Morant Bay. Presently I hear Father humming. We just are passing the dead cotton tree which divides our land from Aaron Dacre's. We enter the dried grass-piece with all o' us a-hum. We pass out of this grass-piece and go down into the small valley where Aaron has planted some mash-mash canes to feed his hogs; only there are no hogs there now, and people have eaten out the mash-mash. Just as we enter into the mango-piece topside, there is heavy bass in front and Father has gone into Bro' Ira D. Sankey's pilgrimage hymn:

> THERE ARE SHADOWS IN THE VALLEY WHERE OUR
> TIRED FEET MUST GO
> BUT WE HEAR THE PEACEFUL WATERS AS THEY
> MURMUR SOFT AND LOW.

Then the chorus, and all o' us singing:

> SUNSHINE ON THE HILL, THERE IS SUNSHINE ON
> THE HILL,
> THERE ARE SHADOWS IN THE VALLEY, BUT 'TIS SUN-
> SHINE ON THE HILL.

Reason is there why my father starts to sing. Tell, I will tell you.

We come out of the mango trees with the end of the chorus, and there looking down on us is Bro' Aaron Dacre's house. Reason of Aaron Dacre why my father started his song.

You see, Aaron does no' like Pastor Humphrey's church, for he is one of Deacon Bogle's men. I saw him the morning when Davie carried me, and there was no man at Stoney Gut who cried out *Secession!* louder than Aaron Dacre.

Like 'most all Baptist people since Eyre sent his constables to nail the *Queen's Advice* on their chapel doors, Aaron hates the Church o' England more than ever, and from since then, whenever times we pass him, Aaron makes a noise like jackass a-bray in sunhot.

I remember one Sabbath morning after Pa John had put on his beaver hat, I saw him go to the buttery-room and take out our mule whip. When Mother looked on his face, she saw there was bad in his eyes, so she sent us young ones to wait bottomside the hill meanwhile she spoke to him. Afterwards, when they came down to meet us, sorry, I was sorry, for I saw my father had not got the whip in his hand. For is nice and no' nice to see someone else get a whipping, and Bro' Aaron Dacre would ha' got the whip this Sunday-day.

But every time after that, whenever we passed Aaron Dacre's house on our way to church, Father would start the pilgrimage hymn. That way, we do not hear the braying at all.

This morning I see Aaron at his doorway seated, sharpening his hoe. Many weeks now since he had not brayed at us, and I had heard Davie and Moses saying the fire was not so hot in Aaron Dacre again.

I saw him put down his file and the hoe and a-come over the ploughed land to meet up with we. Aaron is a big brown man with shoulders like yoke-steer. Broad face and flat nose with the end turned up like a stallion. But he is no' so tall as my father, and no' so strong either. I have heard many men at Morant Bay say my father is the strongest man in the parish.

When Aaron met us at the edge of his ploughed land, he had his *jippi-jappa* hat in his hand, a-finger the loose straws like a banjo player.

"'Morning, Bro' John Campbell, 'morning, Ma Tamah, 'morning, all *pickneys*," said Aaron with manners.

Only Naomi and me answered. There was serious in Aaron's face. Stonewall was Father's face.

Aaron said: "Bro' John Campbell, I be'n asked to bring an invitation."

With stiffness still in his face, by-and-by my father spoke: "Invitation to what?"

Is the first time, this, I ever hear my father speak before he has told howdy-do. You can see Bro' Aaron has noticed too, for the stallion nose widens a little more. But he plays like *cho, man, nothing*, and talked with the same voice as before.

"Invitation to Stoney Gut, Bro' John Campbell."

Wayah! Why, somebody has not told Aaron Dacre 'bout the mule whip in our buttery-room!

The little sound behind me comes from Davie's throat. Fright has come to Davie, and his eyes are a-pop like ackee seeds out o' pod. All o' us are waiting to see Father strike Aaron Dacre.

You can see shoulder muscles a-talk to my father's arm underneath his coat. Worry rides Mother and Manuel; Ruthie is hugging sickly-sickly Zekiel; Naomi's mouth opens wide, a macca-back fish being shored in net. Sammy's face does no' change, 'cept that his eyebrows are telling howdy to one another. All o' us wait to see Aaron Dacre on the ground.

For a long time my father's hand stayed tight on the Book he was carrying. Then his head shook a little, the shoulder muscles stopped talking.

With slowness he asked: "Who sends the invitation?"

"Deacon Bogle," said Aaron, "and Mr. G. W. Gordon."

Now, is funny that. For we know if Mr. Gordon had an invitation, he would have taken it to Father himself. Moreover, Mr. Gordon knows good and well that Father does no' like this Stoney Gut business. Then is who right?

All this time Father's and Aaron Dacre's eyes were making four with each other, and they do no' look away from one another.

"Mr. Gordon knows where to find me. Why has he sent you?"

"The invitation comes from Deacon," said Aaron. "He says Mr. Gordon told him."

Only a bit longer his eyes made four with Father's, then they only made two as Bro' Aaron, head down, watched how grass growed. The laugh a-laugh in Father's throat was not a good laugh. Mirth was not in it.

Hear my father: "Aaron O, the Devil walketh in cool pastures. Tempt, you are tempting me this Sabbath-day?"

Aaron's head came up. The look in his eyes was the one you see in butcher-dog a-beg for scrap meat. Sorry, you must be sorry for Aaron.

"We want you to come to Stoney Gut," he told my father with humbleness. "You are 'most *buckra* white, but more than that, a man o' influence in our district. Though you be Church o' England, we know you are no' blind to what is happening to poor people. We want you to come and sign a Petition to Governor Eyre 'fore next Vestry meeting."

Father said nothing, and Aaron stepped a little closer, talked again. "Listen me, if matters keep like this, young men with few mango seasons back o' them will take the traces out o' our hands. A precipice-road we are on now, and if they take the traces from us and their hands falter, what will happen to all o' us?"

My father's eyes are gone long distance, and none o' us are near to him at all, at all. A good thing, or he would hear the croak in Davie's throat and see that Davie's eyes are mad on Aaron Dacre. Howsoever, he came back from long distance. He held up the Book before Aaron.

"Eh, no, Bro' Aaron. Bro' Aaron O, I stand or fall by the Book. It has told me say, have nothing to do with the Devil and his works, and yon Paul Bogle is a Devil."

Dry weather comes to Aaron's face. His skin is cracking with the heat o' the sorrow inside o' him.

"But, John Campbell, you do no' know that blood will flow!"

"Aaron, what I say to you, is: Respect the grey o' your head and come away from Stoney Gut before too late is the cry. Come we travel, Ma Tamah!"

And my father is leader-bull again, a-stride in front of us with the sun a-gleam on his high beaver hat. We sweep past Bro' Aaron Dacre. Aaron is a strayed dog in a strange town watching the sun set and night come with rainclouds.

SUNSHINE ON THE HILL, THERE IS SUNSHINE ON THE HILL...

I am trotting to keep up with leader-bull and same time turning my head to see what has happened to Bro' Aaron Dacre. Then is over a tree root I am stumbling and Naomi's foot is on the seat of my pantaloons.

We stop awhile and Mother helps me up. I look on Naomi and see there is a grin there. Full time now, that I bend a twig as I pass to slap back under her nose.

CHAPTER 7

Every third Sunday there is church parade at Morant Bay. Every third Sunday-day, Missis Queen's militiamen put on their scarlet and blue to march past Custos Aldenburg.

Our family turn into the square fronting the church just as town clock is a-talk the three-quarters. Militiamen have no' left the Fort yet, so Father says we will stand and wait and watch for Missis Queen's men.

Enough-plenty people are watching for them too. We stand under a big cotton tree fronting the gate, being nice to watch the carriages of the planters driving up to the gate. Shiny horses there, drawing four-in-hand, with negro coachmen sitting straight up on the box. Coachmen wear beaver hats like Father's, and blue ribbons flash from their whips.

Many pretty women step out o' the carriages, lifting their crinolines high. Davie says is no' needful this, but they must show poor people how much silks wrap buckra women from the world. The crowd do no' make any sound. Before times, cheer, they would cheer.

Is thick dust there on the road, and they must step three times before they reach the carpet what takes them into the church. Poor people do no' use the door where carpet is, but use the back door where baptismal font is. Ruthie says is no' the rule that, but the feet of poor people are ashamed to walk on rich carpet since they have not got any boots on.

Father stands with his head high in the air. I see there are many planters who know my father, for every now and again he touches his beaver hat and they bow and smile. That time Davie, who stands beside me, says something in his throat –

Eh, eh, not in his throat, but in his belly, and to me it sounds like butcher-dog at Morant Bay what can get no scrap meat.

But all of a sudden there is noise coming from people standing topside the square. Hold on to Davie's hand me, and lean over so I can see up the road without falling.

Two white soldiers come a-prance on high horses. Sun is laughing with spike-and-chain on brass helmets, with swords and many buttons on scarlet coats. Knee-boots shine so till you can see your face in at them. Back o' the soldiers is a big scarlet coach with two soldiers a-ride postilion and box. Nobody has to tell me say is Custos's carriage this.

Now then. People begin booing and a-caterwaul, but soldier-men look neither to the right or the left; proudness on their faces lifted forward. They pulled up before our gate, and the soldier on the box jumped down and opened the door o' the carriage.

I do no' know if is true it, but Ruthie says Aldenburg's face is always red 'cause he eats raw meat. This morning red and dampy-damp is his face. A fat man is he, with heavy belly folding over his waistband, and cheeks to match his belly. This day his robe of office he wears, scarlet open-gown, hat like Admiral's at Port Royal, and a grand gold chain a-loop at his neck. October sun is a-shine warm on me, but no warmth there in his ackee-pod eyes what walk all over we people.

When his eyes come to my father's, a nod from his head my father gets. Father took off his beaver hat and bowed while Mother swept a curtsy. But when Custos looked on Davie, Custos's mouth corners went to hide in the slack o' his jowl. I looked up on Davie and saw his eyes had gone to bed and not a-look on anything at all. Custos stepped down into the dust and turned around back to his carriage door.

All this time, 'cept for little hissing back o' the crowd, there was quiet on we people, for Custos's eyes were on us, and it was not good to anger him, for you might soon have to face him on the Bench – then woe betide you! But all of a sudden people started pushing for the front.

CHAPTER 8

An old man now, me. Many years bank the flame that was John Campbell. And down the passages o' those years many doors have opened. Some o' them ha' let in rich barbecues o' joyousness, with good things covering the bottom of the pot o' life and no thorns there to give me pain. And others have opened into butteries of hell, and me soul has been scarred with the fires.

But even now when I am old, no door has ever opened that brought both joy and pain like the door which let in Lucille Dubois.

Is remember I remember one August morning when rain was a-drown the earth. For two weeks now the sun has no' shone. Black is the morning, black the evening, and Mas'r God's heaven does not look on us at all. Yallahs and Morant and Plantain Garden rivers heavy so, until you do not know where rivers end and land begins. That was the time when an alligator swam clear up to the barrack and took away my friend Timothy's baby bro'.

Then there was dirging down at the barracks. Day in, night out, you heard it through the rain, a-mark time with the drip, drip, drip of *guinep* and mango trees, weeping.

For two weeks we have not come out of the house 'cept to the kitchen to dry our *osnaburgs* at smoky damp-wood fires. Miserable it is, and mud a-clog your toes outside and damp a-creep into your bones inside and at nights you sleep on sodden kitty-up.

Then one morning when day-cloud was peeping, I woke and did no' hear the rain. Creeping out o' my kitty-up, I went to the door and pulled the latch-wood – *Wayah!*

Look there! Is no' that Mas'r God's heaven looking down on us again?

Blue and clean it is, O! God has washed His Face, and His Right Hand is coming up out o' the Bay with a red poinciana 'twixt His Fingers!

There is a wind coming off the water, pushing staleness out of you so, till your heart pumps and pumps and you must open your arms wide and feed on the breast o' the new day.

So it was when I first saw Lucille, but I did no' know her then. All I knew was that here was such a beauty before my eyes that I had never seen before.

Nobody had to tell me say it was a new visitor to our parish, this lady, for townspeople were craning their necks to see her face as she stepped out o' Aldenburg's carriage, and all through the crowd you heard them ask of one another: *Is who it? Is who it? This new face comes from where?*

'Member I remember how I stood looking on her eyes, on her hair, and saying to myself, "Johnny O, is summer moon it, shining on Maroon Hole, and silver lights are a-twinkle at the bottom o' dark waters."

And then I saw that her eyes were resting on Davie. Davie it was I knew, for I saw her looking long over my head, and when I turned and looked too, there was my bro' Davie. My bro' stands there looking on Lucille Dubois as if other people were not here at all, at all.

Watch them, Johnny O! Stallion eagerness is a-ripple Davie's flank against me shoulder. The sun has brought silver to the black of Lucille's hair, her lips suck at a blood-plum that is not there.

Not for long could they have been standing with their eyes making four with one another, for I remember I did no' draw breath – me, who could no' dive from bank to bank at Maroon Hole without kicking for water-top. So it must have been less than half a minute when Custos saw there something funny going on and followed Miss Lucille's eyes to Davie. Anger brought more red to his face; hear him with sharpness:

"Goom, Miss Dubois."

Soldiermen swords flashed in salute as Custos stepped for the carpet with Miss Lucille at his side. They must pass near where our family stands, so Father tells us low to move back. All o' us move 'cept Davie.

Custos and his lady are stepping for the carpet when she stumbles forward. Nobody has to tell me say her feet must have caught the edge of the carpet, for she was looking on Davie and did no' see that the edge was so near. I am a-look to see Davie reach forward and help her, for poor pot-belly Custos can no' move fast enough. But my bro' does no' do anything and almost she would be flat on the carpet.

It is Father and Manuel who must reach quicker than you can say *Jack Mandora* and stop her from falling. Mother said: "Poor Missie!" and went down to arrange her skirt. Miss Lucille touched her hair little places and said *thankie* to Mother with a smile. But there was wonder and hurt when she looked at Davie.

And Davie? Well then, he is looking like say she is not there. Just like say nothing has just happened here.

Custos is looking on Miss Lucille as if he would like to put trace-leather on her, especially when people around the square burst into little titters. But all he did was make a noise in his throat and step off up the carpet. I am a-think it will be bad to face him on the Bench tomorrow morning.

Before Pastor Humphrey begins his sermon, there is the reading of the *Queen's Advice*. I believe he must know it by heart, for most of the time while he is reading, his eyes are walking all over the church where poor people sit.

Pastor is a tall and pale conger eel, and for mouth he has rat-trap. Every sentence Pastor finishes, mouth shuts tight *ram!* Then he looks around some more, fish-eyes a-stare at we people.

This Sunday-day, Pastor says his text comes from St. Paul's Epistle to the Ephesians. I am sitting 'twixt Naomi and Davie and I feel when Davie's body gets tight. I look on him and see his eyes are shut. I know Davie does no' like St. Paul.

Hear Pastor: "Servants, be obedient to them that are your masters according to the flesh, with fear and trembling, in singleness of your heart, as unto Christ."

Father sits with his head high, beaver hat on his knees. Ma Tamah is 'side of him, and when Pastor reads I see her nod and there is curve on her mouth like she has said *Amen*. That is how Mother is. Every time everybody read from the Book is that what my mother always say. Just like she is telling them that they should not forget that they should say *Amen*.

Pastor Humphrey closed the Book, leaned far over his pulpit, eyes a-search of we people. Hear him:

"Servants, be obedient."

CHAPTER 9

Whenever we go to church, Naomi and me sit side-and-side. First time when we sit down we open our knees wide, but when the sermon begins we close our knees tight, and then there is good space for crab-race.

You know how you play crab-race?

Down on the beach where the mangrove bushes are which never wet feet but at high tide, you find the holes of the little brown deaf-ears land crab. Is easy it, to catch them, for they never hear you until you are right down on them.

Every Sunday morning before church time, Naomi and me get plantain trash and go down the beach for our deaf-ears. We strip the trash down to strings and tie them around their feet, then into Naomi's headkerchief they go. Tied, they must be tied good, for the 'kerchief will go into Naomi's bosom, and is hell and powderhouse if they get away in there.

Sermon time comes, and out comes Bro' Deaf-ears. Then there is Naomi and one string, me on t'other string, and we are racing them on the bench 'twixt us. Father never sees, for his head does not turn from the pulpit after we sit down. Mother never sees for sleep; she is asleep soon after Notices.

So today when Pastor closes the Book and say: *Servants be obedient*, I can feel Naomi drawing away from me and I know she is ready for our crab-race.

"When St. Paul in his Epistle called upon the people of Ephesus to be obedient to their masters, he was writing both as an Apostle of our Lord Jesus and as a man of the world who had held office above men and knew the wisdom of a civilised submission to authority."

That was how Pastor Humphrey began his sermon this Sabbath-day in Morant Bay parish church. Mouth came down *snap* on "authority", long neck shot out, then drew back into his cassock like iguana in stonehole. Mother said *Amen*, and when I looked at her, her eyes were just a-close. I know she is asleep now.

But there are other sounds back o' me like somebody has just groaned deep, and I look back. Church is crammed full, with people standing around the font, and men outside peeping through the windows. Negroes and mulattoes and many barefoot German whites from Seaforth Town are listening to Pastor Humphrey.

Father is sitting straight up, his eyes on Pastor, but Davie's eyes are shut tight, and only the ridge which comes and goes on his cheek tells that he is no' asleep. Naomi is poking me in my side to say it is time for our crab-race. She does not know that something is happening in Morant Bay today-day. For when I turned my head I saw that many Stoney Gut men were standing outside the church windows.

Now then. Every Sabbath-day there is a big *met* at the Gut when Deacon Bogle preaches to his people. From day-cloud broke this morning they should be trudging into the Gut, from Morant Bay and Yallahs and Bath Town. There will be big mountain men a-come through the Cuna Cuna Pass from the Rio Grande Valley. There will be sugar-boat men a-come in wains along the Windward Road from Morant Point. Enough-plenty men go to Stoney Gut every Sabbath-day.

And that time Deacon's big *met-pots* talk all day with juniper-wood flame; that time wild hogs turn on spits all day to feed hungry men. Then how come so many o' Deacon Bogle's men are at Morant Bay church today?

I touch my bro' on his arm and whisper that there are many Stoney Gut men at church today. Davie does no' open his eyes, but his lips form to say *Shut up*.

Well, make Stoney Gut men stay where they are. Davie says I should shut up. A-listen to Pastor Humphrey, me.

"Over a quarter of a century ago our good Queen Victoria in her great wisdom gave freedom to her darker children of Africa. Men there were who questioned the wisdom of that gift and asked whether people who were clearly unfit for responsibility should be made citizens, holding in common with all the inestimable privilege of being freedmen of the British Empire. How has it worked out?"

Rat-trap mouth shuts tight. Iguana neck pulls out, pulls in.

"We pastors, whatever our failings, have never but preached the Word of God to the people. We have taught that the good Christian should be humble in the presence of those set in authority. We have taught that men must eat by the sweat of their brows. That in work, and only hard work, lies the redemption of a race which for centuries has lived in sin and savagery before Almighty God. And by our efforts the whip and the crank and the treadmill have been set aside and the opportunity for their freedom offered. What do we now find?"

Pastor tugs at the collar of his cassock and bobs his head out and in. There is a wind outside, wind a-talk soft with the old cotton tree. There is good smell o' leather and sweat from militiamen in the front pews. I can see Judge a-sit with other *buckras* near to Custos's pew. Morning sun shines on his bald head like crown-piece lying on the road. Wish, I am wishing I had my slingshot for Judge Boltin's head. Naomi can no' bother with me longer so she one is racing two crabs.

Why Davie will no' make his eyes four with Miss Lucille's?

Hear Pastor: "What do we find? Because Almighty God has seen fit to visit His wrath on these people for their laziness and hardness of heart, because He has seen fit to seal off from their lands the rains of heaven for these past three years, they have rebelled against His ordinance and seek to supplant those whom He has set in authority over them."

Groan from the back o' the church, and nobody has to tell me say from Stoney Gut men it comes.

"Yes! I say yes!" Loudness has come to Pastor's voice, and iguana bobs more than ever. "Not many miles from here a black Satan in human form is preaching sedition against the most gracious person of our Queen!"

Cho, man. I must know that he means Deacon Bogle.

"In Kingston, a man who holds office in the honourable Legislature of this colony, moving in the best circles of society, the society he has sworn to protect, a leader of the people, preaches sedition against Her Majesty!"

Well! If is not Mr. Gordon that, then is who it?

This time there is a louder sound from back o' we, and I see

Pastor looks up sharp. Davie too opens his eyes, and there is alarm in the jerk o' his head as he looks around. There are more groans as Stoney Gut men show they do no' agree with Pastor. I see old Mr. Amos, the beagle, get up from his bench near the door and go outside, his gown flapping back o' him like a *John Crow* in north wind. Soon there is tramping in the churchyard, and white helmets bob past the windows as constables begin to move men from the windows. Everybody are looking now, and Naomi and me are climbing on our bench, but Father said something sharp and we sit down quick-quick.

There are people scuffling outside. Someone calls out, and there is sound of a blow. I feel Davie a-stir beside me, but Sammy, who sits on t'other side o' him, whispers in his ears. More white helmets bob past our windows. Then after that, is quiet it, but Stoney Gut men are no' at the windows.

Pastor Humphrey stands tall in his pulpit, no fullness to his lips, glass marbles for his eyes.

"And now they would bring their perdition to the House of God. They would bring their seditious practices to the doors of the church established by the grace of God and Her Majesty."

Pastor leans over the pulpit, rubbing the stone with his palm. Now then there is a cooing in his voice; pigeon a-coo in his voice, but yellow snake looking out o' his eyes. His palm rubs easy back and forth. Hear him softly:

"Saint Paul was a man of the world. He knew what terrible punishment could be inflicted on those who did not submit to constituted authority. He himself had once been an instrument of this authority. He knew that, rightly or wrongly, such authority had the power to flay, or even slay the malingerer. So, he said: 'Servants, be obedient…with fear and trembling in singleness of your heart as unto Christ.'" Then he is a-look down his nose at us. "Let the malingerer beware the might of constituted authority!"

And so, finished he is finished and is turning for the east window to say the final dedication. And I am looking, as I always do, to see Mother open her eyes, as she always do.

"Let us pray for rain," says Pastor Humphrey.

CHAPTER 10

After service Custos will take a salute from the militiamen at parade-ground on the Fort. Before the militia march from the church we will meet under the cotton tree, all we friendly families. We will meet to tell howdy. Every Sabbath-day after service, tell, we tell one another howdy under the cotton tree.

This day the family of Bro' Zaccy O'Gilvie we have met with first. Bro' Zaccy is head butcher o' Morant Bay and a Vestryman. Nearly a black *buckra* he is, prosperity having fattened his belly. Davie says he is the greatest black imperialist he has ever seen; though I do not know if is cuss-word, that, but Davie spits when he says "imperialist", and you only spit when you say cuss-word.

I do no' like Bro' Zaccy. Because of his belt and buckle why I do no' like Bro' Zaccy. Black and crusty is his thick belt with great brass buckle what shapes like wild boar's head. I am a-think that such a belt on my behind would bring smoke and fire to my eyes, and whenever we meet and he shakes my hand, my eyes only reach as high as his belt and I smell the stinking leather.

But, imperialist? Davie says that Zaccy does no' drink mint tea any longer. Says you could no' boil fresh-cut *cerosee* in coconut milk with new sugar enough to tempt him. Only China and Indian tea Bro' Zaccy drinks now, and is more English than Lord Derby.

Zaccy said: "Morning, Bro' John, morning, Ma Tamah, morning, *pickney* all."

All o' us say morning. Zaccy is wearing his black alpaca suit with heavy silver chain riding his stomach. His family are Ma Mary and Hannah and Ebenezer. Hannah is Ruthie's size, so she just nods at me, and I go over to Ebenezer. I hear Bro' Zaccy laugh, and silver chain gallops over his stomach.

Ebenezer shows me a green glass marble with a nick on top. Naomi says *cho* and I say *cho*, for there is a nick on top and not so good. Naomi gives me her headkerchief with the two deaf-ears crabs, and Ebenezer's eyes get shine. Ebenezer's family lives at Braco Hill, where there are no deaf-ears crabs. He says all right, he will take them. I get the green glass marble with the nick on top.

"Bad business in church today, Bro' John Campbell," said Zaccy.

Father nods his head. Hear him: "I got an invitation today."

"Invitation? Who from?"

Father told him about Bro' Aaron. Zaccy shook his head, and silver chain cantered on his stomach.

"Aaron is finding his mistake, yes?"

"Hope, I am a-hope so, Zaccy," my father said.

Militiamen are coming from the church to form in the square. They will march to the Fort and salute the magistrates. Sammy is madding to follow the crowd, which now is running towards the parade-ground; but my father is no' ready yet. All *buckra* planters have gone on to the Fort in their carriages. After the militiamen have marched off, Father will lead we family a-march behind them, our friendly families marching with us. Ruthie says we do this because we are better-class families who have no carriages but who can no' run with street Arabs. So we will march behind militiamen, Father leading us with his head held high.

"I hear say they will call out more men for the Fort, Bro' John," Zaccy said.

Father nods, with dark-night a-settle down on his face.

More families are coming to the cotton tree, and we are saying howdy-do to them. As they come, Bro' Zaccy rubs his hand over his watch-chain and says: "Bad business in church today, Bro'."

There comes Bro' Hezekiah James, a-lead Ma Lucy and their fourteen young ones. Bro' Hezekiah is the biggest blacksmith in Morant, and is a great sport, he. One gold tooth fronts his mouth, and I am thinking how his mouth favours his smithy every time he laughs and you see fire in the blackness of his face. Is a great sport, he, laughing enough-plenty and looking on Ruthie. Ruthie makes monkey-faces at him. Davie says Bro' Heze only stopped breeding Ma Lucy because he could find no more names for the *pickneys*.

But Davie was two-mouthed that time, for I afterwards heard him tell young men at Morant Bay market that Ma Lucy keeps flat 'cause she turns her back at nights.

Then you see Bro' Hans Schmidt there, a-come with his so-so women family. Bro' Hans is a German potter from Seaforth Town whose fingers talk o' glory in clay. Every third Saturday Bro' Hans and his family come to Morant Bay to sell clay pots. After market they sleep in town until Sabbath morning. Bro' Hans never brings farthing for collection plate, for he says he has no' got much coin. Yet still he will no' miss church parade service, so he always brings a water-jar or flowerpot for his collection. A long time now, from since Manuel was a baby, he has been coming with his clay collection; till Humphrey's church and great house are full with jars and flowerpots. But after barrack people started talking, saying Pastor wants the clay collection to hold the tears o' the poor, Pastor stopped Bro' Hans from bringing more. So now only on Harvest Festival do they bring a big Spanish jar.

Bro' Hans and his family say morning to we. I do not say morning but go quick behind Ruthie's skirt. Howsoever, Ma Sara Schmidt has seen me and has got hold of me, and is up in her two arms what favour sugar-boat derrick, me.

What makes her stay so? Must be because there are six in her family and all o' them girl-pickneys. Naomi is talking to them now and showing them the blue drawers what Mother has edged with lace from her old petticoat. Boastie is my sis Naomi, though!

Bro' Zaccy rubbed his hands on his chain and said: "Bad business in church today, Potter Hans."

"Drue, Bro' Zaccy, dree of them has been arres' and in lock-up now."

Manuel was talking to Hannah O'Gilvie, but now he turned to face Bro' Hans. Spoon-talk, Manuel was making at Hannah, for she laughed all the time and peeped at him under her hat though she formed as if she watched grass a-growing. Same way when Ruthie talks to Moses Dacre down by the standpipe at Morant Bay market. Ruthie gets thirsty every minute on Saturdays and must leave her family for the standpipe. That time Naomi and me laugh to ourselves, for we know well about them.

But hear Manuel: "Arrested, Bro' Hans?"

"Eh, yes. Constabs arres' dree o' them."

All of a sudden Father looked around on all of us.

"Is where Davie?" he asked.

We look too, and there is not a Davie in the churchyard. Sammy looks on me. I look back at him.

"Is where that boy!" says Father, voice loud with thunder, leader-bull looking down on his herd. Mother runs quickly to the fence and looks into the square, where militiamen are getting ready for the march.

"Davie O! Davie! Davie Campbell O!" she is calling.

Bro' Zaccy shakes his head so his watch-chain canters. "A wayward boy, that, Bro' John. Bad he will bring to your grey head."

"Davie O! Salt Savannah Davie Campbell!" Mother is calling, her eyes a-search the square. But there is boom from big drum and chatter from side drums and pipes are a-skirl as militiamen march.

Father breathes heavily, vexation in his eyes. His fingers go down the seven brass buttons, but only six he will find when his eyes walk over us.

"Come, Tamah," said my father, with weight a-pull at his voice.

Funny it is how Sammy's eyes shine when he hears bass drum a-talk.

CHAPTER 11

The first time this I have ever played street Arab from our family. Not a good feeling this, street Arab; for big people jostle you and push you and pull you, and there is not your father to say *let up!* Nobody there to hold your hand.

It was easy to get away from my family during the hurry-hurry of stepping off for the parade-ground. I walked side-and-side of Sammy, my eyes on Father's beaver hat high in the air. His hat does no' turn right or left, step and step we march with the bass drum's boom. If anybody can notice what I will do, should be my bro' Sammy. But Sammy will see nothing, for drums are a-sound and pipes are a-skirl and his eyes are blind with shine.

So when we come out o' the square and militiamen turn left to the parade-ground, to the right has turned Johnny. A good.

But I do not know where to find Davie, and I must find him, since thunderhead gathers in my father's eyes, yes? What makes my bro' Davie like this? Sun has not set yet on the day Father brought trace-leather to his back, and yet trouble is Davie looking again.

Morant Bay streets are narrow, and hot is the sun on the land. Walk, I am walking in shady under the piazzas, but big people need the shady too. Street Arab has no father to say *let up there!* so push, they push me all about and I must jump to escape gutter-water. Sometimes when I am looking where to jump, big people's elbows are gone into my side, and my face is gone into gutter-water. Then there is big laugh when I get up from the gutter and am wiping morass from my eyes.

Osnaburg pantaloons wet well and good now, the sun does not feel so hot now. But is miserable and tired, me, for I have fallen down enough-plenty times. The pantaloons which were too short for Zekiel are now too long for Johnny, for the water was too heavy for them, and the rolls which Mother had made in the legs are now down farther than my toes. So stumble, I must stumble along with morass full in my mouth and eyes and people laughing at me.

Hear them: "Coo, *buckra* street Arab! Coo, white-skin street Arab!"

Then I must cry.

Davie O! Davie O!

Johnny O! Johnny Campbell O!

Somebody is calling my name, but it is not Davie, and morass is full in my eyes.

"Johnny! Johnny Piper O!"

Then I know it is my friend Timothy, for he always calls me Johnny Piper since he says I swim like piper fish.

I get the morass from my eyes, and there is Timothy crossing the street to me. But what makes his face stay so? Could not be gutter-water, for he is a boastie boy who has told me he has been on Morant Bay streets many times, he one. Howsoever, I look good and see that Timothy is crying, and that eye-water is making gullies in the dirt on his face.

Hear him to me when he had crossed to my side: "Johnny O – constables have locked up my pappie!"

Lord O! My poor friend Timothy. Heard, I heard once that Mr. Abram, his father, rolled dice at Morant Bay every market-day, but I did no' think he would roll dice on the Sabbath. All the same a nice man is Mr. Abram M'Laren, and how he loves Davie too!

Timothy is a-holler, words coming out 'tween his breaths.

"Constables – lock up my pappie – for making noise at Humphrey's church window!"

Wayah! So Mr. Abram was not arrested for gambling! Three arrested, had said Bro' Hans!

The way he is bawling, Timothy must catch breath before words will come.

"My pappie – and two Morant Bay men and your bro' Davie!"

When something bad happens to frighten you, such a way your heart can jump.

Bup! And pain crawling over your chest and night-time a-cover your eyes, and the talk around you sound like thunder far down the Bay.

Then afterwards, pain leaving your chest, and it is daylight again and people talking around you. So it was at Morant Bay. when Timothy says my bro' is in the lock-up.

Gone, then, I am gone from Timothy, running and stumbling and falling on the stones.

Davie O!

All I am doing is running, running to the lock-up where my bro' Davie is. I run into a tobacco-woman's donkey, and the hamper is on my chest and I am on the ground. Get up me quickly, but she clouts me on the head and calls out loud: "You *buckra* street Arab, you!"

All I am a-do is running. I wipe blood, but no eye-water, from my face. Zekiel's pantaloons are too long for me, so I must hold it up when I run. And then there is no balance on me, so very often I am down on the stones. No softness is on the stones for street Arab. There is pain all over me. There is nobody to say *let up!* so big people clout me all about.

Find, I must find Davie.

Eh, eh, everybody have not gone to the parade-ground. Seems like everybody is in front of the lock-up. A cactus fence it is, with people for cactus. You try to pass through the people, and cactus fence pierces you when people clout you and pinch you and say: *Get, there, street Arab!*

I holler to them that my bro' is in the lock-up, that I should pass and talk with my bro'. But the fences does no' move, only pushes me down on the stones. That time, then, I must cry, so I go by the lock-up stone wall. It is nice and yet no' nice to cry when you are hurt. Crying makes you 'shamed, but there is quiet inside you afterwards.

I lean on the wall, and my arms are soft and warm against my forehead. Nice and no' nice to cry.

By-and-by quietness reached me. Up the street, I could see that the lock-up doors were closed. Four constables stand on the steps with muskets under their arms. People are shouting at them:

"Let them out! Let out the men! You hangmen you! Traitors, all o' you!"

Remember, I remember that was the time a woman picked up the first rock-stone. She can no' throw as good as Timothy or me, for the stone falls on those in the front of the crowd. But the man who stood beside her was good as Timothy and me, for he dropped a stone clear on a constable's head. Then now the stones begin falling on the constables.

Constables call out and are raising their muskets. But before anything else can happen, I hear the Queen's bugler a-sound the alarm, and horses come on the gallop around the corner.

Jesu o' St. Jago! Now watch them, Johnny O! Watch hurricane come on the cactus fence and toss it all about!

Mounted militiamen come a-tear around the corner, and the crowd scatters like ploves out of the reed when they hear gunshot. Glad I am, for I did suffer when they pinched me and pushed me. Quietness goes out of me, cymbals crash inside my belly, and I am waving my hands and screaming:

"Ride them down, soldiermen! Ride them down!"

But all of a sudden I cover my mouth; for street Arab has nobody to say *let up!* and the cactus fence is coming hard for me.

Cymbals are dead inside me now, and a little pain comes at the bottom o' my belly, for I am frightened. Big people's feet catch up with me, down I am gone again. I am close against the stone wall so I do no' get many kicks, but when they pass and I get up, there is blood on my face.

Then now the horses are coming, and Johnny can run where?

I am bawling for the militiamen to let up before they reach me, but I believe they have not even seen me at all, at all. Dead is Johnny now?

But just the same, God is good to street Arab. For then I notice there is a storm-water drain at the foot of the wall with iron bars across it. I push my head through the bars, and Zekiel's pantaloons are fluttering behind me. Inside, me, but most of one leg of the pantaloons is no' with me.

By-and-by, when all my sobs have left me, I look around where I am. There is another stone wall in front of me, and when I see the windows with more iron bars across them, nobody has to tell me say this is the lock-up where my bro' Davie is.

Somebody inside is blaspheming. I listen good, and think it must be Mr. Abram. There are no doors in the wall, so this must be the back o' the lock-up, and the constables will be in front. Well, then, smart, Johnny must play smart. A Maroon hillman, me, crawling up on English camp.

I creep to the stone wall and call softly: "Mr. Abram, O!"

Blasphemy stops a little. I call soft again: "Mr. Abram O! Is me it, Johnny!"

Night-time in our bedroom when Mother and Father talk o' things what happened in the day she calls him Flathead Abram. A flat head, with face broad and black under it, looks down on me through the window. When our eyes make four, surprise brings roundness to his eyes.

"What you do here, Johnny?" he asked.

"Is Davie it," I whisper back. Sobs are gone now but hiccup is in my belly. "They ha' locked up Davie too."

"But how come you bleeding? Who been licking you?"

Why Flathead M'Laren talks so! I fist against the wall with vex a-twist my face.

"I want Davie! Where Davie is?"

Mr. Abram sees I do no' want to talk, so he puts his finger through the window and points. And gone, I am gone.

But this time I do no' have to call, for when I look up, Davie is there. Wildness is in his eyes, flax stand straight up on his head. See my bro' Davie there looking through the bars like monkey at August Fair! They ha' caged Davie, my poor bro' Davie!

"Davie O, poor Davie," I say with sadness.

But there is a grin from him, and softly: "Cho, man."

That is how my bro' is. Fright taking you, and he says *Cho, man*, and fright is gone from you all of a sudden. I swallow on a hiccup and wipe my nose clean on the pantaloon waist.

"How come they held you, man?" I asked him.

He grinned again. "I heard they had taken Abram, so I came and jumped to the lock-up steps, and the constables hauled me inside. Is where Sammy?"

"Militiamen drums are a-sound, and he has got shine in his eyes."

"You must find him," Davie tells me. "He must go to Stoney Gut today to tell Deacon Bogle o' this."

Foolishness this is, I am thinking, for by this time our family will be on shady track to Salt Savannah. And after I go back to Salt Savannah and get my whipping from Father, not one of us young ones can leave again, for Father's eyes will be making four with ours all the time. I speak to Davie o' this.

He nodded his head quick, then his eyes went to long distance. When they came back to me, they went over me like a mule-buyer at Cedar Valley auction. All of a sudden hear him:

"You will ha' to go then."

Eh? Me one? To pass Mother Cruikshank's burying-ground? Foolishness Davie is talking. I can no' go to Stoney Gut, me one.

"You will ha' to go quickly, Bro' John, for the constables soon will pass around here."

Bro' John? Who can Davie be calling *Bro' John*? Only my father is *Bro' John*, and he is not here. Why Davie is talking foolishness this day?

"You will have to go quickly, Bro' John-Johnny, you one," says Davie with grin on him.

"Bro' – John?"

He nodded. *Bro' John* – and me only eight! Nobody has ever said *Sis* Naomi!

"Tell Deacon they have caged us in the lock-up and that we will go before Custos in the morning. Put foot in hand and go light, Bro' John," Davie tells me.

Well then, gone, I am gone.

"Tell Deacon all o' us will be ready," Davie called softly to me.

It is no' easy to get through the bars this time, for no fright is behind pushing me. Howsoever, push and wriggle, me, and I am through the bars, but another piece o' Zekiel's pantaloons is not with me. I peeped back through the bars, and there was Davie a-grin at me. His mouth forms like he says *Bro' John*. I love Davie.

There is quiet on the street, cactus fence has gone. Sun comes down hot on the land. I rip t'other pantaloon leg so both o' them are same length now. I am thinking why did Mother not shorten them as I have done, 'stead of rolling it like cotter cloth what Morant fisherwomen put on their heads to hold their baskets?

Starch is on my face, face stiff with blood and dirt. I wash my face clean with gutter-water and dry it with the piece of pantaloon. Then I stick this piece in my shirt pocket, leaving it a-hang like Father's breast 'kerchief.

It is five miles to Stoney Gut. I turn my face to sun-up and distance.

CHAPTER 12

Davie says that soldiermen a-campaign must live off the land. Davie knows all about our wars. He knows all about Tackey's insurrection at Port Maria. 1760, that was. He knows all about the great Maroon War o' 'Ninety-six. Great tales he can tell of the march o' five thousand soldiermen on Trelawney Town, or the time when the English redcoats hunted the Maroons with five hundred Spanish bloodhounds. Davie knows enough-plenty of our island's history what he has got from books at Stoney Gut.

Often he tells me o' these as we walk through the woodland. Remember, I remember the smell o' oranges and tangerines ripening in the sun, the tune a-pour from the throat of a *hopping dick* high in a pimento tree, and there is Davie, striding through thick guinea grass with me on his back bobbing and listening with all o' my ears to tales of the Spanish occupation and the war with France, and of Admiral Nelson at Port Royal.

Then tell, he tells me of the hurricane of 'Eighty-six when fifteen thousand slaves had hunger riding them to death with white bridles at their mouth corners. When he talks of the fifteen thousand, aloes settle in this throat. For he says it was not long afterwards that the Earl of Effingham arrived as Governor, and that time there was feasting and dancing among *buckra* and soldiermen on the Assembly vote of four thousand pounds. But fifteen thousand slaves had just finished burying one another.

He talks of how the English put red coats on the backs of their slaves and took them to fight the Americans in the War o' Independence. He talks o' the war in Haiti, and I hear of Bro' L'Ouverture and his republic. But Davie swallows more aloes when he talks o' the black redcoats what the English sent to Haiti to fight against Bro' L'Ouverture and his black soldiermen who were a-fight 'gainst France for their liberty.

When we come to the stone wall what fences Pastor Humphrey's banana field, Davie looks around quick and says we are soldiermen on campaign and must live off the land. Then over the fence we are gone. Fat and sweet are Humphrey's bananas; one of his bananas can be a bellyful; but soldiermen on campaign carry long bellies, so Davie and me eat enough-plenty.

Lord O! White road is long and rocky and my feet are a-blister already. Never knew, me, that stones could talk and say: *Do no' put down your feet, Johnny, for we are waiting with Maroon swords.*

But I must put down my feet to follow one another if I must get to Stoney Gut. So I walk on pain, with pain in my head, with pain a-swell my heart. Cry, I must not cry. Hunger is on me.

I am walking with a stone wall on my left, with a mangrove bush on my right. Only the deaf-ears crab can eat in mangrove bush, so I climb the stone wall on my left. I am looking down into a cool mango-walk. Mango crop is 'most over now, being October, but some late Number Elevens are hanging with heaviness down in the mango-walk. Before you can say *Jack Mandora*, I am off the wall and down in the mango-walk.

Poor people do not have stone wall around their lands, so I am thinking this is a buckra place. Is remember, I remember that Timothy always says that if buckra catch you on his property, it is the whip for your backside. But hunger is on me.

I go quick to a tree full in the family way, pull down a dozen mangoes, and inside my shirt they are. Then back to the stone wall, me.

But when I get back to the wall I am frightened. For I had not noticed that the mango-walk was lower inside than the road outside, and here now the wall is higher than my head. I climb, I climb, I climb, but still I can no' climb out of the mango-walk. Smooth is the wall on this side, and my toes which were walking on pain can find no grip on it at all, at all. Well, after I fall three times, that is enough-plenty. Johnny must find the road-gate out of the buckra property.

I walk with the wall, looking for the gate. By-and-by I hear running water, and when I come to a stream which runs through a hole to the road outside, now I know where I am. For this is Coneyman Water, a little stream what crosses the road, goes down into Mother Cruikshank's burying-ground, then loses itself in the sea. I know now I am on Custos's property.

Man can not be frightened to more than fright. After you are frightened enough, you forget there is fear in you, and everything comes steady again. Just like when Father threatens you to peel off your bottom with his trace-leather.

Then you ha' a little pain at the bottom of your belly, and dryness is there in your throat. Then there is sweat-water a-tickle your armpits, and when you look at Mother her petticoat is a million miles away. But after Father grabs you, there is no fear again.

All the same, you holler, for the trace-leather stings, but that is not fear at all.

I find a smooth stone beside Aldenburg's stream and sit down and put my feet in water. *Wayah!*

Pain walks all over my legs, and my legs beg to run up inside my belly to get away from the pain. But presently the water takes away the pain, and my feet are dancing in the stream. Good, I feel now, and am hungry again.

Big people do no' understand how to eat mangoes. They will make a big bite into the golden flesh, then out comes their tongue and they are licking like mad to catch the juice, which is squirting everywhere. But they can no' catch all the juice. When you want to see how to eat mangoes, watch Timothy and me.

You know how you eat *Number Eleven*? Listen to me. You must find a smooth stone, then take Bro' *Number Eleven* and rub him and pound him until he is as soft as pap. Pinch his top with your front teeth, making a little hole. Then suckle on this hole, with your fingers squeezing all around, and up will come the golden juice and there will be music in your throat!

When there is no juice left inside, blow hard in the hole and squeeze hard with your fingers and soon there will be *pop!* – there will be mango meat a-plaster your face. A good.

Well, by Aldenburg's stream, me, eating of Aldenburg's mangoes. My mind has gone on Naomi; wonder if she is calling my name? When your mind goes on people you do not see, it is because they are calling your name. This will be a story to tell Naomi. I will tell her tonight when we play *Moonshine Baby*, and I will watch her mouse eyes a-shine with vex. Poor Naomi, nobody has ever called her *Sis* Naomi.

Six of Custos's mangoes are inside my belly already. I am blowing and squeezing on this last one, and *pop!* – mango meat is all over my face. Behind me somebody laughs.

I have not fallen into gutter-water this time, but Aldenburg's stream wets me all the same. When I get up from the water I brush the hair from my eyes and see standing on the bank the lady who had been to church with Custos.

She has stopped laughing and is stooping by the stream and is holding out her hand to me. I jump to the other side of the stream and stand looking at her. Quick feel of my shirt says there are no mangoes there. Quick look at the water sees *Number Eleven* bobbing under the stone wall for the road. Glad, I am glad, for I do not want her to see I stole. If the whip is coming for Johnny, make it come, but not for stealing.

"Your poor little dear!" said the lady.

Now, hear there! So petting will come before the whip? *Hell and powderhouse!*

My head is twisting side to side. I am looking from where will come Custos.

"You mustn't be afraid, little man."

Is who it is she talking to? Me, Bro' John afraid? I am only looking what way I must run, because I must reach Stoney Gut and Paul Bogle.

"I am no' afraid," I tell her as I knead water from me eyes.

Miss Lucille is looking hard on me; then all of a sudden she laughs. First time, I am vexed; but when she laughed and laughed and laughed with her throat a-trembling like hummingbird before a morning glory, what can poor Johnny do? So I start laughing too, yes?

By-and-by we gurgle a bit, then empty of laughter are we. Her hand came out to me, I waded the stream and stood beside her.

She said she was Lucille Dubois. I told her I was Bro' John Campbell.

"I saw you in church today, John," she said.

What a thing! I thought all she saw was my bro' Davie.

"His name is Davie," I told her.

Puzzle-marks 'twixt her eyes tells me she does no' understand. But presently they left 'twixt her eyes and went down to her mouth, where they became laughter-marks. Fireflies danced deep in her eyes.

But she nodded deep like Father and said: "Yes, Johnny."

"Yours and his eyes made four when you stepped out o' Aldenburg's carriage," I told her.

There was sun a-set on her face and shoulder just like when Ruthie sees Moses Dacre at Morant Bay market and he is looking at her like sheep.

"Is arrested, they ha' arrested Davie now," I said.

Now look there! Sunset gone from her face all of a sudden, and moon is a-shine on white sea-sand as Miss Lucille reached for her throat. Her mouth is a two-day *kling-kling* a-beg for air.

"Ar – arrested – ?"

I nodded me head. "They ha' got him and Mr. Abram in the lock-up."

"Ar – arrested – in the lock-up – ?" says pretty polly parrot.

I nodded me head. "They will go before Custos in the morning."

Hear Miss Lucille: "The – the men at church?"

I nodded me head. "Davie went to the lock-up to quarrel with the constables, and they hauled him inside."

Is now it the worry-marks ride Miss Lucille.

"But – but – John, you don't understand!"

Not understand what? Is what it Miss Lucille is talking of?

She is whispering with her hands at her throat: "The Baron said he would have them whipped in the morning!"

Weep, Jesus O! What is Miss Lucille talking of? Custos to whip Davie in the morning? My bro' Davie?

No sun is there now, a-lace the floor of Custos's mango-walk. No music is there now flowing with the water under the stone wall. I could not ha' just finished eating seven *Number Elevens*, for emptiness is in my belly. Blackness is covering St. Thomas parish, and I am madding to run and bawl. Davie to get the whip like yam-hill thief at Morant Bay!

Miss Lucille has got me by the arm and is shaking me. "Johnny, where is your family? What are you doing here?"

I told her I had left my family and had found Davie at the lock-up and he had sent me out.

"Sent you out where? What did your brother tell you?"

She is stooping low to me, so our eyes made four on one level. I could see her mouth was prettier than Adassa, who Davie plays with. But all of a sudden I remember that she had been in Custos's carriage and now she is here on Custos's land. So she must be Custos's friend, yes? Eh, eh.

Oyster at rock-bottom, me, my mouth pouting, my eyes peeping at her from underneath my brow, no' saying anything at all.

She looked good at me, then she looked all around the mango-walk, then she had me by one hand, and with t'other clutching at her skirts she is running like mad, carrying me with her. Before I can begin fighting real, we are ducking under a thick grape arbour which I had not seen before. Cool and dark it is. She sat down on the ground and pulled me down to sit with her.

"Quiet, Johnny," she whispers, "I think I hear the Baron."

Well then, quiet I am, for I do not want to get the whip. I do not hear the Baron, but soon Miss Lucille peeps through the arbour and says I must not fear any longer.

"Now then, Johnny, tell me what did your brother say."

"You are no' Aldenburg's friend?"

Miss Lucille laughed softly, and it was a nightingale homing in June dusk. "Yes and no, Johnny."

Funny, that. "Are you Deacon Bogle's friend?"

She laughed again and said again: "Yes and no, Johnny."

She is nobody's friend, she is everybody's friend, Miss Lucille is a screech-owl.

"Have you ever heard of a place called Haiti?" she asked.

I nodded my head.

"My parents are from Haiti, Johnny, but I was born here in Jamaica. I am not a *buckra*, I am like you and – Davie."

"Your father is Scotch? Like our grandpappy?"

"French. My grandparents were with Toussaint L'Ouverture and took part in the fight for freedom. My parents used to tell me of it, and what is happening here seem to be the beginning of another Haiti. So you see, you mustn't be afraid to trust me. I am on your side, but I don't want our side to move along too fast."

All this not so clear to me, but Miss Lucille is talking me to her, and nice it is to watch her mouth as she talks. She is talking me over to her side.

"My people knew the sufferings of the poor Haitians and sympathised with them. But when the Revolution came, the poor people forgot who had been their friends and simply killed anyone who appeared to be a white. That was why my grandparents and their family fled to Jamaica. If the Revolution had come slowly, it might have come without bloodshed. I am a friend of Deacon Bogle, but I am afraid he might move along too fast; and what happens when a wagon moves too fast?"

"It turns over, and Father brings the whip to your behind," I tell her.

Laughter comes to Miss Lucille again and she nods her head.

"Well put, Johnny," she said. "The whip will come to you. My father saw what was happening in Jamaica since the three years of drought, and would have warned the government but for something which decided him against interfering. Have you ever heard of a man called François le Seur?"

Is remember I remember hearing of François le Seur. A black Haitian he was, and Eyre hanged him in Kingston because they said he was preaching rebellion to the poor. So I nod my head and say I have heard of le Seur.

"He was our friend. My father kept quiet after that – until he died six months ago."

Nice it is to listen to Davie talking of things which happened long ago. His voice walks on one level, no hill, no valley, 'cept when he is blaspheming. That time his voice walks down into the valley and there is thunder rolling around the valley wall. Miss Lucille talks like Davie if Davie had new treacle in his throat.

Hear me: "Then how come Aldenburg? How come yes and no? Is how it you are living on his property and driving in his carriage with him?"

"But I do not live here, Johnny!" Miss Lucille said quickly. "I am only staying the week. My guardian is here for the Vestry meeting. He is Doctor Creary, you know."

Eh, so she is no' Aldenburg's filly? A good. Davie says a good man is Doctor Creary, even if he is an English *buckra*.

"Then why you do not sleep with your mother?" I asked her.

"My mother died a month after my father," she said softly.

"Poor Miss Lucille!"

Quiet is here. Green lizard creeps in and looks on us and winks at us and is gone.

"I do not want the whip to go on my bro' Davie tomorrow," I tell her.

"No, no, it mustn't happen! It's downright brutality, Johnny! It would be too humiliating!"

I am with Miss Lucille now and will tell her of what Davie told me.

"Davie says I must be at Stoney Gut and tell Deacon Bogle he is at the lock-up and will go before Custos in the morning."

She is looking hard at me. "Nothing else, Johnny? He said nothing else?"

"He says I must tell Deacon that he and the men in the lock-up will be ready."

She held my shoulders tight, and juniper-wood flame danced in her eyes.

"Good, boy! And tell Deacon Bogle that they will not be fined – they will be flogged. Don't forget, Johnny, no fine – *they will be flogged*. For this once the wagon must move fast."

CHAPTER 13

From the time Miss Lucille helped me over the stone wall at Custos's property I have been running. I have left the white road now, and I am going through the track which will lead me to Stoney Gut. There is now no stone wall or mangrove bush walking side-and-side with me. I am trotting through a ghost land o' rock and thornbush and twisty-twisty trees through which the wind runs with fear whistling in his throat.

It is dark down on the track, 'cept now and again where the trees get 'shamed and open a little so the sky can look on the earth. That time I can see that evening star is not yet a-peep.

My ears are ringing again. I do not know if it is 'cause I am tired or is somebody calling my name. If it is Father, there will be *How Long, O Lord?* in his voice, and his fingers will be twitching every time he sees the trace-leather. By now Father will know that Davie is in the lock-up, but is where Johnny?

All of them will be sitting on the barbecue now. Worry will be riding Mother bareback. Manuel will be watching Father and Mother. Naomi's mouse eyes will have got shine in them when she remembers that I will get the whip. Poor Ruthie will be stretching her toes so till they crack. She is thinking of me too, yes? But every time her hands jump to her breast it will be Moses Dacre on her mind. Every time Ruthie sees Moses smiling his white-teeth smile at her, her hands must go to her breast.

I know Sammy must be worrying too. Father will have asked him where am I, but he will have to say he does no' know. Wonder if Father will take the trace-leather to him then?

But what a trouble I have brought on Salt Savannah! Pa John's leather will dance a mento on me before day-cloud breaks in the morning.

Stoney Gut is really far today, bro', but I know I am nearing it when sounds of singing come a-dance through the trees and trip fandango on me eardrums. Breath is not so plentiful inside o' me, but I must trot faster now.

Soon then enter I am entering Stoney Gut and hear Bogle's men singing vespers.

Though the trees are still shaking, there is no sound of wind in my ears. When my feet slide through the loose gravel, I only know by the pain at my ankles. No scents of *cerosee* and *daschalan*, which grow heavy around the houses, come to me. I see and do not see Deacon's chapel, which is a molasses pot, full to overflowing. Only the singing I can hear and see and feel.

Thick it is all around me, beating up under my nostrils, a-push against my breast like the morning swell in Morant Bay and white water foaming 'round my ears.

Breath comes back enough-plenty into me. I walk across the square, and is a cassava-strainer, me, and the rich ripeness of the song is pulping and pressing through me, and I am a-throb to it.

But they come to the long-metre *Amen*, and the wind is a-run through the trees again, and nightingale is a-talk to the dusk again, and men are clearing their throats again, and I am Johnny again.

Big people who crowd Deacon Bogle's chapel are not like cactus fence. Easy it is to get past their legs and creep my way to Deacon's mercy-seat. So presently, when the *Amen* is near done, I am there standing before the mercy-seat and looking up into his face.

The second time, this, I am looking close on Deacon. He stands tall on his platform behind the mercy-seat. Shut tight are his eyes, his long arms stretched out towards we, fingers hooked like he was clutching at something which he has just let go of and does not now want to look at. Climbing around his ears are his shoulders, while all of his body is a-tremble. In his long, black coat, Deacon is a *John Crow* a-hover over Cuna Cuna Pass.

When Deacon has let go of his *Amen*, which has been riding above all others, there is a loud moan from him, his hand drops to his side, then his eyes are opened on us.

What is it what makes Deacon's eyes different from other people? All red and black, and there is no white like the rest o' us. Fright comes on you, and you do no' want his eyes to make four with yours. But all of a sudden there was a little pain in my belly, for remember, I remember I must hold talk with him.

But by this time he is talking with his congregation.

"Brethren, our Sabbath is over. For some o' we this has not been a Sabbath of peace. Some of we have felt the cruel hand of a *buckra* government today-day. Some of we are now in durance vile. But those of we who are here, our hearts beat strong within, our courage is no' impaired!"

Heavy is Deacon's voice, but you can no' hear it over the mighty shouts of *Amen!* and *Alleluia!* which come from the crowd. Then now, see me stand there, wondering, wondering, a-wonder, for nobody has to tell me say that *durance vile* means Davie and Mr. Abram. But how could Deacon have known and I have not yet spoken to him?

But when I look around on the crowd, I can see how it is Deacon knows. For some of the faces which I now see are men who have been at Humphrey's church. They must have walked fast while I ate of Custos's mangoes.

And now 'shamed, I am ashamed and sorry, for nice it is to be first with news, and moreover Davie had said I should reach the Gut quickly.

Hear Deacon again: "We will not change our plans. We will send on the Petition to Eyre come Tuesday, please God."

More shouts from the crowd of: *Come Tuesday, please God!*

"Howsoever, we will not fail our brethren. Three Councilmen will leave for Morant Bay a' morning and pay whatever fine Aldenburg shall inflict."

Away with Aldenburg! Bloodsucker Aldenburg!

But I am no' feeling pain in my belly again, for it is nice to know that Deacon has no' got all the news yet, and to know that Johnny is not too late at all. For wrong, Deacon is wrong to believe that they will be fined.

"No, no, no, Deacon O! They will be getting the whip!"

Kling-kling piping through thunderhead is Johnny crying through the Stoney Gut *Alleluias!* But I must cry, and cry.

"Custos will take the whip to them a' morning! Hear me, O!"

People around me are hushing one another, and Deacon on his platform is hushing those others far away. Soon then there is quiet, and Deacon stoops down to me.

"You are whose young one?"

No fright is on me now. Nice it is to be first with news. Loudness comes in my voice.

"I am Bro' John Campbell, Pa John's youngest, and Davie Campbell is my bro'."

I can feel that all eyes are making four with mine now, and there is quiet but for breathing and *osnaburg* rubbing against *osnaburg*.

"Is who it sends you here, Bro' John Campbell?"

"Bro' Davie is in the Morant Bay lock-up. Custos will have him for the whip tomorrow-tomorrow."

"How you know, Bro' John? How you know?"

Well then, tell, I am telling Deacon Bogle how I crept through the storm-water drain and got inside the lock-up yard and saw my bro' in his cage. How he sent me for Stoney Gut, but how I hungered and met Miss Lucille. Then Deacon is reaching his long hand down for me, and then I am on top of his mercy-seat, standing with my face to the people.

"So now, you hear, brethren?" Deacon is shouting mighty. "You ha' heard what the pickney has said? Say that *buckra* will tomorrow whip honest men? You are a-hear?"

Wayah! Roar comes in Stoney Gut chapel like ordnance in the Fort at sunset.

"Is war it or peace *buckra* is looking? Is war it? Or peace?"

"War! War! They are a-look for war!" shout Stoney Gut people.

Deacon held up a long hand for quiet. When quiet came, his hand came down to my shoulder. His fingers walk over my shoulder, and I am saying to myself that so this is how small chicks feel inside when hunting-hawks swoop down from the banyan tree.

Hear Deacon softly: "Very well then. Very well. Is war it. Return to your tabernacles, people o' Stoney Gut. Councilmen will stay back to make a council. Sing, we will sing the Doxology."

There is a picture which hangs in our room at Salt Savannah which shows young men with horn on their heads, a-sit around a dark-night fire. Ruthie says the writing underneath says: *Plotting in Hell for a Sinner's Soul.*

A long time now we have been sitting around the fire in Deacon Bogle's kitchen. First time I listened good to Deacon and his men as they talked in soft voices. But many times after that, tiredness brought sleep to me. Sometimes when I woke up of a sudden, the smoke in my eyes did not make me see clearly. That time I am frightened, for it seems to me that the Councilmen around the fire have no heads to their shoulders. But after a while I see eyes swimming in the gloom and teeth a-gleam as they talk.

But they swim away again; and am running through dark-night with quicksand all around me. A great Baron Aldenburg runs behind me with a coco-macca stick large as the tower on Morant church. Pastor Humphrey is fronting me, standing beside a big potful of boiling water. Am running fast from Aldenburg and can no' stop, so Humphrey catches me up and hoists me in his arms and is bobbing me up and down before he drops me into the pot.

Davie O! Davie O!

"All right, pickney John. All right, Bro' John. Take time, take time, you are going home now."

I hear the voice in my ears as I open my eyes. I am bobbing up and down in dark-night, and it is time before I know that I am on somebody's shoulder who is walking through the dark. I can make out that there are three or four men around us, talking quietly to themselves.

Nice to be going through dark-night with big people all around you. You do not even notice when you pass Mother Cruikshank's burying-ground. Like say you are like Timothy and me and was born with a caul over your face and duppy-ghost can do nothing to you at all.

CHAPTER 14

A long time now since day-cloud broke, but I am still in my kitty-up, half asleep, half awake. Once when I opened my eyes I saw Father at the door, standing, looking at me. But quickly I formed as if I was still asleep. Two times Naomi came in and tickled my toes to wake me, but I bit hard on the pillow so she thought I was still asleep.

Naomi wants to talk with me and hear what happened yester-day. Last night when the Stoney Gut men brought me home she was asleep. She did not hear when Mother was a-cry and Father was a-thunder at the men. Nor when the men o' the Gut talked and talked about the brave *buckra pickney*, which is me, and told Father that I am Davie's brother and that blood is thicker than water.

That was the time when thunder left my father's voice and *How Long, O Lord* came in. He promised the men that he would not take the leather to me, but that they should have nothing more to do with me.

Poor Father does not know what is happening. Ha' nothing to do with Bro' John Campbell again?

"You have taken one of my boys already. You can no' want this infant," my father told them. Eh! Eh!

But life was not in his throat when he said that, and much of the lantern light was lost in the cockpit country of my father's face.

Sorry for him I was that time, and sorry for Johnny too, so I must cry and Mother must hold my face close against her breast. When eye-water stopped flowing, I wiped my nose and looked at those others of my brethren. Sammy and sickly Zekiel were looking at me like say I am a Kingston acrobat at Morant Bay's August Fair. Is remember, I remember smiling at them just before I dropped off to sleep.

But now daylight is bright outside. Sammy is working the hardwood squeezer to get cane juice to sweeten our tea. He is singing the squeezing song, and whenever the handle cotches at a cane-joint, Sammy sings out:

CANE BUMP O! CANE BUMP O! MASH HIM,
MASH HIM (GRUNT) – CANE BUMP O!

That time Ruthie, who is beating coffee in the small iron mortar, shakes the pestle so it makes music at *Cane bump O!* And there is laugh.

I do not hear Zekiel and Naomi. They must be at the stonehole for water. Monday morning, this is, so Manuel will be out with the canoe to see if any fool-fool mullet will mistake cane-bait for pear. If Davie was here, it would be he and me in the canoe. How Davie can make fool-fool mullet take cane-bait for pear! Nobody has to tell me that Manuel will come back with empty hands and sorrow on his face and no mullet on his string. He does not know fish-style like Davie, 'specially with dry-weather bait.

I wait until I hear Father mounts his mule and tells Mother *God Be.* Then he is trotting out of Salt Savannah on his way to Mr. Gordon's property, where he is head-man. I am off my kitty-up and gone to the kitchen.

Mother is handing out the coffee mugs and journey cakes and singing her matin hymn, her head beating time to the tune. Sammy notices me first and looks up at me with his mouth opened. That makes Mother raise her head and notice me too.

I tell her: *Morning, Ma Tamah.* She looks at me with nothing on her face; then she is handing me my coffee and cake, and I know she will not speak to me this Monday morning.

When I sit down beside Sammy he breaks a bit off his cake and places it atop of mine. I know he wants to hear what happened at the Gut. Naomi's mouse eyes are twisting up and down, her ears cocked to hear what I will say. When I say nothing, hear her softly to me:

"Well, Mas'r Street Arab Johnny, you joined with Deacon Bogle now?"

I tell Sammy we will talk men-things when blah-blah-mouthed women are not around. Naomi makes a sound through her nostril and say she wonders when since Johnny Piper turned Kingfish.

I want to talk with Sammy too. For wonder, I am a-wonder why nobody has gone to Morant Bay to see after Davie. I will talk on our way to school.

When we leave Salt Savannah for school, Sammy and Naomi and me, there is quietness on us until we pass the dead cottonwood into Aaron Dacre's land. Then Sammy tells Naomi she should walk fast and leave us since we must talk of men-things. Naomi is cotching, as if she would make war, but Sammy reaches quickly for a cane-band and she runs and bawls like hell.

Then Sammy and me are walking slowly and I am telling him of things. When I am finished I ask why has nobody been to see after Davie. Then I hear that Father has finished with Davie. I hear how while they were on the parade-ground watching the march-past they heard of Davie being locked up. How say when Mother heard, she threw her bib over her head and was for running to the lock-up, but Father called her back sharp and said he would no' be having a jail-bird for his son. And with that he gathered our family and watched until the march-past was over.

But by that time they have missed me. Then is search, Father searched all over Morant Bay town for me. Not until dusk do they leave town, and only after Father has hired a bell-ringer to cry the town for me.

Good I am feeling now and sorry I did not hear the bell-ringer crying the town for me. Hope, I am hoping that he called me *Bro' John Campbell*.

When we reached the school gate old Mr. Amos M'Donald was ringing the bell for classes. I told Sammy I would go to the privy to make water. I go back of the privy and watch until they march into school. I do not make water, but hide my slate under some dried trash.

For fire and brimstone will be at Morant Bay today and Street Arab Johnny must be there.

CHAPTER 15

I must wait back o' the privy until they have done with prayers before I can get through the gate. When *pickneys* are praying with eyes closed, Mr. M'Donald is always looking through the window and fingering his high collar. Like say he has no need of prayer 'cause the Devil has no' got anything in the Book against him.

Howsoever, prayers are finished, and I am on my hands and knees going past the window. I can hear Mr. M'Donald taking the sixth class with history. You never see anybody for history like Mr. M'Donald. Davie says the *buckra* government pays him to fool poor people's children.

"Now, children, last week when we left off we were at the war against France and America and the Great Divergence in 1783. If the people of the United States of America had obeyed the dictates of His Gracious Majesty, King George III, today they would still be children of the Mother Country, enjoying the wonderful privilege and safety which lies in being a member of the vast British Empire.

"There would have been peaceful emancipation of their slaves, with the Mother Country, in her beneficence, providing millions of pounds compensation to owners, as was done in these colonies. There would not have been this disastrous Civil War, which has most certainly wrecked the future of America. For never again will there be complete peace between North and South,"

A great imperialist is Mr. Amos M'Donald. But I am through the gate and on the road for Morant Bay.

I am waiting in the shade of a banyan tree when the constables brought Davie out from the lock-up. Constables have turned my bro' Davie into a cotter-head plough-steer, for it is like a plough-steer they have chained Davie and Mr. Abram and the two Morant Bay men. Davie and Mr. Abram walk side by side, with the two Morant Bay men behind. The Queen's iron bangles are around their wrists, and all are joined together by a long iron bar 'twixt them. And there is sound there, of *clank clankety clank*. You hear it above the murmur of the crowd under the banyan tree, *clank clankety clank*.

High is my bro' Davie's head, a young stallion a-stride without fear. There are no lips to his mouth, his eyes are gone to bed, but not asleep is my bro' Davie. For every time the constables say something to Mr. Abram, you see Davie's nostrils, and juniper-wood flame flashes in his eyes.

But how Mr. Abram has lips to his mouth! He is talking enough-plenty, and nobody has to tell me that he is blaspheming. His flat head is a mud-back turtle, going in and out, and he moves with quick-quick steps to keep up with Davie's long foot.

I am in the crowd waiting in the shady of the banyan tree to see them pass. The tree is at Main Street corner where it crosses the road to the lock-up. When you ha' crossed over Main Street, turn your face to the north wind and you are looking up the Blue Mountain Valley. Walk for distance, and you will come to the track that takes you to Stoney Gut.

Well, then, *clank clankety clank* is a-come, and *bump bump bump* is in my heart. I am holding my belly for the little pain which is walking in it.

Stand good, Bro' John Campbell! Is now it!

They were not more than six boar-hunter's strides away when I leaped out of the crowd and ran towards them crying: "Davie O! Davie O!"

Davie's head jerked and lips came to his mouth. I cry at him again and am almost on him when a constable pushes his stave in my belly and I am falling to the ground. Up comes Davie's free hand, and such a fist does that constable gets that I am no' alone on the ground.

Aie – war now! The other constables are coming for Davie with their staves raised above their heads, and Mr. Abram is a Wareika boar bellowing down on them. Then I hear the shout that I am a-listen for:

"Take time, Bro' John! Take time!"

Nobody has to tell me that the Councilmen are a-come.

Ha' you ever stood on the beach midsummer morning and feel south-easter a-come with day-cloud? Not like other times, this, other times when south-easter comes with whisper first, then talk next, then louder talk, then shout. Midsummer mornings, the sea wind gets up from the Bay in a mighty rush that would flatten you on the sand if you had not seen the white horses riding in far out on the Bay and leaned your body forward to meet it. Was so, the rush of the Councilmen at the banyan tree that day.

Take time, Bro' John! And there I am in big people's hurricane. Man battering man, women and young ones a-scream, and Johnny rolling for the gutter.

But I only reach the gutter when I am up in the air and riding a Councilman's shoulder. Across Main Street, into the back track, rocking and bobbing all the way along, and in front of me there is music, music, *clank clankety clank clankety clank*, plough-steers racing for clear pastures. And behind me, man is battering man, and women and young ones are a-scream.

Far in front o' me I can see where Davie and the others on his chain turn into t'other track what leads for the mountains. Then I am shouting:

"Go along, Davie! Go along! Whip will no' come to you today!"

When we reached the corner the Councilman swung me to the ground and there was big grin on his face.

"You are the man for the glory, Bro' John," he told me. "No whip for your bro' today! Run home and cover your mouth."

Then gone, he is gone galloping after the sound of the chain, and I am standing in the sunlight with happiness thick in my throat so I can no' shout but must croak:

"Run, Davie! Run! Run! Run!"

Back o' me people are still shouting. Down there, I know the constables will be madding to go after Davie, but Councilmen have worked well and townspeople are many on the streets today. It will be no' easy for the constables to get through.

I know they will not catch my bro' on the mountain track to the Gut. Somewhere on the track Davie will meet more of Bogle's men with sledges and chisels for the Queen's bangles.

Late it is. I will run for the school, no?

Mr. Amos is still talking history and does not see me when I go in, but my eyes meet up with Sammy's and Naomi's and wonder is on them. I slip to a seat beside Timothy. Timothy's eyes ha' got water in them and tremble is on his cheek.

I whisper to my friend Timothy of some of the things that have happened at the Bay. There is a big grin from him and no more tremble at his cheek. By-and-by, when the bell rings for eating-time, I will hold man-talk with Sammy.

CHAPTER 16

'Cept for digging-match and burying-wake we never have visitors on weekday times. Only on Sabbath after services do folks come a-visit us at Salt Savannah. So when we come home from school this evening and see visitors sitting on our barbecue, nobody has to tell me say something has happened. I think on Miss Lucille.

Zaccy O'Gilvie was there in his alpaca suit and big silver chain. There was Mr. Gourzong, tall mulatto with a beard that is a candlewood torch in whirlwind, a-blow on all sides. But what has carried my mind to Miss Lucille is to see Doctor Creary on our barbecue.

All o' them are Vestrymen. Mr. Gourzong and Doctor Creary live in Kingston. A full *buckra* English is Doctor Creary, but Morant people likes him very well just the same.

All o' us. Sammy and Naomi and me, tell howdy to our visitors. Father sits facing the Bay, with sunlight splashing his back and tiredness walking heavy on his face. When we tell them howdy, his eyes do not come on us at all. Mr. Gourzong nodded his head and said: "How Johnny is growing!" Doctor Creary fanned his face and said: "Yes, Johnny is really growing."

What is that then? Should Johnny not grow? How come big people so funny?

Even deaf-ears crab must know that the visit has to do with what happened in Morant Bay today. I am walking to the house with my back holding stiff, a-wait to hear somebody call my name and call for the trace-leather. But nobody calls my name.

Well then, quick into the house and push my slate under the kitty-up. Smart, I must play smart if I will hear what big people will talk among themselves. So I am back out of the house and under the barbecue before you can say *Jack Mandora.* Mother is in the kitchen drawing coffee for our visitors, but if she sees me under the barbecue, I will be splicing a piece of bamboo to my kite. Listening, me, to big people's talk.

I hear Father. "Since Davie has gone and troubled trouble, then trouble will trouble him in turn."

I can no' see my father, but the voice he uses is the voice he uses when he shakes his head like a stubborn hamper-mule.

Snort from Bro' Zaccy. "But, Bro' John Campbell, is of no use that! Trouble has happened already and you must do something now!"

"That is the position, Mr. Campbell," said Mr. Gourzong. "Only right and proper that you go to Kingston and bring Mr. Gordon here!" Zaccy says with loudness.

"That is the position, Mr. Campbell. Nobody knows where this trouble will end. Bogle is an arrant fool, but his influence over the people is only second to Mr. Gordon. The Stoney Gut people are out for trouble, that we do see now. We must have Mr. Gordon down here, and as soon as humanly possible. You are his headman, liked by him, and – well, it might also help your son."

"Davie has troubled trouble," my father says, tiredness walking with his words. "He must lay in the bed he has laid."

"*Jehovah-Jireh!*"

Silver chain jangles as Zaccy shouts and slaps his knee.

"*Hear, God O!* Is what the matter with you, John Campbell! Don't you know what has happened in our parish today-day? You do no' see that the powderhouse will soon go up?"

Doctor Creary is quieting Bro' Zaccy, with sharpness. For a while nothing comes from my father, till afterwards his voice limps back from distance.

"Is what it you gentlemen want me to do?"

Now, hear there! So Pa John had only been listening with one ear!

"To get Mr. Gordon down here quick-quick!" shouts Zaccy.

"Bide!" Doctor Creary says with sharpness. "Bide, Mr. O'Gilvie! Mr. Campbell has his own sorrow."

I am under the barbecue looking up at the floor. I can no' see our visitors, but when I look up, I believe I will hear better. So, being that way, I did not see when Naomi came under till I heard her ask: "Is what it?"

Her mouth is wide, I want to rub dirt in it, but holler, she will holler like hell. So I only look on her like fierce Maroon and form my mouth to say: *Shut up.* She does not hear me, but I will be quiet, for ears that are deaf bring trouble on a secret talker.

Father said: "What happened at Morant Bay today?"

"*Jehovah-Jireh!*" Zaccy filled his belly with air and pushed it out with deep groan.

"Bide, Mr. O'Gilvie," Doctor Creary said. Then he is talking to Father. "You will understand, Mr. Campbell, that we got the story second-hand, for the constables who were escorting the prisoners to the courthouse are now held prisoners by Bogle at Stoney Gut."

Hard it is to hear such news and not able to bawl out *Wayah!* Poor fool-fool constables must have met up with some Councilmen on the mountain track.

"However, we have gathered that while the prisoners were under escort to the courthouse, the constables were set upon by some Stoney Gut men who forthwith rescued the prisoners. Among them, of course, your son David. They ran in the direction of Stoney Gut, manacled as they were. About a mile from town the discarded manacles were found – evidently cut by a chisel."

Take time, Bro' John! What a way Councilmen work, though!

"The constables continued along the track, and I now understand, by, er, devious means, they are being held prisoners at the Gut," Doctor Creary said.

"But nobody has heard from the constables?" Father asked.

"Is so that," said Zaccy O'Gilvie. "Her Majesty's authority is flouted and Her men held prisoners by Paul Bogle. What is a-happen in this land?"

"But why should Bogle put himself in such jeopardy?" Father is asking. "If he wants to help his people, why did he no' go to the courthouse and pay the fine?"

Throats are cleared, and our visitors move their feet on the barbecue.

Hear Doctor Creary: "This seizure of the constables is a very serious turn. If they are not released and the prisoners returned for trial immediately, the militia might be sent against them. You know how Mr. Eyre feels about this spirit of unrest in the island, especially in this parish. It is true the people need assistance, but acts like these will not win sympathy to them."

"Quite true, Doctor Creary, quite true," says Mr. Gourzong.

"Mr. Gourzong, Mr. O'Gilvie, and myself discussed this matter today and came to the conclusion that only one man can ease the situation before it is too late. That man is Mr. Gordon. We therefore decided to solicit your help. We hoped you would see the position and consent to travel to Kingston to see Mr. Gordon as soon as possible."

"And after all, Mr. Gordon started the trouble with his preaching; he should end it with his preaching," Zaccy growls like boar.

"Mr. O'Gilvie!" Doctor Creary shouts, "will you stick to the point?"

But Father has done heard the words already and is quick on Zaccy O'Gilvie.

"Is what it you say about Mr. Gordon? What, Zaccy O'Gilvie? You think such foolishness would come from Mr. Gordon? You do no' know he would have told them to pay any fine rather than this foolishness?"

Hear the belly laugh from Zaccy O'Gilvie!

"Fine? Who is a-talk of fine? Those seditioners were to get the whip at Morant Bay courthouse!"

Father said softly: "What you have said, Zaccy?"

Seems to me that all our visitors are trying to talk one time, but Bro' Zaccy is a wild boar, roaring off *Wareika Mount*.

"Said that Custos would ha' ordered the whip for them this day!"

Doctor Creary is telling Father not to listen to Zaccy, and that they did no' agree with Custos. But Father still talks soft to Zaccy.

"Have Davie whipped? For what, Zaccy O'Gilvie? Ha' my son whipped like a yam-hill thief?"

"How so?" shouts Zaccy. "Then you have no' heard that they were raising Cain outside Missis Queen's lock-up yesterday?"

"But when no violence was there? When no violence came from my son?"

Quiet is in my father's voice, but quietness is in the first wind when it piles black clouds over the Bay.

"Whip John Campbell's second-born? Like food thief?"

"Bide, Mr. Campbell," said Doctor Creary.

But breath left Pa John with heaviness. "*Aie*, then 'fore Mas'r God, and honour to Missis Queen, right, Davie was right to get away from the constables."

Funny it is to be under the barbecue and see mule feet on the walk. There is primness in the straight foreleg while hind-legs glide and roll behind like sugar-boat men who have just come ashore.

I keep quiet while Manuel leads Father's mule to the paddock-tank. Grass roots are brown on Salt Savannah with three years' drought on them, but every step Manuel makes, the mule head goes down and his big yellow teeth nibble at the brown. Manuel does not jerk the rein as how Davie would have done. If it were Davie, there would be tug and tug, he on his haunches, mule on his haunches and the rope like iron bar 'tween them.

Stand quiet, does my bro' Emmanuel, till the mule stops nibbling, and they start off again.

Howsoever, Zaccy is shouting at my father again.

"Right? Say they were right to flout Queen's authority? Do you remember what Pastor Humphrey said yesterday?"

"Shut your blasted trap, O'Gilvie!" bawled Doctor Creary, his feet stamping on the barbecue. First time I have heard loudness in Doctor Creary's words.

"Davie was right to escape, 'fore God and the Queen," my father said with finish in his voice.

CHAPTER 17

After quiet had been on the barbecue for a while, Mr. Gourzong took up the traces again, and off big people were gone again.

"About Mr. Gordon," says Mr. Gourzong.

Father stirred on his stool. Must ha' been two breaths before he spoke.

"Post came today from Mr. Gordon," he said. "Ill he is and will not be at the Vestry meeting this week."

Doctor Creary said sorry he was to hear o' Mr. Gordon's illness, but would Father go to Kingston and tell him of what is a-happen? Perhaps Mr. Gordon would then send a letter to Stoney Gut?

No talk came from Father for a while. I know say now his eyes are gone to long distance while his mind is looking on what Doctor Creary has said.

Then, now, hear him: "Doctor Creary, Mr. Gourzong, Bro' Zaccy, what I said a while ago was that Davie was right. I did not mean that right he was to flout the law, but manhood would be gone from my boy had he received the whip in Morant Bay's market-square."

Father is talking with firmness, in the voice he uses for *Come, Tamah*.

"All you gentlemen know how I feel about Stoney Gut. Sympathy is no' in my heart for law-breaking. But Davie, like many o' our young men, is wild with the wildness of Paul Bogle. Yesterday-day, when I was leading my family to Sabbath service, I heard from an older Stoney Gut man that they would send a Petition to Governor Eyre."

All of Naomi's face has gone into her eyes. She is listening to man-talk but has no' made head nor tail o' what they are saying. Whisper, she whispers to me: "Is what it? Is what it, Johnny?"

My father says: "I say, sympathy is no in my heart for law-breaking, but Stoney Gut people are my people all the same. Yesterday I said I would not sign their Petition. Things have happened today, things which must make a man think. Hear me now."

Mother and Ruthie came out of the kitchen with coffee for our visitors. Softly-softly under the barbecue, me, while the coffee mugs go around and Mr. Gourzong is saying how Ruthie has grown pretty. Bro' Zaccy slops his coffee like hog at buttery door. Mother and Ruthie go back to the kitchen.

"Hear me now," says my father. "My son Emmanuel will carry your letter to Mr. Gordon, and better it is if he leaves tonight. But what about Queen's constables at Stoney Gut?"

"Something must be done about that immediately," Doctor Creary said.

"Then very well. Tonight I go to Stoney Gut and sign Paul Bogle's Petition."

Shepherd Jesus, hear me voice! Is what that Father has said? Cover your mouth, Naomi! Stand steady, Johnny, mind they on barbecue hear you!

All our visitors on the barbecue shout together. Zaccy O'Gilvie cries: "Man, mad are you?"

But my father still speaks with calmness. "Hear me now. Nothing is wrong with the Petition, but yesterday I was blind. Better it is if Stoney Gut men send their Petition than take the law into their hands. Hot-heads, we call the young men, but which of us were not hot-heads when we were green? So till the years bring ripeness, and cool, we grow cool."

"Much in that, Mr. Campbell," said Doctor Creary.

But Zaccy O'Gilvie will have nothing of it. "Man! What treason that you are talking? Say you will help the Stoney Gut seditioners?"

"Hear me, Bro' Zaccy!" my father said sharply. "You have no son who is a-play with hell, so you can no' see the matter plainly as me. Better it is if we older ones take the traces out of young men's hand 'fore all o' us go to the gully. Wrong or right, Doctor Creary?"

Doctor Creary says right my father is.

Hear Father: "What I will do is this: I will tell Deacon Bogle that I ha' come to sign his Petition, but on condition that he releases the constables and send back Davie and the rest for trial. But I must tell him too that they will not get the whip. Can I tell him that, Doctor Creary? I can tell him that?"

A smart one is my father. For Doctor Creary is good friend with Custos, and he can have good talk with Custos that should take the whip from my bro'. Smart, is my father. But –

"You can no' change what Custos has decided!" hollers Zaccy O'Gilvie.

Doctor Creary quieted him quickly, then he spoke to my father.

"I cannot give an undertaking that Baron Aldenburg will be in agreement with that, Mr. Campbell, but I will certainly endeavour to make him see our point."

"Then very well. I will ask Deacon Bogle to send them back for trial as soon as word come to him that they will no' be whipped."

"Wait a minute, Mr. Campbell," Doctor Creary said. "Why don't you suggest to Bogle that he adds the circumstances of this case to his Petition?"

"Is good, that, Doctor Creary," Father said with heartiness. "Good, that."

"What exactly are they petitioning for?" Mr. Gourzong asks.

But what a fool-fool mulatto-man, that! Then dry-time is not on our land? Then people are not starving? And don't they must pay tax and can earn no wage? And must not they pay church tithe and have no crops? And constables and runners after them every day? A fool-fool mulatto-man is Mr. Gourzong.

But nobody answers Mr. Gourzong 'cept fat boar Zaccy, who snorts: "Seditioners!"

"Quill and ink and paper, Mr. Campbell," says Doctor Creary. "Let us draft the letter to Mr. Gordon."

CHAPTER 18

Night-time is glee time 'round our house at Salt Savannah. Heavy throat bullfrogs lay down thick bass for bush crickets to pipe upon, and there are much skirtings from 'fraidy young screech-owls high in the poinciana trees. North wind strides with giant steps from one treetop to another. Down in the Bay, groundswells roll in slow thunder, thundering far away. When night comes it is music time around our house at Salt Savannah.

In the hall, we are now, and our visitors sit with Father at the table. Quill has finished scratching on paper now. There are sounds of music outside and lantern a-splutter inside.

All o' our family sit around on the long wall-bench, but Manuel stands tall by the door, seriousness riding his face. He wears a pair of Father's leggings at which he slaps with his *supple-jack* whip. Ready for his night-time ride, is my bro'.

Doctor Creary has the quill in his hand and is looking at my father.

"Shall I sign, Mr. Campbell?" he asks.

"Is not needful that, Doctor Creary," my father says. "Alone I will sign."

I do no' like Bro' Zaccy in lantern light. Valleys and ridges are there in his face which you do not see in the daytime. He has got his fingers over his eyes, but there is a gleam shining through his fingers, and the gleam is shining on me. I do no' like him in lantern light.

Father closed the envelope and handed it to Manuel.

"Is a long night-time ride, it, Emmanuel," my father said.

Manuel is as tall as Father, and they are big men standing facing one another. "You know the road to Cherry Gardens where Mr. Gordon's house is?"

"I know the road well, Father," Manuel said.

Hear my father: "God be, me son."

Then Manuel is gone through the door, and all o' us stare into dark-night. I am thinking say only three sons in the family now. Father pushed breath out of him with heaviness.

All of a sudden Bro' Zaccy is talking.

"Hearsay says there was a little *buckra* boy with the Stoney Gut men this morning."

Father got up to reach for his coat and hat and does not look at Zaccy at all.

"Hearsay has it that a buckra boy ran with the seditioners this morning," Zaccy O'Gilvie said again.

Doctor Creary and Mr. Gourzong are getting up from the table. Doctor Creary says *Cho!* as if he would like to spit.

Sammy's eyes made four with mine. A little pain has come to the bottom o' my belly. For Zaccy is looking at me through his fingers, and nobody has to tell me he is talking about me.

Father had his coat on before he looked at Zaccy. Then he took his eyes to walk over his family while he buttoned his coat.

"Well, well, well," he said with dryness. "What a thing, eh, Zaccy?"

Buttoned is his coat.

"God be, Tamah. Stoney Gut I am for."

Our visitors tell us good evening, and their riding boots are going heavy down the steps.

Father stopped at the door and turned his head to look me in the face.

"God be, Bro' Johnny," he says softly.

No men left in our family now. Mother sits and rocks herself her eyes full on the lantern.

I am wondering on Manuel and Father. Forty miles it is to Kingston, thick with darkness along the windward road. Wind will be moaning through the trees on one hand, moaning over the sea on t'other hand, my bro' will be leaning forward in his saddle, he alone in dark-night.

I am thinking say Father will have parted from our visitors by this time and now is a-strike up the gorge road, he alone. He has ridden his plantation mule which can do many miles in easiness.

But am I a-think about Davie? *Davie O!*

Mother stopped rocking and got up and reached for her apron.

"Come, Ruthie, gal, we will wring cassava."

Is women work, this, to wring cassava in the kitchen, and only Zekiel used to help the women. But tonight Sammy looks on me, and his eyes say yes. North wind is blowing around the house and we do no' feel to be alone.

CHAPTER 19

Davie says that sweet cassava is our food for manna in the times of famine. For whether you have water-O, or whether you have no water-O, plant your sweet cassava on your dry land, and up he will come overnight.

Davie says God Almighty made cassava to feed poor people in times of famine.

You know how you wring cassava?

Dug, you have dug out the brown roots, and now you are in the kitchen washing them clean. Afterwards comes scraping-time, and the knives are flashing and the skins are peeling, and soon the creamy flesh is thick in your hands.

Then comes grating-time, and you never see anybody that can grate like Mother; one tuber grated to a nobble, and swift she reaches for another tuber while she pushes hair from her eyes. Good it is to see the juniper flames a-paint sunset on her face, and all the while the cassava is rising creamy and frothy in her bowl.

Sammy and me can no' do it as swift as the women and Zekiel, so we find we must suffer Naomi, who grins like Cuna-Cuna monkey.

Afterwards Mother will get out the *osnaburg* wringing-cloths. We will put the grated cassava in these. Then two of us to each cloth, we will wring and squeeze and pulp the juice through the cloth into the bowl. Tomorrow the juice will be on the barbecue to be dried into starch, while the cassava will be dried and pounded in the mortar to make the cassava flour for our bammie cakes.

Come Saturday-day the starch will be sold to Morant Bay produce-buyers, and money will come to buy salt beef and osnaburg. Cassava is poor people's manna when dry is come to the earth.

But we are in the kitchen at Salt Savannah. By-and-by Sammy's eyes meet mine, and he tosses his head to say come outside, for tired he is of grating cassava. We will go out and hold man-talk.

We go outside to the roots of the big ackee tree and talk of Stoney Gut. Firelight from the kitchen has pushed away dark-night, but all the same, frightened I am when a hand comes from behind the tree and holds my shoulder.

When I jump up from the tree-root, there is a chuckle behind me, and a voice says: "Take time, Bro' John."

It is Moses Dacre.

"What do you here, Moses?" I asked. "How come you are not at Stoney Gut?"

"I come from the Gut, Johnny."

"Met up with Father, you?"

"Yes, but he has no' seen me. We passed at Chigafoot Turn. What he goes to the Gut for?"

Well the Turn is two miles from the Gut, and Father was riding while Moses walked foot, so Father must be at the Gut by now.

"Father has gone to sign the Petition," said Sammy.

Moses whistled sharp like a blackbird. His eyes in his mahogany face caught up the firelight.

"Is so that? Good, good. My father will be glad this night," he said with a chuckle.

"How Davie does?" I asked.

"Well he is, and does no' wear Queen's bangles any more."

"How the constables do?" Sammy asked.

"Deacon will let them go this night," Moses told us.

Now hear there! For if my father had known that, he would not have had to fight through dark-night for the Gut. All the same I am glad that my father is going because he has love for Davie again.

All of a sudden Moses said: "Bro' John, Davie wants to see you."

Now I did not expect that, for only grown men will tell one another: *I want to see you.* It means they will hold man-talk in private. This morning I was Bro' John, tonight he wants to see me. A big man I am now, yes?

So all I can say is: "For true?"

"For true, Johnny. You must go to Stoney Gut tomorrow with sun-up."

They are grating hard in the kitchen. North wind is walking with ice in his knapsack, telling us there will be no rain this October. Moses turns his head to the kitchen.

"The women are a-grate cassava?" he asks with nothing in his voice.

Who Moses thinks he is fooling?

Sammy asked: "Moses O, when will Petition go to St. Jago?"

"At morning. We leave with sun-up."

"You are going? How you are going?"

"Yes – walking through the mountains."

There is pride in Moses's voice, although there is no boast like in Zaccy's. But right he is, for young men must be strong like boar and quick like goat and with breath like racehorse of St. Dorothy's parish if they would use the mountainside to go to Kingston. I do not know the trail, but Davie has been there, and great tales I have heard of the bush where man can touch man and still not be seen; of mighty stones with which Jehovah played marbles and left helter-skelter for by-and-by; of cracks in the earth where you throw rocks down and no sounds come back until you draw four breaths; of streams where water never dries out; of valleys whose fat grasses never knew dry-time. Tales I have heard of the Blue Mountains, where Davie says God is no' far from man.

"We leave with sun-up for Kingston," says Moses, hatchet face turned to the kitchen. Then with nothing in his voice he says again: "Women are wringing cassava?"

Who Moses thinks he is fooling? But Moses is my friend and Father is not here. So I go back to the kitchen and presently I am at Ruthie's ears.

She can grate no more. Calmness is on her face, but her body is a young cane in early wind. Her eyes talk with the firelight, her fingers curve sharp to her palms. Stretch, she is stretching her body like when Father stands over you and the trace-leather is coming down for you.

Presently up she gets. Now firelight talks with the corn of her hair, and the blue of her eyes is as black as dark-night. Her hands reach up to her breasts as she walked out into the night.

The wind is a-north from the Blue Mountains, but warmth is there at the roots of the *ackee*.

Must be just before daylight that Father came in from the Gut. I am not asleep in my kitty-up, but form like say I am.

"Tamah O!" I heard him call at the door.

Quick with the lucifer on the lantern is Mother, and is opening the door to him. He came in and stood by the lantern.

"Davie hearty," he said.

Mother nodded and said it was good, that.

Father said: "All the *pickneys* hearty?"

"Fast asleep, Pa John, fast asleep, fast asleep."

Mother sits on the stool and talks like she is not there, her eyes on distance, her head rocking side to side.

Father has got off his coat. He sits on the bed, unlacing his jackboots with fingers that can no' see.

"No good there at Stoney Gut, Tamah."

"*Aie.*"

"Bogle is a madding man, Tamah, but they have let go the constables."

"You ha' signed the Petition?"

130

Father is tugging and grunting at the boot.

"I – *grunt* – sign – *grunt* – Petition."

"*Aie*," Mother said quickly.

Father looked up quickly. "No harm there, Tamah."

Mother's head stopped rocking. "I do no' trust Deacon Bogle," she said. "Bogle does not want peace. He does no' understand what Mr. Gordon talks of."

"True, Tamah. But what must we do? Mr. Gordon is ill and can no' come down here. We older heads will have to do something."

Mother made a grunt in her throat which was neither yes nor no.

"What has Bogle put in the Petition?" she asked.

"Well –" Father is thinking with his eyes closed "– general things, Tamah. But remember, I remember that near the end it says if Governor Eyre does no' protect them from the magistrates, they will put their shoulders to the wheel."

She got up and pounded Father's pillows. "I do no' like that, John."

"I do no' like it either, but the Petition was written from last week and they would change nothing now. Howsoever, they added that they were Her Majesty's loyal subjects. But that is not all, Tamah."

For a time Father said nothing more. Then he leaned his face on his arms so that his voice came out through cotton. He said: "They will march on Morant Bay tomorrow to see Custos at the Vestry meeting."

Mother stopped pounding the pillows and looked up at Father. "Davie too?"

"Davie too."

Take time, Bro' John! Do not jump!

"Mercy, Mas'r God!" my mother said softly.

"Let me tell you of the road to Stoney Gut, Tamah. When I got to Quacko Corner, about forty chains from the Gut, I heard a shell blowing in the darkness. I was on the road, alone. But after I rode a little more, mankind suddenly grew out of the night and the ground and caught the animal's head."

Father rose from the table and sat with his arms across his chest.

"I heard: 'Halt! Is who this?' Somebody lit a candlewood, and then I saw them – *aie*, wildmen there at Stoney Gut, Tamah. Their machetes were out, and eyes rolled, and teeth gnashed at me.

"Somebody said: 'Is a good man, that, Bro' John Campbell o' Salt Savannah. To where you go, Bro' John?'

"I told them I was for Stoney Gut and Deacon Bogle. 'Is a blockade, this, Bro' John,' somebody says. I say to myself: 'What they are playing? Boys a-play at Maroon War in moonlight night?'

"So, patience left me, and I jogged the animal to go on. But before you could say *Jack Mandora*, men were grabbing at the mule head and hauling me from the saddle."

Father cracked his knuckles and looked at Ma Tamah.

"I buried my wrath with soft answer. By-and-by they said I must walk foot and follow a guide who will take me to Deacon Bogle. I went off with the guide, but every chain we went, there was somebody calling out to us in the dark-night, and my guide answers back. I know now this is no play. Bogle's men are girded for war, Tamah."

"Mercy O!" my mother said again.

"*Aie*, Tamah."

Weariness was on my father as he rested his face on his arms. "Men from Manchioneal and the Rio Grande are there at the Gut, Tamah."

"Say what? For true, Pa John?"

Mother must be surprised, for you must cross the Blue Mountains into Portland parish to get to Manchioneal and the Rio Grande.

"Bogle has sent men into the mountains to have war-talk with the Maroons. I hear say the Maroons have promised to join him, but I do no' believe they will."

"God O! Move so they don't!" My mother is a-pray while her head rocks from side to side.

"Ahh," comes from my father as he gets up and goes to the window and peeps out. "Soon be daylight, Tamah. Manuel must be near Kingston by now."

Mother covered her face with her hand. I know she is a-think of Manuel.

CHAPTER 20

Sammy and I have dumbed Naomi. She has taken oath over running water that what eyes see and what ears hear, mouth will never talk. Hard, it was hard to get her to the oath, but Sammy bent down a pimento branch and tied her pigtails to it. Dumbed, we have dumbed Naomi.

So then, now I am going to Stoney Gut and am no' worried about Mother hearing say I had no' gone to school today.

I have heard shells blowing around me, and voices have spoken to me from rock-holes and trees, but I have no' been stopped like Father last night. I have not seen them, but I have heard: *Take time, Bro' John!* and big belly laughs from Deacon Bogle's sentrymen.

Hear the shells how they blow! First a-moan with sadness and loneliness, of earth heavy with sorrow; then there is the swift ascension and no longer near the earth but is leaping from treetop to treetop, a-leap to the wild stones high on one another, and your head is twisting all about, sending your eyes up after the sound of it. So till reached, your eyes have reached the highest crag and there against the sky is the shell-blower.

Watch how he leans against the wind, his cow-horn shell curved away from his lips, taking your eyes with it, till you forget the crag is there and believe the shell goes to shake hands with God and is a-carry the blower with it.

Are where those shell-blowers now? Shepherd Jesus – how they could blow!

Eh, everybody is not at home. Everybody is at Stoney Gut. There are men marching up and down, a-carry sticks on their shoulders like militiamen's muskets; there are men sitting in cool shade, rasping files on cutlass teeth; many men practice to form fours and squares just like Queen's soldiermen; and I can no' find my bro' Davie.

The chapel doors are closed, but there are men sitting on the steps. I ask for Bro' Davie Campbell. Strangers, these, who do no' know Davie Campbell. My eyes are stumbling all over the crowd, and presently I see a flat head bobbing through the crowd. I run and call out:

"Mr. Abram! Mr. Abram O!"

Timothy's father it is, and he stops and turns and sees me. There is a big grin on him.

"Eh, Johnny, tell me you come to join up now?"

Nice it is when you are stranger in a strange land to see a grin what you know.

"I am a-look for Davie," I tell him. "Davie wants to see me."

Mr. Abram scratched his head and formed like he was sad.

"Eh, think, I was a-think you had come to join we," he said. "Your bro' is inside, reasoning in Council meeting."

He pointed at the closed door of the chapel. I tell him I will wait, so he takes my hand and tell me he will show me the Gut. All about the square we walk, and Mr. Abram is grinning enough-plenty and telling everybody that I was the pickney at the lock-up. So all the men say good I am and that proud my father should be o' his blood.

While we are going around, a bell rings and Mr. Abram says Council meeting is over. I want to run for the chapel, but he says wait and soon Davie will be coming out.

Presently I see Davie coming out of the chapel. He walks slowly 'twixt two men, the sun shining yellow on his bare head. He sees me, and his eyes laugh. The two men wear breeches and no more clothes on. They carry long muskets, and powder horns swing at their hips. Tall they are like Davie, and walk as if they would no' like to feel the touch of earth on their heels.

"Maroon-men, they, Johnny," Mr. Abram tells me.

Aie, the wild black men o' the mountains, walking like feet too proud for the earth.

"They ha' joined up, Mr. Abram?"

He bobs his flat head, his eyes a-roll. "Everybody will join we, boy."

My bro' shook hands with the Maroons and came towards us. But he has not got to come all the way, for I am running to meet him and am up in his arms. Good it is to have his arms around you and the smell of him in your nostril. There is everything settling in its right place and quietness there inside of you.

134

I told Davie everything that had happened from the time I had got out o' the lock-up yard. I ha' been talking like a pretty polly till I remember that Moses had said that Davie wanted to see me, and yet he has no' held man-talk with me yet. So I cover my mouth.

Is good that, for by-and-by after he has rubbed my head with his hand, he talks.

"Johnny O, why did she do that? I think she is Custos's filly – then why she did that?"

Eh, so I had no' told him everything?

"No, Bro' Davie, is not so. Daughter to Doctor Creary she is, spending time at Custos's house."

He pulled back my head by my hair so I must look up at him with my teeth showing. "What you talk about, boy? Doctor Creary has no daughter."

So then I must tell him of Lucille.

My bro' listened to me till finish came to my voice. Then he said softly: "Is so, it? Then she is no' near Custos, eh?"

His eyes went to bed while he rubbed my head with his palm. Quietness is on me, quiet till his eyes come back to me.

"You afraid for Custos's estate, Johnny?"

I tell him no, with nothing in my voice. A grin took his mouth, and he pulled my hair down on to my face.

"You are no' afraid to walk on Custos's land?" he said. "Then you must carry *thankie* to Miss Lucille."

Eh, God! What Davie will do with me?

Howsoever, he must think say I am not afraid. So I form like he has not just ask me to turn up my behind to Custos Aldenburg's whip. I tell him I will take *thankie* to her.

"You must tell her that gratitude is on us at the Gut," he said.

CHAPTER 21

I leave the Gut for Aldenburg's land when the sun can grow no higher. When I reach his stone wall my shadow is as long as myself. There is nothing of Miss Lucille in the mango-walk, so I know I must go up to the house.

Hell will pop if anybody should see me, so I am a-walk with cat-and-mouse through the tall Spanish needles to the croton hedge which borders the house garden. And find, I find is a good thing, that, for who do I see when I reach the hedge but Custos Aldenburg.

Heavy from his table is Custos, wearing a white weave suit which looks like sleep was had in it. Stands with feet wide, hands clasped under his belly, head held proud as he looks down his red nose at the County Inspector who is holding talk with him. Doctor Creary is there too, leaning against the pillar of the step, back o' a long cigar.

But what is a-burst my eyes is the sight of the militiaman standing stiff by the head of his horse. Is what this, then? Militiaman in uniform on weekday?

"There are a few old muskets at the station, sir, but absolutely no ammunition," the Inspector said. "We will have to borrow some from the militia."

"Addrociouz zdate of affairs," Custos says down his nose. "Really addrociouz."

Humble is the Inspector.

"Addrociouz. Ve vill have to use the militia for guards and as many gonstables as can get muskets."

"Shall I dispatch the courier now, sir?"

"Eh? Yess, of course." Custos belched and looked at the militiaman: "You have your inztructions, my man?"

No' stiffer the militiaman can be, yet he makes his back come stiffer.

"Yes, sir, Custos. Dispatches to His Excellency, Governor Eyre at St. Jago."

"Very vell. Be off with you."

Hand flash up in salute, then he is a-swing into the saddle. Quick paw of hoofs on the ground, and the horse's belly nearly kisses dirt as his forefeet strike forward for speed.

"This vill zettle those rebel bastards, Inspector," says Custos, his eyes a-hide from daylight.

"I hope His Excellency dispatches the regiment at once, sir. A forced march will bring them here by Thursday."

Doctor Creary stood straight from the pillar. "Will you see the

Stoney Gut people if they attend the Vestry tomorrow, Baron?"
he asks.

"They vill see the muskets of the militia, Doctor Creary,"
Custos said with file in his throat as he turned up the steps to the
house. "Vait for me, Inspector, ve vill go in the carriage to town."

Doctor Creary waved to the Inspector and went into the house
behind Custos. Is cat-and-mouse, me, on my belly in the Spanish
needles with wonder opening my eyes and my mouth.

Presently the carriage rolls around the drive with Custos's
hoity-toity coachman on the box. Little afterwards, Custos and
Doctor Creary come from the house and join the Inspector in the
carriage. I spit through the crotons at Custos's carriage wheels.
Pig, that!

Custos's house is a stone house, with wide verandas all around
and green jalousie blinds to give cool shade. I think say during
rainy weather nice it must be to play around all these wide
verandas over which my eyes are walking in search of Miss
Lucille. Spanish grass tickles my nose, and a hunting bee circles
'round my head. I am backing out fast on my belly when
somebody laughs behind me and say:

"Careful there, Johnny."

I am on my feet, a-spin to face Miss Lucille.

"How come you walk like Davie so?" I ask her.

She laughed with eyes a-dance. "I wish I could *run* like your
bro' Davie," she said.

"You ha' heard about it?" I ask.

"I heard about it, Johnny," she said with graveness like my
father.

"We tear lick on constables – *wham! wham!* – and take away
Davie to Stoney Gut. Is me it who started it."

I am no' boastie like Naomi, but is true, that.

"Good boy, Johnny!" she said like Father. Then all of a sudden
there is clear laugh from her and she is a-kneel in her riding-skirt
on the grass, and kiss, she is kissing mango-face Johnny.

Only Mother I used to have kiss me; for good it is how
quietness reaches you when she does. Ruthie kisses with her
mouth opened, and her tongue is wet and moving inside your

mouth. Once I kissed Naomi, and was a stone wall that. Miss
Lucille kisses like my mother.

"I want to see you," I tell her.

"Yes, Johnny?"

"I got a message from Davie for you."

Her eyes walked on my face. "Come on then, Johnny."

She held up her riding-skirt and is running with her head bent
forward. Although she is laughing I must run like mad. For do no'
let duppy-ghost fool you, Miss Lucille can run though!

We are in the grape arbour and sitting in the cool shady.

"Now tell me what your bro' Davie said."

"Davie says to tell you howdy and *thankie*, and says gratitude is
at Stoney Gut."

No laugh comes from her now. Her hands are passing through
my hair, come and go, come and go, like Davie's. A little time
before she talks.

"Will he be going to the Vestry tomorrow?"

"Davie is a Councilman; he must have to go."

Her eyes make four with mine.

"Johnny, do you think there will be trouble?"

"Davie says there will be none, for they will go and make talk
with the Vestrymen, a-tell of their grievances."

"But the Baron expects trouble – do you know that?"

"Davie says there will be no trouble. My bro' must know."

She laughed. "All right, Bro' John. But suppose the police tries
to hold Davie and the others. Will the Stoney Gut people allow
them to be taken?"

Wayah! My mind did no' think on that at all, at all! For true, if
constables make after Davie again, Councilmen will tear licks
right and left.

"You will come to see me after the Vestry, Johnny?"

"Yes, but no' near the house. We will talk by the stone wall."

Miss Lucille laughed and said it would be at the stone wall.

"I am bringing Davie too," I say from my mind. Is so it
sometimes when you do not cover your mouth truly proper, your
mind talks o' secret things.

"But – won't he – will he want to come?" she asked with breath.
"Do you think he will want to come?"

Gourd-mouth Johnny! You will do it how? What you are? Big man?

"He must want to come," I say with finish.

"All right, Bro' John. I will be at the stone wall."

"When your shadow is as long as you – not before," I tell her.

CHAPTER 22

All morning Mr. Amos M'Donald only bleats in one o' me ears. T'other ear is cocked to Morant Bay way, a-listen for something else. And nobody has to tell me that so are Timothy's and Sammy's.

Mr. Amos is a-talk of the walls of Jericho. Mr. Amos has no' got clear sight, and so does not see me telling Timothy about Stoney Gut men coming to the Vestry meeting.

Mr. Amos does no' stop talking about the horns 'round the walls of Jericho until lunchtime has come. While we are singing the grace we hear the shells blowing.

Take time, Johnny! Mind your heart does no' jump through your mouth!

When we go out into the schoolyard for lunch the shells are blowing stronger now, and there are enough-plenty big people running towards the courthouse way. Naomi has got the shut-pan with our lunch and is walking to the cotton tree under which we will eat. Ackee it is for lunch, with breadfruit fried in coconut oil. Crisp and flaky will be the brown fried breadfruit. There will be oil a-drip from your fingers as you scoop softie ackee, fat and round. Sweet water will be a-gather at the roots of your tongue, a quivering deep in your belly.

Before times Sammy and me would be under the cotton tree quicker than you can say conoo-monoo. But today-day gone, we are gone a-run with the crowd to courthouse way; and there is Naomi one under the cotton tree a-holler like red ants are crawling up her skirts.

Funny it is to me how the shells sound different when I hear them in Morant Bay town. There was wildness when I heard them in the hills, but there was beauty in the wildness, a clean length of sound that did no' snarl at me as it leaped from earth and curved through blue spaces. But now when I hear them in Morant Bay no cleanness is there.

Hunting-bees trapped in calabash gourd are a-talk of hate through throats filled with slime.

When Sammy and me reach the cross street what leads to the courthouse, the first Stoney Gut men are just there too. Thick is the crowd, but I am a worm in *calaloo* field, yes? I am going to the front.

Big people's elbows are bringing water to me eyes. Arm sweat is scenting in my nose from clothes which ha' no' shook hands with soap since the August Fair.

Watch Stoney Gut men! Gut men a-march to see Custos! Take time, shell-blowers! Take time, drummer-man! Mercy, Jesu O! Watch them! And watch me here, a-jump and a-shout too while the shells and the drums moan and boom!

But is where Davie though? I do not see him at all.

Shell-blowers march in front o' the men, but no beauty, no curve, no leaning 'gainst the wind. There is a drummer-man back o' the blowers, and I look good and see is flat-head Mr. Abram it. Timothy's father flogs the goatskin like mad while his head is bobbing and bobbing. But there is not a Davie.

All of a sudden, there comes from the crowd:

See Deacon, there!

Deacon Bogle is a-walk, he alone. He is wearing his pulpit coat and a broad trash hat, under which his sight rolls from side to side o' the street. But otherwise still is his face.

Look as I look I can no' see Davie. There are black men and brown men and mulattoes and poor whites, but none with head like English flax, which would be me bro' Davie's hair. *Davie O!*

You never can hear *kling-kling's* piping when storm-wind is a-howl through the trees. Elbows are taking breath from me, but how must I turn right or left? Heavy is the crowd around me.

I hear the singing from the Stoney Gut men. When men make songs on contented bellies, there is depth and roundness in their throats. Wet earth and full trees bring quiet and content. But Stoney Gut men are a-dirge through three years o' dry earth and Humphrey's tithes, so aloes ha' come to their throats.

★

Aie – I tell you, now that I am old, black was the cloud o' singing that day piling up on Morant courthouse. Did they hope say rain would fall from it?

All the same, rain did fall. Rain, like the rain from the side o' Mas'r God's Son, the Golgotha rain.

Not the soft spring rain which whispers o' hope through the windy March nights. Is remember, I remember some March days when evening comes to you, droopy and weary, and the Blue Mountains has turned to grey. Then sometime in the night-time while sleep is a-walk over you, he stoops to draw his shoelace, and you turn over in your kitty-up.

Then softly, in the little wake 'tween your sleep, hear, you hear water a-whisper in the roof-thatch, and your heart is a-leap at the sweetness o' what you hear. Then droopiness and weariness are gone, and you are a-pray: *Mas'r Jesus, why day-cloud will no' break?*

Come, sweet morning! Come holding up your green, green head!

But at 'Sixty-five red rain did fall, and it drowned some o' me brethren.

I worm from the crowd and run into the lines o' the Stoney Gut men who march to the courthouse. And presently we are in the square fronting the courthouse.

Thick is the crowd, Bogle's men in front and Morant Bay people pressing back of them. Men are climbing the trees around the square, swarming among the scaffoldings of Pastor Humphrey's new church, for which he did take the contract himself. In front o' the courthouse, facing to the square, two lines o' militiamen and constables lean on their muskets. The bottom doors of the courthouse are closed, but now and again I can see heads bobbing past the upper windows.

When I wormed to the front I could see Deacon Bogle a-hold talk with the County Inspector. Mr. Abram has put down his drum and is forming some o' the men into ranks. Since I can no' find my bro' Davie, then I must stand near Mr. Abram. I get through big people's feet till I can touch Mr. Abram.

He looks down on me, and hut-door hanging on one hinge after heavy breeze is his lower jaw.

"John – Johnny! What you do here?"

I do not make answer to that, but ask for Davie while I listen to Deacon Bogle's talk with the County Inspector.

Bogle is asking to see Custos Aldenburg, and Inspector says they can no' see him now, for there is the Vestry meeting there. Bogle says they will wait, for injustices must stop now, now. The Inspector smiled and said that is not his business. Bogle shouts that: *No!*

"No," Bogle says, "is the business of the people, this; and the people's voice which is the voice o' God will be heard in the land this day."

County Inspector slaps his stick against his booted foot and says yes, so long as only their voices are heard, and so long as their voices are no' too loud.

"We should no' talk to underlings!" a Councilman shouted. "We will talk to Custos Aldenburg!"

Eh! Red is the Inspector's face as he champs his moustache like pasture horse mouthing dry grass.

"You had better hold that restless tongue of yours, my man!" he bawled.

All this time, noise is swelling around the square. Morant Bay people are getting restless for the shells, and the drums ha' stopped sounding now. Bogle held up his hands to show that he wants quiet. Quiet comes, then he tells Morant people that he has no' come to the Bay to give them fun, but that he is seeking justice for the poor.

"Hear me now," he tells them. "We will wait so till Custos finish his Vestry meeting, and then we will hold talk with him. We will not go away. Justice we must get, same place here. County Inspector says we voices must no' be loud, but sing, we will sing the hymns o' our faith. One o' the brethren will please raise the faithful servants' song: *Break Down the Walls o' Jericho*."

Long-tongue Bogle, my mother used to call him, and how his tongue is long this day!

Mr. Abram shuffled over to his drum and made a double roll on the goatskin. A tall Councilman with a red 'kerchief around his neck stepped out in front and faced to us. He points his beard to the treetops and sings high: *O-o-o-h-h-h!*

Long is the sound, coming from distance. Then his beard is coming down slow from the treetops, and the sound is coming nearer now till his eyes make four with ours again, and he is a-sing with his mouth opened wide at us:

BREAK DOWN THE WALLS O' JERICHO –
Hear Stoney Gut men: YEA, LORD O!
BREAK DOWN THE WALLS O' JERICHO –
YEA, LORD O!
SEVENTH DAY WALK, SEVEN TIMES 'ROUND
SEVEN TIMES COME-O! SEVEN TIMES GO-O!
BREAK DOWN THE WALLS O' JERICHO –
YEA, LORD O!

Morant Bay people take up the chorus with them. Then in comes Mr. Abram with his drum, and I see shell-blowers take their bull-horns from their shoulders and point them up at Mas'r God.

Funny it is how the shells sound different when I hear them in Morant Bay town. But now clear, I must be clear about what happened next.

Listen me. I ha' heard from Davie about these Vestry dinners. He says whenever there is Vestry meeting, Custos and the Vestrymen always sit down to big banquet. Many tales I have heard about whole hogs with pimento and fresh mint packing their insides in sweet scents. Heard o' great white yams brought all the way from Westmoreland parish and powdering as they reach your tongue; roasted yellow hearts o' breadfruits tasting like goats'-milk butter; booby eggs from Morant Cays boiled hard with salt and pepper; guinea chicks what never ate anything but young corn even in dry times; stewed mango chutney served on kingfish caught on the California banks; and whole demi-johns o' 'Twenty-five Trelawney rum to wash down all this richness.

When Davie talks he spits. I do no' spit, for sweet waters gather at the roots o' my tongue, and I must swallow that.

Morant people have no' been trained like Stoney Gut people, so they sing with raggedness as of small stones being shaked in a calabash gourd. But presently I see cook-women carrying platters from the kitchen to the banquet room upstairs. Morant Bay hungry people see it too, and such a howl comes from their hungry bellies!

CHAPTER 23

If a man would keep well the secrets o' his thoughts, then he must no' sing his songs. For hear me now. I tell you that try howsoever he may try, his thoughts will fly out on the wings o' his song, and see, you will see their colours; sable like carrion crow going to death, or gold o' the solitaire a-wing towards the morning star.

Is remember, I remember something. I call to mind one Saturday morning when I went with Sammy to meet Father coming back from wild-boar-hunt.

Manuel and Davie had been gone with him for a whole week, so this Saturday when we reached Morant Bay market, Mother said we should go to meet the hunters under the cotton tree at the edge o' town. Father is not much of a rummer, but usual it is that after boar-hunt the men will stop at Miss Martha's Tavern near to the cotton tree. This day Mother wants to see him early, so Sammy and me will meet him and tell him this.

'Member, I remember how I heard them singing as they came down out of the mountains. We were sitting at the tavern door, Sammy and me, in the cool shady. We hear Miss Martha calling inside:

"Come, come, Becky gal! Boar-hunters are a-come! Gal, come clean down the counter! Becky-O! You are where?"

Black and fat Miss Martha be, and heavy is her voice. Three daughters she has there, and once I heard Davie say that Martha is a payable mare, for she has proved with three different sires. While her daughters are cleaning the counter for the boar-hunters, Martha is rumbling to them. For a while she will be talking to herself, then all of a sudden out a question goes to one of the girls. Then before the girl can answer good, Martha is a-rumble again, and soon there is another question to another girl, and the said thing happens again. And I am noticing say all of the girls talk with rumble like Martha, but lighter according to size. Then, me there thinking how they sound like Humphrey's organist when he is a-finger on the swells.

But soon my mind goes from them, for the hunters have come on the road in my sight.

They are striding slow and long, wearing their broad trash hats fastened at their belts, muskets slung over their shoulders. Father is there in front of the hunters, fingers o' wind lifting his hair for the morning sun to wash with gold. There are Davie and Manuel walking side o' him, and you cannot with easiness tell one from another, 'cept that colt horse can no' have shoulders like stallion's.

Manuel leads the donkey, burdened down with dead wild boars. A good hunt, this has been, and huntermen are a-burst with jubilee hymns. Tomorrow Humphrey will say a special prayer for them right after he prays for rain. Humphrey's mind will be walking on a fat tithe hanging over his fireplace.

Inside Miss Martha's they go, and after huntermen toast Father for a good leader, and Father toasts them for good huntermen, Father says he must leave them now, for Tamah is waiting on him. While his eyes pass over Manuel and Davie and Sammy and me, his fingers feel for the brass buttons which are not sewed on his hunting-shirt. Davie asks Father if he could no' remain longer with the huntermen. My father's eyes go away for a while, then come back to Davie.

"Very well then, but stand good, Davie. Do as St. Paul says," he tells Davie.

Davie says he will do so. Then he feels my hand squeezing of his arm and asks if Johnny can stay with him too. There is a nod from my father; then he is waving his hand to the huntermen as he goes out with Manuel and Sammy. Davie swings me up on the counter to sit, and there is a grin crinkling his face as he calls me the youngest rummer o' the Campbell family.

But afterwards, as the rum comes to the counter enough-plenty, I do no' know if Davie stands good, for there is wild talking

145

and shouting, and men are cursing Governor Eyre with loudness and calling blessings for Mr. Gordon. Miss Martha and her daughters have no time to play pipe organ, the way they must hurry with the demijohns.

All of a sudden Davie fists hard at the counter and shouts: "All right! All right! Stand good, gentlemen! Quiet!"

Martha looks quick at him, then she is waddling out of the room with her head thrust forward for speed, while over her shoulder she is a-thunder at her girls to come fast with her for the kitchen.

Hear Davie meanwhile: "Is what it we want, gentlemen?"

Huntermen hit the floor with their musket-butts and there are mighty shouts for: "Pepper-pot! Pepper-pot! Martha – you ol' soak! Where the pepper-pot?"

"Coming! We a-come!" she is shouting from the yard.

And then through the door I see Martha coming with the big hardwood bowl, from which steam rises like evening mist. And such a shout for *Pepper-pot! Pepper-pot!* goes up from the huntermen, and such a grabbing for the calabash gourds which her girls are a-hand to the men! Then there is dipping into the bowl, over which Miss Martha bends with perspiration making heat-rash on her grinning face. And there is a gurgling and a hissing which you never hear 'cept where river goes to bed in a stonehole.

Davie says: "Come, Johnny, taste your pepper-pot!"

I take the gourd which he is giving me and go down for a big sip – and *wayah!*

Gourdy drops from my hand, and I am coughing and spluttering while eye-water runs down my face!

Is not soup this what Davie has given me. I am a-swallow scorpions, or else Maroons are at my belly with their spears. All the huntermen burst into laughter. Davie is at my back a-pound, a-pound, and telling me: "Take time, Johnny-boy, stand good." Well, after that you know what I find out? I find out that all soups do no' bring the same contentment. Evening time when Ma Tamah makes her congo-pea soup at Salt Savannah there is a richness and smoothness in peas and pimento and thick coconut milk. But not so Miss Martha's pepper-pot, which shrieks in your stomach a hate-filled discord o' *calaloo* and red peppers, *ochroe* and *soosumber*, green *skellion* and wild Indian cane.

★

I should tell o' one thing though. Remember, I remember that after the huntermen had eaten of the wild soup at Miss Martha's and took up the street into town, nobody could be telling that they were drunk one time. Quiet talk, straight walk, everybody standing good.

Davie says last heat has driven out t'other heat.

CHAPTER 24

All singing is no' the same. Today-day Morant people sing in hate and discord. But presently, when they look long on the platters going up the steps to Custos's banquet room, their mouths shut tight as they work spittle from their throats which the sight o' the platters has brought up.

Now only Stoney Gut men are a-sing, and I look back at Morant people and wonder at how their throats work and work. Only Stoney Gut men are a-sing while Flathead Abram is bobbing over his drum. Morant people suck at their throats, and hate is filling their eyes.

Far up on top o' Humphrey's half-finished church I hear a voice cry out:

And, Jesus Christ, we hungry!

Then now from the scaffoldings, from the trees in the square, from the hundreds on the ground such a tumult of shouts there are that you hardly can hear your ears hearing.

"We hungry! We want to see Custos Aldenburg! Bring out the fat-belly German-man! You in there a-feast on poor people's money while we out here a-starve!"

Mr. Abram is bobbing over his drum, but soon the tumult is gone over him and perplex comes to his face. His head bobs slower over the drum till he stops flogging the goatskin altogether.

"Bring out Parson Contractor Humphrey! Come, preach and tell us the price o' cement in heaven!"

I am a-look towards the courthouse when my eyes notice something. I see a constable shade his eyes from the sun and look

147

to me. But when I look good again I see he is no' looking at me, but at Mr. Abram, 'side of whom I am standing. By-and-by, after the constable has looked well and good, I see him go over to the County Inspector and point to Mr. Abram.

Nobody has to tell me say they have made out Mr. Abram as one o' the prisoners who escaped. The County Inspector talked to two other constables, and they came forward towards we. I drew Mr. Abram's sleeve and told him that constables were coming for him. He could no' hear me in the noise and only grinned at me. I drew his sleeve again and shouted he should get Councilmen, for we must tear licks right and left. Mr. Abram grinned again. I grabbed his belt and shook him and pointed at the constables. But 'fore we could do anything the constables were at the line and had laid hands on Mr. Abram.

Hell, now is hell! For Councilmen and Morant people have seen what is to happen, and down they come on the constables. Deacon Bogle is running up with his coat a-flap behind him and a-shout for quietness. But quietness is not here today. I see the County Inspector talk quick to the constables and the militiamen and their muskets come up from the ground and point at us.

The constables who had come for Mr. Abram are backing with quickness to the courthouse. Mr. Abram is railing and prancing, madding to go after them, but Deacon is talking sharp to him. Then up from out of the bed o' hate which Morant people are spreading from their throats a rock-stone rose, curved through the air, and landed behind the militiamen. Glass window in the courthouse grinned quick at me as the stone went right through it.

As the gap 'tween Judgment Day and me draw shorter, so that I know many months can no' be left 'fore I go to the big Mercy-Seat, I, John Campbell o' St. Thomas-in-the-East, swear say that was how the rebellion o' 'Sixty-five started. And the rock-stone did no' come from the Stoney Gut men.

Morant people back o' us are shoving forward, Deacon's Councilmen are bracing backward, and Johnny is a red herring squeezed 'twixt hot-roast *renta*. Then all of a sudden I hear shell-blowers tearing at our ears, and Councilmen are shouting:

"Let be! Let be! See Custos Aldenburg there! Let be!"

Only then I can stand on me feet, and breath comes back to me. But I do not wait for breath but wriggle through Councilmen feet until I stand by Mr. Abram again. And from here I can see up on the courthouse balcony and see that Custos is standing there.

Pastor is there, too, and Doctor Creary, Zaccy O'Gilvie, and all the Vestrymen. Anger is on Custos, and his belly fights hard at the black band around it. His hand is up as if bless we he would, but I know he is calling for quiet. He looks down his nose at us.

"Vat is all this? Vat iz the meaning of all this business?"

No answer come from the people. I know frighten has come on them. Is like the story in the Book about Saul and the duppy-ghost. They ha' called for Custos and now he is here; but 'member, they have remembered he is Chief Magistrate, and now they feel as if they were facing the Bench.

The County Inspector has run up the steps and is talking to Custos while he points to Mr. Abram.

"Vere is this Bogle?" Custos asks loud.

Deacon stepped forward from among the Councilmen. His pulpit suit gleams in the sun as his head goes back and he looks back at Custos down his own nose.

"I am here, Custos Baron Aldenburg."

Deep and strong is Deacon's voice, a mighty leader fronting his people.

Aldenburg is blinking at him.

"Vat do you vant?"

Deacon Bogle puts his hands under his coat and stands akimbo.

"We ha' come to seek justice for the poor. We desire speech with the Vestry."

"Vat do you mean, justice? Vat do you imply, my man?"

Doctor Creary is saying something to Custos, but he is waved away.

"Your Honour, we desire speech with your Vestry," Bogle says with stubbornness.

"You will get no speech with the Vestry today!" Custos shouted.

"We must have speech!" Deacon shouted back. "Loyal subjects we are to Missis Queen Victoria!"

Eh, now. I think Custos's neck will burst and spray Doctor Creary with purple blood.

"Inspector! Inspector! Get this scum out of here!"

Deacon Bogle turned back to us, red eyes walking quickly over us. He turned back to Custos.

"You see scum here today-day, Your Honour?" he is a-ask. "Scum is no' here today. Free men we are now and loyal subjects to Missis Queen. We must ha' speech with the Vestry."

A cunning man is Deacon, for he has talked back to Custos, telling him that free we are, and has no' been struck dead. So now a thousand freedmen face one big-belly German on the court-house balcony.

You ever listen how March wind starts a' morning when you stand in Cinchona Valley?

Long-legged coconuts see it first and commence shaking his fuzzy head. Then the others get it too, and soon the whole Valley is wheeling and curtsying and a-chatter with a million tongues.

One voice screams out from far up the scaffoldings o' Humphrey's church:

"Is who it you call scum, Aldenburg? Is who it?"

And then the cry is coming from all around the square.

Aldenburg held up his hand and shouted something. People are pressing forward again, and I am up on my toes tripping forward like tightrope acrobat at Morant August Fair. And soon I do no' dance nor trip but just travel on big people's elbows and insteps.

Deacon Bogle is shouting to the people to let up, Custos is a-shout from the balcony for peace, but nothing in these can stop the crowd.

T'other Vestrymen are holding up their hands, crying for peace too. The County Inspector is giving orders to his men. Constables in front go down on their knees while militiamen form at the rear a-stand. Dark and round are the musket muzzles as they look in Johnny's face.

Most o' the cries now are for Custos, asking who is he calling scum. But I think say the crowd is like Miss Martha, for they do no' wait to get answer before they ask again.

Johnny, your feet are where? Johnny, your head is where? Street Arab has no father to hold his hand and tell the crowd let up.

Davie O! Davie O!

Wham! Is a rock-stone, that, landing on a constable's helmet. The Inspector is up on the balcony talking to Custos Aldenburg. We are there halfway across the square now, and I can see the Vestrymen's faces plainly. Fear is a-walk among some Vestrymen now. Bro' Zaccy does no' push out his chest like barnyard rooster any more. Worry is on Doctor Creary, but I think he is a calm man.

More rock-stones are falling. Custos nods his head to the Inspector and says something to the Vestrymen. Bro' Zaccy runs back inside the courthouse. Soon he comes out a-carry a paper which he hands to Custos. Custos begins to read. Somebody who is standing near me cries out:

"Riot Act! Custos is reading o' the Riot Act!"

Well then now it is that fear has come to me. For I know that after the Riot Act has been read County Inspector has all his rights if he tells militiamen to make their muskets talk. Davie has told me all about the St. James parish rebellion o' 'Twenty-nine. Fear has come to me and I am madding to run; but with big people all around me, I can ran where?

"They are a-read the Riot Act! Butcher Aldenburg will shoot we down like blackbirds! *Riot Act O!*"

I can no' hear all what Custos is reading. One hand holds the paper before his face, and t'other is waving over his head. After a while his face comes up from the paper. He takes off his hat, and the other Vestrymen with him take off theirs too. In the little quiet which comes on us everybody hear when all the Vestrymen call out:

God Save the Queen!

Then I see Bro' Zaccy turn and scuttle inside the courthouse, and all the t'other Vestrymen follow him, but slower; all, 'cept Doctor Creary, who stands looking down on us, his head shaking from side to side. Custos is at the door, beckoning to Doctor Creary, but Doctor only shakes his head from side to side and will no' go inside. So Custos goes in and closes the door.

And I am thinking how it is like night-time at Salt Savannah when Father looks out on dark-night one last time before he closes the door. That time sorry, I feel sorry for poor screech-owl,

151

who must screech in cold and darkness outside while warm and with light we are inside.

Doctor Creary stands looking down on we, his head a-shake, his shoulders sad.

Crr-r-r-a-a-ck!

My heart comes up to my mouth, and there is no breath left inside my chest. There is smoke a-whirl in the wind over the constables' and militiamen's heads. I am holding on tight to an arm, and my face is buried in somebody's shirt. Body scent is rank in my nostrils. Is remember, I remember I heard two sounds: the beat o' the somebody's heart behind his shirt, and the rattle when the muskets are reloading. For the space o' two breaths men do no' move.

All of a sudden I shiver, and there is a big sneeze from me. Then somebody laughs out loud and call:

"Blank! Blank cartridge! They can no' shoot down free people!"

Stillness leaves big people, and they are shouting and pushing across the square again, and more stones fall on the courthouse now.

"We want Aldenburg! Come out and talk to we, fat German-man!"

Then over the shouts o' the people I hear the muskets talking again. This time in the silence I do no' hear any heartbeats. Neither the muskets as they reload. Fastened, trace-leather has been fastened around my heart so I can no' breath.

Then, God O, I come back to myself. I am lying on the ground in the square and a dead man is on me.

I see the blood a-pour out of the hole in his face. His eyes are opened on me but are no' seeing me at all, at all. I am watching the blood on the ground, coming, coming, a-come closer to me, a long red snake wriggling nearer to me, coming so till it almost touches my face – and is then my heart swells and bursts trace-leather, and a shriek is a-bubble in my throat.

I am no' the only one shrieking. How could it be me one a-shriek? You ha' not heard say that forty o' we people fell when militiamen muskets talked the first time? And say that seven o' the forty looked at the sun without winking? You must ha' heard that one o' the seven fell from atop Humphrey's new church headmost into a mound of wet mortar and found his death there with his heels a-kick at the sun. Ha' you heard o' the woman who hugged musket ball to her breast, then went slow to her knees, so that long afterwards thought, we thought she was a-pray? Or of the little *buckra* boy who was running 'round and 'round crying for *Davie O, Davie O*?

Is me, Bro' John Campbell, that. I do no' know how I get out from under the man with the hole in his face, but I come to myself when I am swung up into the air and looking down on the face of Mr. Abram.

Cries and moans all around me now, but the cries are getting louder than the moans.

"They ha' shot we down! Shot we down like dogs! Fat German Aldenburg has made militia shoot we down like dogs!"

Good it is Mr. Abram was here to take me off the ground, for now the crowd is rushing towards the courthouse, and not even gunshot can stop them. I am riding Mr. Abram's shoulders in south-east surf, and Custos's musketmen are on the lee shore. Two Vestrymen are at the windows firing pistols into the crowd. Quick as they can load, musketmen are pulling triggers and reloading again.

But south-east surf is still roaring in, and then they are on the Inspector's men.

Shoulders, shoulders are all I see; but ha' shoulders ever talked to you like how they talk to me this day? Men are ploughing there up courthouse way, and their shoulders talk back to me. I can no' answer, for my throat is tight.

They plough and plough and plough. Presently they have stopped working, and the shoulders move away. I can see they had been ploughing at death.

I am sitting on the ground inside Humphrey's church, not thinking of anything at all.

I call to mind that one time at Salt Savannah, Timothy and Quackoo and me were sporting in a morning sea, riding on a bamboo raft. We did no' notice that the sea was coming up till we were 'way beyond the blue-water mark. Quick we turn the raft for shore, racing like mad with the surf coming fast after us. But race as we could race, a heavy sea caught up with us, and up we are gone and down again, down to sea-bottom. And then there was a struggle at sea-bottom, with sand a-fill our ears and nostrils, and water pounding out our breaths. When well bruised and full o' aches we crawled out on to the shore, gasping like groupers in net, we just lay flat on the sand, a-think on nothing at all, at all.

So, is how I stay now, my back leaning on Humphrey's wall. Stoney Gut men are all around, and near where I sit Mr. Abram is kneeling beside a man with blood on him. Mr. Abram is rubbing bush in his palm. From the scent I know it is ma raqui, which is good for any wound, even from musket ball. Mr. Abram opens his palms and spits on the bush and puts it on the man's leg where the blood is. Then he tears a piece of osnaburg and ties it on. The man said *thankie* to Mr. Abram and leaned back to the ground. Then he blasphemed Custos's name with loudness. Mr. Abram helped him with the blasphemy.

Councilmen are sitting in a corner holding talk with Deacon Bogle. Others of the men are sitting on the ground, and others are peeping around the walls to courthouse way. Mr. Abram's eyes make four with mine and he comes over to me.

"What is a-happen to Johnny?"

I shake my head without talk and he sits down beside me. I see now that Stoney Gut men are climbing up the scaffolding inside the church, carrying muskets in their hands and bandoleers over their shoulders. Nobody has to tell me where they get bandoleers from.

When they reach to the top of the wall they lie full out among the scaffoldings, a-peep over the edge of the walls. By-and-by one of the men fire his musket.

Everybody is looking up at them now. Mr. Abram calls out:
"Man, ha' you brushed him?"

There is laugh from many men.

A duck in swamp reeds is the man who just fired as he drops his head quick under the edge of the wall. There is the sound of a musket from courthouse way. Another Stoney Gut man fires from the scaffoldings and plays at duck in swamp reeds again as a musket from courthouse speaks with anger and chips fly from Humphrey's scaffoldings.

"Try and drop a ball under Custos's tool so he will no' chisel stray gals in his buttery-room longer!" Mr. Abram calls to them, and there is belly laugh from the men.

I pull at Mr. Abram's pantaloons and he stoops down to me. I asked him to tell me o' things.

Then it is that I hear that after the shoulders had ceased to plough, nothing of the musketmen before the courthouse had been left alive. Howsoever, some of the militia escaped into the courthouse, and they are there now, a-fire at Stoney Gut men who are up in the scaffoldings. I hear say the County Inspector is there on his back in the square, looking full at the sun without pain.

"What we will do now, Mr. Abram?"

He nods his flat head at where Deacon sits with his Councilmen.

"Musketmen's bullets took forty o' we people, Johnny; drew blood from forty. Only six constables lying out there to keep our dead company. Boy, Deacon wants to see Custos!"

Do no' ask any more, Johnny! Done there with Mr. Abram!

A shell-blower stood up among the Councilmen, and hunting-bees came with anger from his bullhorn.

Come O! Come O! Deacon has ended his reasoning in Council! Up here, Johnny!

Up on Mr. Abram's back me. Mr. Abram is broad in the back like penny-a-ride donkey at Morant Bay Fair. We gallop through the crowd which is rushing through the church to where Deacon stands tall on a platform they ha' rigged for him.

Deacon is holding out his hands for quiet. Talk, he will talk to us.

"Men o' Stoney Gut, hear me! War is here today-today!"

Come O, hunting-bees! Come in anger and hate from two scores o' curving bullhorns!

155

Wild are the shells as they talk o' wartime and the hunt. This is where they are strong, yes? They ha' talked o' these times, many times.

For, hear me now:

Bullhorn O, how often ha' you led into battle your Jamaican men? When first we heard your voice in the hurry-hurry hills and the wild woodlands o' the Cockpit country up Trelawney parish way, was it no' of war you talked of? Did no' the English redcoats and traitor Juan de Bolas sweat in terror as you spoke o' death in the bush? Then again in 1690; did they no' hear your voice in Clarendon parish when African slave-princes would sever their bonds?

And four years later were you no' there at Carlisle Bay in the parish o' Vere, standing side-and-side with the English? That time your voice told the Frenchies say they would no' land on your island. Slaves and free whites in King William's clothes, three hundred o' them meeting Du Casse's fifteen hundred Frenchies; but called you did to their hearts and won the day for the Jack.

But changed, you were changed in 1728. Remember how English redcoats marched side-and-side with baying Cuban bloodhounds to smell out your tracks through the mad mountains? And when too many men and too better muskets made you fall to the precipice at the edge o' Nanny Town, did no' your voices thunder: *Death, yes! But no' slavery!*?

They say the English could no' see the bottom o' the precipice for the broken bodies of those who answered your call.

Talk! You can talk o' war and the hunt, for down through the years you ha' called to us.

'Thirty-eight – you ha' rallied your people, and now there are Mosquito Indians out o' Honduras marching with the redcoats as they hunt your people. 'Forty, and changed again, you ha' sailed to fight beside the redcoats before the Spanish city o' Cartagena. 'Forty-six and 'Sixty, and back you are in your island, fighting for freedom against English soldiermen. But come 'Sixty-four, and now you stand with the redcoats before the Cuban city o' Havana, and soon your voice is a-shout o' victory as the Jack flutters over the turrets o' Morro Castle.

Then in 'Seventy-eight you went to America with the strong youths of our island. 'Member, can you remember how your voice sounded before Charlestown when you stood with the redcoats to battle General Washington?

Run, you had to run that time, for weakness was in your throat when to your shame you saw you were there side-and-side with German mercenaries against the men o' America who had stirred for freedom from England's tyranny.

Aie – then the glory o' 'Eighty, as you followed the beardless Horatio Nelson into Nicaragua and the city o' San Juan. But O, the shame o' 'Ninety-three, when Haiti is offered to King George's crown by the Royalist colonists o' France. That time, for your shame, you went with the English up the Windward Passage to fall on L'Ouverture because he sought freedom for his people.

Glory came to you again in 'Ninety-eight, when you howled for freedom in Trelawney parish, and men felt for their muskets in the dark o' night and leaped upon the English camp.

And yet, back you were in America in the War o' 1812. How your Jamaican men died there! Remember the roll o' musketry in the night? That night when five thousand Americans came out o' New Orleans town and fell on you and your English redcoat allies?

"Well did your Jamaica men fight," "Old Hickory" Jackson said afterwards; but General Andrew Jackson did no' know that you failed because your voice was no' created to howl against men who go into battle for their rights.

Wartime, hunting-time, hear the shells talk! Much glory and much shame ha' you seen. Sometimes against one, sometimes against t'other – *human you are, Bullhorn?*

Deacon is holding up his hand for quietness. Quiet, me, on Mr. Abram's back, and quiet the shell-blowers.

"Stoney Gut people, we did no' want war. We come to Morant Bay to seek justice. You know we can get no justice from the Bench. You know the taxes buckra English has asked us to pay is more than we can bear. How many o' you have no' got blood relations in lock-up right now because they can no' pay their taxes?"

Yes, yes, is true that! True, that, Deacon!

"Is true, yes? Tithes – tithes, me brethren. Don't we know how Pastor Humphrey managed to build a great house for himself? Don't we know say even our Baptist Chapel must pay tithe to Humphrey's Anglican church? So that his stipend will pay for carriage and servant? And no' that only. Is not it plain and straight to all o' we that rascality was in Humphrey when this pastor took the contract himself to build this said church in which we stand now?"

True, that, Deacon! *Aie – Pastor Humphrey thief, Pastor Humphrey robber, Pastor Humphrey go to hell faster than Morant Bay cobbler!*

"But what is bad a' morning can no' come good by evening. What will you expect from a Pastor who in the old days was a slaveholder himself?

"So now we are here today inside this church which Humphrey is a-build out o' we blood, and outside, seven o' our people ha' gone to see God's face, and forty ha' had blood drawn from them. We have reasoned in Council, and Councilmen say blood for blood. Is what it you say, brethren?"

They are saying blood for blood too, Deacon. You ha' heard them? Walls, do no' shake. Trees, stand steady. Make only courthouse to shake. Blood for blood, forty for forty. Lord O! Look on Deacon's face!

"We will do it like the Children o' Israel. Put to the sword our enemies and their household! Forty for forty, then we return to Stoney Gut. Very well then."

Very well then, Deacon. Forty for forty.

"Quietness, brethren. Listen me. We are sending runner-men for Bath Town, Morant Point, Manchioneal, Maroon Town, and everywhere. We will hold talk tomorrow. We will go no farther than forty for forty if the redcoats do no' trouble us. But we will prepare, for they will be sending to Governor Eyre for soldiers. By the time they can reach here we will be prepared."

I nearly fall from Mr. Abram's back. Is what it Deacon is saying? He does not know that Custos Aldenburg has sent courier to Governor Eyre already? Say that troops and ammunition are a-make forced marches even now?

"Man, they ha' sent for soldiermen already!" I shout.

Pot-mouth Johnny! Now you ha' brought Deacon's red eyes on you. Why you can no' cover your mouth?

"Is who that?" Deacon is asking. "Who just talked about soldiermen?"

Mr. Abram is bobbing his shoulders so that a jack-in-the-box I am.

Hear Mr. Abram underneath me: "Here, here, Deacon! See the boy for the glory here! Things can no' hide from him!"

Pride is there in Mr. Abram's voice, but fright is on me when Deacon's coal-fire eyes make four with mine. Deacon looks good on me, then there is laugh from him.

"Bring up Bro' John Campbell here, Abram," he calls. Stoney Gut men who remember my face are cheering for me, and I hear from my Councilman-friend: "Take time, Bro' John!"

Well, I am there on Mr. Abram's back, taller than Deacon; and that is no' good for me, for if I fall, down I will be on Deacon's big teeth. All the same I talk like no fright on me and tell what I heard at Custos's house.

Deacon says *thankie* and tells Mr. Abram he should care me till I ha' found Davie.

"Till Davie comes? He will come here?" I ask.

"Yes, Bro' John. More Stoney Gut men will come. You do no' know say is war this?"

Mr. Abram is walking me to the back.

"Davie will come soon?" I ask him when he has placed me on the ground.

His eyes roll on me.

"Davie will raise his behind when time he comes, Johnny," he says. "Davie will raise eternal hell, for he did no' want it so."

CHAPTER 26

Mr. Abram says that after sunset it will be forty for forty.

I lay on my back and watch through the roof as the evening sky is a-darken. Mr. Abram will not make me go outside in the square, for bullets are flying from the courthouse to the church, and he says he will no' have odd number in his business, for is unlucky, that.

"Forty it is, Johnny, and forty let be. A good Bible number that, and I will no' make you spoil it by being forty-one," Mr. Abram says.

Howsoever, I hear all that is happening, for often he comes to me, his head pushed forward and bobbing on his great shoulders, his feet a-shuffle quick like monkey walking on hot sand. One time he came with a cornpone wrapped in a plantain leaf, and glad I was, for hunger was on me.

I hear how Doctor Creary has come from the courthouse with a white cloth waving over his head. He looks on all the people lying in the square. Nobody fires on him, because everybody say is a good man that. Afterwards he would have speech with Deacon Bogle, but Deacon says he does no' want speech but forty for forty. So Doctor Creary goes back into the courthouse with sorrow riding his shoulders on tight girth.

Deacon and some Councilmen have gone to the powderhouse behind the Fort to look for ammunition. Stoney Gut men are waiting back and front o' the courthouse, and others in the scaffolding still pull their triggers. and play like ducks in swamp.

While I am talking with Mr. Abram I hear a bullhorn outside. Mr. Abram cocks his ear and grins at me.

"Your bro' is here, boy," he says.

Up I am and running like mad for the doorway and Davie. Mr. Abram is shouting that I should come back, for if I go outside I will make the number odd. But I am at the doorway, and there is my bro' Davie before me. One time only I call his name, and then I am up in his arms and scenting the good sweat of him, and his fingers are strong on my back.

"What is a-happen, Abram?" I hear him ask over my head. "Is where Deacon?"

"Hell, here," says Abram, and tells Davie o' things.

Davie did no' want it so. I hear him blaspheme that Deacon has drawn blood when all Councilmen had reasoned yesterday that today of peace they would talk. Presently he said:

"Johnny, how we will get you to Salt Savannah?"

I tell his shoulder that me, one, can no go home, since darkness is on the land now. He lifts my head away so our eyes make four. There is a laugh from him.

"A Stoney Gut man you are now, boy? Eh, boy with the hard ear? Abram will take you to Salt Savannah; then he can come back here."

Howsoever, when he is gone I talk to Abram, for I know Abram will no' want to leave Morant Bay. Well, we talk. I promise Mr. Abram I will no' leave the corner in which he has told me to hide.

Deacon Bogle has come back to the church. Rage is on him, for he can no' get the powderhouse opened. All around in the darkness outside, people are singing and shouting, and muskets talk at the courthouse. Morant Bay townsmen ha' opened the government rum stores, and their voices are loud with strong liquor. Deacon has warned Stoney Gut men that they must ha' nothing with the townspeople.

"We are here on the plains o' Jericho, and the Lord God o' Hosts has commanded say we turn not to the right hand or the left hand. Keep yourself from the accursed thing, lest ye make the camp o' Israel a curse. Hear me, O."

For a long time now Deacon and his Councilmen ha' been talking together. Over the noises outside I hear the town clock tell of eight o'clock. Dark-night it is not good to be by yourself in hiding in the corner of a church. You remember there are seven in the square outside whose eyes will no' blink at the sun any more. You remember that one day last week you spoke the name o' Timothy's dead baby bro' and did not put salt on your tongue. You remember how you passed Mother Cruikshank's burying-ground on Councilman's shoulder and did no' bother to say: *Deliver us from evil*, three times...

Where is Mr. Abram? *Mr. Abram O!*

"All right, John, quiet you now. You want Davie to know you are no' at Salt Savannah?"

Mr. Abram has come softly to my side. I hold his hand and ask what is happening.

"We will get out Custos now, boy," he says.

"You will get him out how?"

"Eh, now, you are not wise," Mr. Abram says. "When conch hide in his shell and will no' move out even when you stick him with your knife, how do you get out Mas'r Conch, boy?"

161

"Put fire on his tail," I tell him.

Mr. Abram laughed deep in his belly. "Eh, but wise you are, boy!"

Hell and powderhouse! Councilmen will burn down the courthouse to ha' Custos come out to them. Then when he comes out, what? Shoulders will talk some more?

But cover your mouth, Johnny. I can see Davie tall among the Councilmen as they hurry out through the door.

CHAPTER 27

I did no' tell you o' the schoolhouse which stood beside the courthouse?

A school for the children o' the rich it was, and all who go there walk in shoes. A *buckra* schoolmaster they have, and Davie says the first morning that Bro' Zaccy's Ebenezer went there, the *buckra* had spasms when Zaccy's boy said *oonoo* instead of *you.*

I heard Mother tell Father one night that to get his boy into the school it meant that for many months Zaccy could no' call on schoolmaster's cook to pay for the best fillet cuts. Mother said Zaccy is a hurry-come-up man. And that hell it is when kitchen towel turns table-napkin.

On this school which stands beside the courthouse my eyes are looking now. Mr. Abram says I can no' leave the church, but I can poke my head around the wall and watch what will happen to the school.

A while ago men were busy inside the church splitting fat candlewood. Then they were gone softly into the night, carrying kindling-wood for the conch's tail. I look on the schoolhouse.

First there was nothing at all. Then the night grows a red tongue, and it licks at the wall o' the school. Then the night grows another tongue, and another, and more, and the night has burst into a red laugh as it eats up the walls of the school.

Then the shells sounded, and men opened their throats and poured hate in a great wildness.

Come, shell-blowers, shock poor Johnny. Rip his heart and make his limbs tremble and his belly kiss his ribs as breath leaves him. Then make him holler like Stoney Gut men when he sees a red tongue lean from the schoolhouse and lick at the courthouse wall.

Bright as red day is the square. I can see Deacon Bogle there now. He runs about in little quick steps, a few steps to his right, a few steps to his left, his cutlass a-flame in his hand.

He runs his little race with his body bent forward, black pulpit cloak flapping around him. Wide are his mouth and eyes, but his eyes are blind with a red shine.

Deacon is a hunter-dog quartering the hole o' the German boar. Deacon is a cult shepherd in Yallahs Valley waiting for the sacrificial lamb. If after the shoulders cease talking anybody should see Deacon there, then he will be a quartering *John Crow*, working up his appetite before he swoops for carrion meat... Watch how Deacon runs his little race!

Fire has got to conches' tails. They come a-seek cooling wind. See them come, Shepherd Bogle? See them coming from the fire into the cool where you are?

Brethren – the Lord hath delivered the Philistines into we hands!

Full of loud and lusty life is Shepherd Bogle's voice as he welcomes the courthouse men. Full of life are the voices of his Stoney Gut men as they come forward with *Amen! Amen!* Throw down your muskets, militiamen! Big people say eyes should be closed and hands clasped when it's prayer time at sleeping-time. Then how come you kneel with your eyes cocked over musket barrels, and fingers a-search for the triggers?

Throw down your muskets, militiamen! Stoney Gut men say now you will sleep...bow your head for the hack.

The Stoney Gut men go forward. Militiamen muskets talk a little, but soon the Stoney Gut men are on them, and their shoulders talk louder, even though you can no' hear their conversation.

Near the end of the line Shepherd Bogle's German lamb comes. Fat he is, fed on young spring grass and running water 'gainst the time when he must come to Bogle. Bogle runs his little race, left and right, till he is up against Custos. Then I do no' see

Custos any more, for he is gone to his knees. Men say he prayed then to Deacon; but from where I am, Deacon shoulders worked in conversation. When they stopped talking, redder was his cutlass.

Then all the shoulders are standing straight now and turning back to us, finished. And, God o' mercy, is believe, I believe I did no' feel the horror before as now when I see that some o' them are wearing militiamen's helmets.

CHAPTER 28

Boom…boom…boom…

Mr. Abram's drum is laying stepping-stones for the shell-blowers to walk on. The courthouse is a torch which shows me the whole of the square. I run to where Mr. Abram's flat head is bent over his drum. But on my way I run into Davie. My bro' holds me by the arm.

"What you do here, boy?" he cried with rasp in his throat. "Where that son of a bitch Abram? Why he has no' taken you to Salt Savannah?"

I mumble something to Davie which has no' got much sense to him since I did no' put sense in it. At that he looks over to where Abram is beating his drum and Deacon Bogle is leading the Psalm his men are chanting.

"Can no' hear you," Davie said with anger. "This damn' puppet-show – chanting Psalm at time like this!"

"Davie, they ha' got forty for forty!" I tell him.

"It looks so," he said with aloes in his throat. Then up I am in his arms and he is taking me to the church.

"Then – Doctor Creary and Bro' Zaccy too?"

Davie puts me down in the corner where I had laid before.

He said: "No. Doctor Creary and Bro' Zaccy and a few others came through the back where I stood guard. All o' them are all right, for I made them pass."

"But, how that? Deacon Bogle will be vexed?"

"Make him be vexed – the damn' fool!" His voice sank like

how it is when Davie talks to Davie. "I told Deacon we should no' kill, but take them to the Gut, where they would be hostages if war comes. But is that what he does? No. Stoney Gut men get mixed with Morant Bay rabble and do as the rabble would do. Will this no' turn even our friends from we? Is what Mr. Gordon and the others will say now? Think say the Maroons will come to we when they hear we ha' mixed with the Morant Bay people? Think say those proud fightermen will want to march side-and-side with riff-raff? Is what it that makes Deacon Bogle such a dam' fool?"

Outside, we hear the chant is finished, and Deacon is calling that Stoney Gut men should fall in ranks. But a new noise comes above his voice.

"What is a-happen, Davie?"

My bro' listens. He spits and says: "Morant Bay carrion – saying they will burn Custos's house."

Very well. Time passes before I remember something. Then I am a-shout: "Davie O! Miss Lucille is there – at Custos's house!"

Without a word my bro' is leaving fast from me. I must run and shout at him. He turns back, and I am off the ground and on his shoulder. Then we are going through the crowd, twisting and turning through Morant Bay streets, making for Custos's house.

Much running through the night, and there is Custos's wall. This is no wall for Davie, like how it was for me. Over, and through the mango-walk my bro' is a hump-back duppy-ghost; through the slender Spanish needles and the crown hedge around the house. I slip from Davie's back.

"Go in to her – quick, Johnny. If Doctor Creary is home, tell him to come to me out here now."

I go to the veranda and peep through the jalousie blinds. Miss Lucille is there, but no Doctor Creary. I call at Miss Lucille. Good it is to see her come to the door standing in the light, and forty for forty leaves your mind for a little while.

"Why, Johnny, why have you come here at this hour?" she says as my hands are in hers.

Back o' me in the night, sounds are building on one another. Morant Bay men are coming with their shoulders ready to talk.

"Hell is a-pop, Miss Lucille!" I cry out. "Everybody dead – bloodshed and fire – they are a-come for you now!"

"What – what are you saying, Johnny? Who – oh!"

A gasp from Miss Lucille, and her eyes are gone over my head. I hear Davie's voice as his hand comes on my shoulder.

"Good evening, Miss Lucille. Doctor Creary here yet?"

Her eyes are making four with Davie's; and feel, I feel just like on Sunday when their eyes first talked to one another. Not a Johnny is on the veranda for them. Out in the night Morant Bay men are a-come.

"Good evening Da – Mr. Campbell. No, the doctor has not returned."

My bro' looks on her just like Father at Golden Grove horse auction a-calculate shoulders and flanks to see if the wind is sound. My bro' told it level.

"Custos Aldenburg and most of the Vestry are killed. The doctor is safe, but the Morant people are coming to burn this house. Come, you must come with me."

'Cept for one quick breath, nothing comes from Miss Lucille. Their eyes are steady on one another.

"What about the servants?"

"I will tell them, ma'am, if meantime – " he nodded his head at the long white frock she had on.

The sounds in the night are howls now. Morant Bay people are coming fast. Miss Lucille hears them, listened a little, and nodded at my bro'. Then she was gone into the house.

Quick she is back with me wearing riding-breeches. Sensible just like Davie is Miss Lucille.

"Where is he?" she asks me. I tell her he is warning the servants, then I take her hand and is leading her through the crotons. I make a yellowthroat whistle, and yellowthroat warbler whistles back. Presently Davie is there with us in the Spanish needles.

"All right the servants are. This way."

Through the night we are gone, rustling through the needles, while Morant men's howlings are a-batter at our eardrums.

Davie puts us over the wall, and we are on the white road and going Morant Bay way. The night is still now, with only a redness in the sky in front o' us. Miss Lucille asked what it was, and Davie said they must be burning the town. But he answers with far voice which he uses when his thoughts are no' steady. I think Davie must be wondering what he will do with Miss Lucille, for back to Stoney Gut he must go.

About where if you hollered loud enough it would reach Miss Martha's quick ear in her tavern on the edge o' town, Davie halts we. Hear him:

"Miss Lucille, bad things have happened today, and worse will happen still. There is no buckra house safe until the soldiermen come in from Kingston. Where can I take you?"

No fear on her as she answered: "Wherever you think best, Mr. Campbell."

"Knows, God knows Stoney Gut is the safest place tonight," Davie told himself.

Miss Lucille laughed. "Then why not there? I always wanted to know a rebel stronghold."

"You mean you would go there with me?" says Davie with a little wonder.

"Of course. Didn't I leave the house with you? You are my keeper now."

"Eh, no," he said quickly. "Stoney Gut is no' for women now. We must find somewhere else."

I am eight, and though I am tall for my years, eight-year-old can no' be long without sleep. After a while I come to myself when Davie and Miss Lucille are laughing as they raise me from the road where sleep had dropped me.

"Salt Savannah for you, Bro' John," he said.

"Miss Lucille is a-come too?" I asked.

For a while nobody answered; then my bro' whistle slow like storm-bound *kling-kling*.

"You know you right, Johnny?" he asked slowly. "You know you right? Salt Savannah it will be. Nobody will trouble you at Salt Savannah, Miss Lucille," he said.

"Where and what is Salt Savannah?" Miss Lucille asked.

"That is we home, where Father and Mother lives," I told her.

If I yawn any more, lockjaw I will have. Make big people talk all night if they want to. Davie's shoulder is good to lay on. Forty for forty. Miss Lucille did no' make it into forty-one. A good.

CHAPTER 29

Father says is a lucky man he to ha' lost a son and gained a daughter. He says it as he breaks his potato roast to scoop up the *calaloo* which we are eating for breakfast. Miss Lucille smiled and said is the best compliment, that, she has ever heard.

She is sitting beside Ruthie, two heads close together, morning-cloud and sunset. Dawn is Ruthie's, dawn on a yellow corn field; Miss Lucille is the sunset, and stars wake in her hair when the firelight dances over her.

All o' us are in the kitchen 'cept Davie and Sammy. From Naomi I heard this morning that Manuel had no' yet returned from Mr. Gordon. Miss Lucille is in our family for true now, for you never see anybody whom everybody in our family must love as quickly as she. When my mother heard say Miss Lucille's father and mother were no' on the land o' the living, and that the ward o' the good Doctor Creary she is, there is a quick hug from my mother for her.

I have no' told of Davie and Sammy? Last night, after Davie had told of what happened in Morant Bay, back to Stoney Gut he returned. Then this morning with day-cloud, Father sent Sammy to find Doctor Creary and to tell him of Miss Lucille. Father will ride for Morant Bay as soon as breakfast is over.

Now he is here, smiling at Miss Lucille, but you can see that sorrow is on him. When he has finished eating, he touched the buttons on his Sabbath coat which he was wearing. He rose and went for his mule.

"God-be, Tamah," Father said as he mounted. His mule is burdened down today. The mule is a-carry both Father and his sorrow.

I go to look for Timothy and Quackoo down at the barrack. Zekiel wants to go with me, but it is no use to carry out Zekiel, for he can no' stand rough play. There is something wrong with Zekiel. Stiff inside he must be, for every week Mother boils castor oil to dose him. Mouse-mouse Naomi he should play with, so

168

when she is following me down to the barrack I wait for her in the cane-field and make a cane-stalk dance on her behind.

Naomi is running back to Salt Savannah a-holler for all fire and brimstone. I go to look for Timothy to hold man-talk with him.

With evening, Father came back to Salt Savannah. We watch him as he lets down the gate and comes riding into the yard. We stand there saying nothing at all, watching if his face will tell good or bad. He is heavy coming out of the saddle.

Mother said: " 'Evening, Pa John."

"Evening all. God stayed with you, Miss Lucille?"

Miss Lucille curtsied and said: "Very well, thank you, Pa John." Her face is grave like Father's. All o' we young ones say well we are.

"I saw Doctor Creary today," Father said. "Well he is, and says this is the best place for Miss Lucille."

Mother can no' wait any longer. "How goes it yonder, Pa John?"

"*Aie* – is bad, that," my father said. The long sun can no' reach every part of his face. There are deep gullies in his face which were no' there this morning. Father is no quick for speech. I am thinking if it was *Johnny Newsmonger* how I would be quick to tell of what happened. *Newsmonger* is what Ruthie called me when I told Naomi how Father found her in the cane-piece with Moses.

Hear my father: "None o' Bogle's men are at the Bay. They ha' gone all over the parish – west far as Roselle, others east to Bath Town, some ha' gone up the Blue Mountain Valley, and some ha' crossed the mountains to call out the Maroons. A burying-ground is Morant Bay, and what shops ha' no' been looted are fast closed. Buckra families have gone into the bush, and some have gone on board the sugar-boats at Port Morant. Mr. Gourzong is dead there in the square. I would be home before this, but I was helping to bury the dead."

My father stopped talking and pulled at the saddle girth. He let fall the saddle on the ground and wiped his forehead with his sleeve.

"Nobody seen anything o' Manuel?"

Mother can no' talk, but shakes her head. My father walks for the kitchen. "You ha' coffee, Tamah?" he asked.

★

Is the first time, this, that Father has ever locked our door so early. We are sitting around in the hall-room, Zekiel asleep on the floor. Everybody is a-think by themselves. Ruthie has her hands on her breasts, and Moses in her eyes. Sammy is a-look on militiamen who will never hear the pipes a-skirl again. Hungry-belly Naomi has brought around her pigtails to her mouth, and is chewing at the ends while she picks at her nose.

I am on the floor with my head in Miss Lucille's lap. Her fingers are nice in my hair. Her face is turned to the lamp, and warm I am inside o' me as I look on the sweetness o' her. Mother mends my Sunday pantaloons while she rocks to a tune which only she one is hearing. Quiet is on the world, only the rustle of the osnaburg and the night-time music outside. These, and Father's voice as he reads from the Book:

Give ear, O my people, to my law: incline your ears to the words of my mouth. I will open my mouth in a parable: I will utter dark sayings of old.

Miss Lucille's eyes are at long distance. I work my head so she looks down at me. I call her with my eyes. When she bends down I tell her ears: "I do no' think anything will happen to him."

A tight squeeze Johnny gets, and when she lifts her head there are laughter-marks around her mouth but sunset is on her face. Coo, Miss Lucille ashamed?

In the daytime also he led them with a cloud, and all the night with a light of fire...

All of a sudden dark-night hammered against the door. Zekiel woke with a cry. All our eyes are there on the door. Miss Lucille's fingers are still in my hair.

Father got up and reached for his musket and said with thunder: "Who comes to Salt Savannah this time o' night?"

Is me it, Manuel.

Nobody beats Johnny to the door. I push up the latch and swing the door open to let light fall on Manuel. There is weariness on him as he stumbles into the room, no hat on his head, blood on his forehead. Manuel's face is old nearly like Father's.

He says evening to we all. Father tells Mother to fetch a stool for him, but quick he gets it for himself. There is surprise on him as he sees Miss Lucille.

Father said: "Miss Lucille Dubois, my eldest, Emmanuel."

Father closed the Book and asked: "How you came, Manuel? I did no' hear your animal?"

"I left him at Yallahs, sir. Is dead, he."

"He died under you?"

"Is so it, Father."

Father said: "You ha' coffee, Tamah?"

On her way to the door Mother rested her hand on Manuel. "A hard ride that must ha' been, son."

Manuel said: "Yes, Mother."

We sat down quiet while Father prayed to the God o' weary travellers. Then he reached for his pipe, pushed in tobacco, lit it, drew deeply, and said:

"Well, how it goes, Manuel?"

CHAPTER 30

Last night we heard many things from Manuel. Mr. Gordon is still ill, but has sent a letter to Father, asking Stoney Gut people to cease all violence and wait till he can come to them. But we hear too how Governor Eyre got Custos's dispatch and troops are now on board the Queen's ship *Wolverine*. We hear news o' the courthouse killings ha' reached Kingston and more troops are now coming on the *Onyx* – these are soldiermen o' the West India Regiment. We hear that this day martial law will be declared and that Governor Eyre will come to St. Thomas parish himself.

We hear that certain o' the Kingston buckras are saying that Mr. Gordon should be arrested. My father fists the table and say they could no' do that, for a good man is Mr. Gordon.

Manuel told us how he had to ride through the mountains to get past troops who march the Windward Road on their way to St. Thomas. We hear say orders are that the soldiers must punish without having mercy.

Then, when Ruthie is gone to the kitchen to help Mother with the coffee, we hear how when Moses took the Stoney Gut petition to Governor Eyre, Eyre had his officers hold him and put the cat-o'-nine on Moses's behind. The soldiers will bring him to St. Thomas for trial under martial law.

Father listened with pain in his eyes; but afterwards he said the English officers will see there is just treatment.

This morning there is quiet on Salt Savannah. Later this day news come to us that the soldiers have come to Morant Bay and that Doctor Creary will come with evening for Miss Lucille. Miss Lucille and me sit under a guinep tree, and I am *Newsmonger Johnny*. Howsoever, she does no' stop me as I talk all the while of Davie.

Father says I must no' stir from Salt Savannah. He wears the trace-leather inside his coat, and there is fire in his eyes. I will no' stir from Salt Savannah.

Is evening now. Doctor Creary is here in his parry cart, and Miss Lucille is ready to go. Doctor Creary is talking to Father.

"You see, Mr. Campbell, the soldiers have come with one idea. That idea is revenge. They do not know the guilty from the innocent. They look on every poor person in the parish – anyone who might have a grievance against the present hard times – as a rebel. We will have to look out for betrayals from those who in times like these will lie to save their skins. Blast it – it's a ticklish situation!"

Father said with steadiness: "All the same, I feel sure the officers will permit no cruelty, martial law or no martial law."

Doctor Creary is quiet for a while. Then he said slowly: "I hope you are right, Mr. Campbell. I certainly hope you are right. Well, thanks again for your kindness to my daughter. Meantime, stay away from Morant Bay – all of your family. I will come out to see you tomorrow."

Just before I jump from the steps of the parry, Miss Lucille bends down and kisses me. She whispered something in my ear. Remember, I must remember to tell Davie that Miss Lucille said he was to stand good.

CHAPTER 31

Next morning, day-cloud has no' broke when from my kitty-up I hear horses' feet madding on our road. Father gets up quickly and makes for the door.

"Mr. Campbell! Campbell! Come out, quickly!"

Doctor Creary's voice it is. All of us tumble out quickly, for we have heard bad things in Doctor Creary's voice. We get on our clothes and are out as he scrambles from his horse.

"Campbell! – God Almighty! – awful things are happening! You will have to leave Salt Savannah!"

Father waits until the doctor has taken breath.

"Morning, Doctor Creary," he says. "What brings you to Salt Savannah so early?"

"Campbell! – Eyre got into Morant Bay yesterday afternoon. He went on to Port Morant last night. At midnight he hung the first man, Campbell! Hung him with his own hands!"

Day is just rubbing sleep out o' his eyes. The sun is washing his face in the sea, and not a peep of him we can see. North wind is coming chilly off the mountains, but Doctor Creary is in sweat.

Father draws breath deep into his chest.

"God's will be done," he says. "Since is martial law it, all rebels must prepare for such." But the pain in his throat tells me he is a-think of Davie. Me, too.

"Rebel fiddlesticks!" cried Doctor Creary. Then his voice went to hide in his collar. "Listen, Campbell. I happen to know Flemming of Port Morant. A blusterer, yes, but he was no rebel."

Father said quickly: "Flemming? Flemming o' Port Morant? I know him too – Flemming was no' a Stoney Gut man!"

"Yet he has been hung by the Governor and a ship's officer because some fool of a Customs man said he been threatened by him. I got the nasty details, Campbell. When Lieutenant Brand of the *Onyx* had kicked away the old door which formed the trap, Flemming's toes were touching the ground. So Brand puts two bullets through his ear."

"My God o' me!" Mother cried, her hands to her cheeks.

Father said: "But what is that for Salt Savannah? What should I leave here for?"

Doctor Creary looked steady at my father. He said: "*Campbell, you have been proscribed.*"

"Proscribed?"

"Yes, as an outlaw – a rebel – all who signed the Petition."

I see my mother fall into Manuel's arms. My father has been hit in the chest with a stone-hammer. Staggering is my father. Then he looked at Manuel and told him he should take Mother inside. My father comes steady again.

"God is on my right hand, Doctor Creary. *Thankie*, but I am ready to face justice."

"Justice! Justice! God Almighty! – don't you realise what is happening? Eyre has brought Ramsey of the Kingston police as his Provost-Marshal, a brute if ever there was one. Eyre has shown the manner in which he intends to settle this business, and right now Ramsey is building two gallows at Morant Bay. There will be no justice, Campbell. Flemming was arrested, tried, and executed in less than one hour. That will be the pattern – any trumped-up charge, and you are at the tender mercies of Ramsey!"

"But why must I flee? What charge they ha' against me?" Father is saying. "I sign the Petition, but you and Bro' Zaccy and Mr. Gourzong – God rest the dead! – were here and knew why I signed. I will only ha' to tell Ramsey this."

Low Doctor Creary's voice comes to us. "I will tell you all, Mr. Campbell. God forbid! – but your name has been given to the proscribing registrar by Zaccy O'Gilvie himself."

Suffering Jesus! Knew, I knew I could no' trust that man. My poor father forms words with his mouth, but time must pass before he can talk.

"Bro' Zaccy – Zaccy O'Gilvie has proscribed me?"

"True enough, Campbell," says Doctor Creary. "I did what I could when I heard of it at about two o'clock this morning, but you will have to believe me when I say the odds were all against you. There were people on hand who were ready to swear that your son is one of Bogle's Councilmen. Add to that these three circumstances: you are a well-liked employee of Mr. Gordon; you went to Stoney Gut and signed the Petition; and thirdly, the marshal's anxiety to use his two new gallows.

"They would not listen to me, Campbell. I told them about

your boy allowing O'Gilvie and myself and the others safely away from the courthouse. I told them how he rescued my daughter. But, prompted by O'Gilvie, they asked was he not at Stoney Gut now? You have got to go, Campbell. They will be coming for you today. You must leave here at once!" "But where I can go from Salt Savannah?" my father says with stubbornness. "The wicked fleeth when no man pursue. I will stay for justice."

I think Doctor Creary will burst. "Man! You can expect no such thing! I tell you this is going to be a reign of terror! You must go!"

"But where I must go, Doctor Creary? Is no' this Salt Savannah my freehold? Was I no' born here? Is no' my navel-string buried on this land? Must old age find me a street Arab running from bank to bank? God o' Abraham and Isaac and Jacob! what are you a-ask, Doctor Creary?"

Fright is on all we as we watch Father's face. First time, this, I ha' heard these things in his voice. There is pain on Doctor Creary's face; pain in his voice when he speaks.

"I know the wrench it will be, Campbell. I too might have felt as you do, but if even for the sake of your family, you must go away. You must not travel alone – they must go with you. You wouldn't know, but one of the cruel things about this affair is that when a man is proscribed, his family is too. Go away – go into the mountains for a couple of months until the reign of terror is over. I daresay an old boar-hunter like you will know caves where no soldier or constable could go. For the sake of your family, go away, I entreat you, Campbell. These terrible days cannot last; they must end, and soon. But innocent blood will be shed before so. Go away, go away, Campbell; you must go away, you must leave, you must go away for the sake of your family."

Father looks around on we, his eyes walks away and goes to long distance. Still Doctor Creary talks to him, but his eyes are gone away to think. They come back to look at us to see if he is thinking right; he looks away again, and when he comes back to Doctor Creary his eyes say the doctor is right. But aloes thick at his throat.

"Go, I will go, Doctor Creary. I will hide in caves like mountain boar. I will flee from the mighty King Saul so till his wrath subsides."

I am thinking o' Bro' Zaccy O'Gilvie. Nana Cobina, the midwife, once told people at Morant Bay market that I was born with a caul over my face and can see things 'fore they happen. Knew, I knew that nobody should trust Bro' Zaccy O'Gilvie. He could and well have no' proscribed my father. *Make him burn in hell 'til his fat guts shrivel, Mas'r God!*

But is wrong, that. Davie says boys should no' swear until they can buy their own breeches. While I am saying *God, forgive* three times, Doctor Creary rides away.

Crying-time is finished now. You never see people with eye-water like Mother and Ruthie and Zekiel and Naomi. Father leaves them to cry, they alone, while with we others he turns the goats and pigs into the open, where they must forage so till we come back from the mountains. Then there were harness-leathers to oil and tobacco-leaves to be taken down from the fireplace and pack away in the buttery.

After that Father says: "Come, Tamah. Crying-time over now."

Well then, Mother uses her apron on her eyes and asked those others if they heard what Father said. Naomi sits on the ground, rocking her head come-and-go, moaning and crying like mad. I pull at her pigtails and say: "Come, gal, crying-time done now."

She slaps at my hand and say: "Listen him! When since?"

Mother looks on me, her arms akimbo, and good it is to hear the laughter that comes deep from her belly.

"Coo here!" cries Mother. "When since kling-kling turn into hawk-bird? *Heh!*"

Good it is to hear her laugh, but when Mother says *heh!* like that, all of your manhood is gone, and smaller than calaloo worm you feel. Is funny it how your breeches drop off any time Mother says *heh!*

But it is good to hear her laugh and watch how she is walking quick-quick to the buttery to find provender for we journey.

CHAPTER 32

Father has got on his brass-buttoned coat. Two full hampers are a-ride the jackass's back, full with cassava cakes and a whole of roasted hog. After crying-time was finished, Mother did no' idle. Quiet we are.

Father took off his hat and turned to face the sun and we. A wind is a-search the strands of his hair. Down in the Bay the sea kneels on the shore.

Our Father which art in heaven, Hallowed be thy name...

If I keep quiet and bite on my lips, I will no' sob like Naomi. Heavy with tears is my Father's voice.

Give us this day our daily bread. And forgive us...

Zekiel must cry, for weak he is. I am a-wonder how he will manage in the mountains. I will bet say he will soon be riding in one of the hampers.

And lead us not into temptation, but deliver us...

Father O! You can no' fool me, tears are there in your throat. I must no' listen to you, I must think on Davie... Davie is a-march the Blue Mountain Valley with a hundred Stony Gut men... Davie is there on the Windward Road leading his men to Bowden. They will march the foreshore road to Port Antonio, then over the mountains past Manchioneal, and down again into St. Thomas, and County Surrey will be circumvented. So, Bogle's Councilmen planned it.

Will the Maroons join Deacon Bogle's men? I do no' know. Mr. Abram did no' sound sure.

For thine is the Kingdom, and the power...

I never before hear Father talk to God with so much tears in his throat. All o' we say the *Amen*.

Father motions Manuel to the head o' the donkey. Both of them carry their machetes, and Father has his musket on his shoulder. He looks around on us, his fingers going down his buttons. Father says: "Come, Tamah."

So then, leave, we are leaving Salt Savannah.

I do no' know how long we have been walking. Our feet make no sound on October leaves. Pannikins are rattling in the hampers ahead. Father speaks to Manuel, and we stop while they wrap plantain trash around the pannikins. We ha' been striking through the bush for a long time now.

In the bush time does no' go by the sun, for not a sun you can see. High trees lock hands over your head, and down here it is dusk even at noon. First time there were miles of levelness, with ebonies and cashaws and twisty lignum vitae shaking hands over our heads. *Pitcharries* whistle howdy-do to we, and *john-to-whits* flit like ghosts from tree to tree.

First time I whistled back at them, but Father says save my breath I should, for soon then I will need it. Howsoever, I must bubble with *john-to-whit*:

To whit! to whoo! sweet to whit! sip, sip, sip!

Well then, afterwards we start to climb; and now, try as I try, breath does no' come easy to me. Father shows us how we must bend our knees with our bodies forward, toes digging into the earth.

We come to a little stream, and glad I am when Father says we will stop for victuals now. 'Cept for Father and Manuel, talk does no' come easy to us. Father's eyes walk over us. When we start off again Mother is riding in one hamper and Zekiel and Naomi in t'other. All the same it is no' long before me too is riding on Father's shoulder.

Oh Lord God of my salvation, I have cried day and night before thee.

Through the bells a-ring in my ears the voice comes like from long distance, but I know it is my father reciting that Psalm for the sons of Korah. You never see somebody who knows the Psalm like Father, 'cepting perhaps Deacon Bogle.

My belly is pressing hard on his back. I feel the move of his shoulder as he fights the mountains before us. Every ridge fights against my father. Every stone is saying: *Turn back, John Campbell!*

Behind me the donkey's forefeet claw at the earth, his hind-legs thrust under him. Nobody has to lead him now. With Mother and Zekiel and Naomi on the hampers, he alone is fighting his battle. Manuel walks back o' Ruthie and Sammy, his arms ready to catch them if they fall. Poor Ruthie breathes through her nostrils and mouth one time. There is tightness on Sammy's face.

The trees are no' shaking hands any longer. They stand far apart as if they ha' no business with each other, as if each is trying to catch his own breath.

Shall thy loving-kindness be declared in the grave? or thy faithfulness in destruction? Shall thy wonders be known in the dark? And thy righteousness in the land of forgetfulness?

I feel my father bow under me. Mountains, you must fight like mad! My father is a great boar-hunter! Mountain-mists, you must wrap us tight-tight in your shrouds! My father has the strength of ten! If there is sorrow a-tear through his throat now, do no' believe is a sign of your victory, that. My father has the strength of ten; a leader-bull is he, leading his herd to the high places.

The clouds rest close on our heads. Father scoops sweat from his forehead. Deep and firm is his voice as he calls back to Manuel:

"How it goes there with you, Manuel?"

"We here with you, Father," my bro' says.

"Stand steady, boy; it is no' far now."

Bend to the pull, leader-bull. Plough forward for the furrow, yoke-steer. Move up, mountain man, with your mighty muscles swelling fit to burst. My father is a mighty boar-hunter with the strength o' ten.

We reach the great rock with evening. The donkey went around the rock and, with no word from us, commenced to browse. An old boar-hunter, he. Nobody has to tell me that this is the boar-hunters' cave.

In great strides from one head to another, the wind walk over the tops of the trees. We followed Father to the foot of the rock, and here there is no wind at all. We face the cave which goes deep into the rock. Cooking-stones, black with soot, are at the door of the cave. I am thinking we should have pepper-pot now, for good it would be for the cold up here.

"We are where, Johnny?"

Is Naomi, that, at my ear. I look down my nose at her, and with my voice at long distance tell her that this is huntermen's cave. Poor fool-fool Naomi!

There is the Lord's Prayer from Father, while we stand

bareheaded and listen to a nightingale pipe his long note, mellow as the sun which is dropping down from us.

"Tamah, you ha' coffee for we?" asks Father.

CHAPTER 33

For two weeks now we ha' no' seen men other than us. I ha' heard and seen all what Davie used to tell of.

I ha' heard the flute o' the *solitaire* piping through the silence of the secret mountains as he floats through the valleys at dawnlight. I ha' watched the sun which comes in far morning thundering over the peaks to beat back the heavy mountain mists. I ha' seen holes whose bottoms no man knows of. I ha' wondered if on top of a tall grevillea growing up into heaven I could no' touch the stars.

For two weeks now we have no' seen any man; but now Father says we will leave the mountains. Is on account of Ruthie it. Listen me.

One morning before daylight I woke to hear Father say: "Tamah, what is wrong with Ruthie?"

Manuel and Sammy and Naomi were gone out for wood and water. Zekiel was still asleep. Ruthie has gone outside the cave to be sick. For three mornings now she has been sick back o' the cave. Mother does not answer.

"Is that the moon which is a-bother her?" Father asked again.

I think Ruthie will retch out her stomach if she does no' try to stop being sick.

"God there upon us, John," my mother said with slowness. "Hold your temper, but I think she will no' see her moon for nine months."

I see Father's hands make fists at his side. A cane-leaf in the wind is he.

Thundered my father: "Woman! What it you say to me! Say I carry a harlot in my family?"

Mother does not answer with words, but she groans softly. Then my father is raging. Never I have heard him so before. And I see him strike my mother.

Mother lay crying softly. It is no' nice to see big people cry, for it makes the world upside down.

My father came quiet, resting his hand on her shoulder. After a while when she came quiet too, he said:

"Tamah, is who it?"

"Aaron Dacre's Moses," she said.

My father groaned. Mother sat up and said: "Have done, John. God is upon us – is our sorrow, this."

"But – what make it so, Tamah?" Father said. "What make it so? Search me life, Tamah. Search me life. We ha' been with each other all our grown years, and you know my life. What ha' I done to God? Why filth must drag at me loins? What have I left undone, Tamah?"

Tears are in his voice, but do no' make him cry, Mas'r God, for if my father brings eye-water, Johnny will be dead.

I can no' tell why, but all of a sudden I am up off my bed and am running for the open.

When I tell Naomi, her eyes got round and shine.

"Ruthie is a bellied woman, then!" she cried.

So we are going down off the mountains, and Naomi says we will go down quickly, for Father will ha' Moses take Ruthie to church.

Going down the mountains, you walk on your heels and spring your knees at every step. You believe that easy it is, but after a while you find it is no' so and you are wishing for a place where you would have to climb instead. Howsoever, we go down faster than we came up.

Soon we pass untidy bastard cedars and dark, sweet-scented pancheleons and the bush is on us again. We stop by the stream for victuals, and I am looking on Ruthie and wondering if bellied women must cry all the time.

Well then, we can no' stay here all day if we will get to Salt Savannah, so Father gets up and says: "Come again, Tamah."

We are ready for the march. My father looks around at us.

"You can use your breath now, Johnny," he said. "We will sing *Christian Soldiers*. Sing, everybody, so I will keep my faith."

But we are only at the second line when I hear Zekiel and Naomi cry out.

Wayah! Is my bro' Davie that, yes?

Davie has stepped suddenly out of the bush by the track, but the bush is still with him. My bro' has come from another world, for on top of his head and all over his body shrubs and tall grasses are growing.

"Davie O!" I cry out, and run forward so hard that he must drop his musket and catch me before I am on the ground.

Davie, man, how your face stay so? You are not bellied like Ruthie; then why all of a sudden old is your face? Like a wary tody-bird my bro' is looking at us but yet looking all around with quick glances. Down he has put me and has grabbed up his musket, looking all around. After a while his eyes stood on Father.

"Is no' wisdom, this, Father," he said low.

Father does no' answer. Manuel said: "Bro' Davie? You forget we ha' no' slept under the same roof last night?"

My bro' jerked his shoulders without patience, but he spoke the howdy. All o' we tell him howdy-do. Father said:

"Now, boy, in what do you no' see wisdom?"

"You are singing so loud they can hear you all over the mountain!"

"Then what is wrong? I am in no man's yard?" said Father, hawk-eye sharp on Davie.

"But do you not know that soldiermen are hunting all over the mountains?"

"Is that why you are dressed up Maroon style?"

"Yes – to fool the English and the Maroons themselves."

"The Maroons?" asks Father quick. "They are against you?"

Light catches Davie's teeth but no' his eyes. "They play safe on the stronger side, sir. The English have armed them to hunt me down."

Jesu o' St. Jago! Now hear there! The Maroons are no' with Bogle!

Davie is talking with nothing in his voice, as if he is talking back at Davie. He stands tall and straight, the bush covering all his body, so till you think the rest of him is killed and only his face has come back to tell us of blood and fire in St. Thomas parish. And nobody asks anything, only now and then there are sobs and groans.

"Far as two days ago about five hundred o' our people are dead. That number again ha' had their blood spilt. We do no' know how many ha' got the whip. Provost-Marshal Ramsey hangs them dozen at a time in front o' Morant Bay courthouse. Colonel Hobbs o' the Sixth regiment o' Foot is using the rope and the bullet together – eleven shot and then hung at Chigoe market, sixteen at Coley.

"Inside Deacon's branch chapel at Fonthill he made them hang one another. At Monkhill he had thirteen o' them dig a trench and then kneel on the edge; then he had his soldiers shoot them when a bugle was blown. Major Nelson o' the West India Regiment goes well too at Port Antonio; howsoever, he only uses the rope."

Jesu, my God. Forty for forty? Five hundred for forty!

A long time goes before any of us can hear what the others are saying, for seven o' us have got heavy sorrow on, and moans and cries are tearing at our throats. Only Father and Davie stand still, looking on one another.

After a while Father got us quiet again so Davie could go on with his story.

"But you say over five hundred killed?" Father asks. "All could no' be Stoney Gut men?"

"They do no' ask if you are Stoney Gut man again, Father. If you are no' *buckra*, then pray hard."

Davie tells us how whole families ha' been taken from their homes, flogged, and hung from trees while the soldiers set fire to their houses; how black and white redcoats o' the Queen marched through the Blue Mountain Valley and fell on Stoney Gut men at Monklands; how Bogle's men forgot all their drills and fired their muskets without aim; how say Bogle swung east far as Bath Town, gathering men to him; but how say many men would no' come to Bogle, for muskets are scarce and the Maroons are no' with him.

Then Bogle met up with Hobbs's men on Sunday by the Plantain Garden River. Across the river they draw and prepare themselves for battle. Then when the sun is falling they march on the soldiermen, chanting Psalms. But Psalms can no' fight red-hot iron balls, and soon Bogle is flying from the field.

They go back to Stoney Gut, and is a village o' the dead, that, for the soldiers have been there. Only ashes to show where the chapel was. Then there is marching, and hiding, and marching through the bush, with sorry heavy on them.

At Torrington the first rains fall. Bogle holds his prayer meeting and say is a good sign, the rain. So he will no' listen to the Councilmen when they say he should go up into the mountains. They stand there till dawnlight comes on Saturday; and with it the wild, howling Maroons, the Maroons who are fighting for the Queen. When the battle is over, Deacon Bogle is wearing the Queen's chains.

"Then Bogle is – ?" Father stops there.

"Deacon Bogle is a-hang from the yard-arm o' the *Wolverine*," says the face which has no' got any body.

Mother it is who starts to ask after our friendly families; and after that all of us are shouting names at him so that Davie only answers when the person is no' living. So a game we play now, calling names one by one at him, and hoping and praying he will not answer.

Mother calls: "Aaron Dacres?" Davie nods his head. My mother swallows hard and said: "Mo – Moses?" My bro' answered.

White covers Ruthie's eyes, and Manuel must jump to catch her.

But I can no' look on them, for I have just called for Mr. Abram and I am watching Davie's lips.

"Let me tell you o' Abram," Davie says, and quiet comes on us. Well I know now that Mr. Abram is gone, and the emptiness in my belly turns my knees to water.

"Let me tell you o' him," Davie says. "Ramsey captured Abram and took him to a room at the lock-up. From the room he can see where other men are swinging from the gallows. Ramsey puts a rope on his neck and a Bible in his hand. 'Swear!' says Ramsey. 'Swear that George William Gordon came to Stoney Gut and told you to rebel. If not, I hang you by the neck until you dirty your pantaloons!'

"Abram will no' swear, so he gets a hundred strokes on his back and then the rope around his neck. While they carry him to the gallows Quackoo and Timothy are in the line o' prisoners. Hot is the sun on his head and on the whip sores. Quackoo takes off his hat and gives it to his pa while he passes to the gallows. So then rage comes on Ramsey, and while Abram is kicking on the gallows his two boys are stretched on a puncheon getting fifty from the whip."

Poor Mr. Abram! My poor friends Quackoo and Timothy! Mas'r God, steady your mountains and do no' make it fall on Johnny.

"Nobody has tried to tell the good from the bad?" Father asks.

"Soldiermen ha' orders to take few prisoners, 'cept if held near Morant Bay. All the gentry ha' gone away; there is nobody to tell who is who. Ramsey is king o' Morant Bay and his dozen gallows."

"What of Zaccy O'Gilvie?" Father asks.

Tight is my bro's face. "I ha' tried to meet up with him," he says low. "But well guarded he is, and saving his own skin by telling Ramsey that everybody else are rebels."

"Very well," says Father. "I must go down."

Davie looked on him. "Go down where?"

"To Morant Bay. If Mr. Gordon was well, he would be there to help them. I will go down and help them."

Davie is smiling without mirth. "Is what it you say? *You* help them? Because Mr. Gordon is ill? You ha' no' heard that Mr. Gordon is hanging from the courthouse gate? Say that Assembly-man Gordon is a-kick at air too?"

Father's hands drop stiff at his side. All o' we wonder if we ha' heard right.

"Boy, you lie!" Father thunders. "Say you lie! Tell me you lie!"

"I do no' lie," Davie said quiet, and know, we know it is true. "Eyre took Mr. Gordon from Kingston by boat to Morant Bay and tried him in court-martial. They did no' call witness, 'cept who Ramsey send."

Stillness took the mountainside. *Orange quits* fly quietly through the clearing. Only the stream is a newsmonger, even death can no' still his tongue.

My father said: "I will go down. Mr. Gordon can no' die in vain. I will ask to see Governor Eyre. I am no' a Stoney Gut man. The English will no' make war on Christians."

"But, Father, you do no' understand," said Davie. "We family is proscribed and they look for you now. All who ha' signed the Petition are dead, 'cepting you. Your head is in the lion's mouth, so take time and get it out. Wait till they ha' lifted this martial law."

Father said quietly: "You it is who do no' understand, Davie. My navel-string is buried at Morant Bay, and it is my own people who are hanging down there – innocent blood is being shed. If only the death o' me can help, then die I will. Perhaps they keep killing the innocent because they can no' find the guilty."

"What will happen to your family if you die?" cried Davie. "What will happen to Zekiel and Naomi and Johnny and Ruthie?"

"I do no' die if my boys live," Father said. "If Manuel wants, he can stay in the mountains with you. Take Johnny too, for his head is full of you. Zekiel must stay with the women, soldiers will no' harm them. I am going down – come, Tamah."

Well then, Ruthie goes on the donkey with Zekiel, and ready they are to travel. But all of a sudden there is no Davie. I call loud for him and am madding to run into the bush. Father held my hand.

"Take time, boy. Davie heard what I said. He will come if he wants you."

The donkey is moving ahead. I am crying a little. Father said: "Sing, all."

Everybody sings with eye-water in their throats.

CHAPTER 34

Now and again on our way down the mountains there is the whistle of yellowthroat warbler. Is mid-October, this, and I know yellowthroats ha' no' come south yet. So I know my bro' is no' gone, but is coming down the mountains with we. I wait till I can do it in secret, then I whistle back so Davie will know I am with him.

We do not sing any more, for sorrow has dropped heavy on us. Soon we will be out of the mountains. I hear Father tell Manuel that we will go into the town by Baptism Valley. Davie had told us that the Maroons had gone east, so this way we will go into

Morant Bay from the west. Father says he wants to meet up with regular soldiers o' the Queen.

The ground is levelling now, but we can no' see anything, for we are forcing through high marshland reeds with mud clogging our toes. Sultanas and bitterns dodge at my feet like clowns at Morant Bay Fair. Suddenly Davie's voice comes to me from up ahead.

"– say is madness to go down into the valley now, for I ha' just seen redcoats in there!"

Father's voice said: "Where are the soldiermen?"

We are standing now, one behind the other, while up ahead the voices talk.

" 'Cross the valley. They are searching for people who run from Morant Bay. If you ran from the Bay you are a rebel!"

"This family are no' rebels. I must go to the Bay."

"I say they will no' ask questions, Father, but will shoot first!"

"Then our blood will be on their heads, David Campbell. Move away!"

"God judge me, Father, mad you are?"

"Do no' blaspheme here!" said Father loudly. "Move away – come, Tamah."

Then we are going forward again and passing Davie standing in the reeds with fire in his eyes.

"You are a dam' old fool, Pa John Campbell! You think say your head is big enough to carry all the blood? God strike you for a stubborn fool!"

Thick with rage is my bro's voice, but my heart is swelling for burst, for I know Davie is talking through tears too. I am turning to go back to him, but quick is my mother's hand on me, and forward I go again.

I hear Davie's voice blaspheming again, but over it comes Father's shout: "Sing, all! Sing the devil away!"

His heavy bass is rumbling out *Christian Soldiers*, and everybody is singing now 'cept me. Everybody singing, and all of a sudden the reeds have opened and there before me is Baptism Valley sweeping down to the town.

Clear at the far side I see red blobs bobbing against the green of the valley. Nobody has to tell me that these are redcoats.

Father is marching with his head high, rumbling out his bass as he leads us down into the valley. Behind him is Manuel, and then the rest of us. Power is in my father's voice.

With the Cross of Jesus going on before...

Father is a mighty boar-hunter whose voice can go long distances. So now the hymn is swelling through the valley as Father leads we towards the redcoats who do no' make war on Christians.

Seen, they must ha' seen we now, for I see the redcoats stop. Then they are coming fast towards us. There must be about six of them.

I hear Davie's voice from the reeds calling to Father to turn back. Then he calls to Mother, then to Manuel, then to Sammy and me. But I can no' turn back when Father is leading us?

Hell's foundations quiver at the shout of praise...

Listen me. I do no' want to talk with my head scattered. Clear I must be on this, and many years have a way of scattering your head. So I will ask to bear with me till remembrance bring back my head.

I think say I will just hum a little o' that tune, and my head will come back to me. Old I am, yes?

Like a mighty army moves the church of God,
Brothers, we are treading where the saints have trod...

Aie – I think I ha' got memory now.

The soldiers came rushing towards us, and Father marches to meet them. Partways to we, the soldiers fall on their stomachs to the valley floor. All of a sudden Father stopped singing. I see him stand tall in the sunlight, his head held like a pointer-dog.

"Father O! Father O! Come back! Come back!"

Davie's voice pleads at my father.

Then I see flame born on the valley floor, and muskets talk sharp to me – one time – two times – three times –

And Father is no' standing any more. And Manuel is no'

standing any more. And Johnny's mouth is opened, pipes are a-skirl in his head, his heart is battering at the walls of his chest just like how Father and Manuel kick at the valley floor.

Presently they do no' kick any more; blood gushes from Father's mouth.

Mother has fallen flat on Father, and her moans and cries are filling my ear, but I can hear Davie's voice calling our names. All we others are running, but we do not get far, for we run in little circles like wounded hound-dogs. There is a whiteness in front o' my eyes through which I see with dimness that redcoats have got up from the valley floor and are running to us.

I hear a voice calling my name, but I do no' think I would have moved right if he had not whistled then like yellowthroat. The dimness left my eyes, and I turned and ran back to the reeds where Davie was calling me.

Partways there he met me and I am up in his arms and we ha' plunged into the reeds.

CHAPTER 35

You never saw anybody that knows St. Thomas parish like Davie. My bro' is rushing through the reeds with me there in his arms, through thick reeds where you can no' see daylight at all, at all. And all the while I hear a whimpering coming from him:

"Fool! – dam' old fool! – dam' old fool! – dead back there 'cause he thinks say redcoats will no' war on Christians! – dam' old fool! –"

I cry with my bro'. Cry for our dead pa and our dead bro' Emmanuel, and for those others whom we must leave behind. Howsoever, Davie says they will no' harm the herd since leader-bull is dead.

We must ha' galloped many miles before Davie stopped in a clearing. Down I am placed on the ground, and Davie searches his knapsack, which is about his waist, under the shrubs.

"Eat, then sleep for you, Johnny," he said, giving me a piece of *bammie* cake. "We will move with the moon."

★

I wake to find that we ha' moved again. My bro' is a duppy-ghost, flitting through tall trees without sound. The shrubs are not on his body longer. Moments come every now and then when he stands quiet by a tree and his hand comes over my mouth. That time I know a ghost I must be with silence.

After a while of walking there are lights on my right hand. We turn that way.

"Johnny?" Davie says, "know where are we?"

Must be Morant Bay this, yes? We must have circled through the bottom hills and come out east o' the town, yes?

I tell him this. He says right I am.

"I am going for somebody, Johnny. You will sit by this tree root and cover your mouth. Maroons and redcoats thick around the Bay like fleas on mangy dog."

I will no' be untruthful; fright has come to me. But how can I tell Davie that, eh? So I must whisper that I am standing steady, and watch him steal away while my heart jumps in my mouth.

He could be not ha' gone an hour when I heard him coming through the brambles calling my name low. I know then something must be wrong, for Davie does no' walk the bush with noise. Jump to my feet and answer softly.

No more words pass before I am in his arms. Is then it a hand rests on my head a little, and I see there is someone else there, and – Papa God! Is is Miss Lucille!

"Quiet there, Johnny!" *Nanka* snake hissing from stonehole is Davie.

Then we are going swift through the trees, across a road, and down through a coconut-walk. Sea-sand talk soft under our feet, sea-scents tickle at my nose, night swell of the sea is a great purring cat. Where Davie a-go?

Quickly we are among the mangroves, and right at the edge of the sea Davie is pulling at something. There is sound of dragging, and the shape of a long canoe pushes out into the swell.

All of a sudden there are other sounds up the beach, sounds of men's feet on the run and men's voices a-shout. Into the canoe I tumble, and Miss Lucille is quick behind me. Then Davie is shoving, and the bow of the canoe is shaking hands hard with the sea.

Shove, Davie! Shove, shove, we are getting off, shove! Up, Davie, grab the oar! Is a wild stallion, this, and he must no' get the bit! Pull in your feet from the water, Davie! Ground sharks come in close with the swell, and if ground sharks get you, then who will dip oars till we are far from the shore?

Pull, Davie! I can see the redcoats in the moonlight now, taking aim on the beach. Muskets talk in lightning and thunder. Davie shouts we must lay down in the canoe while he bends to the oar. Groundswells have taken us, and we are going up and down, up and down. Muskets talk, but we are going up and down. Poor fool-fool muskets! You can follow us up and down though? Musket balls can catch this racer-horse whose belly is one with the ground though?

We are out, and the wind from the land is passing through our hair. Davie goes up to the middle and he is putting up the bamboo mast. I know all about it, for often it is Davie and me alone a-search the seas for snapper-fish. So I go up from the bow and hold the stays while Davie fits the sprit. He and me make fast, and the crocus-bag sail shake hands with the wind.

Davie goes back to the oar. I hear him say:

"God strike that Zaccy O'Gilvie!"

There is aloes thick in his throat.

CHAPTER 36

The sail is singing matins to the wind when I wake up. Green water walks fast past the bow. Davie is leaning back in the stern, the oar grating on the sides as he keeps our head up. Miss Lucille lies on the bottom, her head in his lap. I lay still and listen as they talk.

"They will take Mother and those others to Morant Bay. Last night, 'fore Bro' Zaccy made me run, I asked Doctor Creary to look after them."

"He is an evil man, that O'Gilvie," Miss Lucille says.

Tightness comes to my bro's face. They do no' know I am not

asleep, so I lay and listen and learn that my bro' would ha' taken a wife last night if Zaccy had no' seen him when he went into town. Doctor Creary, who is a Justice of the Peace, would ha' mated Miss Lucille and my bro'. Then they would have taken to the boat.

Davie had planned it that all we family would ha' taken to the boat with Miss Lucille and he, but Father's way would not have it so. For the weeks we have been in the mountains my bro' has seen much of Miss Lucille. He has been in Morant Bay town striving to get near Zaccy O'Gilvie, but well guarded was proscriber Zaccy. Howsoever, my bro' has done much good, for he has talked to Doctor Creary often and had some young ones saved from the rope – Quackoo and Timothy too.

I get up and say good morning to Miss Lucille and Davie. Davie said:

"Man, how you sleep!"

I asked if we will have prayers like at Salt Savannah. Miss Lucille laughed and said I should ha' breakfast first. I get the *bammie* cake spread with molasses. What I could no' see last night I see this morning – that many bundles and baskets fill the canoe. I finish eating and drink from a coconut which Miss Lucille gives me. I will ask questions now.

"We sailing for where, Davie?"

"Morant Cays, boy," he tells with a grin.

I must think for a while now. I have heard o' the Morant Cays and seen the sailormen selling the booby eggs which they gather on the Cays. And I know there are great schooners which gather guano manure to sell to farmers in America. Is remember, I remember that once Davie sailed for a season with the egg-men, and when he came back to Salt Savannah after the June crop, many tales I heard from him of the Cays, where there are only sand and mangrove, and where the sun rises and sets in the sea.

"Morant Cays? We will leave Jamaica?"

"Proscribed people can no' pick and choose, Johnny. The sea is a good neighbour; it does no' tell your secrets like Bro' Zaccy."

"Then we will no' see Mother and Sammy and Naomi and Ruthie longer?"

"We can no' pick and choose, Johnny. We are proscribed."

"Miss Lucille proscribed too?"

A good laugh comes from her. "Not exactly, Johnny," she says, "but I am going to be your mother in our new home." All right that is. If Mother can no' be with us, then glad I will be with Miss Lucille.

"Then Bro' Davie will be the father?" I ask her.

In the east the sun is a-come from the sea, but on Miss Lucille's face I see there is the red of sunset. Howsoever, laughter-marks gather at Davie's mouth.

"Yes, I will be father, *Mas'r Quick-Tongue Johnny*," he said.

The sun is going down when we bring the Cays to our bow. We sail between the first two. Like Frenchmen's pompadours are the coasts, high standing. Davie says they are shaped like saucers, sunken in the middles. He says we will no' stop at these nearer ones, but will go to one he has in mind.

Man-o'-war birds swoop around our heads, and gaulins almost slide on the water-top. But for the slap of the water on the canoe and cries of hunting-birds, silence is there.

We leave the Cays and go into open water again. Sail again for time till Davie points with his chin and say:

"See our Cay there."

Turn my head and look and see low on the water green mangrove bush ahead and few tall coconuts on which the sun is a-glisten. We go in close, and there is a stillness on my bro' as his eyes search the mangrove which walks to the edge o' the water.

Then we go on again and are bucking and jumping as we tear through the surf and ride easy on calm water, with piper and shore mullets a-sport below us.

"Is the new Salt Savannah this, Johnny," my bro' tells me.

CHAPTER 37

Last night we had our sleep on the high shore 'twixt two little sand-hills. This morning Davie says we must work quick, for he does no' know what might happen today.

After we have taken out the bundles and baskets, we hauled the canoe up on the beach to a thick mangrove growth. We put some large rocks in the canoe and soon it settles down into the swampy water. Then Davie pulled mangrove roots around the gunwale till there is nothing to see of the canoe. Then up the beach we travel with the loads till we reach the reeds that grow in the middle of the Cay.

Here the ground is not much of swamp but soft all the same. Davie scooped the mud and made big holes where the bundles go. Then cover, they are covered. After this we eat some more of the *bammie* cakes and molasses. Davie says he will go back to the beach now. Sun is getting up from his bed.

I see my bro' take a crocus bag with him to the beach, and all the way he is wiping out marks what our feet and the bundles had made in the sand.

Green-back mallards and bitterns are a-play at hide and seek 'mongst the reeds. I think say I will go among the reeds to see if there are any plover eggs, but Miss Lucille calls me back sharp.

"Johnny, you must not leave until Davie returns," I hear.

I am a-think she is afraid to be alone, so I tell her there are no redcoats or Maroons.

"There may be soon, Johnny," she says with quietness. Now hear there! Is what this? "You see, Johnny," she is a-tell me, "they know we left in a canoe, and they will search the Cays, among other places. Davie is on the look-out now."

"But why he has no' told me then?" I say, anger on me.

Miss Lucille laughed. "Come now, don't be angry. You were asleep when we were discussing it, and I guess we forgot tell you when you woke."

I can no' look at her, but my face stiff with anger must watch grass a-grow at my feet. She put her hand under my chin and tilted my face to hers. After a while our eyes make four.

"Are you sorry I am with you and Davie?" she asked. "Are you sorry Davie took me too? Eh, Johnny boy?"

I search the sand with my toes and try that our eyes do no' make four.

"Don't you love me, Johnny? Don't you love Davie?"

Well then, I must stamp earth like donkey cub and cry in loud anger that for true I love Davie. My eyes make four with hers, and her eyes are walking all over my face.

"Ssh, Johnny boy! Now, listen, if you love Davie and I love Davie and Davie loves both of us, shouldn't we love each other too?"

I am quiet while love for Miss Lucille and Davie is a-push anger out of me. Quiet, me, while the beauty of her holds hands with my eyes and will not let go. I will no' be untruthful, but I do no' remember when I said:

"Love, I love you too, Miss Lucille."

But all of a sudden I am in her arms, and soft are her breasts on my face, and she is a-tell that she is my mother and my sister now.

Then, without anything from me, she is telling me all about how when Eyre brought Mr. Gordon to Morant Bay, Davie brought some Stoney Gut men into town to rescue Mr. Gordon. How they came in on the night o' the court-martial and tried to get to him. But Bro' Zaccy saw them, and they had to run from redcoats' and blue jackets' muskets.

I hear how they ran through Morant Bay streets and the redcoats trapped Davie in a corner. But a mountain goat is my bro' over a fence and ran into a house. The redcoats ran around to the door, but who they met but Miss Lucille, pointing and screaming say Davie has gone that way. Then when they are gone a-chasing where my bro' is not, Miss Lucille wrapped her scream in a laugh and goes back inside to Davie. For lucky my bro' has been to ha' run into the house where Doctor Creary and Lucille are living.

So in the dark they are waiting for uproar to die down, when Davie will get out of town. Doctor Creary is no' there, but is tending the wounded, and she and Davie talk. She tells him that Stoney Gut men can no' win. My bro' is vexed at this, but she tells him that Governor Eyre has sent to Honduras and Cuba and America for ships and guns and sailormen enough to fight all poor people in the island. And that Eyre will no' have to fight them anyhow, for everybody has heard that five hundred ha' been killed and many are coming into town begging for mercy.

Well then, after more talk there is quiet on Davie, and she

believes he is crying. I tell her that Davie never cries. She laughed and said perhaps is a mistake, that.

Then Davie told her of the Cays and what he has in mind. Miss Lucille says is wonderful, that, for he can live like freed-man. Help she will.

After that night there are many more visits, when Davie talks to Doctor Creary to help save necks from Ramsey's gallows. And with Miss Lucille he arranges for the canoe and supplies. I do no' know when it is she arranged that she will go too, for she does not tell me this. But the night when Davie went back for her who sees him in town but big-belly Zaccy!

So, while Zaccy is gone for the redcoats, Davie picks up Miss Lucille and runs hard for me and the beach. So I am here on the Cay in the bottom reeds with Miss Lucille.

Sun has come up hot on the land; the wind is a-come through the reeds, heavy with the scent of them, warm in your nostrils. If you listen hard enough, *gingi flies* and *water boatmen* will sing noontime chorus in the reeds until sleep walks with heaviness on your eyelids.

I must ha' listened long enough, for I do not know anything till I am waked by Miss Lucille shaking me.

Hear her with tightness in her throat: "Johnny – Johnny – Davie is running to us!"

Is true, that! My bro' is coming through the sand like there is no place on the ground for his feet, but I know say he will no' leave marks of his passage. He calls out to us:

"A gunboat – they are coming!"

Into the reeds he sends us while his crocus bag is brushing out the marks we made. Quickness was in his moves, but when he was finished, you could no' tell that people ha' been here.

"Follow me sharp," he told us as he struck off for the reed-bottom. We stop at a place where the reeds grow taller than man.

"Good enough-plenty," he said. "Come, corn-hair Johnny, rub mud all over your face and head."

I see Miss Lucille is rubbing mud all over her beautiful face already, so I do no' stop for question. Soon we are like *John Canoe* dancers at Christmas-morning promenade.

"Lay down, bro'," Davie said. Down I am on my belly, and he

196

is packing mud all over me and making mask with reeds for my face. Meantime, he is telling me what all this is for.

"Redcoats and Maroons are coming for hunt us, Johnny, do no' even breathe hard, boy, even if they stand on you. Yes, Bro' John?"

I am a tumblebug in the mud, and so is Miss Lucille too. And when he is finished, reeds are growing out of the mud on top o' us.

"Stand good, you hear?" he says, and then I do no' see him any more.

Well then, come, Maroon-man. Miss Lucille and me are no longer we. Even if you stand on top of we, you can no' tell we from the swamp. My bro' Davie will be a great duppy-ghost walking at high noontime. Man's eyes will look for him but will no' see him 'cept he wants them to. Stand good, Miss Lucille, do no' fret; Bro' Johnny is here and nothing will trouble you.

"Ssh, quiet, Johnny," said Miss Lucille's voice. I did no' know I was talking aloud.

I heard men's voice a-talk. Nobody has to tell me that these are redcoats. When Maroons are on the hunt, the trees and the birds and the wind talk for them. The voices grow as they come nearer, and coarse is their laughter. Quiet on me.

When the voices come to the edge o' the reeds, I drop my face on the *cotter* of reeds which Davie has placed there for me. Deep dusk is at the reed-bottom, and when something stirs just a bit from my face, I nearly cry out, for I thought it was. yellow snake. But I know no snake can be here in the mud, so quiet on me.

The voices go away, and I am about to lift my head again when something stirs again – *wayah!*

Listen me. My face is down on the mud-bottom and I can look past the roots of the reeds, and not a spit-distance from me is a man's foot. And nobody has to tell me that it is a Maroon-man's foot.

Johnny is a mouse far from his hole, and a big black cat is a-smile at him. Johnny is a congo worm in a farmyard thick with moulting hens. I do no' know what I am. I watch the foot with eyes what can no' wander. For all I know, the Maroon can be standing tall over the reeds looking down on Johnny's head. And I can no' do more than look back at his foot.

When Maroons are a-hunt, the wind talks for them. For a long time there is no move from the foot, but presently it moves towards me.

My fingers are tight in the mud. No breath comes from my body. I shrink into myself so that nothing is left outside. I bite on my lips so that nothing will come from my throat. I believe if the Maroon-man bends down for me, gnaw, I will gnaw at his toes.

He is beside me. Stand good, Johnny! Hold hard, Johnny! God o' me – will he stop beside me?

But I do no' ha' to shout. The Maroon-man is gone.

A wise thing, this, when Davie did not hide us in the thickest reeds, for the Maroons would ha' found us. Three times I ha' clawed mud as Maroons pass with their feet proud to the ground. And every time they passed, their long swords went down in the thickest clumps with a sound that moved my belly.

But now for a long time I do no' see any more. Then I hear Davie calling to us. *Aie.*

"How are things?" Davie asked.

Miss Lucille said: "We are all right. Have they gone?"

Davie nodded to her. He rubbed my muddy hair with his palm. "Maroons nearly walked on you, eh, Johnny?"

I do no' know how he knows this, for he was no' in the reeds with us. Miss Lucille laughed. "Johnny is wondering how you knew, Davie," she said.

"Eh, boy, I was in a tall coconut, and me and my musket watched the Maroons all the time, even the one who nearly walked on your face."

Is good, that. We are out of the reeds and walk down to the beach. There is nothing but blue water on the sea. Davie pointed Jamaica way.

"Clean water 'tween the Queen's land and we. Mas'r God keep it so."

His arms come about Miss Lucille and me. But I must twist and look on his face, for a while ago it was my father's voice which spoke. Iron and heavy wind.

PART TWO

MAS'R, is a heady night, this. Memory is pricking at me mind, and restlessness is a-ride me soul. I scent many things in the night-wind; night-wind is a-talk of days what pass and gone.

But the night-wind blows down from the mountains, touching only the high places as it comes; so then, 'member, I can remember only those places which stand high on the road we ha' travelled.

Such a way my people are a-sing, though! You know they will sing all night tonight so till east wind brings the morning? Torchlight and long-time hymns, and memory a-knock at my mind. *Aie*, and there is tomorrow what I must ha' faith in.

All the same, it does no' trouble me at all, this tomorrow. I ha' learnt say no matter how you hedge in your life, trouble will come just the same. Moreover, you can no' tell where trouble will come from, for it does no' set like rain.

I ha' learnt say man should no' turn his back to the temple and worship the sun. I ha' learnt say rain and dry-times are always in a man's life.

I tell you this, and believe me, for I ha' seen it with my own two eyes. I ha' seen the abomination o' desolation standing in my holy place; but there was nothing that I prayed for 'cept that my flight be no' in dry-times.

Thankie, God, that my times of flight ha' come when my earth was rich with wetness.

Howsoever, if long years you have seen like me, you will know that on many of them your memory can no' walk; for neither good nor bad happened in those years; there were no high places. Howsoever, I will tell of Salt Savannah Cay and the seed o' Davie and Lucille.

CHAPTER 1

Is the year 1882 it, in the month of June, and I am a-stand on Salt Savannah Cay watching a British man-o'-war heave to. A shining morning it is, with sunlight a-sparkle on blue water. Up in the blue above, pelicans are wheeling left and right like say is guard of honour this for Missis Queen's ship. I stand on the edge o' our shore waiting for the Queen's men.

The boat that leaves the ship's side comes walking to me on six flashing oars cutting smooth water like one.

I stand on the edge of the shore, and back o' me are a round dozen of men standing quiet in the sun. If you can see them and remember faces well, you will see these are Morant Bay young ones who ha' now turned into full men. If good your mind is and remember faces well, you will see that the one in front o' them is my old boyhood friend Timothy. Timothy has grown full man now, and he is the bosun o' my guano-pickers.

Back o' these is my line of barrack-huts, brown and white in trash roof and Spanish walling. Before the barrack-huts we ha' laid out a feast-table with clean white cloth. A flagpole points empty finger high at the sky.

A hand is pulling at mine, so I must look down at the little boy who stands side-and-side with me. When our eyes make four it is the face of Lucille under the corn hair of Davie I am looking at.

Hear the seed o' Davie and Lucille: "Uncle John, is the Queen this coming?"

I shake my head and say no, not the Queen but her men.

Thought make bean-furrows on his forehead, but he does no' say more now. That is how James Creary Campbell stay. This evening when our Bay water turns to orange, and brown dusk is a-creep in from the west, and the guano-pickers sing vespers in the smoke o' their mosquito fires, James will ask me why Missis Queen did no' come herself to take charge of her land. For James, talk must wait till thinking fails. Ten mango seasons he has seen, but they have no' loosened his tongue.

Now bluejackets have hoisted their oars, and the boat is sliding to the beach. I see the officer in the stern. Full-dress uniform he has on, with his dirk lying on his knees. Is a young officer, this, and I am thinking he can no' be more than my own years of twenty and five.

The boat is shored and a dozen o' marines jump to the sand. Sharp command from the sergeant, and their carbines go to their shoulders for the slope. The officer has stepped from the boat and is coming to me.

I tell James to wait while I go to meet him. When we meet face and face, his hand comes out to me.

"Mr. John Campbell?"

I say yes, is John Campbell, me.

"I am Lieutenant Harvey of the Royal Navy. Are all the arrangements complete?"

I wave my hand to show him the feast table and the flagpole. He looks over at the table brimmed with pineapple, mango, brown naseberry, and thick, ripe bananas, and calabash atop o' calabashes full with cooling lime beverage.

He laughed. "Rather more than we expected, Mr. Campbell. We only thought to see a flag-mast, y'know."

Howsoever, in front o' his men and my men we walk to the flagpole. Quick, sailormen knot the Jack to the ropes. Then there is sharp roll from side-drum, and the Jack is going up, up, catching morning sun on red, white, and blue.

A great gun from the man-o'-war thunders for Missis Queen Victoria. Coconut trees tremble at his thunder, but the Queen's men stand stiff like ramrods. I ha' got my trash hat in my hand, and all my men take off theirs too.

I count till twenty-one thunders and the Royal Salute is finished.

Great gun covers his mouth again and coconut trees stop a-tremble.

Hear lieutenant: "In the name of Her Most Gracious Majesty, Victoria, Queen of England and the Empire across the Seas, I take possession of these Morant Cays. God Save the Queen."

Lieutenant Harvey feels that time now he should shake my hand again. Timothy closes one eye at me. By-and-by, when sailormen have feasted, I will tell Lieutenant Harvey that I will go

203

back to the mainland with him. I will ask passage for James and me. I am thinking that it is full time now that James Creary Campbell should know his mother.

Eh, how come all this? How comes this fruit o' Lucille does no' know the tree? How come I stand on Salt Savannah Cay and not a Davie is here with me?

Aie – Davie what was head cook and bottle-washer; Davie what was top and bottom of my life.

I must no' take you too fast. I must tell you o' things what have happened. But, 'member, I must remember that the night is going and day-cloud must no' see me by the window. Tomorrow is a tomorrow which I need strength for.

But I will go back till you know.

CHAPTER 2

As 'cording to the palm what Lucille marks each day, three months now we ha' been living on the Cay. But things are not so good for us, for man is no' built to live on fish alone, and coconut can no' take the place of rice and good yam.

Davie and me have been all over the Cay, but we can find no good earth for planting. In the quiet years, before times, men have no' done more here but hunt birds' eggs and dig guano manure. Guano, which is the droppings of noddy and sooty terns, is a rich food for the earth, and it is this that after times brought food for Davie's mind. This and the mud-bottom of the reeds.

For, hear me now. One day when we dug the sand for a new water-hole, Davie sat back and wiped his face and almost blasphemed aloud. Lucille looked up with surprise on her.

"Water and manure enough-plenty on the dam' place, but no soil for planting," Davie said. Lucille looked around on glistening sand, out to the round blueness o' the sea and sky.

"It's a picnic island, Davie," she said with quietness. "Not for living."

It is no' the first time that she has said this, and now my bro's eyes are walking on her face; but her face is turned to the shining sea, and her eyes do no' make four with his.

"Why?" Davie asked.

"Nothing grows here but coconuts, and they are really made for the sand." She looked back at him, a little smile on her. "Coconuts and picnics go together, Davie."

"Then is how the reeds grow, Miss Lucille?" I say. "There is no sand at the mud-bottom?"

Davie turned his head to look on me. I think he will say to shut up, but after a while a grin comes on him and his hand reaches for my shoulder.

"They grow how, Smarter Johnny? How they grow? Reeds do no' grow in sand? Eh, Lucille, you see it? Reeds grow in sound earth and water!"

I think Davie must ha' got the sun to his head, for up he has jumped and has grabbed Lucille and me. Then at Morant Bay Fair we are, and fiddles are a-rip in a first figure, and round and round he is dancing us.

"Eh, Lucille? You see what Bro' Johnny is telling us? There is sound earth at the mud-bottom, there is guano manure in the sand – then why we can no' have a big plantation, big as Custos Von Aldenburg's?"

I did no' mean it so. But good it is when big people say that the small ones are smart, so I keep my mouth covered.

That was six weeks ago as 'cording to Lucille's markings. Davie has been a-work every day from day-cloud till evening star stands by the sun. We ha' pulled up the reeds from a good two acres, and now the rich mud has eaten of the sunlight, and sound earth is ready for the plough.

We have no hoes, but if you peel away the coconut boughs and bury them in the hot sand, after a while when you take them out they are nearly as tough as mahogany.

We have saved some yam-heads and cocoa-heads from our stores, and there are enough to fill two squares. We ha' dug a deep trench around the squares for drainage, and now we sit and wait for our crop.

But things are no' so good. Is 'member, I remember that at Salt Savannah when Father used to talk o' his plans, Mother would nod and say: "Good, Pa John, but 'member that while the grass is growing, the horse can be starving." While we were at work from day-cloud to evening star Miss Lucille had eyes for nothing but the earth. Now, while we wait for our crop, there is nothing for her eyes but the sea and long distance.

Davie is away most of the time now, fishing the shallows for sprats and mullets. One day at late sun Lucille and me were waiting for him when she asked me a funny question.

"Johnny," she said, "are you happy here?"

We were on the edge of the beach. Davie was around the point so we could no' see him. Out yonder white water foamed over the reef. Late sun was a-play at hide-and-seek in the dark-night o' her hair. Beautiful, she was, and I was thinking how good it is that Davie has forgotten Adassa of Port Morant and is yoked with Miss Lucille. Up in the Blue Mountains Naomi one time told me that Davie should no' put his mind on Adassa. For hogs must be rooting in his plantation now, what with so many o' the Queen's soldiers in Port Morant, Naomi said. I am a-think it is good to ha' Davie and Lucille all day with me, and nothing to do but bathe and roll in the sand. Then, how come if I am happy here?

So I nod me head and tell Miss Lucille that Johnny is happy here.

"Do you never long for Morant Bay, Johnny?" she asked with her eyes close on me. "Wouldn't you like to hear laughter and the fiddles playing? Or see your mother drawing coffee in the kitchen at night and hear hymn-singing down at the barracks?"

Is what Miss Lucille saying? She has no' remembered that Deacon Bogle marched from the Gut?

"You do no' remember that there is nothing more o' that? You ha' no' heard that there has been five hundred for forty and that people are no' people longer?"

"But it could not go on, Johnny," she is telling me. "It must be all over now – and how can we know if we are never to go back?"

"My bro' Davie knows what he is doing," I tell her. "If Father did follow Davie, he and Manuel would no' be in Baptism Valley now."

Miss Lucille rubbed her forehead with her hand, teeth tight on her lip. I asked her: "You are no' happy here?"

She turned on me quick, loudness in her voice: "Don't ask me that!"

I am looking close on her; her eyes moved away from mine. Quieter now, she said: "I am happy with Davie and you, Johnny boy. But –"

Her eyes on the sea, I see Miss Lucille's body get tight. Her hand closed on my shoulder.

"Johnny!" she is whispering, "isn't that a sail out there?"

Well, when I look to sea, for true there is a sail out there. Faster than a mountain goat is me to my feet and hollering at Miss Lucille:

"Come! Run fast! Maroon-men are coming back!"

Lucille is quick up too. "Davie – Davie – we must warn him!"

Then we are running up the beach, running like mad to where Davie is fishing the shallows. I holler to him: "Davie O! Davie O!"

We tear through heavy sand warm with the sun; we take a short cut across the point, and when we top the lip of the beach on t'other side, there is Davie riding the swell in the canoe. Off with my shirt quick and waving and shouting at him. He has seen us, and now his oar is out and fast he is coming through the swell.

While we tell him of what we ha' seen, we helped him haul the boat up on the beach. There is quietness on him. Lucille said we should hide the boat quick, but he said it is of no use, that.

"There is our cultivation and our huts to show that people live here," he said.

We have got the boat up on the beach, and now we stand like sailors on Sabbath nights when the rum shops are closed and there is nothing else to do. Miss Lucille and me are watching Davie's face.

"I will see the sail," he said, and we went along the beach.

On our way he tells us we should go to the hut for his musket while he will go to the beach. We get the musket and quickly go down to the beach. Davie meets us partways with puzzle-marks on his face.

"It is no' the Queen's ship," he said.

"No? Are you sure?"

"A Morant Bay schooner it is with a Montego jib. They ha'

207

anchored already." His eyes met mine. "Johnny, go back to the hut."

Davie speaks with finish in his voice, so I must go back to the house. But, smart, I play smart, and when they turn to the beach I drop behind a sand-hill and crawl up, so that I am like them laying in the sand and facing where the schooner is.

The sailormen have drawn in the tow-boat from the stern, and now men are going down the rope into it. There are five of them. I think from how they row they will land farther up the beach than where we are. I am a-wonder if we should no' make for the reeds when all of a sudden there is madness from Miss Lucille.

Up she has got and is running along the beach to where the boat will land and crying something at the top of her voice. And there is my bro' behind her, running without his musket in his hand.

But no time after I am on my feet too, running and shouting like them, for nobody has to tell me say that the good Doctor Creary has just landed from the boat.

CHAPTER 3

Deep into the night we have sat before the hut listening to Doctor Creary tell us o' Morant Bay. From him we have learnt say not until men's habitations from the Bay to the foot of the great mountain ha' been put to fire did Governor Eyre stay his hand and say: *Let be.* But that time there was no more fodder for his guns.

Like when we had talked with Davie in the mountains and waited in fear for him to nod his head, so now do I see Davie and Lucille watching Doctor Creary as they speak o' names they have known. Many times does Doctor Creary nod his head.

Now and again when there is no knowledge in him one of the four Morant sailormen who brought him to us will tell us what we want to know.

My mother did no' die of violence. She lived to be brought into the Bay with my brethren, and there Doctor Creary shield them with his influence so Provost-Marshal Ramsey did no' take them. Howsoever, my mother did no' linger long behind my father.

Of my brethren there are good words. All ha' gone to Kingston to Doctor Creary's estate. Ruthie was ill to death, but well she is again now and governess to the daughter of a city merchant. Zekiel and Naomi are at school, but there is health trouble on my bro' Zekiel. He was not so strong before times, and now the malaria is on him.

But of Sammy? Eh! What has my bro' Sammy done but joined up with the soldiery! A Boy of the West India Regiment he is now, stepping proud in the scarlet and white-top boot o' Missis Queen's men. Davie smiled and said his eyes always did shine when militiamen pipes skirl.

Then we hear o' the Royal Commission.

Quiet are Davie and Lucille as Doctor Creary tells us of the anger of England when they heard of the wickedness of Eyre; and now the Commission has been sent by the good Victoria to find out why her children ha' been put to the sword.

"It is this that has brought me here especially," he said.

"How did you know we would be here?" Davie asked. "You must ha' heard that the Maroons searched the Cays and did no' find anybody?"

Good laugh comes from Doctor Creary. "That I did, but your sister Naomi told me that no corn-footed – these were her exact words – no corn-footed soldiermen can find her bro' John if he meant to hide," he said, looking at me.

They all laugh while a small grin I grin and think say Naomi is no' so bad.

"These Morant men knew the Cays well, and together we combed every nook and cranny – this was our last bet."

A little silence came on us. Davie asked:

"What did you say of the Commission, sir?"

Doctor Creary cleared his throat and moved a little on the coconut thatch on which we sit.

"See here, Davie, I will not beat about the bush. I want you to return with us to give evidence before the Commissioners. I want the Commission to hear the other side of the story – the Stoney Gut side. And, though God forbid that I have to say it, you are one of the few left alive and certainly the only Councilman that I know of."

In the light o' the mosquito fire I can see Lucille looking hard at Davie as we wait for him to talk. His voice was low.

"The Commission can no' bring back to life my father or Emmanuel or any of the dead ones. What use of taking evidence? They will gallows Eyre? or Colonel Hobbs? or Butcher Ramsey?"

"What they will do, son, I am in no position to state. But have no fear that British justice is any respector of persons."

My bro's voice was louder: "British justice? Is that what they call Ramsey's drum-head court-martial? Or is the new name, that, for the *Queen's Advice*?"

"Now, Davie –"

"Sir, I am no' quarrelling with you, but I ha' had my taste o' this justice. Aloes it has been for me."

"I do not call Eyre's actions justice, nor those of his minions," Doctor Creary said. "Those actions were unjustifiable. But what we seek now is justice."

"Has it no' always been like this?" my bro' is saying with his eyes on the fire, Davie talking to Davie: "Like this always? Down on other people go the hounds o' Britain, running without leash, savaging and mauling the poor ones who have been sinful 'cause they talked for freedom. Then when we bowels ha' been ripped out, Mother England plays like soft and begin to holler that she did no' want it so; that the well-trained hounds she has sent out ha' only gone mad because they scented blood. Or if she sees her hounds getting the whip, then she hollers all the same and call them back quickly. Was it no' so it went in America?"

"But even there, Davie, you must not forget that in the long run, justice was indeed done. Remember how the people at home faced solidly against the government for pursuing that war? I know it was wrong in the first place, but they made amends, my son. And since then, there has never been trouble between Britain and America. It is that which makes a great nation, Davie. Britain is never vindictive."

"I will silence my voice, Doctor Creary. I will no' argue against you. But this I know, not for me this British justice which first kills, then wakes for the dead. I am out o' the Queen's land, on my own island with only sun and wind for king and queen, and here I stay."

"You mean you will never return to the mainland?"

Davie looked into the mosquito fire. Then he raised his head and looked at Miss Lucille and me, and back to the fire again.

"Never go back, me," he said with finish in his voice.

Doctor Creary said slow, his eyes not on us: "There is a list of names posted to the courthouse at Morant Bay. It is headed: *Executed Rebels*. Under C, there are two Campbells, John and Emmanuel. Those names, and many others like those, will never be cleared from that list if the Queen's Commissioners can hear but one side of the black story."

I am a-wonder if my bro' has heard him, for never a move does he make. But after a time he laughs a little.

"Rebels?" he said, looking at the doctor; "what is wrong with men calling you a rebel? A body ever rebels against good? Did Jesus Christ and Wat Tyler and L'Ouverture rebel against good or bad? Eh – if Governor Eyre had put *Executed Mice* atop his list and had my father's name under it, come talk to me, Doctor Creary, and then I would sharpen my cutlass and go to St. Jago for his guts! But, rebel? Is a good, good tombstone that!"

"Your father would not think it that if he were here, Master David!" Doctor Creary said with sharpness.

"*Aie* – you did no' know my father well, Doctor Creary," said David with softness. "A rebel worse than me he was. But there were many mouths to feed; and a man who has his two hands to the plough can ha' no use for the sword. 'Stead he takes to the Book and waits for time to be full."

I am thinking that my bro' is talking away the full of his belly which has been on him these many months now. For these months he has worked with his hands leaving little time for talk. But now his eyebrows are walking up his forehead and his voice is mocking on Doctor Creary.

"I must go back to Morant Bay and tell Commissioners say we were wrong to kill fat Aldenburg? But that the redcoats charged too high for only one fat German? I must go down past Bath Town and 'member that a dozen were on one limb, clutching on each other like men a-drown while they kicked air? I must be a-visit at Monkville and see thirteen on the edge o' the trench and Hobbs's musketmen taking aim? I must watch him in Fonthill Chapel hanging nine 'fore the altar? Then after this I must go in before the Queen's fat Commissioners, cool in their silk suits, and bow and say: *Pray Your Honours, in duty bound* – and all the while my fingers itch to send a *tengre* lance clear through their bellies to their behinds? I must –"

"Davie Campbell! You are a stupid fool!"

Is Miss Lucille that. She was sitting straight up and firelight was snapping in her eyes. Davie took his eyes to her, and I see the mockery is gone from his face, leaving a surprise. Nobody has to tell me why surprise is on him, for is the first time, this, I ha' seen her vexed at him.

Doctor Creary reached out for her hand.

"Bide awhile, Lucille," he said. "Davie has seen more than any of us, and it will take time for him to forget."

She turned on the doctor with quickness. "What can be the use of his memories? He says the Commission cannot bring back life to the dead. Will his bitter memories do that? Is he the only one who has suffered?"

"Bide, Lucille. Let me speak again," said the doctor.

"No – no – I will talk to him," Miss Lucille said, as she took her eyes back to my bro'. "Look at these men. Ask which of them has not lost close relations. Ask which of them has not suffered, and see if their suffering cannot be compared with yours. Is that any reason why they should leave their homes and loved ones to live bitterly and miserably by themselves? You are only being a slave to defeat when you think like you do. You have not got the courage to fight back to freedom. You are –"

"Shut up!" my bro' cried with loudness.

Tongues o' flames crackle at mangrove wood. This was the only sound in the night.

After a while Davie took his eyes from Miss Lucille, but I can see that anger has gone from them, leaving only hurt in them. My bro' is a house dog what has been slapped. For a time nobody says anything. Doctor Creary went down on his knees, searching the fire for a small coal that will fit into the bowl o' his pipe. I am watching the quick jerk of his fingers as he picks up the coal and tosses it from side to side of his palm and then gets it into the bowl.

Hear Davie: "The Commission meet where?"

Doctor Creary spoke quietly: "In the Morant Bay church-hall, Davie."

"Will they hear me? A man who marched with Bogle?"

"The Commission bears a mandate to erase all of that, son. They are only here to get the facts. Anyone who testifies before them is immune from punishment – you come and go as you like. When the findings are promulgated by London, the law will take its course. But I think I can assure you that all punitive measures are at an end so far as the populace is concerned."

"Yes – we ha' paid enough-plenty already," Davie said.

Bullfrogs down in the mud-bottoms throat a call to the screech-owl what flies low over our heads. Good it is to me to see other faces on Salt Savannah tonight.

"Very well," my bro' said. "I will talk to the Commissioners." Davie will go to Morant Bay!

He looked sideways at me. "The night gets old for you, Bro' John," he said.

Doctor Creary smiled at me. "John, the second," he called me. Then he turned to Davie. "I have brought something for you, David. Your mother asked me to hand it to you."

One of the Morant sailors brought up a large package. Doctor Creary opened it and shook out my father's black Prince Albert. Firelight talked merriment to the brass buttons. I see Mother has darned up the holes what the bullets made when they were a-seek my father.

CHAPTER 4

We went back to Jamaica with the good Doctor Creary and his four Morant sailormen.

I remember I did no' see there what I expected to see. For to me the thoughts in my mind were that most of the town must ha' been burnt flat, and that Mr. Gordon must still be kicking air under the courthouse steps. True, the courthouse was only black skeleton, but they had long since cut down Mr. Gordon.

Neither was the town burnt down flat. Afterwards I learnt say much o' the damage done by the soldiermen had been done outside the town.

I went back to Pastor Humphrey's half-finished church, where I had watched with Mr. Abram as he started for his forty for forty. I could almost see his flat head bobbing up and down in the corner where I waited for Davie, and hear his great voice a-thunder: "Take time, Bro' Johnny!"

All the time I am alone. Reason for this, Davie spends all his time at the church-hall where the Commission is taking evidence. Miss Lucille has gone to Kingston to see her friends who had picked flowers 'cause they thought she was dead.

Every evening I meet Davie when the Commission stops listening for the day. Every evening he does no' look happy. Came the fourth evening, and when he came in to where we lodged, there was deep thinking back o' his eyes. We sat down for supper, but he does no' eat much of the food. I see his eyes searching the lamplight and presently he said:

"Is of no use, it."

I am glad to hear him talk, even though he is no' talking to me.

"What is no use, Davie O?" I asked him.

"Eh? No – nothing, Bro' John," he said, a little smile in his eyes.

I go on eating of yellow *ackee* and codfish.

"Johnny?" said Davie after time, "I am thinking say we have come for nothing. I can no find Bro' Zaccy."

I must jump. "Bro' Zaccy? You were a-look for him?"

Davie nodded. But what has brought surprise on me is that there is no anger on him when he calls Bro' Zaccy's name.

"What you would do to him, Davie?"

My bro' is looking at me with distance in his eyes. "I do no' know, Johnny. Funny it is that before we left the Cay I was a-think o' many thing I could do with Zaccy, but –"

Silence came on him. His eyes are standing steady on something in the corner of the room, and when I look too, I can see only Father's coat hanging there.

"You ha' no' got many years, Johnny, but you are my bosom bro'. Hear me. Much o' what was in me seem to ha' gone from me since Doctor Creary gave me Father's coat. You ha' no' got many years, but listen me. Know, you know now that I am the oldest Campbell?"

I tell him know, I know he is head o' us, now.

"Bro' John, to the plough I must put my hands."

"But how Bro' Zaccy comes into that?"

My bro' smiled at me again. " 'Fore we left the Cay, I wanted to lay hands on Zaccy. Since I have been here I ha' looked for him. Nobody knows where Zaccy has moved his family to, but he is no' in St. Thomas parish longer. Yet still, though my mouth is a-breathe of vengeance, my heart knows I will no' hurt a hair of his head even if our eyes make four."

"Then what of the Commissioners? You will no' talk to them?" I ask.

Nice it is to feel my bro's fingers in my hair. He shook his head.

"For Doctor Creary I will talk to them. But they have got their minds sealed, Johnny. They will no' interfere with Eyre's recommendation to Missis Queen that she take away representative government and bring on Crown government. Deacon Bogle and the Stoney Gut men fought for freedom, but they ha' got the chains hammered on tighter instead."

I asked how that? If you ha' battled for something and you ha' lost even what you had, is not the time that when you should fight harder then?

"My hands are on the plough, Johnny. Mother has sent me Pa John's coat."

"Then you will no' hurt Bro' Zaccy and you will no' battle for what Stoney Gut men lost. Is what then? Zekiel you will be?"

A good laugh comes from Davie, and his fingers pull at my hair. But heaviness is in his throat when he says: "Is a harder battle this before me, Johnny."

Next day Davie does no' go to the church-hall but says to Salt Savannah we will visit this day. So with the sun still young we take the shady track for our old home.

215

As before times I am up on his back, and trees are walking quick past my head. We pass Bro' Aaron's house, empty and lonely topside the furrowed three-acre which he had left without planting when the shells sounded at Stoney Gut. Now grass and chicken-weeds riot in the calm furrows.

We came out of the hollow and climbed the hill and there was Salt Savannah before us.

Funny it is how even a whisper is loud in a house where there is emptiness. Believe, I am believing that the family chairs and tables must have taken up some of the loudness in our voices so that behaviour will be in their house. And when these are gone, there are no wooden kinsmen to help keep high the pride o' the family.

"Every stick gone, Johnny. Is a house o' the dead, this," Davie said as he stood in the doorway and looked in the empty hall-room.

We went down the beach to the barracks, and here things were no' so bad. For people were crowding around us, and dogs barked and fowls clucked and Timothy and me shouted at each other over all the noise.

We stayed there till past noontime. I rolled on the sand with Timothy while he talked with pride o' getting Ramsey's whip and showed me the place where he was wealed. A full rebel, Timothy was, for he has got the whip; but I bring shine to his eyes when I tell him of musketmen firing at me as I took canoe for the Cays. We did no' talk much of Mr. Abram, though.

When we went back to Morant Bay, Doctor Creary told Davie that the Commissioners would hear him next day. Davie said that was good, for afterwards he could go to Kingston and see the rest of his family.

CHAPTER 5

Humphrey's church-hall could never have been big enough to hold all the people who have come to hear the inquiry. Davie and me got in easy, howsoever, by the pass which Doctor Creary had got for us. We got seats on the witness bench right up in front near the rail.

Chairs for the Commissioners were on the platform under pictures o' the Saviour and Pastor Humphrey in his robes. But silent is Pastor today, and his mouth does no' snap at us. People were talking plenty to each other when we went inside. But soon as Davie stepped in, down the talking went till there was nothing in the room 'cept secret whispers and rub of *osnaburg* cloth. Everywhere I turn I look on eyes – eyes on the flax o' Davie's head and the young one beside of him. Nobody has to tell me say Davie is known for the only Councilman who is left to blink at the sun. Today-day they know they will hear from a man who marched close with Deacon Bogle.

A man with many eyes on him can no' but feel stirrings inside o' him, and I am thinking if I open my mouth wide at all the eyes whether they will all shut tight. But same time the clock begins to tell of ten, and a big voice cries out to us:

"Order!"

That time then the eyes swing from me, and it is the Commission which is coming into the room should begin to feel stirrings inside o' them now. The Usher is calling the *Oyez, Oyez,* and I am looking at the men whom Missis Queen Victoria has sent from England to listen to my bro'. There are three of them, and all overseas Englishmen, but in the old light which comes through the jalousies I can no' see their faces plain at all. Howsoever, the *Oyez* is over and the Commissioners are bowing to us. All o' we bow back to them and sit down.

There is much whispering 'tween the Commissioners and the Clerk, and once all o' them looked full at Davie. Then there were more whisperings and nodding of heads. The Clerk went back to his seat, whispering to the Usher as he passed. The Usher looked one time all around the room, then loud is his voice as he called:

"David Campbell o' Stoney Gut!"

My bro' got to his feet and went to the rail. The Usher gave him the Book and is a-ask whether my bro' will tell all o' the truth as God help him.

You can hear down in the Bay where Morant sailormen are

217

walking the capstan on a Cayman Island schooner, hear the rattle of chains and the bawl of the crierman:

Walk i' up-O! Walk i' down-O! Morant Bay sailormen, walk i' round-O!

The Usher said my bro' should kiss the Book. The Usher said my bro' should face the Commissioners and keep up his voice.

People move a little, then sit back on the benches and open their eyes wide on the man who did march close with Deacon Bogle.

CHAPTER 6

By the time the clock has said it is eleven, the Commissioners have got all from Davie of what they call the Morant Bay rebellion. He told them of how the constables had arrested him and of how the Councilmen had rescued him. Of the march on the Vestry by the Stoney Gut men and the burning of the courthouse. Of the coming of the redcoats and the battle in Blue Mountain Valley. Of my father and Manuel going to earth in Baptism Valley, and of how we went to the Cays and ha' been there ever since.

And all the while his voice walked on one tread, neither going up nor going down, just as if we were by Maroon Hole and he was talking to himself.

When he was finished and the Clerk was kneading his finger-joints where they ached with the much writing, the Commissioners bent their heads together. After a while they looked back at Davie again, and the man in the centre spoke:

"Campbell, my brother Commissioners and I are not here to try your case; you are not bound to answer any questions put to you. But, we are anxious, very anxious to get to the bottom of this rebellion, and whatever you can tell us may assist us in our findings. Do you understand?"

"I do that," Davie said.

"Very well. Now, from your replies during the examination, we have arrived at some conclusions. You are the son of the deceased John Campbell, a man who held responsible office in the employment of the deceased William Gordon. By the nature of his employment and from what we have gathered, he was a fairly well-to-do man, owning his own property, house, cattle, and other livestock. You and your brother, the deceased Emmanuel, did the work on your father's farm; and by all accounts, a thriving farm it was.

"The – er – colour of your family made you also – er – well thought of in the community. We even understand that the late Custos had spoken of appointing your father a Justice of the Peace. In other words, the point we are making is that you had everything which should make you sympathetic to the – er – rulers of your country. What made you join the rebels of Stoney Gut?"

My bro' came erect on the rail. Hear him: "Your Honours, because hunger came to my door and I was no' blind."

"After my remarks how can you say that?" said the Commissioner sharp, anger riding his shoulders.

"I will tell you. Where my family once locked their door everybody around us, 'cept for the wealthy *buckras*, hungered. Everybody around me were my people, and when they hungered, hungered me too."

"But why should you, the son of a hard-working, thriving father, cast his lot with people of whom Her Majesty wrote as being unprofiting because of their own indolence?"

My bro' said with teeth in his voice: "Stand steady there, Your Honour!"

People stirred and the Usher said: "Order!"

Hear Davie: "Do you know how we came these last three years? Or how come we before that? Tell, I should tell you?"

"Just what do you mean, Campbell?"

"*That now I would speak for the dead ones!*"

My bro' is a-talk to the Queen's men without fear in his voice. My bro' is standing tall and strong, and his head is golden in the green gloom o' the room. Hear Davie, Mr. Abram O! Is the man for the glory, this!

"I would speak for such as do no' speak any more! I would tell you that for two hundred years before October gone, men were a-march on Morant Bay courthouse. Say it was not from Stoney

219

Gut they marched, nor Bath Town, nor Port Morant, nor Cuna Cuna Mountain. Say that they marched from all over the island, and ha' been marching for two hundred years!"

People in the room are stirring again and the Usher is bawling for order again, and believe, I believe that he will burst into blood. Whisper between the Commissioners, then they looked at Davie again.

"My brothers and I are not quite sure of your line of talk, Campbell, but we will hear what you have to say."

Davie's voice came back quiet: "Is good, it. I will tell you, Your Honours."

It was so he began that day before the Commissioners in Pastor Humphrey's church-hall, and he spoke things which I had no' heard him spoke before. Not afterwards either.

"Man was no' built for slavery, Your Honours. In him are the Image and Likeness, and it is no' of the skin. Inside o' him there is the dignity of God, whether he was birthed in a hut or in a *buckra*'s mansion. And that dignity o' God tells him say he should no' a serf to another. But for two hundred years on this island, men ha' been serfs to the buckra planter.

"They did no' take it quietly. Often much blood flowed. For although they read no books of history what could tell them of the road followed by the bonded before them, yet the dignity inside every born man would 'low no rest to these slaves. There was something else too.

"For these two hundred years they saw the shaming of man's highest calling – the calling o' labour with the hands, the sweat by which the Big Master said we should eat our bread. The shaming o' labour? Make me tell you of this, Your Honours."

The Commissioners have no' made any moves, but you can sense say they are saying that Davie should tell them of the shaming. My bro' will.

"Not all of the English who came to the colonies came as *buckra* planters. Many were men who sailed out o' England with no more than their own two hands and no coins in their fobs. They came a-seek a name and a home in what you called the New World.

"They came and took their tasks in the cane-fields, side-and-side with the bonded; and for a time, they worked. But by-and-by when they looked around and saw none of their own people on the hoe and on the mill-bed, shame took them. They cursed the labour o' their hands and left the fields to the bonded men who toiled under the lash. So then, here was something to vex the dignity inside the bonded: to them also came the sense that only serfs should toil in the fields."

The Commissioners were forward on the table, their eyes leaving nothin' o' Davie's face. My bro's voice was walking on one level, neither going up nor down. 'Member, I remember how 'twixt his times for breathing, never was anything heard save the clock telling of the seconds. By now the sailormen's song was finished, for their sails had taken in the wind which will walk them out of the Bay.

"For six days, and a half on the Sabbath, from sun-up till evening star, the bonded toiled so that the *buckra* planter could drink his rum and dance, so his women could wear silks 'gainst their skins. It came so that the bonded could no' bear the sight of the cane-fields. The silver arrows what come with the ripe stalks in October were no more than their badge of shame. It was no' that they wouldn't work. They still stirred the earth to plant the yams and potatoes for their own bellies; but the sugar-cane had become to them what holy water is to the devil.

"Howsoever, Emancipation came in 'Thirty-eight, and the *buckra* said they were free and gave them some acres of rock and cactus."

My bro' took a breath. His voice came easy again.

"What happened when this freedom came? What happened when *buckra* said he would now pay them wages for their work? Did they take tasks in the fields for money where not long ago they took it for the lash?

"Ask the government in Kingston-town. You will hear that never was the cane crop so poor as after the Emancipation; that estates after estates pawned their titles. Hand labour did no' have beauty to men longer, for they did no' like the scent of sugar-cane longer. Stir the soft earth 'tween the rocks and the cactus, and enough-plenty yams would be grown for their own bellies. Then they work from day-cloud to evening star longer?"

Heads of the Commissioners on the Bench nodded to each other as my bro' took breath and pushed his hair from his forehead. Now he talks straight at the Commissioners, leaning forward on the rail.

"*Aie*, Your Honours, it is no' whether one was right or wrong, but I am telling of the case for they who marched on Morant Bay courthouse. I say there would ha' been no march if *buckra* had made it well for them to stay home.

"I do no' say that they did wisely by leaving the land to starve while they lay in the sun; but show me the one who can say that men who ha' been bonded for two hundred years, without wages, without rest, and under the lash, would act with wisdom when at long last the chains ha' been struck off? Show me the one, Your Honours!"

Quiet, bro'. Make your voice come back to one level.

"But this did no' last for ever. After time they grew to freedom. Saw, they saw there were other things which freed-men must earn for themselves. There were clothes and shelter and education for the young ones. Arose, they arose and looked around them and saw that cactus and rocks could no' bring the coin they wanted. Canny buckra had given them such land as they could shrivel on, easy. They opened their mouths to cry, but laugh, they laughed instead – just like how they had done for two hundred years. They went back to b*uckras'* estates.

"Very well then. *Buckra* was there waiting, with ninepence-a-day wages in his hands. They laughed and went back to the hoe and played canny too. For they worked hard and saved, Your Honours – yes, *saved* out of this ninepence a day. Saved, so till one after another they bought their own pieces o' good land which had no rocks and cactus. These same people what the *Queen's Advice* says will do no work – 'member, Your Honours?"

Talk it, Davie O! We back o' you down here on the floor are nodding and saying soft to one another: *Is the man for the glory, this!*

"Order! Order!" I think the Usher will soon burst into blood.

"One after t'other they became their own landmasters, and leave *buckra* planters' estates. That time, then, there is no labour, and there is making of new laws in the House o' Assembly which will prevent people getting good lands to buy, so they will return to *buckra* estates. There is even talk among the plantermen of bringing indentured labour from India and China.

"Well then, they ha' left the estates, but they can get no more land to buy. And when one whole family must live off a little acre, soon the acre will be tired because everything is coming out and nothing going in and there is no time for rest. Good it is to remember too, Your Honours, that for these two hundred years the English plantermen had also been taking from their lands and putting nothing back. They too would ha' been in the same trouble, but they had enough-plenty to leave many acres every year to lie fallow and gather strength. Howsoever, this is how it went.

"Men who ha' become their own landmasters will no' easily work for another. When they saw that their lands were getting sluggish, they petitioned and petitioned and petitioned the Governor of St. Jago to put more lands on the block so they could rest the tired acre. But will the Governor? No' him, when all his tea-table friends are telling him that these freed-men are becoming too big for their pantaloons. And so our people lived on their one little acre with only enough food to keep breath a-pant in their breasts. So it was until 'Sixty-three."

Take breath, Davie. Commissioners ha' ceased whispering one to another and only sit a-watch of my bro'.

"'Sixty-three was the year when rain stopped falling and the land died under us. Is the year it when the Americans fought their war o' the ports, and no schooners could enter their harbours to bring the flour and salted cod to us. Is the year it when hunger really buckled down on our people for the ride which would last three years. For three years the heavens were dried up.

"Our people hungered, Your Honours; and meantime they saw *buckras'* tables loaded and heard buckra plantermen laugh in his fat. They groaned as they saw their land going back to the Queen because there was no money to pay taxes and tithes and buy the little food too. Meantime plantermen grin and wait, for labour will be soon cheap.

"Petition after petition goes to Governor Eyre at St. Jago, to the Queen's Ministers in London, and what comes to us but the

Queen's Advice, which says we are hungry 'cause lazy we are. *Aie* – the feet began tramping with loudness then!"

My bro' stopped talking and took his eyes over the Commissioners' head to where Pastor Humphrey stood pompous facing the Saviour.

Hear my bro', softly: "Funny thing it is, but though men talk and say mightier is the pen than the sword, time comes when they will no' be able to read your writings 'cept the edge o' the sword is there to point it to them. I am a-think o' the young King Richard standing on Smithfield Commons and listening at last as Wat Tyler and his poor come to London Town marching behind their sharpened pikes. I am thinking o' other times when the edge o' the sword has made holes in the castles o' the rich and leaked out some of the good things to the poor.

"'Member how even the rich barons one time took to the sword to pierce the deafness o' King John's ear? 'Member how it was no' until the Americans took to their long muskets that the English knew that their cries o' 'Injustice!' came from the heart and no' from the mouth? I know that representative government is a-leave us. Common talk it is now that at the next session, Governor Eyre will ask for Crown government. But yet still I am thinking that even if the little is taken from us, time will show that St. Thomas people did no' die in vain. That the shells 'fore Custos Aldenburg's courthouse were a-talk of a new day. Say that good has come o' this march.

"How so? Representative government will come back to our island one day, one day. And mark me, Your Honours, there will be no *buckras* making the laws then, but the said poor like whom they have killed, and a Governor of the people will be sitting in St. Jago. For we will ha' learnt that sympathy for the poor must come from the poor. Then who can say that time that St. Thomas people died in vain?"

Softly Davie's voice has finished talking to the Queen's men. Easy-easy his voice goes down till at the last it was like he was talking to Davie. *That they did no' die in vain.* Say that Father and Manuel will see God's face, even though I hear the Anglican pastors would no' pray over them because they were no' obedient servants.

My bro' looked back at the Commissioners. Then he is

bowing and walking back to where I am sitting, and people are talking to one another again.

When will the Usher burst into blood?

CHAPTER 7

Today, Saturday, we will go into Kingston to see our brethren and to bring back Miss Lucille. After that my bro' says we will go back to Salt Savannah Cay, for he has something on his mind. I wonder if our brethren will go back with us, and I wonder if Miss Lucille will like to go back.

Of late there has been much talk between Davie and Doctor Creary. Since the Commissioners saw him my bro' and the doctor ha' been often closeted with many different people. First it was the Methodist minister, Reverend Mr. Logan. Pleased were Mr. Logan and Doctor Creary when they came out of the hall to the veranda where I sat; but serious is on my bro's face, like say he is on Plantain Garden River and Hobbs's redcoats are a-form line on t'other side.

Then there were meetings with a Caymanian sea captain and many Morant fishermen, who talked enough-plenty with my bro'. Many letters have Doctor Creary written to Kingston, and once there was a fat lawyerman who came down on the stage, whom I did no' like. He gave me something to smell which made me sneeze while he laughed until his belly creaked up and down.

But yesterday a constable brought a letter to the doctor, and afterwards Davie said we will go into Kingston today.

We left early in the stage, and now the sun has reached manhood and we are rocking and rolling on the Windward Road past Rock Fort. We ha' passed the fishermen's huts, and I can no' sit still but must get up beside the driver and look hard forward for the first glimpse of the town, which Davie says can put Morant Bay in its pocket and you would no' see Morant Bay longer. Must be a big town, this, I am thinking.

We roll past the Pens east o' the town and presently are at the edge, by the lunatic asylum. We stop by the trough, and Davie says we will freshen up here. I scrub my face clean and put on a clean *osnaburg* shirt. My bro' scrubbed too, then he took out Father's Prince Albert. When he is finished with the buttons it is my father with years off his face who is standing before me. Brown and beautiful is my bro' and the sun on his hair and his face like a smooth, shining rock.

What a way life busy in this town, though! Never knew me that so many carriages could gallop among so many people and not run over them. My eyes can no' follow all the sights o' Punch and Judy shows, handless man playing the mandolin with his toes, the *John Canoe dancers* in their tall feathers, the feetless man dancing on his fingers for penny a time. My ears can no' hear all at once the ringing o' Herring Jews' bells as they show us the little herrings in their beds o' coarse salt, the roar and rattle o' lumber wains and two-wheeled buggies, the cries o' street sellers: *Buy your white yam!... Buy your Lucea yam!... Yellow-heart breadfruit!... Hard boiling sweet potatoes!...*

All I can do is open my mouth and turn my head round and round like poor German at Morant Bay Fair.

Howsoever, we leave the town and go into quiet roads again towards where the mountains go high into the sky. Presently we turn from the main road into a drive 'tween tall cabbage palms, until a bend in the drive shows us the house.

Is a fine house, this. Long and low it is, with many jalousie windows and deep verandas where cool-shady makes a man want to go in out of sun-hot. The driver pulls up sharp before the steps so the wheel must drag in the gravel, and same time his foot is hard on the gong. I am waiting to see Naomi's face when she sees how like Custos in his carriage I am.

Davie says I should get down.

"Johnny! Johnny! Johnny come home!"

Nobody has to tell me is Naomi, this, and I jump to the ground quick before she can tumble me over the way she hugs me tight. I get her arms from my neck and say grave like Father: "God be, Naomi."

She looks at me awhile, then laugh is shaking her all over and her arms are on my neck again and she is calling:

"Boastie Johnny come home! Johnny come home!"

Very well then. So our brethren hear her, Ruthie and Zekiel, and they are rushing from the house and there is much hugging and kissing and Ruthie crying.

I am wondering how Ruthie is no' fat in the belly. I will ask Naomi.

Miss Lucille did no' return from downtown until late in the afternoon. Meantime I ha' had my talk with Naomi and hear how Ruthie lost her belly because of the trouble she had seen in Baptism Valley. Naomi rolls her mouse-mouse eyes and says although Ruthie was sick to death, is a good thing that she has lost the belly, for she would have birthed a bastard.

Of Sammy she can no' tell much, since he is a Queen's Boy and they will no' see him until his six months in barrack is ended.

When Miss Lucille returned, surprise was on her.

"But – why didn't you write to say you were coming today?"

Beautiful was my bro's woman, beautiful as June midnight is beautiful, white stars and velvet darkness in her muslin frock.

Davie said: "I did no' think it necessary since we did no' intend to stay at all."

"Not intend to stay? What do you mean, Davie?"

"I am a-think we could start for Morant Bay this evening. Travel in the cool o' the night would be no' fatiguing for you."

Miss Lucille looked on him for a while without talk, then she laughed a little and walked over to a table, where she turned to face Davie.

"Really, you will at least stay the night. Surely you – where is the doctor?"

"He has no' come, he waits for us at the Bay."

My bro' took out a letter from his pocket and held it to Miss Lucille. She walked over to him and took the letter, her eyes on him. After that, jump, I nearly jump from my skin. For a little cry has come from her, and there she is in my bro's arms kissing him 'fore all our eyes.

Afterwards Naomi and me find the letter, and there is much spelling out of words as we read that Davie has got a full pardon and is to take Miss Lucille back to Morant Bay, where they will be married by Mr. Logan. And no' only that, but my bro' has got a lease on Salt Savannah Cay, where he will collect guano and booby eggs to ship to Jamaica. A big man is my bro' now, says Doctor Creary in his letter to Miss Lucille.

That night Naomi shows me how we must no' go into the dining hall before a bell rings, for they will ha' company to dinner tonight.

Dazzling it is to my eyes. White cloth and candlelight, beautiful dresses of the women, and light gleaming on the men's stiff shirts, six guests. I am glad that the buttons on Davie's coat are shining more than anything else.

Shake hands, I shake hands with His Honour Judge MacGillivray and Mrs. MacGillivray, Mr. and Mrs. Stenford-Taylor, Mr. Moody, and Miss Patricia Lovell... I am a nice boy, and how I favour my bro'!...

My bro' is very handsome in his Prince Albert coat, and what did he think of those nasty rebels?... Is it true that the rascal Gordon confessed?... Governor Eyre acted with promptness and must be commended... Did those devils want to make a Haiti of us?...

"I hear that Mr. Eyre will ask the House to vote for a Crown colony."

"And he will get it sure."

"Good thing hadn't yet got the vote, otherwise they would have packed the House with others of their ilk, and perhaps Mr. Eyre wouldn't have had this support."

"Never again must we allow the Gordons to get power into their hands."

"Crown government is the only government for these irresponsible fools who want to change God's order of things."

"Those hurry-come-ups who forget their origin!"

"You look very distinguished in your Prince Albert, Mr. Campbell."

"Rather."

Leave my bro' Davie alone, you! Think I do no' know that you laugh at his dress?

"Are you not feeling well, Johnny?"

"Well, me, Miss Lucille."

Stand steady, Johnny, says my bro's eyes.

Voting for Crown colony. I am no' too young to know. Enough-plenty talks I have had with my bro', and he knows all our island's history.

"Do you people know that Gordon was a bankrupt and a – er – bit of a rake?"

"No – ! Do tell! Really?"

"His Cherry Gardens property was mortgaged to the hilt –"

"*Perhaps he used the money to pay off the mortgage on his spendthrift English father's house!*" says my bro' as he speaks for the first time.

Tell them, Davie. Leave my bro', Miss Lucille, make him talk.

"But – I say! Really, sir, do you believe that canard?"

"Prove, the records will prove it. And while t'other rich men laughed, Mr. Gordon helped the poor, too."

Quietness, then little laugh.

"Perhaps Mr. Campbell was one of the rebels!"

"Ha, ha, good Lord – no."

"*I was. Marched, I marched and killed too.*"

"Oh, Davie! What are you saying!"

"*Stand good, Lucille. Marched, I marched, gentlemen, and killed too.*"

Davie O! Tell them.

"Really – I say – ! This has gone far enough already."

"Oh, Davie – *please!*"

Leave him, Miss Lucille. White is his face, a smooth rock in the moonlight...

All right, Miss Lucille. My bro' has looked on your face and seen sorrow there. He will no' hurt you more this night.

You red-faced back-draw bulls and your stringy cows! You do no' dazzle me longer! My bro' is a man what marched with Bogle and who told the Queen's Commissioners. He has walked the deep Blue Mountains like a ghost, and you could no' tell him from the trees. His own self, he has sailed out from the Bay and brought up on the Morant Cays. Think say you could be like him?

Is the man for the glory, he!

Next morning we are off for Morant Bay, Davie and Miss Lucille and me.

CHAPTER 8

When we returned to Salt Savannah Cay my bro' and Lucille were man and wife. When we returned to the Cay it was no' like how we went first time. This time we ha' travelled in a schooner, and six Morant Bay men are bowing to Miss Lucille and calling my bro' "Mister Davie". The men are guano-pickers.

Doctor Creary has given my bro' what he calls a stake. Carpenter's tools and cloths are there in the hold of the schooner. There are seeds for planting, and pigs and goats for rearing; moreover, we will no' ha' to turn the soil with sun-baked coconut boughs since there are many hoes and forks.

Doctor Creary has even given Miss Lucille primers and higher schoolbooks, for he says she must see that I do no' grow up into a savage.

But 'fore we sailed from the Bay I heard my bro' with finish in his voice tell Doctor Creary he would pay back all o' this.

Davie was first ashore from the schooner. That night, when the schooner had filled sails for Jamaica and the guano-pickers were singing low around the mosquito fires and Lucille dozed away her tiredness and bedtime had come for me, I heard my bro' praying by himself for the first time. Like Father's was his voice; certain sure in his prayers that Big Master God was a-listen to him.

I would rather be a doorkeeper in the House of the Lord than to dwell in the tents of the ungodly.

Lonely it is on the Cay at night. The wind talks to the reeds o' journeys over miles o' empty waters where even the sails of a dirty seine-canoe would be welcomed to stop and gossip to. The moon comes up out of the sea, looks on us awhile. There is no mountain on which he can sit, so he drops to the sea again. Men only sleep here 'cause a schooner came today.

CHAPTER 9

I will no' worry you with the tears of many years. Neither say with the laughter. We ha' walked well with the years, and truly to God none o' us on Salt Savannah Cay could say our pots ha' no' been well filled and without thorns. We ha' prospered well on Davie's plans, and bareness has left the land.

Coconut trees now go with even steps all around the beach, breadfruits cast shady all around the swamp-bottom; and moreover, there are no more swamp-bottoms, for all the reeds have been taken out, and now bananas, peas, cane, and potatoes flourish in the black, rich earth.

And me, John Campbell, in my seventeenth year, feel nothing of loneliness in my days or nights, for there are now thirty souls on the Cay.

Sawn lumber rises around each family, roofed with thatch bound deep and strong. Near the west beach the sand has been packed hard and firm around a real pitch made of Morant Clay brought to us by schooner, and here every Saturday there is cricket. Soon to go up will be a chapel.

Of the thirty souls on the Cay now, one is the seed of Davie and Lucille, James Creary Campbell. James is by Davie out o' the Book, and Creary Miss Lucille will have for the doctor.

Thirty here now, and if Davie had not studied his head well, there would have been more than thirty. For when in 'Seventy some of our pickers went back to Morant with the guano boat and told of the things we had done on the Cay, many families would have left the mainland to come and live with us. For here on Salt Savannah we have prospered, and hunger do no' ride us with white bridles.

Another of the thirty is my friend Timothy. Glad I was when Davie, on the power of his lease, wrote Doctor Creary that he could take another dozen Morant people and that Timothy should be one. Howsoever, when the schooner came back there were more than a dozen, for some of the men brought their families.

"Davie – look!" Lucille had cried when the schooner came,

231

"they have brought their wives and children! How can we feed them all? What shall we do?"

"Is well they have, Lucille. Stay, they will stay. Howsoever it goes, the Lord will ha' mercy. 'Lift up thine eyes round about and behold all these gather together.'"

Much does my bro' goes to the Book today-days, and I am thinking my father is alive in him.

That same evening after the schooner went back, Davie called all together in the yard before our house. 'Member, I remember he wore the Prince Albert that evening and Lucille must stand by beside him. 'Member, I remember that from that day my bro' did no' smile much to my eyes. Old and with his hands to the plough was my bro' from that day.

"Is a new land, this, you ha' come to, Morant men," he said, "where what you get for your bellies shall be no' gauged by the colour o' your skin or the weight o' your pocket. Work, we must work for what we must eat."

Timothy is madding to tell me of Morant, but I must listen good to Davie, for different is he this day.

"A new land, this, where only Mas'r God is king. It is perhaps no' known to you that this Cay is no' owned by the Queen, although her governor in Jamaica has since 'Sixty-three been granting leases for guano rights. So, till it is taken over by the Queen, Zion it will be to us. The Sixty-fifth Psalm tells us: 'Praise waiteth for thee, O God, in Zion and unto thee shall the vow be performed.'

"To Zion I bid you welcome. What is for one is for all."

Morant people sang a hymn in long metre while my bro's eyes spoke with the mosquito fire; but I am wondering why Miss Lucille stares at him with nothing in her eyes.

Timothy must talk of Morant Bay. Hear, I hear how Eyre was taken to England and that soon he will be tried before the Queen's judges on a charge of murder. How officers o' the regiment ha' been recalled, and that Ramsey and Hobbs have died by their own hands. He tells me too that the House of Assembly has been broken up and the Constitution taken away, and that the Queen is a-rule from London town.

What a way things began when Timothy's father sounded his drum at Courthouse Square!

CHAPTER 10

Davie has got new plans for our fatness. From American sailors on ships which sometimes come for our guano we ha' heard that bananas are now being carried by fast clippers for sale in America. We ha' heard o' the large prices, and how say many northside-coast people are building great stone houses and ride in rubber-wheeled carriages. Green gold, now, they call the bananas.

My bro' says we will grow bananas in our rich bottom lands so from sun-up to night our forks talk deep with the rich earth as we strive to make our first crop before the October rains. We have found a ship's captain who will take our crop altogether. Captain Adam Grantley is his name; young, and with face that does no' talk 'less he wants it to. Something like Davie is Captain Adam, like Davie before laughter went from him.

We acquainted him not long ago when one day he put into the Cay for water. A tramp schooner, does he call his boat, but we know that Captain Adam is no tramp. While he waited for repairs to his schooner we had many night-time talks with him, and learnt that cruising around the south seas for jobs is more sport than work for him. Rich American *buckra* son is he, and only love for blue water has taken him from his home in Newport.

For ten days he lay with us, and many books came off his schooner for Miss Lucille. I think he could ha' left before, for barnacles had no' fouled the bottoms much; but I believe that like Davie he is loving Salt Savannah Cay. When he was ready to sail he had arranged with my bro' to take our egg crop in May to Jamaica at much lower rates than the Morant schooners. Such a way he was our friend.

Is the year it, 'Seventy-four, and all January to March we ha' been planting our acres in *banana suckers*. We still gather guano, but much of it we have been using for our own planting. Very little are we in the house during daylight, for we must hurry with the planting since March will soon be here. March will bring the booby birds, blackening the sky as they fly in wing to wing, and men will be quiet for weeks while the boobies cover the sand with their speckled eggs. Middle April we will begin a-gather them for shipping to Jamaica by Captain Adam.

We ha' laboured hard in the field. From day-cloud to dusk we ha' forked our long furrows and covered them well with the guano manure. First time Davie had said he and me would do the overseeing, for we must see that no man idles in Zion. But one evening, when we sat still with tiredness and listened to Morant men singing deep hymns, my bro' took his eyes from the fire and turned to me.

"Johnny O, we will no' have to drive them," he said. "The Lord has taken hold of their hands, and idleness can no' come to them."

Is true it. Never have I seen such labour in men. Not even in gone days when Father would ride past the planters in Mr. Gordon's fields, and that time they would bend double to the ground with labour, for the headman was a-pass. No headman rode Salt Savannah, yet the furrows grew longer with faster speed across our bottom lands. By the time the north wind had ceased with February, and March came quarrelling from the south-east, our land was ready for the *banana suckers*.

All days and part nights we planted our *suckers*, for we must be finished soon since men must be quiet when the birds come.

Then one evening we stood on the edge of the land, and all the way ahead, row on row, young bananas marched line and line down the moist earth.

"Only to weed bad grass and watch them grow, John," said my bro'. "Come autumn we will load the American schooner with stems and stems."

Next morning booby birds began coming to us.

Wings beating on wings. Cry on tearing cry. Ten thousand grey-white messengers are coming down from heaven heavy with speckled manna in their wombs.

We see them coming in from over the sea, flying face into the dawn. We stand at the edge of the Cay where the houses are and watch them wheel in, quartering the land while they search for nest-spots to lay the manna they ha' brought. For two weeks more they will be coming wheeling in heavy from their spring mating.

All of us stay at one end of the Cay. For six weeks we will leave the land to them, so they can lay their manna in peace. With May they will rise and go in lightness, leaving their gifts in the sand.

Then will come the schooner, and our people will gather the eggs for market in Jamaica. Davie has planned that this crop will build our schoolhouse and bring a teacher from Jamaica. It is no' like first times, when Lucille had only me to teach. Enough-plenty children are on the Cay now, and there is their own James Creary.

So with quietness we live during the laying season. Only in threes and fours do we go into the field to see that the rows are weeded and that the yam-sticks ha' no' fallen. But there is no idleness, for there is much to do around the houses, where tomatoes and okras and calaloo serve our tables with greens. My bro' has planned that there must be no bare spots on the Cay, 'cept where the birds lay. But he will ha' no flowers.

"No flowers on Zion," says my bro'. "God's earth is given to man for his food. Flowers are planted in idleness, grown for devil's garland."

I too ha' read the Book, and am a-think that the thorns around Mas'r Jesus' head must ha' come from a flowering plant.

But, "No idleness in Zion," my bro' says.

CHAPTER 11

Last day in April we began a-gather the eggs. Is a fine crop, this. Davie has marked off places on the Cay where no eggs will be taken from, for there must be young ones to mount with the elders when they fly again. We gather fast since we must be on time for Captain Adam's schooner.

Howsoever, the wind must ha' been full behind him, for we were no' quite finished when one morning at prayer meeting we saw his masts standing off the shore.

Sprucey in white was Captain Adam as he stepped from his boat to the beach. Sprucey he was, so that all of a sudden we are looking on one another and seeing how thready our *osnaburgs* are. All 'cept Davie, who is a-hold out his hand to Captain Adam.

"How the morning, Captain Adam Grantley? Wind must ha' talked sharp to you all the way," said Davie as they shook hands.

"Fine passage, Mr. Campbell," says Captain Adam. "Good crop, I hope."

"*Aie* – the Master has been good to Zion," my bro' said with gravity.

Just a little does Captain Adam raise one eyebrow, and then he is bowing to Miss Lucille as they meet up.

"Morning, Mrs. Campbell. Seems we are a bit early for you all, but we ran all the way before favourable winds."

"Well, you know, it's an ill wind and all that," said Miss Lucille with laugh in her voice.

"It certainly blew me to some good," Captain Adam said.

"You should no' be held up for more than two, three days," said Davie.

"I can use those days. *Lady High Water* has been fretting in her sticks at those winds these last few days. Sure, she could stand some going over."

"We will get to work right away, right away, Captain. Zion is yours and your crew's," answered my bro'.

So our people are trotting back and forth, fast-fast, with basket loads of eggs to the beach. Meanwhile the sailors are tightening up on the schooner, and Captain Adam is showing Miss Lucille the new books he has brought. Good it is to me to hear her laugh when he showed her the new fashions he has brought in the books from America and she tells him *osnaburgs* were no' made for fashions.

Once she used to laugh like that for Davie, but of late there has been no laugh on Davie's face and his voice is like Father's when he reads from the Book.

Captain Adam brought a present too for Davie, but although my bro' took it with *thankie*, when we were out on the sands I saw him toss the bottle of old brandy to a rock, where it broke.

"We will no' have that devil's broth in this place," he said.

236

'Member, I remember Davie when he used to return from boar-hunt with Father and stop for many hours at Miss Martha's Cotton Tree. Soon, high he would be, until afterwards pepper-pot brings him back to earth. But how my bro' has changed!

At the end o' the third day we have got the last basketful inside the holds. That night Davie penned his consignment to the Morant agent, acquainting him that Captain Adam must be paid from it since we ha' no cash on Salt Savannah.

When he had finished he stood up beside the Captain, and nobody has to tell me that brothers they could be, 'cept that laughter is no' living in my bro's face any more.

"God be, Captain Adam Grantley. October, please God, my bananas will be ready."

Next day Captain Adam went with the early wind.

CHAPTER 12

I will no' bother you with the tears or laughter o' many days. We ha' prospered. Our chapel and school ha' gone up, and every Sunday-day Davie goes to the pulpit and tells us o' the Zion above.

Since the lady teacher came out from Jamaica, Miss Lucille has no' had to take classes again, but I do no' know if this is good; for there have been times when I ha' seen her on the beach standing with nothing in her eyes.

Lucille is no' an idle hand. It could no' be good that she sits on the beach with a fashion book on her knees and nothing in her eyes.

One day it was like this. With Timothy I was on the beach looking for a place where we could build a pool for the children to bathe without fear o' sharks. We came on Lucille. My mind spoke to me, and I sent on Timothy, telling him we would talk it over later. I sat down by her and watched the sea with her. By-and-by, since nothing came from her, I spoke.

"August, and no rain, Lucille," I said. Since I was a grown man she had become "Lucille" to me.

Beautiful she was. No' even the *osnaburg*, which all of us now wear, could take what was hers from her. Her dark eyes did no' turn to me at once. I watched the sadness on her face, waiting for her to speak.

"Johnny, it shouldn't be like this. Remember once I called it a picnic island? How long ago was that?"

I could hear our people singing in the field. *Pickney* shouts came to us from the cricket pitch.

"Happiness is still here, Lucille. A picnic island it still is."

With that she turned to me, light a-glimmer underneath the dark surface o' her eyes.

"Oh, Johnny – surely you understand! These poor people have never known better – there is food in plenty – security for they and their children – they will not ask for more; but surely – you know there is something missing – something that's out there – something we've left behind!"

Her palm, flat out, waved Jamaica way.

"Eight I was when we came to Salt Savannah Cay, Lucille," I told her.

For a time she did no' answer, only her eyes stood steady on my face.

Then hear her: "I see. But I wasn't eight when I came here. I came here a woman, with the man I loved to make my life with him – to make life, not living death. To work, to fight, but yes – to live and love and laugh also. He wanted to work and fight, and I have done so because he wanted to. But has he given me what I wanted, Johnny? Has your bro'?"

Now, God o' me! Know, I know what Lucille means, but I can no' say that my bro' has changed and he would have us all live in his drought with him.

"It is his way, Lucille, and he is your husband," I said.

Lucille said with aloes: "He is not my husband. He is my overseer. No flowers. No singing except old hymns. No books, except the Bible and *Pilgrim's Progress*. Do you know that last night he more than hinted that I should destroy the books which Captain Grantley brought me? And do you think I do not know that he must have destroyed that bottle of brandy?"

Davie O! Is no' needful, this?

"Last night I suggested that he send to Jamaica for some bright prints to make dresses for the children instead of this –" she laughed without steadiness and touched her *osnaburg* "– this thing we all now wear. It was then he looked at the fashion books on the table and said something about 'spoils from the camps of the unrighteous,' speaking in that horrible Bible-quoting manner he has adopted. I could not trust myself to answer. Oh, Johnny, what has happened to Davie?"

There is the weep of a lost *kling-kling* in Lucille's voice. Her eyes are searching my face for answer, but how can I tell her that before times he could no' stand being governed, and yet now he is up in the saddle and is riding us all the way he wants to go? Yet I must answer. My bro' has got his two hands to the plough and has taken to the Book while he waits for time to be full. Time, we must give him time to forget what 'Sixty-five did to him. I must speak o' things what ha' lately grown in my mind.

"Lucille, when Bro' Davie went before the Queen's men at Morant Bay, he never made fun to tell them how our people did no' have a level road to walk upon. The Queen's Commissioners heard how our people had thrift in them, 'cause out o' their ninepence a day they bought lands and grew crops. How only drought and poor lands made hunger ride them for these years. Believe, I believe the Commissioners did no' believe him. Afterwards we came to Salt Savannah Cay, and –"

"You mean Zion," she said with a laugh that was no' a laugh.

"Zion then. Good it is if a Zion it could be, Lucille. We came here, and Davie planned that we will build a place to show the *buckra* English that we people are no' benighted. Is the work that he is doing."

Lucille's voice is low, but something grates at the bottom of it.

"But does the end justify the means? Must we walk to Zion in a strait jacket? Then he and I will come to the Pearly Gates wearing fixed frowns and osnaburg wings! Oh, Johnny – don't make me blaspheme! You know as well as I do that everything is not right here. Do you think any of us are happier than Ruth? or Zekiel? or Sammy? or Naomi? Can you see Naomi being unhappy because she laughs and wears a satin petticoat? Would you be unhappy because you wore broadcloth and went to an occasional ball in Kingston? Johnny, Davie has gone crazy with an obsession and would like us all to go the same way!"

"He will no' be like this for ever and ever, Lucille. It is no' his nature. It is like he is building an Ark and must hold himself to put in so many nails a day, no' mindful of the feasting and dancing around."

Lucille got up from the beach. The book fell from her lap to the ground, and a lady in a pretty dress and carrying a parasol smiled up at me from the sand.

"Johnny, your brother is building a Tower of Babel. By the time he is finished we might not speak the same tongue!"

I watched her walk away, and the tears I had heard in her voice was come to my eyes.

CHAPTER 13

When early October came with no rain it did no' bother us much at all, at all. For, long full grown were our bananas, and great bunches hung to the ground, round and glistening in the sun.

I walked through the fields with Davie one mid-October day. Down the long rows we walked in the shady of the broad leaves, and there was depth in my bro's voice as he talked o' the things this crop would do.

"Captain Adam Grantley can come any time now, Johnny. Ready, we are ready to cut."

"Good is this, bro'," I told him.

Davie has planned our planting well. Over in the next three-acre we can hear our people singing as their forks bite deep into the soft bottom where they are turning it up to the sun. Seven days it will look up at the sun, gathering strength before the mating with the seeds. Seven days, and then the long beds o' furrows will begin a-wind over its length. By the time the autumn rains ha' watered the land young shoots will be waving in the wind. No idleness in Zion for man or his land.

"Davie, after we ha' reaped I want to go to Jamaica."

"The mainland? Why so, Johnny?"

"A few things to get, bro'. Good if you would ask Lucille to go with me too."

Davie stopped walking to stand and stare at me. There was puzzlement on him.

"Lucille? To go to Jamaica?"

"She can help me get the things I want. 'Twill be a good holiday for her too."

I would no' say my bro's face was harsh. There was just graveness like my father's when he spoke to us of evil.

"Would no' be right that, John, you know? We ha' come here to live our lives, to work this Zion. None o' us are thinking of holidays. Holidays are devil-*buckra*'s arrangements for drunkenness and carousing. We do no' want that; we must find our happiness in work and fastings."

"But work and fastings alone can no' bring happiness to everybody?"

He did no' answer for a while; then he nodded his head towards the three-acre where the men sang in the fields.

"Would say you that these are no' happy?"

"I was no' speaking of they," I told him.

"Then –"

He did not finish, stopped all of a sudden. I said nothing either.

"What things you want to get from Jamaica, John?" he asked.

"Lucille will know what to get, Davie."

I saw stiffness quiet his body. He spoke with edge to his voice:

"Lucille has been a-talk with you? Is it of pretty clothes and ornaments you speak? For so then I will no' countenance it!"

"Davie, you would no' have Lucille unhappy?"

"Is she unhappy? Say she told you so?"

So terrible is my bro's face that for a while I think he will fist me. I did no' want to cause him pain, for he is the Davie whom I still love. But too I love Lucille; Lucille, who has been my mother since I lost my mother at Baptism Valley; who has been mother and wife to Davie and has worn *osnaburg* for him. Young she was first time, and beautiful, and sadness never came to her. If loved my bro' loved her then because of what his eyes looked at, then how can he no' see that sadness has come to the beauty of her?

I could ha' told my bro' that nightingale will no' sing as sweet if bamboo *springe* has caught her feet. Say that night jasmine will no' scent as sweet in a vase as growing on a rock in the moonshine. Could ha' told my bro' these, 'cept there are things man does no' speak to man of until all is over. That time, then, too late it is.

"She has no' said so, Davie; but think, I am a-think it will do Lucille good to see old-time sights once more."

Davie took his hand to my shoulder; the anger had left his face.

"Not far from two-day *tweet-to-whit* you are yet, John. Lucille and me were big people when you could no' change your pantaloons. We ha' made our bed. Lucille is no' unhappy, but a woman she is, and women sometimes do not think straight. Soon she will come out of the dark passage and see the light."

I do no' know why I said it, but I remember it just came from my mouth:

"But suppose she does no' see *your* light, bro'?"

His hand left my shoulder, and his eyes went to long distance. When he spoke, it was Davie talking to Davie:

"What then? And if thine eye offend thee, pluck it out and cast it from thee."

No rain came with October. Every morning the sun came out o' the sea with noontime heat, quailing the land. We looked at distance with squint in our eyes, and men did no' walk fast longer, but were glad to stop under shady trees every time they could stop. Every morning we went into the sea, but it did not help much at all, for no sooner do we come up out of the sea, sweat-water run down from our armpits.

The bananas were ready for cutting any time Captain Adam came, but with little wind blowing from the sea we knew he could no' make fast passage. Howsoever, each sun-up we go to the beach and have look-out for his sail. If his vessel does no' come soon-soon, the fruits will get too ripe for shipping and we will ha' laboured in vain.

Anxious is every face 'cept Davie's. 'Member, I remember one morning at prayer meeting. Old Mr. Matt, who had come to us from the Cuna-Cuna, got up from the back o' Chapel and asked my bro' to pray for a wind which would bring Captain Adam to us. But my bro' held up his hand and shook his head.

"No' so, Bro' Matt," he said. "The Lord dwelleth in Zion and know our needs. Is no' needful that we should pray so."

Not like Pastor Humphrey, who used to pray for rain, will be my bro'.

But I am thinking Davie must ha' been right, for what should happen but next morning 'fore I could leave the house for the beach I heard shouts coming to me. Nobody had to tell me they had seen a sail, and quick I am galloping for the beach.

Far out, low on the water, we could see the speck o' white, and there was dancing and singing and everybody shouting: *Hosanna! Hosanna!*

Howsoever, presently there was quiet as Davie and Lucille came walking down. My bro' looked at the speck, which had grown but little bigger.

"We will no' begin cutting too quickly," he said. "We ha' to watch the wind till it gets better, for it would no' do to have our fruits in her holds and she can no' sail out because there is no breeze. But we will give thanks for this."

So all of us kneel on the beach while Davie prays our *thankie*.

CHAPTER 14

I will talk now o' heat, and stillness, and of a high wind.

There is heat coming from the sky and from the ground and sometimes like it comes from inside us. There is no talk among us. We lay on the ground under the trees and wave breadfruit leaves for breeze. Bad for us it is, but worse for the sailormen from Captain Adam's ship. Like butcher-dogs at Morant market before the scraps come off the hooks, so Captain Adam's men as they lay on the ground and pant for a wind.

There is stillness all around us. Leaves do no' talk among themselves o' things they ha' seen in the night-time. Gecko lizards do no' pad among the leaves watching us through their eyes without lids. We do no' see *water boatmen* rise to the surface of the pond for their little gasps o' air. No mourning songs come from pea-doves this day; not even a black-faced grass-quit looks at us this day.

A sailorman lying beside me yawned. Sweat-water runs down his face when the muscles smooth out in the yawn. The water went down his cheek, down his nose, dripped off the tip o' his nose.

"*Jesus Christ!*" said the sailorman.

Heat and stillness and breath drawing hard to our nostrils. Down on the beach I see Lucille going into the boat with Captain Adam. Captain Adam has asked her to see his schooner, which today is spick and span and does no' need any repair. Lucille had laughed and said she would go, for she has been longing to eat by silver and linen napkins. Davie did no' say anything, but his eyes did no' speak happiness at her words.

Nothing must be done about the cutting of the fruits till we see how the wind will be, said Davie, but now he has gone to walk among the bananas. Timothy and me and all the others do no' feel like walking today. We lay on the ground and would say *Jesus Christ* like the sailorman, but we can no' take the name of the Lord in Zion.

The sailormen side o' me wiped his nose again and got to his feet. He blasphemed about going aboard out of this oven. The other sailormen rose with him, and we watch them walking to the beach.

Is Old Mr. Matt it who starts it. Mr. Matt has been a Morant sailorman who has gone through the Windward Passage enough-plenty times on guano boats.

He sat up and squinted through the trees at the sky.

"It is no' good, this," he said.

Nobody gave him answer.

"Weather is a-come," he said again.

Timothy yawned and said: "Make it come."

Mr. Matt grunted. "I do no' speak of good weather. I mean breeze-blow?"

Breeze-blow. Mr. Matt has been through the Windward Passage and has seen many mango seasons. He does no' speak with young tongue. When he speaks o' breeze-blow he is talking about hurricane.

I sit up and make my eyes four with him.

"Why you say so, Mr. Matt?" I asked.

He looked up through the trees and pointed his finger. Up, up against the glare where man can no' look easy in daylight I see specks racing to the west.

"Birds are flying high, west. Is no good, this," said the old man.

The others are sitting up now looking up to the sky. Heat and stillness still press on us. I am a-think if breeze-blow comes, Salt Savannah bananas will no' reach America. My mind is on Davie among the bananas.

"Sure, you are sure?" I asked Old Mr. Matt.

"We can no' be sure till we see what our own birds do," he said.

"I ha' no' seen any birds since day-cloud," I told him.

"That is what I do no' like 'specially," he said.

One after another the others lay down again, but Mr. Matt rose to his feet.

"*Pickneys* are in the schoolhouse. Batten, I think we should be battening the schoolhouse," he said, looking at me.

Mr. Matt is an old sailorman; Davie is a-walk among the trees. I call to the men and tell them to help Mr. Matt batten the schoolhouse. I want to find Davie.

I found Davie in the banana-walk and told him of Old Mr. Matt. He looked around and up, nodded his head, and said we must go to the beach. We are walking to the beach when we saw the birds. From reeds and mangroves which we ha' left growing around the fields for wind-breakers, wings flap and beat as they roar up and point their beaks for the west.

No cries come from them. They march in silence, leaving out o' Zion before trouble can take them. Davie and me commence a-run.

Timothy has got the sharpest eye, so he must go to the top of our tallest tree and look out to the east. All others of us hammer at the windows and doors as we batten up all the houses.

We hear a shout from Timothy, and then he is sliding down the trunk.

"*Weather! Weather! Weather a-come!*" he is bawling.

Timothy has seen the line o' white far out to sea, and while he is telling us, even from the ground we can see great banks o' clouds sliding up the sky to us.

Weather! Weather! Hammers and nails and ropes and rock-stones! Batten up! Batten up!

Banks o' heavy, wet clouds sliding up the sky to us. Where is the wind? No wind? Then 'fraid, you are afraid of what? All the same – *batten up!*

Keep the children inside. Leave the outside world. This is no' our world...are sojourners, we...so everybody leave the out world...for here comes the wind now...

Sweet wind, light wind, a-ripple the sullen sea so he must laugh a little. 'Fraid, you are afraid to laugh, Big Sea?

Eh, but wait! Lucille – ? Lucille – ?

Lucille! Lucille O! Is where Lucille? Eh! Eh! Forgot, you ha' forgotten say that Lucille has gone on the sea? the gentle, laughing sea?

Lucille! Lucille O! We must go for Lucille!

But *Lady High Water* has lifted her skirts and is a-step daintily with the dancing sea. Many sailormen on the *Lady High Water* have been through the Passage often. They know why the sky is a-laugh and why clouds are sliding up the sky to them. So men are caressing the long, round arms of the *Lady*, wounding her white garments with heavy stays so she will no' burst them when the dance gets faster. One small jib to take her to the open so she will ha' more room for the dance... *Lucille O!*

"Come, John. The Lord will be with her there as well as here. We ha' work to do."

We ha' work to do. And weeping on the beach with the wind a-toss my hair in my eyes will no' have the work done. I look one time, no more, on Captain Adam's ship racing to sea on her single jib. Then I turned and followed my bro'.

The wind is no' gentle longer. Great fistfuls of it are pounding at my face, pounding at the tossing trees, a-pound on the battened windows and doors. The heavy black clouds have come over us and ha' brought dark night and rain.

Darkness, and sheets of water to wrap you from the darkness. You must feel your way through the darkness and listen for the crash that will mean a house or a tree is gone to the high wind. You must crawl your way on your hands and knees, for the high wind has come and man does no' rule the world longer.

I hear a crash and get up in the darkness to try to run where I heard the sound. But I am over and eating sand. Down on your hands and knees. Man! Stronger, you are stronger than a tree? Why, darkness and the winds o' God were on the earth from the first day, and the trees o' God were on the earth on the third day, and you, Man, did no' come until the last day before He tired and rested on the seventh. Then stronger than a tree you could be?

I crawl to where I had heard the crash and found it was a tree that had fallen. Now I can hear other sounds – voices o' people with fright on them shrieking and dirging in the blackness… tattered ends of voices of frightened people.

Trees are falling all around, awful sounds as their heavy roots come tearing out o' the earth. The first house went soon after, and I creep quickly towards it. I hear faintly Davie calling me. I answer, and we find each other in the darkness. We feel around and find the people who were in the house. Two o' them, a man and his wife, who will no' cry again. I can hear my bro' praying in the darkness.

When he was finished he shouted in my ear that we must get over to the schoolhouse. Most of our people ha' taken shelter in the schoolhouse, since it is the largest and strongest building. We crawl through the tossing world with trees and houses all around us going with the wind. Those who are alive and no' badly hurt we get them following close behind one another, a long snake o' humans grovelling along in the dark.

Most o' the night it continues. We have made the banana-walk with the homeless and ha' shown them how they must get down 'twixt the fallen banana trees and lay there. There the wind will no' blow them about, 'though there is no shelter from the flood above. Then Davie and me go back to the schoolhouse, where we lay in the rain and pray say it will no' fall.

Towards day-cloud the roof o' the schoolhouse went. We know the walls will not hold much longer 'cause the wind will now be battering them from the insides too. We got to a window in the lee and tore the battening away. We took some rope we had found and tied the children into a long chain. We tell the elders to follow on their hands and knees. Is so it when we begin the last crawl to the banana-walk.

Through the awful night we go, through flying branches and falling trunks…

Lord ha' mercy!…Lamb of God O!…Jesu, son o' David O!…through the night o' moanings and shriekings and the sudden quiet when a trunk falls on something soft.

We lost one *pickney*. Ten of the elders did no' reach the banana-walk. My bro' David was one o' the ten.

CHAPTER 15

When I found him breath had no' gone from his body yet. Day-cloud was peeping on his face through the tossing trees. My bro' was no' in much pain. The trunk that lay across his middle had done its work before we found him, now he was just waiting.

Strength came to me that I should lift the trunk, me one; but Old Mr. Matt and the others held to my arms and told me I would no' save him but only put more pain on him. When strength left me after I found I could no' fight them all, they made me kneel so I could cry on his face.

My bro' did no' die without looking at me. When we all believed he had gone, he opened his eyes and whispered with his throat like how the dying do when their lips die first.

"Wrong, I was wrong, Bro' Johnny," he said from his throat. "She should no' be caged on this Cay – tell her for me. *Osnaburg* is no' for her."

We prayed on the ground while the wind ran through the trees, then we sang a hymn. When we had sung it to finish, Old Matt looked close at him, then told us to sing on. So we started again at the beginning, and at the third verse Old Matt looked again and said we could move the tree now.

We brought up James Creary Campbell, Timothy and me, and he knew not his father or mother. For nothing more of Lucille had

I seen to this day since Captain Adam Grantley's ship ran before the storm eight years ago.

But now it is the year 1882, and I am asking the Queen's man for passage to Jamaica, that James Creary might know his mother.

CHAPTER 16

James Creary and me bring land at Kingston on the Queen's frigate before sun-hot has reached the town. Frightened is James at the people and the carts and the wagons and the great carriages on the cobbles, and truth to tell, no' comfortable is me either, for it's a long time since I ha' seen the habitation of so many men.

We leave the wharf and walk to Harbour Street, where I have been told we will find lodgings. I will no' go to seek Naomi and the others till I have found Lucille. I have no' told James Creary of this yet. I think I will see with my own eyes before I tell him of his mother.

Meantime I will tell of the *Lady High Water*. I will tell you of what I got in the letter which Lucille sent me a year after – poor Lucille, at whom in my young-head foolishness I cast the first stone.

I will no' beg pardon with excuses. But what I will say is that in the love I had for Davie hate would go from me towards anyone who seemed to hurt him. And in me young-head foolishness, when Lucille turned to me for the help she wanted and could no' get from her dead husband, I did no' give it to her. But, God be my judge, sorry, I ha' been sorry since then.

I will no' beg pardon with excuses, but I must tell what made me do so. When the blackness had left the world, the beauty of the Cay was no more. Gone were the coconut palms that waved in the breeze. Flat were the banana fields, where my bro' and his people had planted their faith in the new Zion. Homes, where we had laughed and cried and borned our young ones, were level with the sand. Desolation had come to us, and I did no' have the faith to make our flight-time be summer. I did no' have the faith, for much of my strength had been in Davie. My bro' Davie had taken all our strength unto himself; and even though sometimes his strength had no' been comfortable to me, still he had been my rock. Now we dug a hole and put him in the earth.

"I am the Resurrection and the Life..."

I did no' say the words clear. I waved one hand telling them to cover him. We covered two dozen that day.

I buried my strength and, clothed in weakness, cursed Lucille Dubois. For thought came to me that my bro' had no' been happy at the last. And moreover, she had no' been there to help him over the Bar, and though it was no' her fault, such was the weakness on me that time that for this too I cursed her name.

But I am telling of her letter.

Captain Adam Grantley's ship danced her wild dance for three nights and days with the hurricane of 'Seventy-four, and when the blackness had gone from the world there was no' anything left but the shell of her.

For four weeks men knew naught of her until one morning she rolled up on the beach in Oriente Province, Cuba. This letter I am talking about came from Havana to me at Salt Savannah Cay in November of 'Seventy-five. Lucille wrote me saying she could no' get home, for there was no money for passage, and that I should send for her. I put fire to the letter. I would ha' nothing with Captain Grantley's whore; for, if conscience was no' bothering her, why did she not write to Davie, whom she could not know was dead? Or why not to Doctor Creary, whom she could no' know had died also?

That was what I told myself and put away Lucille's responsibility.

Nothing of her came to my ears again until five years after. In 'Eighty Timothy went into Kingston with an egg-schooner. The day he returned he told me his eyes had made four with Lucille's in Kingston. She had been in satins and feathers, said Timothy, and did no' see him, for her eyes were for the tall ship's officer whom she walked with. Timothy was no' sure if it was Captain Adam Grantley.

It was partly because of this why Salt Savannah Cay became the Queen's land. For my people on the Cay, when they heard of this, said they would water no more American schooners. We had turned back two when a large boat came in with many crewmen. They had heard we would no' water the others and so came ready to draw blood. Only after much peace talk to the Caymen did I ha' them allow the Americans to water their ship. Yet all the same there were fights and some of my people were injured. So we petitioned the Governor at St. Jago telling him we could get no redress if American sailormen molested us, and begged that Her Majesty cover us with her flag.

Howsoever, my conscience will no' leave me in peace and now I have agreed with it to come and see with my own eyes if hogs are a-root in my dead bro's garden.

Timothy is a trickified fellow whom a pussy can no' catch asleep. 'Fore he left Kingston he had found out where Lucille was living. So then after I leave James Creary with the woman at the lodging-house it was no' hard for me to find the house in a narrow street leading off the waterfront on the edge o' town.

A large house it is, but many rainy seasons must ha' passed over it, for the banisters 'top the steps were leaning all about and the paint had peeled and hung like September leaves. All the windows were shut tight.

I went up to the gate, which was wide open. Knock, I knocked, but no voice answered. I walked in and went up the steps to the veranda. I had no need to knock then, for the door is flung open and a woman is smiling at me. Such a woman as I had no' seen in my born days.

All red and white, she. I can no' believe that a woman's mouth can be so red or her face so white; and even though she smiles, I want to run from her. Clothed in a silken dress, she is, and though I can see nothing of her but her hands and her head, yet it was like she was naked before me. There was laughter of men and women coming from behind her in the house, but the laughter was of people who had taken too much rum. Timothy is a trickified fellow, but I believe he has been tricked this time.

"Nice blond boy – what does nice blond boy want? Come inside, nice blond boy, and ha' your bellyful!"

Is a mistake, this, I am trying to tell the woman, but she is passing her hand through my hair and smiling while she talks. I can scent the rum on her.

"Make Madam take care o' you – plenty nice women here, sailorman!"

"I am no' a sailorman," I tell her with quickness, backing from the door. "I must ha' got the wrong address."

The smile on her face grew wider and she was poking her tongue at me while she reached for my arm.

"Eh! Madam has found a nice young planterman! Come to bed, nice blond boy! Madam will grind with you herself!"

"Is a mistake, this, I tell you! I am looking for somebody else!"

Our talk has brought people to the door. A man in the scarlet of the garrison with his arms around two girls, and all o' them are grinning at what is happening on the steps. I can no' get rid of the woman's hand 'cept I strike her.

"Who are you looking for?" she is asking me soft. "Won't Madam do for you? Is a good mare, this, what knows the distance!"

"I tell you I am looking for somebody else!" I shout at her, striking at her hand.

She left my arm alone but kept following me down the steps, talking.

"Nobody in town better than Madam, nice boy. Who ha' you heard about?"

I do no' know why I named a name, but I could no' run from the woman, and I must ha' done so to hide my shame at the soldier and his girls laughing at me.

"I am looking for Miss Lucille," I told her.

She stopped following and looked at me awhile before she burst into laughter.

"Nice blond boy taste her and liked her, eh? Ho! Ho! Ho! –" she threw back her head and hollered, "– Lucille! Cuba Lucille! Nice blond boy has come back for some more!"

I am walking away, glad to be free of her, when all of a sudden I realised what she had just shouted. Cuba Lucille! I stopped and looked back at her. Still laughing, she beckoned to me.

"Your fashion woman is inside, blond boy –" Then she is calling again: "– *Lucille Dubois!*"

Now I am no' saying I remember everything I did. Much o' that evening and what followed is a dark-night to my mind. But 'member, I remember going past the woman and up the steps and into the house.

I went into the house, and just inside the doorway my eyes made four with Lucille's coming towards me. How long we looked at each other without voice I do not remember. But after a while we spoke each other's name.

She took my hand and led me down a passage into a small room where there were no chairs so we sat on the bed. I do no' remember if she asked me, but I began telling her of the hurricane and Davie. Then she is telling me of the hurricane and Captain Grantley and Cuba. God see and knows the sorrow that came on me, for wronged, I had wronged Lucille.

We do no' cry. Crying is for penitents who can wash the page clean and start over again. I will tell o' what I learnt.

Is the year it 1874, and for six years now the Cubans are battling with Spain for their independence. My bro's wife in a useless vessel rolled up on the Cuban beach. She is one woman in a boatload of men. Second day of the hurricane Captain Grantley was killed by a falling mast, and now, with his knowledge of Spanish, he is no' here to tell war-mad Spanish soldiers that this lone woman in a boatload o' men is no' a wanton.

My brother did no' suffer much at all after the tree fell on him. By the time day-cloud came, quiet was he, just waiting on the Call. Eight years now Lucille has had this weight o' shame and day-cloud is no' in sight for her yet...

I tell you I do no' remember much of that evening. I must ha' walked from the house and down the lane to the waterfront; but the next I remember is that I am in a rum shop pouring white rum down my throat as fast as the barmaid could serve me.

Drunk I am now, and when a woman comes up beside me and say I should go to her room with her, my mind says right, I should go with the stranger. I put my body on a grindstone o' sorrow while she thought there was pleasure in it for me.

Before day comes I leave her bed and walk through the cool streets to my lodgings and James Creary. Fast asleep he is, with the corn hair spread on the pillow around the face that is Lucille's.

I went to my knees, begging that if tears will no' wash the page clean, then the Master might make me live for the seed o' two dead people.

CHAPTER 17

You ha' heard o' the fire o' 'Eighty-two? Forty acres o' the port o' Kingston burnt to the ground, and many dead and injured. From just after the sun reached manhood it started, and did no' die until the stars were many hours old. Terrible was that day, with the red flames racing in mighty leaps north from the waterfront, while rum-vats and gunpowder stores shook and rumbled. Then after it had reached the centre of the town and the sea-wind had died with evening, south it went again before the land wind, sweeping back to the sea.

I had lain down beside James Creary to sleep off the rum and tiredness. It must ha' been noon when I got up. The landlady had got James his victuals, and now he was a-play with her own son in the yard. A bath brought some sense once again to my head, and I was sitting to a bowl o' warm pepper-pot when a mighty thunder shook the house. Outside quick, me, and just in time to see flames rising to the sky a few streets away.

I got James Creary to my side and stood him there. Another thunder shook us a little, then all of a sudden there came shouts: *"Fire gone to the gunpowder stores! Run O! Run O!"*

Well then, I am a-run with James Creary in my arms. I gallop with hundreds of screaming people mixed with wagons, carts, carriages, horses, and mules; and meantime behind us rum-vats and gunpowder stores are flashing and rumbling. We do no' stop running until we have reached the open pens and fall panting on the grass.

From there we watch the town burn. Black is the world and we can no' tell when day goes and night comes. Surprise is on us when a man told his neighbour it was nine o'clock. At ten o'clock the flames, which had turned with the land wind, died in the sea.

Next day when we went back into the town I went to Lucille's house. Madam was there by the burnt rubble, which was all that was left. Drunk she was, but her face was no' red and white any more. I can no' recall what colour it was.

I went by her side and asked for Lucille. She peered out of squinted eyes at me, then she laughed, no' a good laugh.

"Is the pretty boy come back, eh? Is a eunuch, you? Cuba Lucille got drunk after you left 'cause you would no' cover her! Drunk all day, drunk all night – There she is, still drunk, eunuch boy!"

I saw her dirty fingers point at the rubble.

PART THREE

NOW then I am a-wind up this tale. I ha' talked enough-plenty already, and there can no' be very many hours left before the night goes into day. Yet still our people are a-sing out there – what a way they ha' brought fire and music to my soul tonight!

I can no' tell you everything that happened since 'Eighty-two. I can no' call everything back to mind, but howsoever, I will tell some of what happened to those o' our family who have no' been with me.

First of all, my bro' Sammy. Sammy has been a soldier of the Queen. No' only that. My bro' has been to England and marched before his Queen. 'Twas the Diamond Jubilee that was in 'Ninety-seven, and proud was I when in Kingston I saw my bro' in his blue and scarlet coming back from marching before his Queen. Sergeant Campbell, they called him then, but he was my Sammy, quick to talk with me o' the days when we were young. Since then he has stopped marching and is tending his farm in St. Catherine's parish.

There is a mast outside his doorway, where every morning with sun-up the Jack is hoisted to the head. That time my bro' is a ramrod, and there is salute from him. Born was my bro' to soldiering and he will no' die without it.

With him is my bro' Zekiel, who has grown little stronger with the years. Zekiel has been married to a Cuban lady and has had a daughter. But no' happy was Zekiel in his marriage, for he was no' born with the cut of a leader-bull. Years ha' passed now since his Cuban wife went back home, taking her daughter with her. Now Zekiel lives at Sammy's tend, for never a wife did my bro' Sammy take.

But Ruthie and Naomi? Eh! Well matched ha' been my two sisters, with heavy litter a-crowd the skirts of the eldest, Ruthie. Ruthie is the wife of an English soldierman who went to help the English fight the Dutch in the second Boer War. Like many o' the regiment, after Vereeniging, he sent for his wife and settled to farm in the Transvaal and has been there ever since. Sometimes-sometimes I hear from Ruthie, and know that she has got a round dozen of her own and many grands.

Then now, my little mouse-mouse Naomi. Eh! A lady o' fashion is she, with a great house in Kingston. A good marriage Naomi has made to a sugar-wharf owner in Kingston, and when he died, all his wealth went to her. And though there is no want o' kindness in her, boastie is my sis Naomi when I go to Kingston to stay with her.

I am a-think there is nothing nicer to her than to order the motor which will drive us for cool breezes in the hills. Noisy and no' nice-smelling it is, but there is pride in her as she sits straight up in the back seat with her broad pink hat fluttering in the wind.

All the same now and then I feel her fingers pinching my hand under the shawl, and when I look at her there is merriment in her eyes, which ha' no' changed though wrinkles ha' come to her. None of seed has Naomi got, but there is content in the merriment of her eyes.

Bible-livers, we Campbells had always been, 'cept for Father and Manuel, and even sickly Zekiel has managed to stay with us for over his three score and ten. It is to Naomi that I talk much o' Son-Son, who is Garth. Twelve is he now, with tallness and strength too much for his years, with nothing o' fear in his eyes. He has been through the schools, and Naomi and me are a-talk of England. For a lawyer we say Garth should be.

I ha' no' told you of Garth? Eh, I am running too fast. Well, James Creary has given us a seed, who is Garth on his age-paper, but Son-Son to me. Howsoever, I will tell you o' him.

CHAPTER 1

It is the year 1925. I ha' prospered. Mas'r God has opened his storehouse to me, and no thorns are covering the bottom o' my pot. Three ships o' the Davie Line do the trade to Boston with bananas from our acres in Yallahs Valley. The sugar and rum from the Campbell Estates bring wages to hundreds o' St. Thomas men. For true we ha' prospered.

A long time now since I ha' had done with Salt Savannah Cay. 'Twas after the quake o' 1907, when God shook his earth and took a thousand souls. No man died on our Cay, but the quake sent back a goodly portion o' growing land into the sea, and we were no' sure that the rest wouldn't go back some time soon and take all o' us with it. For in that month o' January when all of Kingston was shaken flat, no less than thirty times ha' we felt the earth groaning under us.

So fright came on our people, and one day we hauled from the Cay, lock, stock, and barrel. All of us sailed back to Jamaica, only leaving Davie and others who will no' watch day-cloud break again. Our people were no' sorry to go, and I will tell why later.

Long swells marching easy up the white sands o' the beach, the wind pulling at the uncombed heads o' our standing coconut trees, the cries o' booby birds, and the scent o' mangrove roots at low tide – all these I am leaving without much water coming to my eyes, even though forty of my fifty years were lived there. For, truth to tell, goodness I did no' see in them longer, since I ha' known so many sorrows there.

I went back to Salt Savannah, Morant Bay, with James Creary. There we will no' dwell longer either, but while we are looking around for new lands, in the old house o' my family I will stay. Funny to hear me telling James Creary o' the things what happened here, and to see him listen without much in his eyes – this seed o' Davie who has grown man now without knowing his father or his mother and what mighty happenings brought his conception.

History o' our people brings nothing to James Creary's eyes. Two high-bred colts ha' mated and brought a good cart-horse.

Do no' misunderstand me. Love, I love James Creary. But still yet sometimes I ha' wondered: how comes this offspring o' Davie and Lucille whose eyes do no' light when he hears of Mr. Abram and forty for forty?

Tired of me he is sometimes, I know, when I talk o' the things past and gone. But one thing I can say: a good businessman James Creary is, for look what he did with our Cay?

When he came of age to manage with me, first thing he did was to put our men on wages.

"Times ha' changed, Uncle John," he said. "We will not keep a nursing-home for destitute gentle people. A business we will run."

My heart was no' with the Cay, so it was no' hard for me to pass the traces to him. Very well then. James Creary does business.

So many rows hoed, so many squares planted, so many roots o' banana manured – into his black book is an entry gone against the name o' the workman, to remain until the crop is sold and payment will square the book. First times the people were no' over-pleased, but James is no' a stingy man; and when they felt the hard pieces in their palms, where once they would have got new clothes and big feastings and a new cow to give more milk for the young ones, why then – James Creary is the man for the glory!

In our house James smiles at me that time and says: "Watch if they do no' work harder this crop!"

And is true it. Davie would no' like this, but the younger generation of our people on the Cay were no' agreeable to a Zion where they did no' earn and spend their own hard coin. Times had changed, said James Creary. *Aie* – it was no' say times had changed, but men had forgotten.

Listen to a proverb o' my people: When dry-time comes to stonehole, huntermen suck on wet cocoa-leaf and say it is spring water.

Howsoever, is true, it. From that time the harvest times grew heavier as more and more acres went into bananas. No' long afterwards James had saved enough to buy our own schooner to take our fruit to America. With that we earned more money for our crop and paid our people better. But he did not see what that would lead to. I told him: "The higher monkey climbs, the more he exposes his underpart." He called me a foolish old man.

Do no' misunderstand me. We did no' quarrel. But remember, old heads can say: *I know.* Young heads must say: *I expect.*

Year after year our people got their coins for their labour, and much of it they have saved, for there was nothing to spend it on. James opened a shop on the Cay, and for a while things went level. But soon there were no' enough of us to admire and clap hands as the young ones promenaded and preened in their ribbons and satins like peafowls in Maytime.

First times, Sunday afternoons on the road we had made by the beach had our young ones full in their finery, walking up and down the sands. But after times they would no' walk much again, but stood in their finery looking lost and pitching flat stones out to sea and laughing a little when the stones skipped four times before sinking. After more times they do no' laugh again.

One day at evening star Timothy and me were sitting on the beach watching the day go away. Many young ones in their finery stood looking at sea too. James was no' with us. He is sitting in his house bent over his books with eyes for nothing but the figures before him. Make evening star rise in the west, James Creary has his stars in front o' him, done in his own hand on the white ledger leaves.

Hear Timothy: "Bro' John, is no' good, this."

I do no' answer, for Timothy will talk again.

"Looking-glass can no' clap hands and say pretty-pretty," he said.

Well then, I know what Timothy is saying. I took off my *trash hat* and blew in it, for the evening was dying in heat. I must see if wisdom has left me.

"Good money goes into their pockets, Timothy," I told him, with nothing in my voice.

Timothy shook his head. "Money never any good so till you can spend it to bring you happy times. Like a man with carriage and no wheels to it. Better than this it was in Bro' Davie's time – God rest the dead! – when wages went to feastings and building new homes."

I must see if wisdom has left me. Hear me:

"But even if Davie was still here, he would have changed, must ha' changed; else what would we do with our profits when we had no' need o' more houses?"

Timothy did no' answer for a while and I am thinking he has no' got answer to my talk. But after a time he said with quietness: "We would no' ha' had such like profits, Bro' John. Zion would grow only what her children needful of."

Now then. That is what I am thinking too. Timothy and me have come a long distance together and we have no' separated on the way, but things have happened which we can no' change 'cept we will bring more trouble on the land.

I say: "We can no' change it now, Timothy."

His head is nodding to say I ha' spoken truth. The young have grown up and they have tasted o' the pots and good is the taste to them. How can they know o' three years drought and the feel o' Ramsey's cat on their backs?

No aloes ha' reached their pots, theirs or James Creary's.

"They will no' find content on the Cay longer, Bro' John," says my friend.

James Creary had no' known that this was what I meant, so he called me a foolish old man. I could tell him that often I ha' sat at evening and made my mind take me back to years past, trying to make things that are gone set me for things still to come. I ha' thought o' Zaccy O'Gilvie, and beside him my mind has stood up my bro' Davie. Zaccy O'Gilvie prospered on his butcher stall, so he bought heavy silver chain for his belly and sent his son to *buckra* school. Davie prospered on his Zion, so he sent away laughter from him and put his woman into *osnaburg*, even though he had marched with Bogle because his women could no' wear silks against their skin.

Hear me. Best that prosperity comes when the mind is ready for it. Otherwise you will no' take it easy along with you, but either flaunt what you ha' got or fear will turn you from the shekels your thrift has brought to you.

Well then, it was no' long before many o' our young began striking for Jamaica on passing ships. Some few came to tell me before they went, that they would see the land of their parents and would no' be from us long. Others we do no' know have gone until their elders come a-shake their heads and speaking in sorrow o' the young generation.

That time James Creary's face gets tight, and swearing bursts from him, for he can no' work the banana fields with people who were old when he was young. That time Timothy and my eyes make four, and there is nodding of older heads.

So, in 'Seven, when the earth groaned and shook and some of our Cay went back to the sea, 'twas no' with sorrow that we left. We knew that the Cay was finished for us.

CHAPTER 2

Our purse was fat with coin when we went back to Morant Bay. I did no' cast around much at all, for my mind was made up what to do. Bananas we will plant; for although the stormy weather means that all your trees are grounded, yet still, if things be lucky on your side, five crops can make of you a man o' means. So bananas we planted.

The hurricanes came in 'Fifteen, 'Sixteen, and 'Seventeen. The winds blew, the seas boiled up on Morant Beach, coconuts and canes and bananas buried their heads in the earth. And too the Great War was on us; so many people suffered badly, we Campbells too. But I must tell that we had had many years o' prosperity back of us, and so there was still fatness to our purse.

James Creary is a good counting-house man, so our savings are heavy and year after year our fields are laughing with the sun. Meanwhile James Creary has got a wife to his bed.

He has made a fine house for himself on a hill topside the town o' Morant Bay. He has asked me to come and live with him, but I know that would no' be wise for me, for I must talk of the old things often times and James does no' think much of the old things. Do no' misunderstand me. He will listen without telling me to cover my mouth. But I know he does no' want to listen to me, for he has got a wife to his bed who is of the English. So I am still living in the small house which we bought in the town.

Near-near our wharf it is, and from my window I can see our

boats loading the Campbell sugar and rum and see Timothy on his stool by the gate, where he sits and dreams all day. Sometimes I too stand and look on Timothy and 'member things of old. Like me he has taken no wife, so sometimes loneliness comes to both of us, and on my way to the office I stop at the gate with him. When our eyes meet up, nobody has to tell me that he too is dreaming of things gone.

Young ones passing on the streets stop to look at us and wonder what we two must talk of all the time. They do no' know what we have seen, for no place has been found in their English history books for the fire that burnt us in 'Sixty-five. Men ha' forgotten. Even the son o' Councilman Davie Campbell does no' speak of what I tell him.

'Twas in 'Thirteen that James Creary had his first born. Garth, they called him. 'Member, I remember when first I saw him; four months only he was, and his face was no' anything to go about with. I had taken his necklace of the dried cashew nut hanging on a chain of red jancra beads. Old-time custom, this is, that new-born babes must wear their cashew nuts until four mango seasons are behind them.

Now then, this day when he is four months old I tell James Creary that I will go to his house to see my grand. James said we would do that.

We left the counting-house together in his carriage. Sun-hot is on this August day, but James has got robes over our knees, for so does the English papers show that men ride in London. When we pass Timothy at the gate, laugh is in his eyes, I can see. I look back at him, and if Timothy's mouth it not forming like *Johnny Piper*, and if there is no' a shake to his greying head, then my eyes are not good to see with.

I am a-think I will sit with him when I return and talk o' old things.

This is the first time that I am at James Creary's house. There is a man in a blue velvet suit to help me from the carriage and take my *trash hat*, but I do no' make him help me from the carriage, and he would no' ha' got my hat if James had not taken it and given him himself.

A fine house this is. Verandas sweep wide from the steps, mahogany doors swing open for us, and I am walking in soft carpets like Maroon-man through the Blue Mountains. My eyes are wandering up and down the high walls, which have got tall pictures to them, over deep chairs that would take strong arms to move, and saying to myself, me: *James has done well.*

"Tell the mistress we have gone to the nursery, Matthews," says James.

The man with my hat bows but does no' speak. I am madding to tell him not to hold my *trash hat* as if it was alms-house rag. Howsoever, I follow James Creary to the nursery.

This Garth is laying in the crib with his eyes wide on the ceiling. A nurse, that I know is English 'cause she sits in the deep chair like there is no depth to it, is a-sew on a piece of lace. Like Baron Aldenburg is the wave o' James Creary's hand as he send her from the room. She got up with the same straight back. I go over to look at this Garth.

Eh, eh, he is a-look at nothing at all, even when I bend over him and say soft: "Coo, here now, Bro' Garth, coo the old man, Bro' Garth."

Hear me again: "Coo, Bro' Garth, you do no' remember me?"

James Creary is at t'other side o' the crib with grin on his face. After a while Garth says something in his throat which we do no' understand, but laugh comes from us since he has spoken and we begin talking foolishness to him, and then Mistress James Creary comes in.

Magda is her age-paper name; but although I am her in-law, I can no' call this woman who has got no warmth in her body anything but Mistress James. Mark me, I do no' dislike her, but sweetness is not betwixt us since she would no' allow Timothy to drink wine with us at her marriage feast.

We tell one another howdy, then I am talking to Garth again while she stands beside James Creary.

After time I remember cashew nut. I take it from my pocket and bending to slip it on his neck when I hear with sharpness from Mistress James:

"What on earth is that?"

I answered without looking up: "I ha' brought his cashew nut."

"His – *what?*"

The red beads ha' shone in Garth's eyes and now he is looking at them. I shake them at him.

"Coo, Bro' Garth! Grand has brought you your neck-guard!" I say.

Nice it is to see how shine comes to his eyes and hear gurgle in his throat.

"*Don't!*"

Is Mistress James, this. I look up at her and see anger is on her. I do no' know why. I look at James Creary. Surprise is on him, I can see, but the surprise is a-change to understanding, and understanding is a-change to seriousness.

"*Don't give it to him!*" says Mistress James again.

I raised the beads back again out of the crib, but stopped when I felt it would no' come easy. I look down and see Garth has got a finger to the chain. I dangle it on one finger and laugh with him.

"I will not have these barbaric customs in this house – and with my child! Take it away this instant!"

Well now, I must look back at her again. Is what it she is saying? Barbaric custom? This custom o' my people, who bring cashew nuts to their newborn 'cause they ha' no' got gold, frankincense, or myrrh?

I look on James Creary. I ha' told him of the old things time and time. Light, he must bring light to her.

But the son o' Davie is a he-ass who does no' know whether he should lie down under the whip or kick. It is me who must bring light to this house.

"Is an old custom, this, ma'am," I tell her. "Out o' the Book it has come."

"It is witchcraft – that's what it is! I will not have it here!"

"It is no' that, ma'am. Gifts must be given to the young, like in the Book."

"Do not blaspheme! It is necromancy!"

This Garth does no' understand his peril, so he is still a-tug at the beads. I look on James Creary. He-ass will lose his pasturage if he bucks at the whip. He is shaking his head at me, telling me: *Let be.* Perhaps I would ha' taken the beads and gone, but just then Garth gets them from my finger and now the gurglings are heavier in his throat. Mistress James made a noise and bent for them.

I went out from James Creary's house with anger in my heart. I will no' wait for the carriage but will walk back into town. On the way I must ask for the daily bread o' charity to sustenance my heart.

CHAPTER 3

Many months passed before I saw Garth again, and then he was toddling. James Creary brought him to the office. For the whole o' that morning until noontime bell I did nothing but watch my grand. I do no' recall when first I said to myself: "Bro', for true is Davie, this."

Must be that time when he could no' get through the wicket which parts our desks from the main room, so he climbed on a chair and went over on his head before I could catch him. Hurt he was, but no cry came from him.

Or must be when he got up from the floor with the corn hair covering his eyes and rubbed the hurt on his head while his eyes went with anger to the wicket.

I believe that must be the time; for just then Timothy, who stood outside looking on the child through a window, looked up at me. We nodded to one another. And from that day Davie was for Timothy and me living in the fine house topside the town.

A little after, the war came down on us. I knew then that the name o' Campbell had been wiped clean, for invitation came to James Creary and me that we should serve on Recruiting Committee. So day after day we rode through the districts, calling on men for the colours.

Up Yallahs Valley, through the Hagley Gap, cut into the Rio Grande Valley, and cut out again, riding and calling to our people: *"For King and Country – Come O!"*

Up Yallahs Valley, through the Blue Mountains, calling with my tongue while my heart is a-wonder how say time can change many things. For, look you, now I am using the same paths where the men of 'Sixty-five had walked; calling now the sons o' the men who had battled England to give battle to the enemies o' England. Then up to Kingston with our first contingent, the tall, young growth of St. Thomas parish, seeing them in khaki marching to the ship which will take them to the land o' the King:

BULLDOGS BARKING IN THE TRENCHES, BARKING
AT THE UNION JACK –
TO LET US KNOW, TO FEAR NO FOE, WHEN WE HEAR
THE BUGLES BLOW.
WHAT A TIME O, WHEN WE CATCH THE KAISER AND
THE GERMAN WAR IS OVER!

Hear them singing on the march that song which was to put fear on the Turks when our Jamaica men charged back o' their wall o' bayonets:

ONE KING AND ONE EMPIRE! ONE FLAG AND
ONE DESIRE!
ALL UNITE TO FIGHT FOR THE RIGHT AND TO
CONQUER GERMANY!

Even today-day I can hear that song and see our Morant youths a-march, a-march, the sun strong in their faces, and knowing say some o' them will no' come back home.

The next year came the first o' the three hurricanes which grounded our trees. 'Fifteen, 'Sixteen, and 'Seventeen, black clouds spewing down on us from the sea and turning daytime into dark-night. Blessed thing for James Creary and me that we ha' had prosperity before and did not need to give our land titles for mortgage.

But now I must tell o' 'Twenty and what happened that time.

A Wednesday morning in June it was, and James Creary and me were in the office. James, who was a-read of his paper, said to me:

"The paper says there has been an outbreak of smallpox in St. Andrew parish, Uncle John."

A-whittle of a pimento stick, me, and looking through the window to sea. I told him: "They must no' make it spread. We can no' stand much of that now at all, at all."

My mind was thinking of 'Eighteen and the 'flu which came on right after the last of the hurricanes; many people died that time.

"The paper reports that a quarantine will be instituted at once."

"Good that. Then it will no' spread like in 'Eighteen."

But next day there is more of the sickness in the paper. Death has come with it, and there is news from other parishes that men are coughing there too. Friday, Saturday, and next Monday week things have got worse. Schools close in many o' the central parishes; roads are blocked so men can no' pass from one stricken parish to another. Soldiers ha' been called to help the police in the quarantine.

For a while we in the east parishes were free. But one day trucks with armed soldiers rolled into our parish, and we learned that men had begun coughing at Bath Town and that the red quarantine sign was up.

Aie – goodness is a turtle flapping through heavy sand at low tide; badness is a racehorse. A good wind blows easy in from the east, stirring the hairs on your cheeks and fanning woodsmoke so it cuts figure dance on the blue of the sky; a bad wind comes howling down from the morning, tearing and destroying all before it.

The ill wind was on us now. Before three days were over, all through our parish there was mourning. Before three days were over, the ill wind was beating on my door.

The knocking at my door came at late dusk when it was no' yet lamplight. When I opened, there was a servant o' James Creary's household.

"Mr. James says quick you must come, Mr. John," she said. I nodded my head and turned back inside for my hat and stick.

There was sickness in James Creary's house; sickness of his wife. James is a good businessman, but now with death a-stand in his doorway he is a boy alone in dark-night, fright on his face and in his voice.

"All the servants have run away except Garth's nurse and the woman I sent to you – What can I do, Uncle John? What must I do?"

271

"No' be so fearful, James. Ha' you called the quarantine?"

"No – no – ! They will take her away!"

"They will no' do that. Your house is big and outside o' town. They will bring the quarantine to your house, and you can ha' the doctor here."

I do no' think James Creary has heard me, for he is still babbling in his throat and walking up and down the long drawing room.

"Why did it have to strike here! What must I do?"

"You can report to the quarantine board and ha' the doctor in," I said with dryness as I got up.

I do no' waste time with him longer, but go outside, where I harness a light buggy and go to town for the doctor and the board. After the doctor has seen Mistress James I went back to Morant Bay with him. There was a soldierman with his rifle standing at the gate when we left, but I am no' interfered with for I ha' been registered as a volunteer medical helper. I can go in and out past any red sign.

I am tired when I reach my house, tired and sad that James Creary is feeling of his ill wind and has no rock inside of him where he can hide. My eyes are watching of my thoughts inside, so I do no' see somebody waiting for me on the steps o' the house until I hear my name called. Timothy it is.

"Bro' John, is true it?"

Nobody has to tell me say bad news has travelled fast to Timothy.

"Trouble reached James Creary," I told him.

"Garth?"

"Eh, no. On his wife."

"Then what now?"

"They ha' put up the red sign, and a soldierman is at the gate."

"Well, what now?"

"Prayers only, Bro' Timothy. Prayers only."

"Eh, no, there is Garth."

"How come, that?"

"Bro' Davie's *pickney* must no' stay in that plague house."

I had no' thought o' that before. James Creary is my own, and all his sorrows are mine; but Timothy has no' got all these sorrows on him, so his mind can jump to the lone one of the family that has his love. Now my mind too has gone to Garth, and some o' Timothy's fears have reached me.

"He must no' stay in that plague house at all, at all, Bro' John. For if the sickness gets to him, you and me will no' live to see Davie at manhood again,"

"But there is the red sign – and the soldierman at the gate, Timothy."

"Then what now? So die, he should stay there and die?" Timothy cried with anger. "One soldierman and the red sign must end the seed o' Davie?"

"What to do, Timothy? Is the law it!"

Timothy got his hand to my sleeve and looked close at my face. There is a laugh from him.

"Eh! Mean to say I ha' lived to see *Johnny Piper* leaving his blood to perish 'cause of the law? How the time when Davie and my pappy in the lock-up sent to tell Deacon Bogle what happened? Who is it crawled out o' Morant lock-up to run all the way to Stoney Gut? Eh? Who it is start the fight in Main Street and made the Councilmen get them away? Eh, Bro' John? 'Member, I am remembering now – who it is really start the Morant Bay rebellion? And for what? 'Cause his blood would get the whip! The whip, *Johnny Piper*! And now Davie's offspring is facing death, and you stand there talking o' the law?" Timothy is shaking me strong. "*Johnny Piper*! Mad, you be? Stop talking foolishness to me!"

I pushed his hand from my sleeve. "Cover your mouth, Timothy M'Laren! It is no' time to talk o' things that happened before we reached our age o' reason!"

Timothy has no' grown up yet; for why then is he stirring an old man's soul with things that happened before reason came to us? How can harm come to Garth when the doctor has spoken of vaccination against the plague? No harm will come to Davie's son-son, for I ha' spoken my prayers all the way down from the house, spoken them in secret where a man should speak his prayers – locked in the upper closet o' me heart.

"Make Garth Campbell die then. Make him die with the rest o' them in the plague house, and old John Campbell will breed a woman in his evening to carry on the family o' Campbell."

That is Timothy talking with thickness in his throat. He is moving away from me. Make Garth die, he has said. But Garth will no' die, eh, Mas'r God? Garth will no' cough if we can help it?

"Very well then, Timothy," I tell him. "Go, we will go for Garth."

CHAPTER 4

So we two old men go through dark-night, walking with silence. Timothy and me do no' talk at all since we came in sight o' the house. James Creary has turned on all his lights, and we do no' like this.

I ha' thrown away my stick, and both o' we are creeping through the trees to get behind the soldier-guard. We get to the back fence and we are over the wire. Clumsy soldierman can no' see or hear ghosts who had cut their milk teeth in the Blue Mountains long before he was born.

We creep to a door near the outhouse and find that this is opened. Inside, we, with my friend's mouth opened wide at the splendour he sees. But we do no' see a living soul. Leave Timothy in the long hall and go to look for James Creary. I find him in his library, his face buried in his hand as if he is hiding from everything. I have made up my mind how to talk to James.

"James, I ha' come for Garth," I tell him.

He looked up at me. His face had agony on it. "Magda is worse, Uncle John," he said.

"I know, but you will ha' to stay with her, James. I want to take Garth with me."

"Garth? You want to take him?"

"To stay with me till this is over, for you do no' know if the nurse will be ill soon. He is where? Sleeping?"

"Garth? Why?"

James Creary is no' thinking straight, so I will no' have to reason with him.

"He is where? I will ha' him well wrapped."

His hand waved towards the door, and he covered his face again. I go to find Garth.

A blanket wrapped around my boy, and his body hugged close to mine.

"We will go down the hill to town, Son-Son. We will play like Maroon in the mountains – no talking while we creep through the mountains."

Seven he is now; nearly tall like me when I went footing to Stoney Gut for Davie.

"I am going to your house, Uncle John?"

"To spend time with me, Son-Son, till your mammy is well again. Maroon – no talking now."

He is smiling at me, then he draws close to my chest and says he will no' talk. Nice it is when a child to close your eyes and go through dark-night in the arms of an elder. I know he will no' talk.

I believe eye-water will come to Timothy if we stand in the room longer.

CHAPTER 5

James Creary and his wife are buried side and side under a tamarind near the gate. I ha' made a head-cut to say they went with the plague o' 'Twenty.

There were tears from Son-Son at first, but Timothy and me have healed his wounds. Much of his happy times comes when we take him into the mountains and tell o' the things dead and gone. That time such a way his eyes light up, and Timothy and me must talk and talk.

Now he has grown tall and strong, and there is no sorrow in his heart.

Such a way he is like my bro' Davie! Same strong talk, 'cept say there are no aloes in him, for we ha' taken the thorns from his path.

I have spoken of him with Naomi. England it will be, to learn to wear the black gown and wig and talk strong but with reason before the King's Bench.

We ha' seen him a-wave to us from the deck of the banana ship which is to take him to London town. Our 'kerchiefs flutter at him, Naomi's and Timothy's and mine, while the blue water walks fast 'tween him and us. But Naomi's does no' flutter much at all because it goes often to her eyes.

"Naomi, you must no' cry. Back he will come to us."

"Cover your mouth, *Johnny Piper.* Old women do no' cry – it is the smoke from your ugly old ship which has gone into me eyes!"

What a way time has no' changed my sis Naomi!

So Garth goes to learn o' things in England. In letters we get we learn how well is his work. Many honours has he got from Cambridge and has passed his Bar finals with honours too.

We wrote to him of our happiness and how we would be waiting for him to come home; but he lettered to say he would no' come home just yet, but would practise for a while among the older ones.

That time hell and powderhouse does Naomi raise; for, says she, we ha' spent our money on our boy, and she must see his wig and gown before she dies.

Howsoever, we can do nought but wait while our young cockerel fits his spurs. So we wait for Son-Son to come back to us.

CHAPTER 6

And a score and one he was when he returned to us full with the right to reason before the King's Bench. Cambridge and Gray's Inn ha' made a man of Son-Son. There is depth to his voice and his eyes as his arms went around Naomi and me, while Timothy's old voice is raising Cain at the stevedores with the bags.

"Uncle John – Aunt Naomi – I have missed you both!"

Then what? He thinks we ha' no' missed him too? Old men and old women do no' cry, only smoke from the old banana boat in our eyes. All the same the old should cry when the young tells them they ha' been missed, you understand? Both of us are lonely now, for now my sis Naomi is a widow.

I asked: "Son, you will practice right away?"

"Stop talk, John Campbell! Holiday he must ha'! You think the English ha' starved my boy these years, and now he must work right away as you say?"

We can no' help but laugh at Naomi, for look at the height and breadth of Garth.

"O.K., Aunt Naomi, I will have a holiday. In any case I must look around first for a decent partnership."

Hear Naomi loud: "Partner? You will no' ha' to run double-harness with any man! If Tight-Purse John will no' set you up, then your aunty will!"

"No, no, Aunty, it isn't that," Garth laughed. "All young barristers should go in with an older man. That way you learn the ropes faster."

"But all the long years you ha' been in England? Mean to say they ha' no' taught you enough?" Naomi cried.

I told her: "See, Naomi. You teach young colt to haul on log so he knows how to brace to the pull when you put him in the shaft. But even then, when in the shaft he goes the first time, an old mule must be there to steady him. Otherwise your harness will be torn and torn. See it?"

Naomi will no' see it; this is man-foolishness. Howsoever, Garth will stay with her in Kingston while he is looking for his partnership.

When he came back to me in Morant Bay a month afterwards, he told me he had found his partnership.

"I am going in with another Gray's Inn man – named Stanley. You must have heard of him? Rather famous criminal man."

"Think you said the civil division for you?"

"It's good to start this way, Uncle. It sharpens your wits for one, and – well, I will get to know my people better."

We are sitting in the office looking out of the window to sea, Timothy with us. Whenever Garth is in the office, Timothy does no' stay at the gate longer.

"Know your people, Son-Son?" I asked. "A stranger you are?"

"In certain respects, Uncle John. I don't know enough of them."

"But – your navel-string is buried here, boy! You cut all your teeth here! What is it you are a-tell me?"

He laughed. "Yes, all that is true. But if you reflect you will see that these things simply happened without any help from me. I grew up a *buckra* boy who wore shoes and had his daily quart of milk as a matter of course. When I played, there was no fear of destroying my only suit of clothes. Really I grew up *among* my poor friends, but not *with* them."

My thoughts have gone long distance. Out there I meet up with Mas'r God's hand hammering a mould together, and I do no' need to ask of the pattern.

I come back and my eyes make four with Timothy's. His old head nods at me.

"It is this awful poverty that gets one," says Garth, low.

"A long time it has been here, Son."

"I've only really seen it since I returned from England."

"Poor are no' in England?"

Garth turned to look full at me. "Yes – yes," he said slowly. "There are poor people in England, but not like our poor out here. You never saw them dying on their feet from starvation. There is poverty, yes, but not the awful variety we have out here."

"Worse it was in 'Sixty-five," I tell him.

His eyes went away from me. Davie is sitting on the chair beside me, wearing English tweeds.

"My grandfer knew, didn't he? It made him very unhappy, didn't it?"

I do no' speak. He turned to me again.

"Tell me, Uncle John. You have often spoken of the old things, but you have never given me an opinion. We have been taught in our history classes that Gordon and Bogle were devils while Eyre was a saint who only did what he did because it was necessary. You knew both Gordon and Bogle. Were they as bad as painted?"

Well, answer, I must answer now.

I tell him: "I do no' know. A small one I was then, no' knowing right from wrong. If Mr. Gordon or Deacon Bogle did wrong, it was because the times we lived in were no' right to them. Worse was the poverty then than now, with hunger riding men for three years. But, right or wrong, no good came of it. Secession was what Bogle asked for – and what he got? Constitution taken away and the Crown a-rule from Whitehall. And that happened 'cause we went too far too quick."

"Which was bad, Uncle John? Crown government, I mean."

Garth is a barrister of the King's Bench. Many men o' high learning have trained him to make men talk of things what they do no' want to talk of. He knows already all what I can tell him, for many learned masters ha' taught him many things. Still, he is a man who will no' open his chambers till he can serve his 'prenticeship with older Benchers who can teach him of their experience. Garth is a wise one who has learnt that knowledge o' things to come is no' spoilt by learning of the past.

"I am thinking that was bad, Son," I tell him.

"You think that if we seceded from the Empire our economy would be stronger? Our people happier?"

"No' altogether that. No' altogether. But now, take a steam train. I am a-think that steam train would soon blow up and destroy all if men had no' made pipes to lead the steam into ways which will drive the wheels. But still, if the engine stands quiet in the yard without ever moving, then the fires must be banked; and fires banked overlong will die. And yet still, steam would no' be steam without the engine. You understand?"

Laugh from Garth. "Now, let's see. You say we should remain in the Empire, but our energy for life should be guided into ways that would spell progress for our people – and not just to let the engine stand still in the yard of Crown government, for soon our fires will be out. Right, Uncle?"

I nod my head and look at Timothy. Timothy's eyes are close on Garth's face.

"Good," says Garth. "Conceded. But how can we get White-hall to see our way?"

"By rumbling in our boilers, Son."

"Aha!" cries Garth, putting a finger at my stomach. "But that was just what my grandfer and his Stoney Gut crowd did in 'Sixty-five, and look what happened! When Whitehall would not listen to their rumblings – *pouf!* Explosion! Right?"

Now then, I can speak to Garth o' things I want to tell. I put my eyes on him. Hear me:

"Take steam engine, Son. When they are drawing our canes to

279

the factory and the engine is going downgrade with too much steam a-boil inside, the driverman reaches hand for a lever. They call it the safety valve. You ha' studied the laws o' our country, Son. You ha' got education, so the safety valve you are. Mount to the footplates if you can and drive off from where your grandfer left. But remember this safety valve and you will no' hear this – *pouf!*"

For a while Garth does no' speak. His eyes walk over my face, then over Timothy's. Then he whistled a tune through his teeth, and a smile did a dance in his eyes and danced down to his lips.

"You old devil, you," he said with slowness. "So that's it, eh? That's your little plan, eh? Garth must get his education so he may take over from where your rapscallion of a brother Davie left off, eh? But Garth must not make the mistakes he made, eh?"

His eyes went from me to Timothy. Timothy is looking through the window with nothing on his face.

We do no' speak with this son o' Davie, neither Timothy or me. We stand and watch his face, and what we see on there tells us we ha' no' laboured in vain.

That is the year Samuel died. We went to St. Catherine parish for the burying. The flag at his doorway is a-speak of his passing. Flag goes part-ways up the mast. It can no' go higher since it is weighted with sorrow for my dead soldierman bro'.

Naomi took sick-sick Zekiel to Kingston to stay with her.

CHAPTER 7

The days o' Garth's apprenticeship ha' been days o' learning for me too. I have been up to Kingston sometimes to hear him plea to the Bench. I have sat in the well o' the court and listen to him walk musty passages o' the law a-seek for the little-known door which will take some poor one out of trouble, and proud I ha' been as I watch how Davie's seed brush away the cobwebs and show a clean and shining doorway to the poor one caught in the maze o' this justice.

For that is how Son-Son stay. Many rich has he taken trouble from; but then, hear him a-plead for one of the poor, and mighty is he that time, standing tall and straight in his gown and wig, easy-easy voice pouring out the words that will clear away the thorns from his path.

Then when all is over, and tears from the poor speak the *thankie* which their throats can no' bring, full is my heart.

Yet still, Garth is no' a bad-minded lawyer. Often he has told me he will no' take a case which will let off some bad one to trouble the world again. It is the poor that has his heart, no' the wicked, says Garth.

Meantime he is running his race.

"The plight of the workman in this island could not be worse, Uncle John. Underfed, underpaid, without a decent roof over his head, God knows how they live. Do you know there are men, men with families, working on sugar estates whose average wages are less than ten shillings a week?"

I nod and say: "Working from sun-up to night-time."

"And do you know that most of the sugar factories are owned by English aristocrats who have never been on the island in their lives?"

"If eyes do no' see, hearts can no' speak o' shame, Son."

"That's it. They sit at home in England and boast of the thousands of colonials who look to them for a weekly pay-cheque. Why the dickens do we take all this lying down? What's the matter with us?"

"Backs which ha' felt the whip for long grow a second skin," I tell him.

"A second skin!" Aloes come to his voice. "I am going to tear away that second skin and make them feel the whip!"

I tell him: "You will no' forget, Son." I say again: "You must no' forget."

Quiet comes between us for a while. Then, hear me again: "I hear say you are no' in Kingston many days, Garth?"

Tobacco must go to his lips before he answers me.

"I travel around sometimes talking to my people."

"Tell them wise things, Garth. Make them grow, but straight up."

"Old trees cannot grow higher, Uncle, unless –" his voice went away.

"'Less what, Son?"

"Unless you graft on new growth which can at least be straighter than the old tree."

"You are a-do what?"

"I believe I am doing that."

He said again: "Yet I fear it will take some doing."

"Nothing good comes easy, my son."

Garth nodded. "You are right, Uncle John. There is a second skin – a second skin of complacency toughened by illiteracy. Do you know that fifty per cent of our people are illiterate? Fifty per cent cannot read what the newspapers are saying!"

"That is no' so bad –"

"Yes, yes, perhaps that's so, when you consider that many of the newspapers are anxious to preserve this *status quo*. Yet they could read the foreign papers and know how workers in other countries are battling for a better order. I am convinced that this new growth will have to be tackled from two angles – long- and short-term angles."

Garth is now speaking his full thoughts with earnestness, so only a-listen, me.

"I will continue talking to the older ones. I will continue this – grafting. This is the short-term plan. But for lasting benefits I am convinced we will have to go to the young ones, the almost children. There must be more schools. People must be found who will give of their time unstintingly to cultivate and water this young growth. It's the only way out of this mess, the only way out of these centuries of darkness. They must grow tall and strong, fearing no man. You hear me, Uncle John? Without fear and without this second skin. Just one thin skin that will feel the whip quickly and resent it! They are my people, all of them, regardless of the colour of the skin. We are all Jamaicans – in the sun on high places or in the deep valleys heavy with life! In a land where every prospect would please if we had the chance of handling those prospects as we pleased!"

Well then, talk your talk, Son-Son Campbell. You know my heart is with you, yes? Am I not at Maroon Hole with my feet playing in water?

I am young again. Davie's voice is a-talk to me, but there is no helpless bitterness in his throat; he is running his race with confidence. And if there is quickness in his voice, it is only 'cause racehorse can no' sprint his race if excitement does no' build nervousness in his flanks.

"You know what? My life is mortgaged to this dream – this dream of seeing our people what they ought to be. My life, whatever I possess, is sold out to this dream. You see me in the courtroom an advocate for the poor? Let me make a confession. It is not because the courts are not fair. I have no quarrel with the judiciary. Thank God it isn't like in your times! They are fair enough. But what I am doing is to obtain the confidence of these poor devils. I must have their faith in me. When I have that, the road will be clearer."

Quiet awhile he is, then: "Even now the way is clearing. I believe I can make the first step."

I ask: "You see as far as the first milestone?"

He nodded at me, looking at me.

"My eyes are no' as good as yours, Garth. What the markings on it say?"

There is a little laughter in his eyes. Hear him: "That if redcoats straggle while on campaign, the Maroons will pick them off."

I do no' see it plain. I ask him how come.

"That the poor must march together. Simply, Uncle, the time has come for trade unionism. We must have collective bargaining with employees. A fairer share in the profits. Or otherwise no profits at all."

"Plunder will no' be given up easy, Son. What buckra has, he will holler to keep."

"I have no doubt he will, but he cannot holler louder than a million angry people."

"Howsoever, 'member, you must remember."

My boy laughed. "Oh, never fear, Uncle John. I won't lose the safety valve you made them weld on to me in England."

CHAPTER 8

Garth is running his race. Garth is a-run his race with speed, but he is no' forgetting his turnings. In letters I ha' got from him I learn of his work among the estate-workers.

He is a-preach the new way to them. He has found that much o' the soil he is ploughing is not altogether rock-stone and cactus. On all the estates he has found men whose eyes were no' blinded by years o' suffering, and these ha' rallied to his call.

Garth is running his race with one foot on the longer road too. All over the parishes young people who ha' spent time in the schoolrooms take their learning to children o' the poor who can no' get to schools.

All this I hear from his letters, but nothing of what is happening must reach the papers, he says; for there are trickified *buckras* who will see the peril to them and put fire at the root o' this young growth.

My boy is no' forgetting his turnings.

All this time often I must tell Timothy how our boy goes. Many mornings when I get to the gate where he sits on his stool in young sun I must stop.

"How the morning, Bro' John Campbell?"

"Hearty, Timothy, hearty."

Then: "Heard, you ha' heard from Garth?"

"Well he is, and standing steady," I say.

"He is no' ready for his march yet?"

"But he is on the march already-already, Timothy."

Then he brings his eyes to me, and there is shake to his head.

"Eh, no, Bro' John. Son-Son will no' march so. When he is ready, shells will sound and you will hear feet a-move on the road."

I must smile and put my hand to his shoulder. "Time has gone by, friend. Men do no' seek right with the sword longer."

"Eh? So, Bro' John?" says Timothy. "Then how is it that right comes, *Johnny Piper*? Those who ha' taken your right by their

284

blood will give it back to you without taking some o' your own blood? Eh? Do no' talk without sense!"

I did no' know Timothy was thinking this way.

"Put mark 'pon my words, *Johnny Piper*. Bro' Garth Campbell will ha' to march like his gran'pappy and my pappy!" he said, his head going from side to side.

I have now penned a letter to Garth, telling him that time has come when he should be visiting me, and I ha' heard from him that down he will be to spend a Sabbath with me.

He came by motor on the Saturday night, just after lamplight. There were two of his friends with him, whose hands I shake while they tell me they are Christopher Langley and Gregory Crawford.

"Chris and Greg, Uncle, two of my best friends," Garth said.

I tell them glad I am to see Garth's friends, and show them Timothy, who is there sitting in the hall-room with me.

"Boys," says Son-Son with laughter, "I have told you of these two old cronies. Meet two of the biggest rebels that ever pulled trigger at constituted authority!"

Chris and Greg are looking at Timothy and me with wonder on their faces. They are no' big, either of them, but they ha' got tightness in their bodies that tells of strength there. What I do no' like is the looseness of their mouths and the leap of stray fires in their eyes. Nobody has to tell me that they talk enough-plenty and with wildness.

Down on Timothy and me come their questions.

"You were at the courthouse during the attack, sir?"

"You actually saw the courthouse burning…and the Custos killed?"

"Did you ever see Gordon and Bogle? What were they like?"

"Is it true that there was a fortress at Stoney Gut?"

I can no' answer all the questions which fall fast from Garth's friends.

"Fellows! Fellows! Take it easy! You will smother the old men!" cries Garth, getting between them and me. At that they all laugh, and me too.

"*We marched back to Stoney Gut with them. Saw, I saw my pappy get the cat and the rope.*"

Timothy's voice, that, from the doorway. His eyes are on Son-Son's face. For a while nobody says anything; we stand there looking at him.

"Black like me, white like you, everybody who were no' buckra plantermen got the cat that day, for cat and the rope are made for the poor whether they be black or white," says Timothy.

There is a quick laugh from Greg. "My God, old fellow, you have the right ideas! I'll bet you're a good red!"

"Shut up, Greg!" said Garth with anger.

"Timothy," I said, "I am a-think time now that you go to bed."

Timothy looked up at me. Then he rose and nodded his head and spoke to Garth:

"You are no' ready for your march yet?"

Puzzle-marks went to Garth's forehead but did no' stay long.

"I am on the march now, old-timer," he said with gentleness, holding out his hand to him.

My friend would ha' spoken more, but he saw I was no' pleased. He shook Garth's hand and placed his trash hat on his head and told us *God be*.

CHAPTER 9

Garth told me: "Our first real test is coming up, Uncle." He said it with graveness.

I said: "How come, Son?"

We ha' done well by the victuals and are holding talk in the hall-room. I do no' take the strong much at all, for I reason that when a man is going down the hill o' years he must foster what is left o' his body to take him to the bottom, where he can lie without much pain. Do no' misunderstand me. I am not against the rum, for the Campbell Estates make it enough-plenty. And all the same, Garth's two friends are still going uphill, so I should no' complain even though they ha' drunk a quart 'twixt them and are broaching another bottle.

Chris leaned over and touched my knee with heavy finger.

"Mean to say we are getting out of swa-swaddling clothes, Uncle John," he said with earnestness.

"Did I write that we have formed a union in Kingston?" Garth asked.

"Union? No, Son."

"A real union, Uncle John. Te-test of strength with the fat ca-capitalists."

"Quiet, Chris. Not so loud." Garth's face is no' so pleased at the new bottle. "Yes, Uncle, a union among the labourers. We are trying to see whether collective bargaining can bring – "

"The fat capitalists to their fa-fat knees," says Greg.

A little ridge comes to Garth's cheek. He said quietly: "Ease off the bottle for a while."

Greg pushed the bottle with his elbow a mite away. "You are eased off," he told it. Chris laughed at him. Garth smiled and turned back to me.

"They are all right, Uncle John, but this is their Saturday night out," he said. I nod me head. But I look at them and think say red noses only come when a man has many Saturday nights.

"This union, Son?" I ask Garth.

"Yes, sir. Now the Corporation has announced a big street-reconstruction programme to begin in another month or so. They will need hundreds of labourers, and the union proposes to serve them notice that the men will not work for the three shillings a day offered."

"Good, that. You will ask for how much?"

"Much, much more, ol'-timer," says Greg.

Chris laughed. "Won't old Vinegar be surprised?"

I hear Vinegar is the Mayor, and a man with vinegar in his veins.

Garth said: "We think it should not be under five bob, but we will ask for five-and-sixpence, allowing the sixpence to be scaled down after negotiations."

"I say we should ask for seven bob!" Greg said with loudness.

"Or eight!" Chris hollered.

"You will never get that," Garth says. "Are you two drunk or what?"

Garth is frowning at Chris and Greg. He got to his feet quick, reached for the bottle, and walked to the pantry with it.

"You've had enough for the time being," he told them when he came back.

"O.K., O.K., we will talk now," Chris said. A grunt from Greg, for he is no' pleased.

Hear me: "Believe, I believe there is reasonableness in Garth's."

"Too reasonable, Uncle John," says Chris. "The biggest *buckra* is the government, and we should crack down heavily on them – it will be a lesson for private concerns to remember. See what I mean?"

"See, I see," I told him. "But you are no' forgetting you must creep 'fore you walk?"

Greg's hand comes up like afraid he is of me. Hear him: "Good God, sir! None of those old quotes, please!"

Chris and Greg are water-mouth men who must flow and flow. What they are thinking? That old-time sayings are no' born out of old experiences?

"You chaps seem to have forgotten that the union has already voted for the five bob," Garth said.

Chris cried: "We said at the time that they were unwise!"

"Nevertheless they voted."

"Because of your lawyer's tongue!"

"And his lawyer's head," I tell them. I asked Garth: "Suppose the government does no' agree to it, Son?"

"Good question, Grandad!"

"Why 'good question', Greg? Don't you know what we will do?"

Greg turned to me. "He says the men should then remain at home."

I nod my head. "Seems there is sense there, Greg. In dry weather a horse can stand beside the stream, but the stream is no' bound to give him water."

Poke at my knees again from Chris. "There you go again with your nineteenth-century quotes. We say this horse should go to the spring and raise all muddy hell with his hoofs!"

"How that? I do no' understand."

Garth told me: "These two half-baked rebels are suggesting the workers should turn out, then strike on the job –"

"Otherwise the government would not know we mean business – otherwise there would be no test of strength!" Greg calls out. "They will simply sit back and starve us out!"

Garth shook his head. "I don't see it that way. If we build up sufficient faith in our men, they will stick it out until the pendulum of public opinion swings their way, for after all, it was public opinion of the conditions of the streets which made the Corporation in the first place decide on this reconstruction programme."

A-listen, me, but my mind is thinking.

"Suppose say the men turn out to work and then strike on the job, what will happen then?" I asked.

Garth said with slowness: "That is exactly what I fear, since I don't know. Certainly the police will be called out. There might be violence."

Empty glass at Greg's elbow rattled on the table. He called out: "And what if there was violence?"

"Nothing!" said Garth sharp. "Nothing except that unionism would be set back in this island for another couple of decades!"

"I don't believe in this dam' cautiousness," comes out of Chris. "It is too near to dam' cowardice for my stomach!"

I am on my feet, anger pulling at my voice.

"Cover your mouth! Is who it you are a-talk of cowardice to? Davie Campbell's grand? Listen, you drunken blabber-mouths, talk o' cautiousness, yes. Cautiousness would ha' been good for his grandfer if he had it in him. But do no' talk o' cowardice to the boy who is Davie Campbell's self!"

Tall I am. All we Campbells are tall. And now I know I must ha' been no' nice to look at as I stood over those two. They are gone back deep into their chairs, and their eyes are a-stare up at my face.

Garth has got me by the arm and is coaxing me to sit down.

"They didn't mean it that way, Uncle John, they spoke without thought."

"Speak, they speak without thought always! Bred horse should no' team with scrub, Garth Campbell! I am a-think I do no' like your friends!"

"Never mind, Uncle John," Garth is a-coax me. "It's all right, never mind."

After time, anger sank down from my head. I took my arm from Garth and said *let be.* I sit down again.

Garth said: "Cut, you two. Some sleep should do you good."

Before we went to bed, I asked Garth of them.

They do no' work at jobs. Idle sons o' idle wealth who are a-seek for shell-blowing in this new movement, it seem to me. Yet still Garth says they ha' helped him much in his organising.

"Things work how strange," I told Garth. "Sons o' wealth, these two, yet they are a-seek to fight wealth now. I will bet say the prosperity o' their families was built on poor people's sufferings."

Garth laughs fit to burst.

"What's this now, Uncle? Am I not fighting capital? And am I not a son of capital? Eh? You old Croesus, you!"

Well, I ha' prospered, but no' on poor people's eye-water. So must be one o' the mysterious ways, this, what the Book says God moves in.

Howsoever, I tell Garth he must no' lose cautiousness; and must watch his heavy-mouth friends.

CHAPTER 10

Work was to start on Monday on the Corporation's streets. Work was to start the Monday, so I went to Kingston on Saturday. I must be there to see how things go with Garth this first step o' his race.

Now then, I am a thrifty man who does no' believe in waste. It is no' that I have made of money the offending right arm which will keep me from seeing Mas'r God's face; for true I believe that my measure has been pressed down and running over 'cause I do no' fail to give to men who ask. But for true I do no' believe in waste.

Bear with the old man. I tell you all this because o' what happened later.

This Saturday morning I would ha' gone by motor, but when I am ready to leave the counting-house, 'member, I remember that one of our launches would be going to Kingston today. Well,

I am no' wasteful, so I tell the clerk he should no' bother with the car as I will go by the launch.

We made the run in six hours with a good south-east back o' us, and I ha' saved eighty shillings and the sufferings in a stinking motor car.

I found Son-Son alone in his chambers.

"Uncle John, why didn't you wire me that you were coming?"

"No' needful, Son. How it goes with you?"

We ha' got our arms around each other and our faces near each other's.

"Fine, just fine; I believe we will pull it off."

I do no' believe what Garth says, for worry is riding his forehead.

"The men will no' turn out, Son?"

He shook his head, a smile on him. We sat down at his desk, and pleased is my heart to see a picture o' me on the desk.

"How is your Aunt Naomi?" I ask.

"Fine, just fine, Uncle John."

"And your Uncle Zekiel?"

"Fine, he's fine, sir."

"First I ha' heard that o' Zekiel," I said with mildness.

He looked at me, then he laughed in silence. "You are a cagey old bird," he said.

I nod me head. "What is worrying you, Son?"

"We-ell, I am not exactly worried, but there has been a slip-up."

"How that?"

"I don't suppose you've read the papers today, Uncle," he said. He handed me a sheet and said, pointing to it: "Read that."

Well then, the papers have met up with Garth on his road. They ha' told it all over their front pages that my boy has formed a union o' workers and that they will ask for more silver when the Corporation works open on Monday. They say there might be trouble, so the police are a-gird their loins. "Not so good, this is?" I asked Garth.

He shook his head. "It's not so good. I fear this might stir excitement in our men. Excitement or curiosity might bring them into the streets on Monday. If they leave their homes and go to the labour office, anything might happen; for, on one hand will be this excited crowd of men, and on the other, the police with their notoriously trigger-nervous English Inspectors ready to shout '*Riot! Riot!*' at the first unexpected sneeze. It's ticklish."

"Well, why not call a meeting? Why do you no' give them extra warning to stay home on Monday?"

He took the paper from me and pointed finger at another passage.

"Read this."

Now I see there is Governor's proclamation that in view o' things, men can no' meet or march together 'cept there is police permission.

"Then, get police permission, yes?"

"I have tried, Uncle, but I am afraid I am a marked man. Nothing doing."

"What now, then?" I ask.

"I am doing what I can. I have got together some level heads and have sent them around to as many houses as possible to warn the men. But that is a tall order. We have no home addresses. It was not necessary before. They simply came to meetings and heard what I had to say."

"What about your Councilmen?"

Puzzle-marks go to his forehead. "Councilmen? Oh, you mean Chris and Greg?" Frown on him. "I haven't seen them since yesterday."

I said: "No matter that. Much sense is no' with them."

"I have done everything possible, Uncle John. I have been to the authorities and told them I represented the union and would be prepared to negotiate before the works begin. They told me they knew of no union. That the jobs would be given out at the original rates and none other. And that the police would be on hand to see that law and order prevailed."

"Has your Aunt Naomi talked any talk with you on this?"

A grin came on him. "Yes. She said I should wire you. She said you have been breaking the law since you were eight, and bullets had not caught up with you yet; so you would know what to do."

I am a-think Naomi does no' know the years are a-hang heavy on me. I rest my hand on his arm.

"We will go up to her house, Son. Nothing to do now but wait and watch. When day-cloud reaches pointer-dog in bird-swamp and he is waiting for ploves to rise, he can do ought but stand steady and keep his eyes clean to see where to point."

My boy smiled on me.

CHAPTER 11

Where the Corporation's employment office is, is on a wide piece o' wasteland. They ha' built a two-roomed office in the middle o' this wasteland. Naomi's motor has stopped on the edge of this land. I am a-sit with her in the back of the motor.

I can see nothing before me but many backs of men. I have been in the motor since this Monday morning was one hour old. Before time, Garth was with us, but now he has gone from my eyes in the middle o' the place built of men's backs.

The crowd is thick; many hundreds of men are here. I hear men's voices far up inside the crowd, and their voices are like morning swell a-thunder soft on Roselle Beach. If the wind comes up higher, thunder will talk louder on Roselle Beach.

How come we are at this place? Tell, I will tell you.

We stood steady all Sunday, waiting to see where the ploves will rise. But by Sunday evening we knew that men would no' stay in their homes this Monday morning. The people Garth has sent out to give warning came to us at Naomi's house. They told us that though they had found many o' the men at home, anger had come on them when they heard that police riflemen would be out. A test case, they had called it; they will see if British men can no' refuse work at starvation wages.

"Hold!" I called when Garth's men were leaving. "Has any seen Mr. Langley or Mr. Crawford?"

One o' the men held up his hand and said: "Mr. Crawford."

"Where did you see him?" Garth asked with quickness.

The man did no' answer, and Garth asked again, sharp.

"I saw him in one of the houses where I called."

"Doing what?"

"Telling the men that police riflemen would be out and that those who had fear should stay home."

Garth's and my eyes made four.

After the men had gone Garth said he would ha' to go down to the Corporation this Monday morning. I nod and say must be. My sis Naomi tucked in her mouth and said she would go to see after her motor. Funny how when time comes like this, Zekiel does no' seem to be a Campbell.

So at the Corporation wasteland Naomi and Garth and me. When we got here the crowd was no' very thick. Soon police riflemen wearing riot hats came down in Black Marias and passed through the thin crowd to the offices. I could see their helmets as they wrapped a circle round the building.

It was after this that the crowd grew thicker and thunder began sounding deep in men's throats. Garth said he would go up in front to the office. When he left the motor and the men saw his face, there were many hoorays and hand-clappings. The crowd is thick and has come right back to the motor. I tell Naomi's driverman that best it would be to back a little – but, eh! Naomi is shaking her head and there is light in her eyes when she says we will no' move the motor.

"Trouble might happen, Naomi," I tell her. "Best it will be if you are where the motor can turn away easy."

"I ha' no' come out here to turn away easy, John Campbell."

I look on the light in her eyes and the silver on her old head, and grin, I must grin. " 'Member, I remember you were thinking of your motor yesterday; but now, today what you want? To play like street-Arab woman and pass up bricks for men when fighting starts?"

"If I was no' respectable, help, I would help *toss* rock-stone 'stead o' passing them, John Campbell. Fighting will no' happen, but I must stay and see how Garth comes out."

But that time I must say with graveness: "Men fight easy, sis. One little match can blow powderhouse."

Naomi shook her head. "Grey *pitcharrie* on her limb thinks owl hoots 'cause he is afraid o' dark-night."

"No talk! You are no' the only one who knows how men fight."

Well, I must grin again; for nobody has to tell me that inside this motor the years ha' gone back and Naomi is a girl at Salt Savannah who is vexed because she was no' at Morant to see Councilmen fight their fight.

Meantime, the wind is coming higher and thundering comes heavier. We in the motor could no' know the reason, but afterwards I heard that this was the time when the Corporation officers said there would be no work for the men this day. 'Twas because the Inspector had told the officers that the police he had with him could no' handle so many men.

Many of the men have come out with their pickaxes and shovels. Those with picks ha' knocked off the heads and are waving the sticks in the sun. I watch their hands wrapped on the sticks, gripping like say they would like to use them for other than waving in the sun. Bad, things look to me now.

"*We must ha' work today-day! We want to start today-day!*"

So the men are shouting. After the officer had spoken, the Inspector ordered the crowd around the office to go away.

"*We will no' move away! We ha' come for work!*"

Garth is in front o' the crowd. Now he holds up his hands for peace, for he would talk with them. Those in front who can hear him are quiet but men at the back are still a-shout:

"*British taxpayers, we! Why ha' you brought police riflemen?*"

Garth turned just then to the office and saw an officer pointing the Inspector to him. He stepped for the office, but riflemen stood before him. Garth called to the Inspector that he would speak with him. The officer and the Inspector just stand and stare at my boy. He called again. They stared at him. My boy tell me afterwards that helplessness in life had never come so close to him.

He there a-call at the two men loud, and they only staring at him while riflemen in front o' him are fingering their arms, and workmen behind him are shouting and shaking their axe-sticks.

After time the Inspector stepped to the line o' police and spoke to Garth across their shoulders:

"What do you want, mister union-leader?"

"I would like to get a chance of speaking to these men," Garth says.

"Well, go ahead, talk to them!"

"I cannot – they cannot all hear me. I want to get on a window or somewhere high where they can see me. They will stop to listen then."

"You will not set a foot inside this office!"

"I do not want to go in. I only want a high spot where the men may see me."

"The only high spot you will get is– Afraid of what you've started now, eh?"

"I started nothing. Had these people not been dared by this display of force, they would have remained quietly at home."

The Inspector is slapping his leg with his cane and grinning at Garth. "On strike, eh? That's what you wanted."

Annoyance is coming on Garth. "Will you order your men to let me pass!" he shouts at the Inspector.

The Inspector turned away.

All this what I am a-tell is what I learned afterwards, you understand?

Garth says then he called again at the officer, but that one only stares at him. Garth says he could hear thunder coming nearer in men's throats, and he knew it would be no time before trouble come on the land. He stood there, looking on the red-face Inspector, at the long-face officer who is fingering his necktie and looking down his long nose while trouble was forming at my boy's back.

And my boy pushed through the police line towards the office.

I am no' saying it was right, that, but times comes sometimes when for right you ha' got to be wrong.

A policeman raised his rifle and hit Son-Son on the shoulder. Two constables grabbed him and pitched him so he must fall to the ground. So then the match has been put to the powder, and trouble comes to the land.

From in the motor Naomi and me see the crowd go forward and hear a rifle-shot. Naomi opened her mouth wide, without sound. We hear more rifle-shots, and thunder in men's throats has reached stormy weather. I feel Naomi's hand tight on mine and hear the scream from her:

"*John O! John! God o' me – they are a-kill our boy up there!*"

Cymbals crash in my belly. I am out o' the motor and running through the crowd. Men, many men are rushing past me, screams tearing from their mouths; but others ha' reached a stone-heap, and now stones are a-whistle over my head towards where I know Garth must be.

I am running with breath full in my mouth. Sounds ha' left my ears, and sight only points one way – to where I know Garth must be.

Come, John Campbell! Run one foot, draw breath, run another foot again. Tiredness can no' drop you now when you know your boy is up there. Sun-hot, dust, and scents o' gunpowder. Scents o' gunpowder, and your feet a-stumble? What kind o' old war-horse you?

The man for the glory was my bro' Davie – he did no' stumble when he took me from Baptism Valley. Will I leave his seed eating dust in Corporation wasteland? Go, John Campbell O!

For, dead, I said Garth was dead now, and I talk to myself as I run that he will no' die and meet up Davie alone. For what will I tell Davie when time to come, me, in my bed will turn my face to the wall? Tell him I could no' reach his boy, so left him to fall alone in the dust...?

Hold your bullet, police rifleman! Just let me reach where Son-Son is.

That time I will no' argue. I will no' argue, for I ha' had many years since I left Baptism Valley. Many years I ha' had, and failed them all.

"*This way, ol'-timer!*"

I hear the voice and shadows clear from my sight. There are Chris and Greg, and 'twixt them is my boy. He stumbles along with blood on his face, and his arms around their shoulders.

"Come on, ol'-timer! Back out of this!"

Gay is Greg's voice, and I see that both he and Chris ha' no fright on them. Fun this is to them two, like butcher-dog going into fight with wide laugh on his face, for life is nought but eat and fight to him.

The rifles are still talking, but stones are no' going through the air longer. Men are running all over the wasteland. Some ha' gone to earth and bite the earth every time the rifles talk. Is bird-shooting, this; rifleman stand up straight and make their rifles talk from their shoulders. I look on my boy's face and sees he is almost no' with us.

"Defender's goal, ol'-timer," Chris calls to me. "He caught one of our own men's bricks on his head."

"Bring him to the car, quick O!" I say with breath.

When I had reached them, there had been many men between the police and us, but slowly we had to go, and by the time we reached the motor few there were who had no' passed us, leaving nothing 'twixt the riflemen and us.

My sis was alone in the car; the driver must had run when the rifles talked. She opened the door quick and was out o' the car, her hands stretching for Garth, but all of a sudden her eyes went behind us and I saw her face break and a scream is a-tear from her.

A pebble falling in morass is the sound the bullet makes in Greg's back. He went forward on his face in the dust. Chris and Naomi get Garth in the car while I look on Greg. Police *mark-seven bullet* has no' left any life in him. I shake my head at Naomi and Chris.

"Inside, ol'-timer!" calls out Chris as he gets into the driving seat. Quick he has the motor a-run and wheels holler in anger as we rock from wasteland into the road. Police mark-seven bullets put two holes in my sis Naomi's motor.

CHAPTER 12

We are heading for Naomi's house. Garth has fainted 'cause of the blood that has gone from him, and now his head is in Naomi's lap. There is a little pain in my belly when I see how his face is like Davie's under the tree. Naomi looked too and said we should get a doctor quick. But my mind has gone long distance.

Is remember, I remember how a long time ago our family walked the Blue Mountains for safety. Safe we would ha' been there, if my father had no' taken us out before men's blood cooled. Men's blood will be hot today, and my mind tells me that Garth will no' be safe until time has passed.

Hear me to Naomi: "We will no' go to your house, Naomi. My

launch is at the wharf, and by sea to Morant we will take him."

At first Naomi wanted to war at this; but after I brought things to her memory, understanding came to her eyes. Chris grinned one side o' his mouth and said an experienced rebel, me.

So we drive down to the wharf, and Garth is taken on the launch by our Morant people; Chris too, for blood will be hot for him. We do no' ha' fear for Naomi; and howsoever, derrick could no' get her to go to sea.

We made for open water same time, and did no' feel well until we had cleared the police station at Port Royal. By this time Garth has come out of his faint. Like Naomi, he did no' like it at first.

"It is desertion, Uncle John! My God, Chris, how did you allow this?"

Chris showed his palm. "I thought you'd be better alive and outside than half dead and in prison."

"Stow it!" He looked around the cabin. "Where's Greg?"

Chris hooked both thumbs to rest on his palms. "Croaked."

Garth looked on him for a while, then his face went down to his hands, and sorrow is on me when I hear him crying.

After time he asked: "When will we make Morant Bay?"

"About after seven days," I tell him.

He and Chris looked sharp at me. He nodded his head.

"I see, old fox."

I am a-think of many good coves where we can lie for a week while men's blood get cooled. Our Morant sailormen will know where to buy food.

CHAPTER 13

We sailed back to Kingston when two weeks were finished. Garth had healed well, and now he was strong again. While we were keeping from men's eyes I had sent our men to a nearby fishing village to swop money for food. From them we ha' learnt that police have made out warrant for Garth.

Warrant says that my boy did riotously assemble with others to break the peace o' King George.

We sailed back to Kingston so Garth could give himself up. There we learn that three died and a dozen got gunshot wounds when riflemen had heat in them. I ha' done well to ha' waited, for now heat is gone and they are content to put Garth and Chris and a hundred more for trial before the King's Bench.

I am a man of substance. I can put my lands in bond and go bail for Garth and Chris, the magistrate tells me. The hundred are poor people who are no' known to men of substance.

When he is released I tell Garth: "We will go up to your Aunt Naomi now. Her heart will be in her mouth for you."

He shook his head at me. "Not yet, Uncle John. I have got to get these men out too."

"Hundred and more? Plenty that, son. Think say the government will let them out?"

"I must find a way. Let's go down to my chambers," he said.

So then with Chris we go down to his chambers. There I see how many men o' high learning have well taught Garth in the laws o' the land. For through tangled woodlands o' many old books he has gone a-search for the matter that will make his hundred see light again. He is gone a-walk through musty old books, seeking for the marks what generations o' freedmen ha' made for us to walk by; marks that tell us why we are free who live under the Jack. Every time he stumbles on a mark I see him nod his head like he is saying *thankie* to the men o' ancient times.

"Think say you ha' got it now, Son?" I ask with anxiousness when he has nodded his last *thankie* and closed the books.

He grinned at me. "Habeas corpus, Uncle John, the Magna Charta of us criminals."

Chris laughed. "That old corpus still around here? I thought only American gangsters used it nowadays."

"Still here, but little used," he said.

"But won't it take some time to get it going?" asked Chris.

"Not if we use the old come-on."

"Now what's that?"

"Threaten to cable London – the Secretary of States. Out here in the colonies they particularly dislike that move, you know."

Well then, ask, I must ask of this marking that Garth has found in his woodland. I hear then how he travelled far. 1679, he says, the mark was made. It says man's body must no' be held without trial before a magistrate. Garth says the Crown will no' be ready with their case yet, so they will heed the writ.

Howsoever, to make a long story short, Garth gets his writ, and his men are looking at the sun again; but I ha' gone bond for them for five thousand pounds. I am a-think that if men go to hide in the mountains, much o' our prosperity will go with them.

But my boy is no' worrying.

"We will beat them yet, Uncle," he said, after he had spoken to the men warning them not to go to the employment office. "We have won the first lap. We will win this race yet, mark my words."

CHAPTER 14

The Crown had fixed the Wednesday for the trial. Wednesday, the Crown says they will run their race with Garth, but on the Monday before, they took the purse. My boy will be galloping for nothing at the end. Now hear me, let me tell it.

When hunger comes on men and their women and their young ones too, you can no' talk to them o' principles. Is food it, no' principles their bellies are a-ask for. And now if the Corporation wanted a thousand men, they could ha' chosen from ten thousand who need this work. For Garth's hundred who stayed home on Monday, there were tens of hundreds who turned out that Monday when the Corporation said the work would start.

My boy will be a-gallop for nothing at the end, for hungry men ha' taken the three shillings a day.

He came home to Naomi's house that Monday evening with dark-night settling on his face. Naomi and me were sitting on the veranda watching of the sunset and thinking our thoughts. Chris came in with him.

I said: "Trouble happen, Son?"

He, no answer; but Chris said: "The whole god-dam' trade-union movement is smashed for ever, ol'-timer."

"How you mean?" I ask.

Chris made to answer, looked on Garth, shook his head, and

301

begged Naomi for a drink. Naomi said he could drink of his piss until she learned what they had done to our boy. A grin from Chris as he went inside to put Saturday night on his nose.

"The Corporation launched their project this morning," Garth said.

"How you mean, launched? Where ha' they got the men from?" Naomi asked.

I can no' say anything, for my heart is bearing Garth's sorrow.

"Any o' the men on bail ha' taken the work?" from my sis.

Garth laughed with aloes in his throat. "I wish to God they had! Now all that they can do, and rightly, is to hate me to hell. *I* told them not to work. *I* made them join my precious union. *I* got them into trouble. *I* made them bury some, and others face a prison term – my God! Hell of a leader I am!"

Naomi is saying something, but quiet on me, for I can see that something is bursting in Garth and we must wait for it to come out. He is standing on the veranda with late sun on his face, tightness on his body.

"Why did I start it? Who did I think I was? What kind of Messiah to change the order of things? A puffed-up, half-educated country yokel who thinks that wearing a wig and gown is enough reason to go about bleating of the rights of men! Rights! God Almighty! – the only right we can claim is the right to die. We should have the right not to be born, then I could have turned crosswise in my mother's womb! A curse is on us – a curse is on us Campbells, I tell you!"

His eyes are wide on the sunset. His voice walks on one level.

I am a-pray: *God O, who lives inside o' men, stir inside Davie's seed today and make him no' forget the high places.*

He turned on Naomi and me, his eyes a-stare.

"Look on all of us. Go back, you, Uncle John, you, Aunt Naomi, go back and look. Where is your father? Rotted in Baptism Valley with a piece of lead rattling around with his bones. He thought he was a leader, leading you all into the straight and narrow. Look at your brother – my own grandfather – hounded like a rat from his own country to be ground to a pain-twisted mess under a tree. Didn't he think himself a warrior-statesman leading his people to a promised land? What of my own father? A hulk of putrid flesh in a plague house! Wasn't he a great leader of industry, building a great house to swank in ever after with his English wife? A curse is on all of us! You too! Two lonely old people watching the sun, and inside the house another lonely old man who has been puny from the day he was – !"

"*Cover your mouth!* You blabbing like the bottom o' sick barrack people who ha' taken castor oil!"

Naomi has got to her feet and is facing Garth with war in her eyes.

"Dam' mongrel mule stumble on one rock-stone and lay down a-bawl that his feet will no' walk again – cover your mouth! Think say you ha' suffered more than any o' we? More than puny Zekiel inside? Yet still, anybody ever hear Zekiel bawling? Yes – we Campbells ha' had many leaders, but you are no' one of them! All o' them who died, died while they were a-lead! When you do, death will take you with your head in the ground and your rass in the air – death will go into your backside!"

My sis Naomi is a-war, and lady-talk has gone from her. I go to them and put my arms around Naomi. Tight she is, with anger a-tremble inside of her. I think she will start again, but then the trembling gets heavier and anger bursts from her in a flood of eye-water. Weak she is now.

I walk her inside to her room.

"John – John O – never know me that I would ha' to talk to Davie's seed like this!" she is sobbing to me.

I get her to lie on the bed and sit beside her.

"Is a weakling, he, John?" she is saying. "Think say he will be no good?"

I shake my head. "Is the safety valve, that, Naomi," I tell her.

Perplex came to her. "How you say?"

"Davie is sitting outside on the veranda, Naomi. Davie with much education in him pushing out wildness from him."

Perplex walked on her forehead some more. "Talk clear, John Campbell."

"If you could see inside o' Garth while he was a-curse of his family, you would see a devil a-wrestle with his angel. The devil wants to break out in one big piece and blast everything front o' him. But sense says: 'No, little bit at a time.' When Garth talks like he has just now, it was the little bits o' the devil that were coming out. If all came out one time, he would be downtown leading his unionists a-march on the Corporation offices. Strength, no' weakness is in Davie's seed," I tell Naomi and can see puzzle-marks leaving her face.

After time she smiled a little. "Good, Garth and me are," she said. "A real Campbell, he, for blaspheming."

I smiled with her. I tell her I will go out to Garth now.

"Talk your talk with him, John, then send him to me," she said.

Well then, I must go out front now. I must help Son-Son to catch up the fire which wind is blowing to little flame.

CHAPTER 15

Wednesday has come and we are going to the courthouse in Naomi's motor. There are Naomi and Garth and Chris and me. You never see a young man what laughs at tomorrow like this Chris. Speaking the tongue o' Lucille Dubois, he shouts as we enter the motor:

"*Avant, mes enfants* – to the *place de la* neck in your shiny tumbril!"

He is driving today since Naomi has told her coward driverman that there is no place for mangy dogs in her household.

But: "No' wise this is, that you should drive," she says as we move away.

"Why, old thing?" Chris flings back at her over his shoulder.

"Think, I am a-think the Magistrate might say we must leave you with King George for five years," says Naomi, nodding her head and hiding the corners of her mouth. "Then who will drive us back?"

"Never that, sweetness," comes gay from Chris. "Not with old Garth here pleading the case of the hundred and odd."

From where I am a-sit I can see ridges in the cheek of Garth going up and down as he keeps chewing on nothing at all.

★

No more visitors can go inside the courtroom, for the hundred and odd defendants do no' leave room for many more people. Howsoever, witnesses we are, so we get past the constables at the door. Back o' we, hundreds cheer in the morning sun. They are cheering for Garth, whom the newspapers say will speak for himself and all.

Inside the courtroom they ha' allowed the hundred to sit on the visitors' benches since they can no' all go into the dock. Garth and Chris go to join them, while a young policeman with a good face on him brings chairs for us two old people.

No' long are we there before the courtroom is standing for the Magistrate. He comes through a little door at the side o' his platform, bows to the Clerk below him, then to all o' we. We bow back to him. Everybody sit down again.

The Clerk takes up his papers and looks at the Magistrate. Their eyes make four and there is a little nod from the Magistrate. The Clerk looks back at where the defendants are a-sit.

"Your names will be called one by one. As you hear your name, stand and remain standing," he says.

Garth has got to his feet.

"You wish to say something?" the Clerk asks.

Garth says: "I do."

The Clerk makes his eyes four with the Magistrate, and a nod he gets from the Bench.

Hear Garth: "May it please Your Honour. I am a defendant in this case, and also a member of the Bar and a Solicitor of the Supreme Court of Jamaica. As such, I crave the Court's indulgence to allow me to exercise the rights of my profession and represent myself and all the other defendants."

A pin drops, you must hear it when Son-Son has spoken. The Magistrate sits back in his chair and nods to Garth.

"Very well, Mr. Campbell, you may do so. Who appears for the Crown?"

A man sitting before the Clerk rose and bowed to the bench.

"Very well, Mr. Solicitor-General," said the Magistrate to him. "We will now take the pleas."

Garth bowed. "I am much obliged, Your Honour."

One by one the names are called, and after twenty names ha'

gone, people in court who were counting with quietness now whisper the numbers. To one hundred and five they go. Everybody called say they are no' guilty. The Magistrate wrote in his book, then made his eyes reach the Solicitor-General.

"May it please Your Honour. This is a case in which the defendants are charged with disturbance of the King's peace, in that on the tenth day of October, in the city and parish of Kingston, they did riotously assemble."

And so the Solicitor-General talks, a-tell of bad things what the Crown says Garth and his hundred ha' done...

"The Crown will bring evidence to say that the defendant Garth Campbell was the ringleader of this fracas that ended in the death of three men. The Crown further states that it is proposed to indict the defendant Campbell on a charge of manslaughter –"

Garth has got to his feet. "I wish to object, Your Honour."

The Magistrate wrote in his book, then looked at Garth.

"Yes, Mr. Campbell?"

"The case of the defendants should not be prejudiced by the Crown inferring that the matter will be taken higher. The future intentions of the Crown has nothing to do with the matter before the Court. If –"

"Surely my friend is not suggesting that the decision of the Bench will in any way be –"

Garth cut across the Solicitor-General: "I am suggesting nothing. This is a court of law, but above even that it is a court of justice. Anything outside the orbit of this case that bears even a theoretical or anticipatory damage to the character of any defendant must not be mentioned by the Crown until and unless he is found guilty and character evidence is being taken."

"Your objection is taken, Mr. Campbell," the Magistrate said. "Mr. Solicitor-General, kindly refrain from mentioning any intentions of the Crown which do not arise in this case."

"As Your Honour pleases," says the Solicitor-General.

Well then, my boy has bloodied his sword. Everybody stirs and there are nods from one to another. Naomi tucks in the corners of her mouth and there is a noise through her nose. The policeman says: "Order!" Naomi looks down her nose at him like is an

306

almshouse rag, he. I tell her, quiet, *let be*. She shakes her head sharp, and then her eyes are filled with Garth again. Nobody there in the courtroom for Naomi but Garth.

All that day the Crown brought evidence to say how things went at the Corporation's office and how they saw the defendants there. Garth does no' cross-examine much at all, but from every police witness he must hear where the constable saw the defendant whom he has identified.

"Now – this crowd. It was quite large, I take it? Thousands, eh?"

"Yes, thousands of men were there," says the constable.

"And this defendant whom you identified, where was he? In the front ranks, I expect, since you saw him so clearly as to remember his features?"

"Yes, he was quite near."

"Positive it was he, constable?"

"Positive, sir. I am sure I saw him."

"And in front?"

"In front, sir."

"Thank you, constable," says my Garth, as if glad, he is glad to know that the constable has no' made a mistake.

That time the Solicitor-General looks sharp at him, and frown walks 'tween his eyes on three tracks. Four o'clock had come when the Solicitor-General rose and told the Magistrate that was his case. Weariness was on the Magistrate's face when he closed his book and looked at the clock.

"I propose we take the adjournment now," he said. "Mr. Campbell will have all day tomorrow to examine his witnesses – although I suppose it will take a couple of days to hear all the defendants."

Garth went to his feet with quickness.

"With respect, Your Honour, my case will take much less than an hour, for I expect to call no witnesses."

Nobody can sit still. What this Garth is saying? Say men will no' talk for their freedom?

Mouths of Solicitor-General and Magistrate open wide with their eyes when they look at Garth. Solicitor-General and Magistrate look on one another, then look back at Garth. Hear the Magistrate:

"Did I hear you rightly, Mr. Campbell? Did you say you will call no witnesses?"

Nothing is on Garth's face.

"Quite right, Your Honour. All my witnesses have already testified."

"I have no time for riddles, Mr. Campbell," says the Magistrate, sharp.

"Very well, sir," says Garth. "I propose to make my submissions that no case has been made out for the defence to answer."

"Are you taking a point?"

"Yes, Your Honour."

Puzzle-marks are on the Magistrate's face. Hear him: "And you will ask for an acquittal on this point?"

"I will, Your Honour."

"Well, in that case I certainly shan't adjourn until I hear your point. Kindly proceed."

Now then Naomi's hand is on mine, tight, and her eyes are filled with Garth. A-listen, everybody.

"Your Honour, I am submitting that the defendants have no case to answer and that all the witnesses for the Crown have really been friendly to the other side. Observe, Your Honour, that my cross-examination was confined to just one point, a point of identification. In each instance the witness was emphatic that the person or persons identified by him were in the front ranks of the crowd. And that must be so. For in a crowd which the Crown's witnesses estimated to run into thousands it would hardly be possible for these witnesses to identify anyone beyond the first few rows. Especially as they were all on ground level and they were seeing people whom they had not known before."

Is true, that, everybody's eyes were saying.

"Now all the witnesses agree that not until I was struck down did the crowd advance. If the Court rules for the defence to reply, I say here and now that each defendant will testify that he was carried forward when the rear ranks pressed forward.

"Your Honour is an experienced jurist. Your Honour knows what can be expected from a mob of that nature. There were policemen with rifles just a few yards away, and it is entirely unreasonable to suppose that unarmed men would attempt an attack when those rifles were in plain view. These men would not have gone forward unless forced to do so, and so they were, by those behind. It is the way of mobs all over the world."

Garth stopped for a while, while the Magistrate wrote in his book. I can no' take my eyes from the Solicitor-General. Anger is a-ride him with heavy bit.

"As for the defendant Campbell," Garth says, "described by the Crown as the 'ringleader', on the evidence brought here today I submit it should have been the other way around with the defendant, Campbell, in the role of plaintiff. Surely this man could not be a ringleader when it has been deposed by the Crown that he has asked permission for an attempt at pacification; when it is known that before the day in question he had urged that everyone remain at home and not go to the Corporation's office.

"I will say no more now, Your Honour. With respect, those are my submissions."

So then nothing in the room but the clock a-tick.

"Adjourned until ten o'clock tomorrow morning," says the Magistrate.

CHAPTER 16

Garth says is a formality, this, being at the courthouse at ten o'clock, for the Magistrate can no' find them guilty on fact after the submissions he has made. Howsoever, all o' us go down again on Thursday.

Today you would think that it is Christmas Eve on the waterfront promenade, for heads o' people pack the square before the courthouse, and hard it is for us to get inside.

The clock said ten, and the Magistrate comes in through his little door. Then there are bowings again, and we sit down while the Magistrate is searching his papers. Afterwards he took his eyes to the Solicitor-General.

"Mr. Solicitor-General, I would like to hear you on the submissions of defendants' counsel," he said.

The Crown's man rose. He said: "Much obliged, Your Honour. Before the court adjourned yesterday my learned friend submitted that no case had been made out against his clients. But –"

Garth is standing tall before the Bench. "I don't want to interrupt the learned Solicitor-General, Your Honour, but I do not think he has represented me rightly. I never submitted that no case had been made out against my clients. What I said was that the defendants had no case to answer since the witnesses for the Crown had all deposed to certain facts which made the defendants *ipso facto* not guilty of riotous assembling."

"That is quite right, Mr. Solicitor-General," the Magistrate said.

"As Your Honour pleases," the Solicitor-General said. "I can take my case no higher. Witnesses, many witnesses have told this Court that all the defendants were involved in this mobbery that resulted in deaths and injuries to several. Whether they were in the van or in the rear of the mob has no bearing on the case in my submission. The fact is they were there and acted in a common purpose –"

Hear Garth on his feet again: "There was no common purpose since their actions were not voluntary, Your Honour."

"I submit, and it is for the Court to rule, that a case has been made out and that the defence should be called upon."

So the Solicitor-General is sitting down and people are a-whisper to one another. Eyes ha' nowhere to look now but on the Magistrate. Little taps with his pencil on the edge o' his desk calls the Clerk to him. Whisperings 'twixt them, and the Clerk goes back to his place, where he stands and faces the Court.

"The defendants in this case will please rise," he said.

So now the Magistrate is telling them all just what my boy says he must. No' guilty of having disturbed King George's peace are they. True it is to say that they were there at the Corporation's office, but facts brought out in Mr. Campbell's cross-examination ha' shown how it was that they were no' to be blamed for trouble what happened that morning.

All the same, says the Magistrate, well it would be for them in the future no' to find themselves in such company. Everybody know say there is unemployment, but problems will no' be solved by violence o' the kind what took place that day.

So says the Magistrate, and then he is bowing to us and is gone through his little door, and Naomi is a-tell me through her eye-water that a man for the glory is Son-Son.

CHAPTER 17

Garth went back to Morant Bay with me. Davie's seed what favours Davie's dead stamp has come back to his Uncle John Campbell.

"I've served my pre-med. course. Now I think I will get down to some hard clinical work," he said when he told me his practice in town he would give up to come back to Morant with me.

"How come that talk, Son?" I asked him.

He smiled with nothing of laughter in it.

"Didn't you know I am a medic student? Sure! I wanted to learn how to purge out poverty and ignorance. Only trouble was I tried to practise on the smattering I had picked up in the pre-med. course, and nearly killed the patients."

Much words are no' needful 'twixt Garth and me when he talks with bitterness in his throat.

"Men would no' know so many things if they did no' try and learn from mistakes, Son," I tell him.

"This is one mistake I have learnt from. I have learnt that our people are not ready for the things I would bring them – and don't think I am not aware of my luck in escaping with my neck! Why, speaking on that, if we hadn't won this case I would have been tried for manslaughter!"

"Well, you did well there. I am thinking Solicitor-General could no' ha' rested well for weeks after."

"Yes, I hoisted him nicely, I think. Those poor devils thought so too. Remember how they lifted me from the courthouse steps and carried me to the car? *Our heroic leader – Garth Campbell!* And all I had done was to lead them out of the morass I had got them in. Yet, that was easy, for it's my job. But for the time being, the union is scotched, and they themselves helped to block the way because they couldn't think far enough ahead. If you talk to them now of a union, they will just smile and whisper among themselves about how lucky they were to have got safely away."

"You ha' no' finished with it, though, Son?" I asked with quietness.

"Finished? Not on your life!" There is good strength to Garth's voice. "When I have learnt myself what it's all about, I will begin again."

I am glad that even if my boy has stumbled, he will no' give up his race. Back to Morant Bay we went.

CHAPTER 18

My grand is no' a man to make grass grow under his feet. There was nothing of practice for a barrister o' the Temple in Morant town, so Garth says he will no' sit down but will work in the business with me.

I am not sorry, for many years ha' greyed my head and oftentimes I ha' felt to sit down. So into the office Garth went to learn how the Campbells found prosperity in cane and banana. He studied the ways of our ships and how to stay in his island and put long finger on soft spots in foreign markets. Tell, I must tell that after few months Garth could find more soft spots than all of us. But then, he has lived in foreign lands and ha' walked in the ways of foreign people.

After months in the office he said to the fields he would go. We had spoken of it often, that Garth should take the traces from me, since I ha' grown overfond o' slippers. But he will no' take my chair until he knows why some banana trees will not bring nine full hands, or why forty tons o' canes will no' grow on certain acres.

He is studying production of the sugar and spends much of his time in the factory. He has told me that he does no' agree with forcing of the land, and thinks that 'stead of heavy fertilising, best to study how to make the factory to get more molasses from the cane.

Yet still, he has no' forgotten his race. Many books come to him at our house, and often at evening he has gone from me early to learn o' things from his books. After time many letters came and went from him to foreign lands.

So now, he has been manager for weeks. He comes in from the fields where he has been all day. Late he was, and I asked if the day had been hard.

"Not until a while ago," he said.

Short, he sounded to me. "What happened?" I asked.

"Took a man to the hospital who had hurt his hand while cutting canes."

"Bad cut?"

"Lost a lot of blood by the time I had got him to the hospital."

Silence came on him, but I know everything has no' been said yet, so sit with quietness and wait.

"Look here, Uncle John, I am going to build a dispensary on the estate. Moreover, I think we should move out and live there also."

"You do no' like Morant Bay?" I asked.

"No, it isn't that. Only that living off the estate reminds me too much of absentee landlords. If I hadn't been on hand today I wouldn't have seen one of the major difficulties of our workers – the lack of medical facilities. I think we should build a house out there."

What Garth wants is my want. I told him I did no' mind. He touched my hand. "Thanks, Uncle John. I knew you wouldn't."

He built the dispensary, and, weeks afterwards, showed me on his books how much time was saved by men not going to the town hospital for treatment.

We ha' now ridden together over the properties and have come to a hill where the Blue Mountains are at our back and Morant Bay a-wash at our feet. From here at evening I can smell the mountains and hear the sea chanting vespers. Is good, it. I tell Garth here I will live.

So then up into the mountains pack mules are gone, and men are seeking mahogany and yacca to build such a house as will be well to live in. While the house is going up, he tells me of his plan to help young ones of promise.

"Without education our future is hopeless," he told me. "As it is, most of our youngsters only attend the elementary schools, and a few go on to the secondaries. They come out half-baked. And that's bad for our national digestion."

I nod me head. Though I will no' tell him, my mind is a-think that his grandfer had but the little knowledge what makes men dangerous. Books what Davie had read at the Gut did no' settle down in him as books should settle. Much o' the good did no' go in at all, and the bad only floated on top like scum in molasses tank. When he wanted to reach for the knowledge that could make him tell o' his country's history, oftentimes only the scum could my bro' Davie see.

"Is true, that. But we can no' bring such education to them, we two?"

"No, but we can *send* them to it."

"How we will, Son?"

"We can provide a few with scholarships to England and America. We have the money, more than you and me will need in a lifetime."

I look good on him.

"Then you are no' thinking that time has a-come when wife you will take?"

Laugh from Garth, good belly laugh.

"My intentions are strictly honourable, Uncle John – to you."

"No' right that. There will be nought of our seed left when we are gone, then."

" 'Course there will be," he said. "There's Uncle Zekiel's daughter who went to Cuba, and Aunt Ruth's got a big litter in South Africa. Why should you and me bother?"

Eh, that is no' it. There must be Davie's direct seed.

"Well that you should marry and ha' a man-child, Son," I tell him.

Another laugh comes from Garth as he got up and placed his arm around my shoulder.

"Never fear, Uncle John. Your boy won't die a bachelor, and you might have that man-child yet. But for the time being we'll let it slide. Let's talk about these scholarships. What do you think of the idea?"

For the time being. Tall and strong is he, with the good-looking features o' his dead grand and all o' his fire. I think say Davie's seed will no' die out.

"Is a good investment, that, Garth," I tell him, "to weld on safety valves so our engines will no' explode, eh?"

Garth nodded and grinned at me.

So then, before the year was out we had three young ones from St. Thomas parish sitting before learned men in Canada, America, and England. Garth laughs and says that, scattered that way, our engines will no' have all one-track minds.

Meantime, our house is nearly finished. Many days I ride up the smooth road which Garth has built up the hillside and sit many hours a-watch our workmen how with cunning they turn and polish mahogany so till you can see your face in at it. Stonecuts from the Rio Grande Valley has gone into the foundations, and I am thinking that if the wind comes heavy up out of the Bay, there will be a house here to split the wind and stand without shake. A good house is this.

"We will fetch Naomi and Zekiel here to end where they began, in St. Thomas parish, Garth," I told him.

"That's it, Uncle. The Campbells must come back, hurrah, hurrah!"

"Joke is no' there, Son. None o' us ha' died here since your great-grand and Manuel went to bed in Baptism Valley."

His arms are around my shoulders quick, repentance in his throat.

"I'm sorry, Uncle John, I didn't mean it that way! I was just larking – why else do you think I am building such a large place? And guess what name I am carving on the gateposts?"

I look at him and shake my head.

"Salt Savannah, Uncle! Naomi and Zekiel will be coming back home!"

I must swallow down on heaviness.

Howsoever, it was no' willed that they should come back to Salt Savannah. Zekiel went in August when sun-hot was sweating the land. My sis Naomi turned her face just as canes were arrowing in October.

Old men must no' cry, I told myself when they threw the sod down on Naomi. While Garth is alive our seed is no' perished. Cry, and purpose will leave the old, leaving just a waiting.

CHAPTER 19

It did no' seem right when Garth told me he had formed a union on
our own estate. It did no' seem right, for why should he make cat-
o'-nine for his own behind? I tell myself I must no' shout at him.

I asked him: "Was needful this? When trouble is in the bush
why bring it to your own doorway?"

The grin of Davie was on his face.

"Physician, heal thyself," he said. "Sure, I have formed, or
rather encouraged our workers to form, a union. Thus, Uncle
John, I have forged the thin end of the wedge."

"Wedge for what? Will benefit come to you from this?"

"A little, a little. Wait and see, Uncle John."

"I will no' wait! I must hear now!"

"Very well, you'll hear. Listen. This union will be the first
apostle of the Campbell creed. I am using it to make the men see
the strength that lies in collective bargaining. They in turn will
preach the gospel according to the Campbell Estates all over the
parish. From here it will travel all over the island."

"But will they no' demand much things from you? Why did
you no' ha' this union among government workers? Government
is the biggest employer – forgot, you ha' forgotten?"

"No, I haven't. I haven't forgotten either that government has
the strongest arm ready to squelch any union; therefore, the
wedge must be forged and inserted before they can mobilise. Let
me tell you more. Our work-people will soon feel the power in
their union and ask for certain benefits. Now, I know they should
have these benefits, and, in any case, *I had intended that they should
have them.* But they mustn't know this. They must believe they
were only successful because of their bargaining power, *and they
must go out and preach that conviction.*"

Confidence is on him as he sits forward pointing his finger at
me.

"Who will lead this union?" I ask.

"A foreman on the mill-bed – named Bogle." He grinned.

"*Bogle!*"

"Any similarity is only coincidental. This fellow is from Westmoreland parish. No kith or kin to your illustrious Deacon."

"Ha' they held meetings yet?"

"Sure, it's a month old, you know."

I moved my feet to find firmness on the polished yacca floor. I found it and got up without a-touch of the chair-arm. Garth grinned and said I was younger every day.

"You ha' got requests for these benefits, then?" I asked.

Garth got up too, with Davie's grin on his face again.

"That's it," he said. "I told them to send a deputation to us here. They will be here at seven o'clock."

Seven o'clock I am sitting in my chair watching the deputation come into the hall-room. Bright electric lights in the room makes them stand and blink at us a little. Four o' them are here, two o' them I know to be old workmen who ha' been with us many years.

Graveness is on Garth's face as he goes over and shake their hands, then they come over to me. I did no' know this Bogle before, and a younger one with him.

"Sit down, gentlemen," Garth said and showed them chairs. "We'll come to business at once if that suits you."

There is hesitating on them, then one by one they are looking towards the foreman, Bogle. I am a-think the foreman is no' used to eyes as much as he puts eyes on others. Howsoever, he clears his throat and speaks to Garth.

Not much are our people asking for. After he has got used to where he is, Bogle talks well; and I am liking him for his clearness in saying what he has come to say.

"So, we think, sir, that you could perhaps see your way to letting us have our wages on Friday morning instead of afternoon. That way our families can market on Friday afternoon 'stead of Saturday as now."

Garth does no' give in easily, saying how the money would ha' to be drawn from the bank on Thursday to be ready for Friday morning. But one by one the men are talking braver now, and arguments are a-show that to market on Saturday means their

317

families will no' have many hours to do their weekend house-cleaning. After time, hear Garth:

"Very well. I will discuss it with my uncle and give you my answer tomorrow morning. Is that all right?"

"That will do. Thank you very much, sir," Bogle says. Then they are wishing us *God be* and are leaving the house.

Before we went to bed that night, I am having good laugh with Garth at what the other estate-owners will say when they hear of our union. Before I sleep, my mind walked back many years ago to when Davie told the Commissioners that in years to come there will be no buckras leading his people, but the said poor like whom they had killed.

I am a-think my bro' was talking with his eye at far distance.

CHAPTER 20

I have got an invitation to attend a meeting in the town o' Morant Bay. Invitation says the meeting will be o' all estate-ownermen and attorneys. Garth and me look on the invitation and grin.

"Here it comes, Uncle John – capital moving up for the counter-attack!"

"And here we stand 'twixt and 'tween," I tell him.

"Betwixt and between," he says slow. "Funny, isn't it?"

"No' if round-shots start dropping on us from two sides; not funny then, Son."

He nodded. Quiet on both of us while our minds look on what will happen if cross-fires begin with us in the centre.

Garth said: "You are going to the meeting, of course?"

"I am a-think *you* should go, Son. You know more o' our business than I do now."

"But the invitation is to you, Uncle."

"Very well. You will come with me as manager o' our business."

So we go to this meeting, Garth and me. Nobody has to tell me why this meeting has been called. Since the months that the union has been on our estates, good name of it has spread all over the parish. Workmen on other estates have heard how men on the Campbells' estates ha' received an acre o' land to each family to grow their home crops on. They ha' heard how our cottages ha' been fitted with showers and that electric lights are making their nights brighter. And lately they ha' heard that a *bit-and-fippence* has gone on to the daily pay rate of the Campbell workers. Sevenpence ha'penny a day more they earn.

Well then, one butcher-dog sees t'other butcher-dog has got scrap meat from the stall, whine, he will whine for scrap meat too, yes?

So, workermen on t'other estates talk much o' how the Campbell Estates do well by their own workermen.

Garth and me are late for this meeting. We are late because Garth wanted it so. There was a grin on him when he told me this morning:

"Let's be a little late for the meeting, Uncle John."

"Eh, no, why we should be late without reason?" I asked him.

"There is a very good reason, just to prove something."

"Riddle-me-ree, tell me this reason," I said.

Garth laughed. He said: "I will bet you any money that late as we may be, they will not start their meeting without us."

After a little thought I told Garth I saw with him.

And right he was. We got to the Bay an hour back o' time, and yet the chairman of the meeting had no' yet knocked the table to say he was ready to start. There were there a score o' estate-owners and managers for absentee owners. There are looks on the faces of the men there not of friendliness.

"You are late, Mr. Campbell," the chairman tells me.

Name of Watson-Smith is he, but I know his name had no' got shaft to it until lately when prosperity came to him. That time he could no longer be Mr. Smith alone.

"That we are," I said. "Sorry, we are sorry."

He nods his head sharp but does no' look in our eyes as he waves us to a chair which is in front of everybody. Many whisper and look at my boy. A chair is found for Garth, and I am a-think that we are so late yet chairs ha' been found for us in front o' everybody. I take my eyes to Garth, our eyes smile at each other. Watson-Smith knocked on the table with his pipe.

"Gentlemen, shall we begin?"

A grievance meeting, this is, and men are no' slow to tell it. Men are anxious to talk o' their grievances which ha' come on them since the union came to us. Leading off is old Mr. Reeves of High River Estates.

A mighty man of influence is he, who has got more prosperity than his years can live through, and many here ha' given him their land titles in 'change for coin he has lent them. Hear old Mr. Reeves:

"I tell you, gentlemen, there is little doubt that a rot has set in, in our parish. Day after day, on estate after estate, you hear the same chorus: *'We want this – we want that – we want – we want – !'* Where is it going to end? I am telling you it will only end when all our lands are in the hands of the receivers! Our workers have become a dam' group of Bolsheviks who would like to pull us down into the gutter with them! What will happen to our wives and our children if we pour out our reserves in meeting demand after demand? What will be the result? Receivership, I tell you!"

I know say goat-beard Reeves has no' got kith or kin hanging to his purse, since he has never married, and none o' his bedded women has ever called on his name afterwards; so what is he talking about wives and children?

Howsoever, a mighty man of influence is he; a man who we would do well to have with us. I whisper this to Garth while others are a-tell their grievances. Garth nods his head, his eyes walking all over the room.

"It must stop at once! We must get together to put a stop to it once and for all!"

That comes from long-head Garfield, English manager of Bluefields Estate, whose owner, a lord of England, could not know yubba cane from watergrass if you held them up before his eyes. But you could no' do it, for this lord has never been to Jamaica since his lady-mother birthed him. Small-sized, fighting cock o' a man is this Garfield.

All this while, during the vex-talk, none of the men looked on us. They fist at their desks while they talk and push out their necks towards Watson-Smith. But by-and-by Watson-Smith looked first on old Reeves, and then looked back at me. Hear him:

"We haven't yet heard from Mr. John Campbell."

Well then, the eyes in the room now come to me and there is sudden quiet. Know, I know now that they were waiting for this.

Make estate-owners be canny. John Campbell is a canny man too.

"Well, gentlemen," I tell them, "I ha' not come here to talk to you. Old horse has gone to pasture, leaving young colt to the shaft. Here, 'side of me is Garth Campbell. Is the man, this, who signs the pay-cheques on the Campbell Estates. Hear, you will hear him?"

I ha' cast chain-shot in the midst of them and wait now for them to catch breath. For everybody knows that Garth is the man who has taught the workers how they should raise their tails.

"You will hear o' my nephew?" I ask again, my eyes on old Reeves.

Watson-Smith looked over at him, too. There is a nod from Reeves. Few who have seen him nod their heads too. Then t'others see these nods, and they look at old Reeves too. Old Reeves nods one time again, and now everybody are nodding and there are belly growls saying they will hear my manager. A mighty man o' influence is old goat-beard Reeves.

"Yes, we will treat young Campbell as your spokesman, Mr. Campbell," Watson-Smith says.

I say: "Good, he will talk for me." Then I turn and whisper to Garth that he must talk his talk. He nods at me, while his eyes are walking all around on their faces and he is getting up to be tall before them.

"Gentlemen," he said, "I agree with you. These conditions must be ended. We must move to prevent these demands after demands for more and more. As Mr. Reeves rightly said, if we don't, we might end up in the hands of the receivers."

Some of the score ha' got their mouths open; some are a-whisper to one another; all o' them ha' got looks on their faces which tell me they did no' expect this. Old Mr. Reeves sits quiet, his eyes close on Garth.

A-listen to this boy, me, whom many learned men ha' taught how to speak before the King's Bench.

"I said I agreed with you, gentlemen, and I meant it. But the question is: how can we stop it? We, or rather, my uncle and I, believe I can make bold to say that what he has is mine – " his hand comes to my shoulder and I put my hand to his to show them he has no' spoken untruth " – we have as much to lose as any man here, and surely more than some. So, I can say that we all agree that indiscriminate demands will blow such a hole in our businesses that may prevent us functioning any longer. But how can we stop them? How?"

"We can starve them out!"

"Shut down the dam' mills for one crop! That will bring them to!"

"Bring in labour from other parishes!"

Garth is shaking his head, his eyes on Mr. Reeves, who has no' spoken. My boy raised his hand, a little smile on his face.

"Gentlemen, gentlemen, just a minute. You are all experienced businessmen, and in doing business you know there is one cardinal rule, never act in haste. Right? Today this matter we are discussing is big business – perhaps the whole of our business. 'Smatter of fact, on how we put through this deal depends the future of all our business. Let's not make hasty decisions in, shall I say, the heat of the moment."

Watson-Smith knocked his pipe on the table for quiet. There was a cat-laugh on his face as he spoke.

"Gentlemen, let us hear from young Mr. Campbell how we should – er – go slow."

Dryness is in Watson-Smith's voice. A little smile tiptoes at Garth's mouth-corners.

"Thank you, sir. Now, gentlemen, let us say there is a river on your plantation which, during the mountain seasons, comes down heavy from the head. Much of your land is drowned, and worse, water you badly need runs to waste. You are all experienced planters; need I ask what would you do at that time?"

Now, then, Garth is no speaking truth. He knows that many o' the men here today-day, 'cept Mr. Reeves, are no' like him and me. These estate-owners run the properties from their office desks, leaving field work to their overseers. But Garth plays smart to make them all feel smart if one of their number can say what they would do when river rides over the banks.

Garth jumps his eyes over all o' them and makes his sight come to rest on old Reeves. Hear old Reeves, slow:

"Sink the bed, of course, then lead the overflow into irrigation canals to wet the lands on which no rain has fallen."

Everybody nods heads at goat-beard Reeves, and Garth and me nod too. My boy is looking on old Reeves as if great wisdom has come from him. Goat beard waggles at us in pride.

"Right, Mr. Reeves," says Garth with loudness. "Quite right, although, to be frank, I hadn't thought of sinking the bed. There's experience for you."

Garth is no' speaking truth. We ha' done just that on Salt Savannah already. But if ownermen think they are canny, Garth is a trickified fellow too.

"But to come back," he says after heads ha' finished nodding at old Reeves, "since we cannot stop the flow, we will control it to work for our own ends. Out of this apparent evil has come good. We find that rain in the mountains is really good for us on the plains."

Garfield is leaning forward, his eyes four with Garth's.

"Just what are you suggesting, Campbell?" he asks.

Garth says with seriousness on him: "Just what Mr. Reeves said – and I entirely agree with him – guide this workers' combine to good ends."

"But we are not here to discuss how to guide anything!" Garfield says loud. "We want to stamp out this combine, as you call it!"

"You cannot stamp out the mountain stream, Mr. Garfield," Garth tells him.

Eh! Garfield is hammering at his desk.

"It must be stamped out! Don't give me any dam' metaphors! What do you think we want in this island? Anarchy?"

My boy is no' troubled. He speaks with calmness.

"Thank you, Mr. Garfield. We certainly do not want anarchy. And as long as there is sensibly controlled unionism there can be no anarchy."

Garfield has jumped to his feet and is pointing finger, that shakes with anger, at Garth.

"You – you stand there and defend this unionism!" he shouts, voice thick with fury. Then he is turning and barking at the others, so they must yap at Garth too. "Did you hear what this – this – !"

So now, in full voices now, they are a-shout at Garth, shouting that this union business began on our estates and that much o' the blame must be lodged with we. But well I feel to see that Garth has dropped round-shot in old Reeves' belly and that now the old one is looking around, perplexed.

A man of influence Reeves is, and if he be with us, much of our task is finished. While ago Garth rubbed his old goat beard with gentle hands and had him in good mood. Now my boy is a-look at him sideways with a smile as if to say they are the only two wise ones in the room. Garth is collecting what Reeves owed him when a while ago he said the old man had spoken wisdom. Play it smart, Son-Son O!

Garth put up his hands. "Wait a minute, gentlemen, please!"

Quick Watson-Smith looks over at old Reeves, and when he sees he has no' joined in the shouting, down comes his pipe on the table.

"Quiet, everybody! Quiet, please!" Watson-Smith says sharp.

"Wait a minute, no heat, please," says Garth when there is small quiet. "Mr. Reeves – and I am sure you gentlemen agreed – pointed out that wisdom lay in harnessing the swollen river. Now once again I will appeal to your reason. You are all wide readers. You know much of world affairs, and by your years of experience, much more than mine, you can gauge for yourselves better than I can what the future holds for us."

Eh, how my Garth is lying there today-day! Much o' these men ha' no' even read the newspapers for years 'cept the part what tells of shipping. I must hold myself and do no' laugh while he is fitting heavy-belly pasture-bulls with nose-rings.

"Mr. Reeves and some of you gentlemen remember the years between 'Fifteen and 'Twenty when wartime demand for sugar pushed the price up to unheard-of amounts. I daresay –" smile tiptoeing at his mouth again "– many of us made a pretty good thing of it. Now, and again I call upon your experience as businessmen, I don't have to tell you that Europe is rapidly moving towards another war. Mr. Hitler is determined that

Germany should expand, and in this close-fitting world, expansion by any one nation means that somewhere there will be a tear. Wherever this tear occurs, there will be resentment, and there you will have your war and a terrific demand for our sugar."

"Where is all this getting us? What have we come here for? A lecture?"

That comes from Garfield, who is on his feet. Garth looks at Mr. Reeves. Old Reeves squeezes his eyes, and his whole face shuts so he is like a gnarled cashew nut. Watson-Smith looks on Reeves, sees the old one is no' pleased at Garfield, so he brings down his pipe sharp again.

"Quiet, Mr. Garfield. We must give the young man a chance to explain further. Sit down, please. Continue, Mr. Campbell."

A mighty man o' influence is Mr. Reeves.

With quietness in his voice Garth tells them: "If we allow our labour situation to deteriorate to the point where our output cannot be guaranteed or stabilised, we will lose a valuable first choice when that demand comes. Always remember, gentlemen, that we are not the only sugar-producers in this part of the world. Just ninety miles away is Cuba, ready to expand, with hundreds of thousands of acres of land ready for the plough. We must keep the good will and confidence of our customers."

A nod comes from Mr. Reeves, on whom Garth has fixed his eyes.

Hear Garth, slow: "It is no use trying to dam the river during mountain seasons. Unionism will come to our island because it has come to almost every other part of the globe. Modern conditions demand it. The old days of benevolent master and dependent servants are passed. These are days of capital and labour, not master and servant. The days are gone when at Christmas a few steers are slaughtered and served with hogsheads of proof-rum to your workers as season's gifts. The days are gone when the sick wife of a worker receives a visit from the master's wife with medicines and instructions how to get well.

"And I tell you another thing. The workers themselves aren't sorry that those days are passed. They are grown up and their sense of values have changed. They prefer to stand on their own feet, to handle their own cash – to buy their own Christmas gifts and to call in their own medical man. This change in the working man's attitude has come to every corner of the globe where he has been educated out of his dependent complex: in England too, Mr. Garfield."

Now they are listening to Garth, and all 'cept Garfield have got interest in their eyes; but I am watching Reeves, for where the leader-bull points his head, the herd will follow.

Nothing on old Reeves's face, his eyes are closed. A-listen to Garth, me.

"In some countries, unionism was born in blood. In others, wise heads who saw the inevitableness of the birth took steps to prevent violence. It is up to us to follow the wiser course and protect our industries. After all, gentlemen, if we view this problem a little more objectively than we have been doing, what are the workers demanding? Nothing really unreasonable? And if you have received unreasonable requests, it is because they are in the dark to your own problems, your own difficulties. Take them into your confidence as we at Salt Savannah have done, and you will see their manifested reasonableness. After all, they must realise it is in their own interests not to wring the neck of the gold-laying goose."

Laughter comes from the men, and even old Reeves show the five teeth which he has saved from the years. But Garfield? No' him. Barnyard rooster sees the dawn a-come and believes he can stop it with much angry crowing and flapping o' his wings.

He is on his feet again: "Stop it! Stop it! This is all bloody tomfoolery! This will get us nowhere! We came here to formulate plans to stop this nonsense, not to listen to silly theories. I for one, and my principals, will never give in to any –"

Old Reeves is moving without ease on his chair, his face folded up till only his sharp nose you can see. Garfield's shouts ha' caused men to cease their laughter, and men do no' like people who cause them to cease their laughter. Down comes Watson-Smith's pipe again:

"*Mr. Garfield! Mr. Garfield!*" he says sharp, "you are interrupting this meeting too often! If you have anything to say in disagreement, kindly wait until the present speaker is finished!"

"I cannot wait!" cries Garfield, a-fist at his desk. "This fool has

326

been the root cause of all this trouble, and now he comes here today trying to win us over. What is he trying to do? Frighten us? There are laws in this country, and arms to enforce those laws! If these obstinate sons of bitches want bloodshed, we will shed it for them!"

Mr. Reeves opened his eyes and looked down his nose at Garfield.

"And what then of our industry, sir?" he asks.

"After we put them in their places once and for all, there will be no further trouble. It was done here before, in this same parish. It can be done again, I say!"

Well then, old John Campbell must get to his feet. Watson-Smith sees that I am up, and his pipe is hammering that all should get down, for the old one is on his feet. I put my hand on Garth's shoulder.

Sit down, Garth O. Years will talk now, no' learning.

I look all around the room and see eyes are full on me. I look on them, pair after another. None has got the tracks under them what tell o' the passage of many years, save old Mr. Reeves. I make my eyes four with old Reeves.

"It can no' be done again," I tell his eyes. "Mr. Garfield is a young man who has no' been long out of England. He speaks with temper. Good it is that the young should ha' temper; young colt that does no' frisk will be no good for the long pull ahead. But all temper and no sense can break the harness and send the hamper tumbling down the precipice, scattering all our goods."

Old eyes I am looking at tell me I am speaking rightful things.

"Very well. The young man with temper says it can be done again. I say it must no' be done again. Most o' you here today-day are young people. Most o' you have only heard hearsay o' what happened in this parish seventy-odd years ago. I do no' know if Mr. Reeves was in the parish then, but if so, a young one like me that time he must ha' been."

Old head nods, telling me that young he was and in the parish then.

"Very well. We saw bloodshed, Mr. Reeves and me, and tell, we are telling you, Mr. Garfield, that it frightened we. It frightened us 'cause we saw how bloodshed can make men forget how they are made on the Image and the Likeness. It frightened we when we saw how hell comes on earth when brother fights with brother. High and low, rich and poor, black and white, they who kill and they who die, none are men in that time. We do no' want that time to come again."

My eyes walk slow around the room. I shake my head as I look on each o' them.

"That is all I got up for, I will no' say more, 'cept this: the union is on the Campbell Estates. It will stay there. I am a-think that nevertheless prosperity will remain with us – my workermen, Garth, and me."

Mr. Reeves and my eyes are making four across the room, and we are looking on things what these young ones ha' never seen.

CHAPTER 21

So the union stayed on our estates. The union found root with us and spread branches all over the parish; for old Mr. Reeves is a man o' great influence, and he it was who told the planters at the meeting that it would no' be good to dam the swollen river. They told Mr. Reeves they saw with him.

He spoke after me. Everybody was with him, 'cept rooster-chicken Garfield, who walked out on the meeting. Howsoever, old Reeves sent a cablegram to London, and sun was no' set on the second day before Garfield received a wireless from his English lord telling him he should no' be against us.

And from that time, men began to see that Garth had spoken sense. That first crop after the union came, mills turned over night and day for the months, making what the papers say was the biggest sugar crop St. Thomas parish ever saw. For truth, although workermen earned more than ever, they worked harder than ever. No stoppages came like in other cropping times; night and day our mills turned over.

Best to my heart is the workers' committee. This workers' committee has been set up for the whole parish, and there owners and workers meet and uncover their stomachs to one another. And after our workers commenced to hear o' the problems of the ownermen, proud I was to see that my people did no' take long to understand what percentages and margins and other learned business talk meant.

All o' we prospered in the parish, workermen and ownermen. Peace and fat was in our parish, but no' so in other places. For the newspapers ha' told us that police ha' had to be called out to quiet labour troubles in city Kingston. Howsoever, Garth says we will leave them to paddle their own canoes to the bar. We ha' partly crossed over already, and now we will teach our people how to handle the rudder in the harbour where many other boats are. So Garth tells me one night when we sit in the hall-room.

Garth has got his pipe in his mouth and has let drop the book he was reading.

"What kind o' rudder you talk of, Son?" I asked him.

His head is back in the mahogany chair. He turned off the light he was reading by, and now his pipe scents good in the dark.

"Politics, Uncle, the rudder by which governments are steered."

"Eh, yes, but if we ha' no ship, then why will we want a rudder?"

"We *are* getting a ship," he said with finish in his voice.

I do no' make answer, I will wait for him to talk again. I listen to crickets and toads playing music in the trees outside, and enjoy the scents from his pipe. He will talk again. "The scene is changing, Uncle. We are growing up. We are getting out of the chrysalis."

"We? We who?"

"The Colonial Empire. Once it was the British Empire, now it is the British Commonwealth and the Colonial Empire. Soon it will only be the British Commonwealth – each of us with our own pair of wings, but flying together."

"And how will we get our wings?"

"We will ask for them, but first we must learn how to use them."

I listen to tree toads and think on what my boy has said.

"We had them once, you know, Uncle."

I nod me head. "Yes, true that."

"We lost them. We flapped too heavily, so mother bird clipped them. For our own good, she said. She was probably right. They would have flapped us into trouble."

"And now, Son?"

He switched on the lights and got up from his chair and stretched his arms over his head. "And now I am a little tired tonight," he said.

"You work too hard, Son," I tell him.

My boy smiled and came over to rest his hand on my shoulder. "Nonsense, Uncle. The hard work is still ahead."

"How is that?"

Hard is his hand on my shoulder, shaking me just a little. "You and I have been indulging in mixed metaphors tonight. Not that I mind it, rather enjoy it, guess it's a Campbell trait. Uncle John, I intend launching a series of political study groups as the prelude to representative government. Study will bring the objectivity we so badly need."

Aie – simply so, Garth is telling me his apprenticeship is over. I looked up at him.

"Ready, you are ready now, Son?"

His eyes stand steady to mine. "What do you think?"

Garth has come a good way. "You are ready now," I tell him. Gently he shook my shoulder so my head nods to him.

"The climb back to where we fell from, eh, old-timer?"

Me head nods to him.

CHAPTER 22

All this time now all is well inside our parish, 'cept on Garfield's estates, where barnyard rooster still crows at the dawn. Tales o' dissatisfaction ha' come to us at Salt Savannah by way of Timothy, who hears everything. Then again, men from Garfield's estates who sit on the workers' committee ha' voiced their troubles at the meetings, and twice I know old Reeves has summoned Garfield to attend so we could ha' talk on it. But, will Garfield come? No' him.

The committee can do nothing 'bout it but ask the men to keep patience. About this time good news has reached us that a great English sugar house will build a factory in our island. In Westmoreland parish this factory will be. Garth says it should help many men who ha' no' laboured for long time now.

But he says there must be much care there, for many of Kingston's unemployed will go to Westmoreland for work, and if there is not care, trouble will come to the parish.

Timothy came to me an evening at Salt Savannah. Early May month it was, and crop-time was near end.

"God be, Bro' John O."

I tell him *God be*. He sat down, his *trash hat* on his knee. Much old I see Timothy is getting now, for electric lights can no' reach many deeply hidden places on his cheek.

"Men are going to blow shells on Garfield's property, Bro' John," he said.

I come up straight on my chair. "Blow shells? Mad you are?"

He shook his head. "For true. Men are going to march, I tell you."

Timothy is an old head that listens to much barrack talk. What he has said might be truth, might no' be truth. I sent a servant to the factory to call up Garth.

When he came I told him o' Timothy. He turned quickly on Timothy.

"Are you sure, old man? Where did you get this?"

Timothy nodded many times, his eyes close on Garth.

"Men will march, for they are no' satisfied."

"When will they march?"

"Tomorrow-tomorrow, sure. They will no' work longer if they do no' get two bits on their pay."

"You mean they will go on strike?" Garth asks.

"So I say." Shine is in Timothy's eyes. Hear him: "You will march with them, yes?"

But Garth's eyes are gone to long distance and he is no' listening to Timothy. I sent old Timothy to bed.

After time I asked Garth: "What to do now, Son?"

"I am going to see Mr. Reeves and take him over to Garfield's place. Better get some members of the committee over too. Together we might talk some sense into that short-arse fool!"

★

We went in the motor to Reeves's. Meantime we sent a truck around to pick up as many of the committee as we could find. We found Reeves at home and told him what was a-happen. Round blasphemy came from him as he went out to the motor with us.

Through dark-night we motored to Garfield's house, but when we got to the gate we found the truck with the committeemen standing outside, and constables with rifles barring them entry.

Mr. Reeves called over the sergeant to our motor. The sergeant saluted when he made out old Reeves, who is a Justice of the Peace.

"What's the meaning of this?" Reeves asked him.

"Mr. Garfield asked for the guard, sir. He received information that there would be an attempt to burn his house tonight."

"Is that so? Well we aren't arsonists. Will you let us pass?"

"Certainly, sir. But I am afraid I cannot allow in all these men."

"Very well. We won't argue that now."

So we leave the committeemen at the gate while we drive up to the house, where many lights are on. We must tell other policemen near the house that we are no' men who light houses afire.

When we met Garfield in the hall-room there was nervousness on him; but strange it was to me to see that though there was nervousness on him, Garfield was no' unhappy.

"Good evening, my dear sirs, good evening to you. Good evening, young Mr. Campbell. I hope you are satisfied now."

Bantam Garfield rubs his hands together, smiling cat-smile and bobbing his head. None of us say more than good evening. Old Reeves does no' wait for anything.

"What do you intend to do about this business, Garfield?" he asks.

Garfield showed us his hands: "Do? Why, nothing! I have no –business. That is, none of *my* choosing – *I* am no union man! It's up to you gentlemen, isn't it? To young Campbell here – our fine-talking labour leader, eh?"

"Man, do you realise there will be a shutdown in your factory tomorrow?" old Reeves asked.

"So I've heard – so I've heard."

"Well, what are you going to do about it?"

"What am I to do? I didn't bring this union here?"

"Don't you intend to negotiate with the men?"

"Of course not. Why should I? I am paying them the rate at which they were taken on."

Bantam Garfield is a-jeer at us as he shows us his hands again. Old Reeves champed hard on his goat beard. Hear him sharp:

"See here, Garfield, I verily believe you are enjoying this dam' affair!"

"Don't you realise that if your men go out, it can likely force other workers on other farms to go out in sympathy?" Garth asks him.

Jerk comes to Garfield's neck as he turns to stare at Garth. The smile left his face, and a bristling bantam cock he is.

"Suppose it does? Suppose it does, Mr. Campbell? Who will be to blame? Who brought this dam' union to the parish? Wasn't it you? Who supported it when I suggested we stamp it out? Wasn't it all of you?" he shouts, galloping his eyes over us.

I see now why Garfield is nervous but no' unhappy. He believes is a way, this, to destroy the union. If all estate-owners have their workers out on strike, they might come together with him and starve out the workmen and their union. Garfield is no' thinking on what Garth said at the estate-owners' meeting. His navel-string is no' buried here, and time will come when he moves on again; then what will our island mean to him?

"So, that's your little game, eh, Garfield?" Garth says slow. "That is why you wouldn't cooperate with us."

Eh! What a way the bantam is a-bristle!

"Cooperate with whom? Your riff-raff labourers led by your foreman Bogle? Labour union! Hell! A barefooted gang of cane-field muckers! Having them in your drawing rooms to discuss how to run your estates! Some of you colonials make me sick!"

"Shut up – you little English leftover!" shouts old Reeves. "What the hell do you know? If I were a younger man I would twist your balls! Do you know we are all the better off since the union came to this parish? If you had come in with us, you wouldn't be in trouble now – surrounded by police like you're in a dam' fort!"

"To speak of it, sir," says Garth, "I for one don't believe he has been threatened at all. He's simply trying to provoke an incident, to make his crisis-mind happy."

Cat-smile comes back to Garfield. He walked to a table and picked a cigarette from a box. Flourish in his hand as he lights it.

"When you gentlemen have finished, you might let me know," he said.

Old Reeves stamped in anger. "Come along, Campbell, come along! Leave him to stew in his own piss!"

"Don't forget, all of you will stew with me, Mr. Reeves," says Garfield.

Old Reeves turned back to him. "Get this: I am sending a cable to your principals tonight. I will see what London thinks of your attitude."

Laughter from Garfield. "Cut down on your expenses, Mr. Reeves, you might need it. I have written a full report to London on everything that has happened here. My owner agrees with my plans."

Eh! Garfield has no' forgotten his turnings. Prosperous already is his absentee English lord, who does no' know the sufferings of the poor in our island and so does no' bother about it.

"You – you – you – !" Old Reeves can no' find his words.

Garfield said: "Another thing, tomorrow, if those men do not report for work, I will have the police throw them out of the barracks on this property. It's my right y'know!"

"You – you – ! Why – I – !" Old Reeves can no' find his words.

Laugh from Garfield, who is rocking on his heels and toes, looking down his nose at the old man.

"You – you English swine!" hollers old Reeves.

A little jerk takes Garfield. Anger fixes him steady on his feet and puts tightness in his body, his head thrust out at Reeves.

"Swine? Swine, am I? English swine, eh? Very well, Mr. dam' colonial! Your black bastard brothers will get their bloody selves off my property by morning, see? No black son of a bitch is –"

"Shut your goddam mouth!" hollers old Reeves and my boy together, and I see Garth lean forward as if he would reach Garfield with a striking hand.

Well then, time is full for old John Campbell to talk his talk now. I go between them and set my hand on Garth's shoulder and say *let be.*

Garfield is a just-come Englishman who has no' been on our island many years yet. He does no' know that here men are no' measured by the quantity o' daylight under their skins. Or say that black foreman Bogle and near-white John Campbell and full-white Reeves are hoeing the said row without a-shoulder of each other. Say that, march, we are marching together.

"Wait everybody, cover your mouth," I tell them. "Mr. Garfield, you will no' reconsider?"

Bantam rooster crows with laugh, for he believes the dawn will no' come again.

"You will reconsider, no? Very well," I tell him. "Mr. Reeves? Garth? Stand good with me while I talk. Mr. Garfield here figures say the strike will come to all of us too. I say it will no' that. Mr. Garfield figures that say his workmen will be idle. I say they will no' that. I say all we ownermen must take up Mr. Garfield's workermen 'tween us so that none o' them will be idle. You stand good with me, Mr. Reeves? That 'tween us all no man will be idle and there will be no strike in our parish?"

A mighty man o' influence is old Mr. Reeves. He with me, then all other ownermen will be with me too. Old Reeves's eyes are wide on me, goat beard pointing at my chest. Then there is a little chuckle from him, then a belly laugh from him to match my boy's.

"Ye Gods!" shouted Garth. "You old owl, you!"

I ha' flung round-shot in Garfield's belly. His mouth opens and will no' shut. I do no' say anything. If smile, I did smile, good it is for an old man to have humour in him, yes?

Why Garfield's mouth will no' shut?

CHAPTER 23

Nobody burnt down Garfield's house; but all the same, a desert his plantation is. We worked hard that night, visiting all the owners in our parish. Everywhere we go old Reeves tells the story and there is heavy laughter from men when they learn how we will cut Garfield's coat.

Next morning before day-cloud Garth and me were at the gate of Garfield's property. We ha' got some old shell-blowers with us. We are no' allowed inside the gates this time, but that does no' bother us at all.

For, up goes Garth's hand, and shells are a-talk loud to the dawn.

Blow, they blow; around and up the sounds wind.

Cooee...coo-eee...cooee...coo...coo...coo-eeeee... a-talk again in St. Thomas parish, but no wildness in their throats this time. I look at Garth standing with his head high, and I make my mind think back...

The shells are sounding loud, and men and women and children on Garfield's estates are running to the gates where the sounds come from. Garth mounts to a dead stump of a tree, and many scores pass through the gates and surround the stump on which he stands. Shell-blowers take their pipes from their lips, and quietness comes on the land. Dawnlight is soft on us. Easy-easy, I hear a john-to-whit bubbling in his throat:

John-to-whit? Sweet john-to-whit? To whoo! Sip-sip-sip.

I listen to my boy as he talks.

"My friends and parishioners, God be. I have come to speak to you. I want you to listen in perfect silence – no interruptions, not even if you hear something that arouses anger in you. I will speak as simply and as plainly as I can. Quiet now, please."

Day-cloud has broken. There is a little wind and sweet scents. Day-cloud has broken over my boy, and glow from the east puts gold on his head.

Quietness on us. Hear him: "This morning you intended to strike. Mr. Garfield knows this, and he in turn intended to exercise his right of putting you off his estate. It is his right, but *– quiet, everybody!* But we, the other estate-owners, have taken care of this. You will not even lose a day's pay. Every one of you will be placed on various estates in this parish; placed with your families too, of course. You will, orderly, in perfect order, return to your barracks for your things and immediately return here to the gate. The members of your committee will be waiting to deal with you in groups, telling you to which estate you have been posted and arranging for your transportation.

"I have often spoken to you of the necessity for keeping cool heads in time of crisis. Well, now is one of those times. Go to it. We will be waiting for you."

I make my mind think back...

CHAPTER 24

So there was no violence in our parish that May month. But there was much violence in other parishes where men had no' learnt the objectivity Garth talks of. Hear me, I will tell it.

First, it was in Westmoreland parish where the English sugar house of Tate and Lyle were putting up their mighty factory. It was no' wages that brought violence there, for this English house paid well, better than anybody else. Howsoever, I am thinking that when scrap meat falls among many butcher-dogs, fights there will be, because the scrap meat can no' feed them all.

One morning the newspapers hollered at us that constables had taken up their rifles in Westmoreland and men had died down there. I came in to breakfast and saw the paper on the table in front of Garth. I saw he had no' yet touched food. I saw there was distance in his eyes.

Some days passed. Then hungry men marched in city Kingston. Then wharf-workers struck and there is rioting. Men died for a week in city Kingston, and we hear say the governor has called out the military. Radio in our hall-room tells us that King George's man-o'-wars are a-race to the island to land sailormen and guns. And say that airplanes ha' left the decks o' their ships and are flying to our island to see if they should drop death on us from the sky.

"Like stuck pigs, Uncle! Like frightened sheep! My God – can't somebody lead them? Can't somebody teach them how to demand a livelihood without getting killed?"

Garth was no' praying. But next day it seems as if answer has been given to prayer. At breakfast he does no' look up from the paper when I come in. His fingers are tight on the paper.

"How the morning, Son?" I ask him.

He looked up then, flame in his eyes.

"Somebody is doing it! Somebody is leading them! Listen, Uncle!" His eyes went back to the paper and he is a-read:

> A NEW FIGURE HAS ENTERED THE SCENE IN THE PERSON OF CARLOS FERNANDEZ, CITY BUSINESS-MAN. MR. FERNANDEZ YESTERDAY TOLD THIS PAPER THAT HE WOULD BE ORGANISING A LABOUR UNION AS FROM TODAY. LATELY FROM CUBA, WHERE HE WAS BORN OF JAMAICAN PARENTS, HE SAID HE HAD HAD CONSIDERABLE EXPERIENCE IN UNIONISM IN THAT COUNTRY. SINCE THE TROUBLE BEGAN, MR. FERNANDEZ HAS BEEN ADDRESSING STRIKING WORKERS ON THE WATERFRONT.

Garth dropped the paper to his knees. "Somebody is going to try it. Wonder who he is? His picture is striking enough – tall, white-haired, strong face, bit of a showman – well, that's all to the good. God! I wonder if he can bring it off?"

Day after day we saw pictures and stories of Fernandez fighting his fight in the troubled city. We read of how he has faced constables' rifles, daring them to shoot him while he talks to the workers.

"The fellow has guts, Uncle! If he has the brains, he can do it! If he hasn't, he must get help."

I look on the picture o' Fernandez. There is strength to his face, strength o' a man who has seen many things and has lived to tell his tale. With Garth I wonder if he can do it.

"Uncle," Garth said next day, "I am going into town today."

Well then, surprise does no' come on me.

"You will ha' to, Son?" I ask him.

He pushed the paper across the table to me. "Read this."

I read that they ha' arrested Fernandez and there is no bail for him.

I look back at Garth. I say: "They ha' caged him."

He rose from his chair. "He must not remain caged. I am going to get him out."

CHAPTER 25

Garth used the old habeas corpus. He has got out Fernandez from the government cage and now writes me that he is with the lion, grooming him, for a lion of our own den he is. I could no' understand what he meant, but he writes that soon he will be home.

Garth writes too that the people of city Kingston will march behind Fernandez, for mighty is his roar. Yet, still, my mind reads of things which Garth has not written in his letters, but which tells me that he does no' approve altogether.

Howsoever, he came home weeks after and brought Fernandez with him. I met them coming into the house, with the light at their backs, and my eyes wonder at the height of them both and how the heads could ha' been cast from the same mould. They stood in the doorway saying nothing at all while Garth grins at me.

"Look good, Uncle, do you know this gentleman?"

Well, old I am, but I ha' not lost my sight. I know I do not know the stranger, but I must say that his face is stirring my memory. Garth laughed.

"It ought to, Uncle, since he is your nephew!"

"*My – nephew!* Is what this?"

"*Meet Carlos Ezekiel Fernandez, grandson of your bro' Ezekiel!*" God o' me!

I turn him to the light and look good. Yes, there is the Campbell in him, something of the lion of Davie in the shape o' his head. Puny Zekiel has ploughed back his seed and brought out another lion to stand 'side of Davie's own.

So then, I must question him, and I hear he is the son o' Zekiel's daughter, who went back to Cuba with her mother. Dead, she is now, after she had given her Cuban husband this son. After his father went too, he came out to Jamaica to live.

"But why ha' you no' seen any of us, your family? You ha' never seen your Aunt Naomi (God rest the dead!) in Kingston?"

"No, sir," says Nephew Fernandez, "I am a stranger, and I wanted nobody to think I was seeking charity."

"Eh, charity? You could no' be a Campbell and a stranger," I tell him.

The shake of his head was no' humble.

"That I am, sir. My grandmother left your brother, you know."

I glance at Garth and his eyebrows lift at me. There is iron in this man's face, and the toss of his head tells me he will no' play second to any man. I shake his hand with respect, but I find I am wondering if two bulls can rule in the same pen.

They stayed with me a few days, then went back to Kingston.

For the month after that, newspapers tell me many times of how they both took over the strike of the longshoremen, feeding them and talking strength into them. The newspapers tell that rifles are no' talking longer, and says that Nephew Fernandez and Garth ha' done well to keep the strikers from violence. And that now government will settle the strike.

All this time Timothy is near me, and I must tell of everything that is happening to Son-Son. I tell him of the peace which Garth has brought to the strikers, and sorry I am to see that Timothy is no' pleased. A man of war he is.

"Look, Bro' John, what is he a-wait for? Think, he thinks that prosperity will come to them if the shells do no' sound for it? If the poor ha' got fire in them to march now, why does he no' lead them in the march? Soon-soon long banking will out the fire, and he will ha' to start all over again."

Eh, only in the middle of his span is a man a man, but at the start and the finish, a child he is. While he was a grown man Timothy did no' remember the blood let from his brethren in 'Sixty-five. Content was he to ha' food and drink and bed down with a woman to take away his fire. But now, when he can no' ride a woman longer, old fires in him would spend itself in warring. I am a-think if that is not why leaders in wars are mostly old men going down into their evenings?

"Take time, Timothy," I tell him. "Garth will no' fight his battle with a sword, yet the victory will be longer for it. We will wait and see, yes?"

Sorry I am to see he is no' pleased when he leaves me.

But I do no' think on Timothy much, for news has come to me

that Garth is building his rudder. This is how it went. Nephew Fernandez has formed his union, and thousands of men ha' come to it, putting in their threepence a week. He is leader of his union, with my boy beside him. Not long after this, our committee had a letter inviting our parish union to join with Fernandez. Our committee held talk on the invitation.

The invitation did no' fully agree with us, for many o' the men felt that while we had come a long distance with safety, we should no' give up our walking-stick till we had come out o' the bush.

Hear old Reeves: "We know nothing of this man Fernandez except by newspaper reports. He might be sensible, well balanced, and capable of conducting our affairs properly. But this is a peculiar arrangement we have in this parish – it is practically a union of employers and employees. How can we know that Fernandez's ideas will not clash with ours? I feel we should adopt a policy of wait and see."

Words o' wisdom these from old Reeves, and though my heart is a-holler that I should go with my boy, old head tells me that words o' wisdom, these. We will no' make any moves now, we tell Fernandez. We will wait until they can come to visit our committee and talk with us.

That was the time when I heard of Garth's rudder. He wrote back telling me they could no' come down to us just then, for he was forming his political party.

Garth wrote:

THIS PARTY WILL MARCH BESIDE THE UNION, SUPPLYING THE SPIRITUAL WHILE THE UNION BRINGS IN THE MATERIAL. IF WE ARE TO HAVE A SQUARE INDUSTRIAL DEAL, WE MUST ACCEPT THE LARGER RESPONSIBILITY OF MAKING OUR PEOPLE FULLY CAPABLE OF ABSORBING THIS DEAL WITHOUT BECOMING SWOLLEN AND, PERHAPS, BURSTING. BY THE TIME THIS STRIKE IS OVER, WE SHALL HAVE GAINED SOME GROUND. THE TASK AFTER THIS WILL BE TO RETAIN THAT GROUND.

My boy is running his race, but he is no' forgetting his turnings.

One morning the woman who keeps our house came to me at breakfast.

"Mr. Campbell? Ha' you seen Mr. Timothy?"

I had no' seen him since days before, but that was how Timothy goes off sometimes to listen to barrack talk. Moreover, I thought he was no' pleased with me since I said Garth was marching without shells. I told her no, I had no' seen him.

"Nobody can find him," she said.

"Can no' find him? Since when?"

"Since Sabbath gone." Was a Thursday now.

"Likely he has gone visiting on t'other estates, Hannah," I tell her.

She shook her head. "Maybe so. But he is a-visit very long."

"Send 'round and see if there is news of him," I tell her.

But we hear nothing of Timothy. Saturday came.

Saturday noon, telegram comes from Garth to me, telling me I must motor into Kingston now-now. Well, then, gone, I am gone since Garth wants me.

I live through stinks and bumps for a long time until I got to my sis Naomi's house, in which Garth stays when he is in town. He was there at the gate to meet me, a young woman with him. Sorrow has brought dark-night on Garth's face.

His arm hugs my shoulder. "I am glad you got here so quickly, Uncle John. Timothy is here."

Surprise comes on me.

"Timothy? Here? How come that?"

"We'll talk about it later. Come, let's go in."

I went up the path to the house with him. The young woman was no' yet introduced to me, but I could no' help staring at her, for my mind knows her face, only it will no' tell me who she is.

Inside the house we go, but I do no' see Timothy. Howsoever, I follow Garth to the bedroom that was Naomi's, and there on the bed is my friend.

His eyes are closed, asleep I can see, but my heart comes to my mouth, for nobody has to tell me that Timothy is near the river.

His breath comes out with noise. I turn to Garth and speak with tears thick in my throat.

"How this? How come he is here?"

"He walked from Morant Bay."

I can no' believe Garth.

"*Walked?* Walked the Windward Road to here? But why so? Why so?"

I must ha' been shaking, for Garth puts his arm around my shoulder and holds me close.

"Let's go outside awhile," he said.

We go into the hall-room. I must find a chair, for weakness is in my knees. Timothy, my friend Timothy, with whom I ha' come a long way. Sorrow has brought a pain to my eyes, and I must try no' to cry.

Garth said: "This morning about ten o'clock he was brought in by an ambulance. He had collapsed downtown, but before he fainted he gave them this address. I've had the doctors in, but I'm afraid it's no use. The poor fellow's heart is gone."

"He has no' spoken since?"

Garth nodded. I wait for him to tell me. His voice comes low to me.

"Uncle John, he came to march with me. He said the shells were blowing but I couldn't seem to hear them."

Timothy O!

Timothy went with evening star. I was with him all the time until he crossed the river.

Before that he opened his eyes and looked at me. Knowledge of me did no' come to him at once, but after our eyes had made four for a while, a little smile touched his mouth. Whispered he:

"Johnny Piper O? Come, you ha' come to march with us?"

I nod me head, for sorrow does no' hold hands with speech. We took back Timothy with us to Salt Savannah, for he must lie near to where one day I will lie. A long way we ha' come together, Timothy and me.

CHAPTER 26

Garth and Mary could no' visit long with me, for much work waits for them in Kingston. King George has said his Royal Commission must go to Jamaica to see why men died, and Garth is working hard on the evidence which he will put before the Commission. Much typewriting does Mary while Garth dictates to her, and very well it is to me to see how her fingers do with the machine what writes for one.

Fine fingers Mary has got, long and beautiful to watch as they skip over the keys o' the machine, with her hair like shining copper framing the sweetness of her face as morning sun pours through the window. Since then I ha' seen those fingers wrapped around a chisel and hammer, and her swift body held in halted flight over a block o' heavy granite which she is fashioning into a figure o' the wind. And remember, I am remembering her grand, who had those fingers too.

But I am a-wind up too fast. For I have no' told you of Mary?

Very well. 'Member I told you my mind knew her face? I was not wrong. Man's mind does no' forget easily the things which are marked there when he is young. But I will tell you as it came to me.

Timothy had just gone to sleep his good sleep, and we were seated in the hall-room, Garth and me, telling one another o' the things which Timothy did in his lifetime. Our voices were low, for people who undertake were in the house doing the things which will make my friend ready to be taken to Salt Savannah.

"Pity it is," I told Garth, "that in Timothy's lifetime I did no' have a picture made. A long way he has come with me. I should ha' something to remember him by."

Garth nodded at me. "Your tales about him make him one of the family, Uncle."

My mind jumped to Abram. Forty-for-forty Abram, father of Timothy he was, and a man 'twixt whom and Davie there was much love. Timothy was one of the family for true.

344

"He was that. One o' the family o' Campbells."

"We could have a photograph taken before burial, Uncle. They do those things pretty well, you know."

I shook my head. "I would no' like to have a dead face to mind me o' Timothy M'Laren. Full of life he was, even in the evening when he was turning to the wall. A mountain mahogany was he, old and brown and full o' life."

"Wait a minute, that gives me an idea. Mary could do it."

"Do what?"

"Yes – that's it. We could have a death mask made, and from that she could carve a bust of mahogany, rich old mahogany. What do you say, Uncle?"

Well, what could I say? I did no' know Mary could carve. I did no' even know who was Mary. I tell Garth this.

My Garth looks long on me, then bursts into laughter.

"Good Lord, Uncle! I have not? Why – I – I –"

More laughter from him, then his eyes are searching my face.

"Does she remind you of no one, Uncle? Nobody you knew in the old days?"

My mind is working hard. My mind knows something of her face, but try as I try, it will no' tell me of her.

"She does that, but I can no' recall," I tell him.

Garth is on his feet and goes to the door to the veranda where Mary is arranging flowers for Timothy's room.

"Mary, will you come in for a moment?" he calls.

He walked her to my chair and they stood a-face me, his arm around her waist. Laughter is in his eyes turned to me, wonder is on her face turned up to him.

"Uncle," he said, "meet Mary Smith-Evers. Once you told me you knew her people very well."

I had got to my feet too, and now I take her hand, for I do no' want to shame my boy; but when did I ever tell Garth Campbell that I knew the people o' his girl?

Garth has laughter bubbling in his throat while he talks to me.

"Being good Britishers, her people changed their family name during the war, but once it used to be – *Schmidt*."

I must just stand and open my mouth like shored mullet.

Schmidt? Old potter Hans? This beautiful girl with hair like shining copper is the young one of Ma Sara Schmidt? Eh, what a merry-go-round life is. You start one place and you go right around and back you are where you start from.

I take her hands in mine. "Whose are you?" I asked.

"My father is Dixon Smith-Evers of St. Andrew parish," she said.

"Dixon? I did no' know of him. Go back further."

A little smile walked around her mouth. She said: "Well now, further back, let's see. His father was Charles Schmidt-Evers."

"Go back further," I tell her. "Old Hans had no male."

She smiled. "Well now, Grandfather Evers was the son of Julia, who was Schmidt before she married into the Evers family."

Good. She I knew for one o' Ma Sara's six. My mind brings her face to me now.

"You are one o' my friendly families, Mary. Knew, I knew your people well."

Old men who will no' live long can kiss a glad kiss even though the house is a house of sorrow, yes?

CHAPTER 27

All this time now the war is on us. German soldiermen ha' commenced marching again under Mr. Hitler, and King George has sent out to stop them. But yet, good it is to me to see that King George has no' forgotten us and has sent his Commission to see why men died.

Much evidence they gathered, and Garth was much with them. He has also talked with them in quiet places and had them agreeing to go with him to place where working people live in houses which men should no' live in.

This Commission will no' be like that before which his grandfather stood.

"Physical evidence, Uncle," he told me. "Even if I have to kidnap them, I will see that this Commission not only hears about the mess, but see it for themselves. When they return, they must not only tell England, but *shock* England too."

He showed them. And when the Commissioners went back to England, they told King George that what he had in his West Indies was no' fit for buttery-hogs. Told him to his face that his gems o' Empire must ha' never been on the polisher's table.

We did no' get the details o' the report, for too dark it would have been for us to look on. Garth said the men of Downing Street thought the report would ha' sent men marching to riot again.

Meantime, Garth is running his race. His party is waxing in strength, and he believes now he can see the road plain. Hear him on his platform:

"We must have a new constitution. This archaic system of Crown government must go. We want full representative government within the British Empire. Adult suffrage, complete adult suffrage is the first step. No longer must the privileged classes be the only people allowed to exercise the vote. We must handle our destinies ourselves, and every man and woman in this island must be allowed to share in the shaping of this destiny."

Hear my boy talking his talk! Night after night he is up on his platform, sometimes in city, sometimes in country. I ha' been around with him now and again sitting proud on a chair on his platform and nodding me head when he says something big, so that people can see that the old one agrees with his talk.

Day after day the newspapers ha' got full columns, full columns o' things he has said and of how thousands o' people stand solid back o' his banner. London town has heard o' him, and often he shows me the English papers which have reprinted things he has said. I think he would ha' ended his race had no' war been on us.

"The war is a terrible setback for us," he told me. "There is nothing we can do – much – until this ghastly business is over."

"How long do you think they will march?" I asked him.

Dark-night was on his face. "Years. This will be a long war. Britain will spar for a long time until she can gather strength."

So there was quiet on us in the island while King George was a-shape his arrows.

But this did no' meet agreement with many o' the men in his party. Many felt that this was the acceptable year for pushing for what they wanted. England would no' oppose much now.

347

'Member, I remember a Sunday-day at Salt Savannah when Garth brought down friends for the weekend. Chris Langley and Nephew Fernandez was with him. All morning on the rum punch they argued and argued, saying now was the time or now was no' the time for them to press for a new constitution.

Chris Langley was the one who led the talk that now was the time. Garth did no' disagree with him, but held say it should be done with wisdom. I listen to the quick words tumbling from Chris, and I can no' help but looking towards where Timothy in mahogany sits and watches us. Seems to me that Timothy is nodding at Chris to say he agrees they should march now-now.

It went on until Garth jumped to his feet.

"Listen, you fools! Do you know what will happen if you don't use your heads? The government will intern the whole darned lot of us for subversive activities! This is wartime you're living through. The Governor has extraordinary powers – powers which make it possible for you to be imprisoned without trial. Use your heads if you don't want to lose them. Keep quiet and wait. I will tell you when to start out."

Nephew Fernandez's face did no' agree when Garth spoke. I told Garth of it later, and this was the first time Garth told me of his fears for Nephew Fernandez. A show lion is he, Garth says, who will no' thrive 'cept men clap hands and cheer every time they see him.

"He means well by the people," Garth said, "but the glory must be shed on himself first, and then to them. I told him to call the union by some other name, other than Fernandez. But nothing doing."

Loud-mouthed jackass brays even when braying will no' ease the pack-saddle. Chris brayed until the King's men came for him and caged him. Not long afterwards barbed wire went around my nephew Fernandez too.

CHAPTER 28

But, eh now – there are no' many days left for me to tell of? Wind up, I can wind up this tale soon. For how did it go after this? Only that my boy ran his race alone at the end. Say that he was the leader-bull and the brake-iron o' both the party and the union since everybody else had barbed wire 'round them.

How come Garth was not back o' barbed wire too? *Aie* – many high learned men ha' taught Garth Campbell how to watch his turnings. He does no' talk with his mouth too far before him.

Garth tells his meetings that they must agitate for self-government; but same time he tells them too that this is a common war and they must no' do anything which will put hamper on the back o' England while she is a-struggle up the hill. Not so did Chris and the rest of them. So now they are caged behind the wire.

But still yet, the wire came close to my boy. I remember the morning they took Nephew Fernandez away because his mouth went too far before him. Like at all times when dark-night comes on Garth, he travels to the old one at Salt Savannah. He talks to me of the men behind the wire and how he is left alone to finish his race, but how he is afraid they will no' leave him outside much longer. Mary was with him, and sadness came to me when I saw what was in her eyes as she looked at him, Nobody has to tell me that in double harness they would be if say this race was over.

"If they take me away too, it means that all will be over for the party and the union – at least until the end of the war."

That is Garth talking to me. I nod me head to show him I have heard and believe with him that all will be over. My mind has gone to look it over.

"How you stay with England, Son?" I asked him. "Is England friendly with you?"

"What do you mean?"

My mind was thinking on all the high men in England today whom Garth might ha' known in his days at college there. Garth's is a labour party. Many labour men are a-stand close to Mr. Churchill now in the government. Perhaps can he no' find strong hands what can keep him from going behind the wire?

When small boy must run from street Arabs, run, he should

run to the elders o' his brethren, who can tell street Arab say: *Let up there!*

I talked to Garth o' this, telling him it would no' be bad if he should go to England and get strong voices to stand with him. As I talked, daylight came to his voice.

"Uncle, you are still a wily one," he said. "I believe it should work. I do believe it should."

"But do you think you'll be allowed to travel now?" Mary asked.

"Why so?" I asked her.

"Shipping restrictions and all that, Uncle John," she said.

Uncle John, I was to her by then, and good it was to me to hear it.

"They can't stop me," Garth said. "I could get away on one of our own ships. Stowaway or something."

"That would no' do," I told him. "England would say you are no' a lawful man. Think again."

"Hell! – I didn't really mean that, Uncle," he laughed. "I could go on business – sugar business."

"Eh, no," I told him. "Forgotten, you ha' forgotten that the Ministry of Food has bought all our sugar till the end of the war? Think again."

"Well, I'll sign on as a crew member."

"And go into Whitehall to talk o' government with your identification papers marked 'Able Seaman'? Salesman wearing patched trousers will no' do much business. Think again."

Laugh comes from Garth and Mary.

"Nothing left inside, Uncle John. You think now."

"You can no' go with ease, boy. Ask the government, yes, but suppose they say no? Well, we will ha' to take our pen in hand. Listen me now."

I get Garth's and Mary's eyes on me listening full to the old one.

Hear me: "Many high men in England hold that stronger she would be if in the fight against the giant squid she would loosen up some o' her own holds. Many high men in England say that then the colonies would no' tug against her, but would swim up alongside o' her and help throw chain-shot at the German squid.

These are the men whom we must write to. If the government says you can no' go to England, then we will get a petition signed by our thousand-thousand and sent it to Whitehall. See with me?"

Garth nods and says he has seen with me.

So then, when we found he would no' be allowed to London town, we had the petition done in secret and sent it to one who Garth remembered as a man with whom he had learnt o' the law.

Many months passed, while Garth walked on tiptoe and covered his mouth, for power was no' yet with him.

North wind was a-whisper down the Blue Mountains when he found our seed was showing growth. December morning I heard Garth's voice calling to me outside the house. Breakfast I was having when he burst through the door like sea-wind at sunup.

"Uncle! Uncle! Look here! Read it – no, let me – !"

Well, I am looking at the newspaper what he shows me, then I am no' looking as he jerks it from me, then I am watching his mouth and the trembling o' his hands, and listening to great happiness pouring from his throat as he reads:

CABLE ADVICES RECEIVED FROM LONDON IN-DICATE THAT SIR BALFOUR BRIGGS IS DUE HERE BY SHIP TODAY. EARLIER ANNOUNCE-MENT OF THE ARRIVAL OF THE EMINENT BRIT-ISH JURIST AND POLITICIAN COULD NOT BE ANNOUNCED BECAUSE OF SECURITY REASONS.

Aie – what a fruit our seed has borne! We have only begged for his powerful voice, and now we are getting the whole man himself! Glad, I am glad that Naomi and me had sent Davie's offspring to learn of the law in England.

CHAPTER 29

Sir Balfour Briggs came to we and did no' even raise his voice much at all, at all. While the government held many receptions for the Whitehall man, Garth and me ha' had him often in quietness at Salt Savannah. We ha' sat and talked all through some nights, and while often I can no' follow them through the woodlands o' the law, pleased I am to see that Sir Balfour turns to me for talk o' the old days.

A little while before he left to go back to England, Garth told me that soon he would hold the launching of his party. I did no' understand.

"But the party has been launched already-already!" I said.

Garth grinned at me. "This is the *official* launching, ol'-timer."

I was no' surprised when I read in the papers that the party had been launched in Kingston in the presence o' the Whitehall man.

And, no' long after the Whitehall man had reached back to England, Nephew Fernandez and the others were released from the government cage.

My boy has no' forgotten his turnings.

Then now Garth started to march. Sad I was that Timothy was no' here to see how men can march with the banner o' the law waving over them 'stead o' shells talking of blood and fire. And now I must tell o' Nephew Fernandez.

Puny Zekiel has ploughed back his seed and brought out a Campbell lion. Fernandez is a lion who must fight in front. When Garth went into the finish o' his race, Nephew Fernandez did no' like that he should be behind. He had built his union with his own hand, and they should clap and cheer for nobody but he. A union man he, and no' much o' a politician, but he will be head cook and bottle-washer o' both the union and the party.

So then a quarrel he has had with Garth and is moving out his close followers from the party.

Aie – how the government people liked it! For the smitten

house can no' stand, and soon both sides will go to earth and they will come and walk heavy on the ruins.

But not so. For from Westmoreland parish to St. Thomas-in-the-East Garth is telling everybody that they must follow who they will, but not to cease a-holler for the new constitution. From Westmoreland parish to St. Thomas, from Trelawney parish to the bottom lands o' Vere, men hear the voice o' Davie's seed talking without fear in his throat.

"Full self-government within the orbit of the British Commonwealth! – Universal Adult Suffrage! – Give us a chance to shape our own destinies! – Let us stand beside you, Mother England, but free and self-respecting – not as whining children, but as adults, with full respect to the obligation we owe our parent! – Get rid of imperialism! – Let us have no decline and fall, but a permanent institution that will stand as long as free men live! – Implement the four freedoms – do not allow them to drift down into the Atlantic! – Get rid of these horse-and-buggy concepts, Mother England, before the rest of the world speeds out of sight leaving you wallowing in the mire of prejudiced tradition!..."

Hear my boy a-thunder in the finish of his race! No turnings now for him. He is marching along the road what his grand spoke of to the Queen's Commissioners. He is a-lead us up the trail to high places, fighting his fight with the up-road, like how his great-grand pitted his muscles 'gainst the mountains. Many leaders ha' gone into his blood. My boy is a-thunder in the finish o' his race, and man has no' been made yet that can stop him.

Hear me. He has come down from a man who had the strength o' ten, a man who was a mighty boar-hunter. His grand is a man who walked the Blue Mountains, and birds could no' know when he passed. A man who went in and out o' Morant Bay when redcoats and Maroons, thick like fleas on dogs, were seeking for his blood. He is a man who took his bro' and the woman he loved and sailed blue water to his own island, where he built his land with his own two hands and made the sand island to flourish with green. His great-uncle is a man what rode the mountains through dark-night, rode the mountains from Kingston parish till his horse died under him.

"Give us the right to walk hand in hand in the march of the new Commonwealth – not as subjects, but as citizens – in our island we have proven that race is but skin-shallow and that we are brothers in the depth of us – give us liberty to walk as Jamaicans, and we will walk up the same road as you, England!"

My boy is thundering in the finish of his race. Mighty things ha' gone into his conception. He is leading his people to the promised land that his father's father had reached for. From Westmoreland parish to St. Thomas, from Trelawney down through the wild mountains to the bottom lands o' Vere, my boy is telling everybody that they must follow who they will, but no' to cease a-holler for the new constitution.

So, they followed who they would, and did no' cease to holler, and lately word has come to us that we ha' hollered loud enough. Say that they in Whitehall ha' heard our voices and will give us what we asked for. Say that they will give it to us tomorrow.

THE MORNING

EH, NOW, you know say day-cloud is there in the east?

A lightness is rising top o' the head o' the east mountains, telling me that I ha' no' bedded down this night. My mind has been a-walk back through the years.

And Lord O – how our people are a-sing! They ha' seen the young light o' new day, and like deep-running water is the song that pours from their throats to greet this new day. With steadiness they sing, just like how I know they will go steady with one another when we march on the new road England has shown us.

Clock is a-talk of the hour. Is what it the clock is saying? Five o'clock? Eh, you mean I ha' been here till now?

Watch-night is over. This is the new day. Today the Governor will proclaim from before Missis Queen Victoria's statue in the parade at Kingston that from this day King George has said that Jamaica-men should look after Jamaica things ourselves. Say that King George has found agreement with what my bro' Davie told the Queen's Commissioners. Say that now we will govern ourselves. Say that Davie's grand has thundered in the finish of his race, and this day the new constitution will be proclaimed.

God O – look what me eyes live to see!

I ha' seen it all. I ha' walked the years from 'Sixty-five, when fear came down the mountains with my family, and now, this 'Forty-four November, I am standing on high places with the grand o' my bro'.

Davie O, you will be there with us on the platform near the Governor and the Colonial Secretary and the Chief Justice? If see, I could see you, tell, I would tell these high men that here is a man who marched with Bogle and was a rebel Councilman. What a way wonder would fill their young eyes!

Garth is a-stir in his room. Soon he will be coming out to me, and wonder will shine his eyes when he sees I ha' no' been to bed. I will walk with firmness across the polished *yacca* floor and watch how he smiles and says I get younger every day. Good it is for the old to walk with firmness alongside the son of a son.

Hannah is a-stir in the kitchen. I scent the good smoke o' juniper wood, and know heavy provender will soon be on our table to pack our insides for the Kingston ceremony. I hear Garth moving to the door, and I turn from the window to make my eyes four with his. Good sleep has taken tiredness from my boy; quiet is his face.

"God be, Son-Son," I tell him.

Quick eyes, like Davie's, look good on me and see there is no crush to my sleeping-suit. His finger points at me sharp.

"Uncle, you haven't been to bed at all! Mean to say you've sat up all night because of the singing?"

I shake me head at him. "Refreshed I am, Son, I ha' visited the places o' my young days," I tell him.

Understanding reaches his eyes. He nods his head at the singing outside. I nod me head at him to tell him that my mind has been walking the Blue Mountains on this singing all night, all night.

"But will you be fit for Kingston today?" he asks me.

Eh, this boy has no' remembered everything. Forgot, he has forgotten that I am of Pa John, who had the strength of ten? Say that I am the seed of a mighty boar-hunter who Morant men speak of with respect.

I nod me head to tell him that the old one will be fit this day.

GLOSSARY

ackee (also *ackie*), a popular West Indian vegetable.

aie, expression of sorrow or weariness.

bammie, cassava cakes.

banana suckers, young banana shoots (plants).

bit-and-fippence, sevenpence ha'penny or fifteen cents at par.

brawta, extra given by one party to the other in a barter.

buckra, wealthy conservative, sometimes applied to all whites.

buntung, species of mango.

calaloo, spinach.

cerosee, shrub used for making tea.

coco-macca, stout wood used in making walking-sticks.

conoo-monoo, colloquialism for a gullible person.

cotter, pads placed on the head for carrying loads.

croaker, a lizard that croaks.

daschalan, shrub used for making tea.

duppy-ghost, a wandering ghost.

gaulin, water bird.

gingi flies, tiny flies.

guinep, small round fruit liked by children.

hopping dick, bird.

jancra, a vulture (shortened form of John Crow).

Jehovah-Jireh, Biblical name for Jehovah.

jippi-jappa, native straw hat, similar to the better-known "Panama".

John Canoe dancers, mummers at holiday parades.

john-to-whit, a singing-bird.

kitty-up, old-fashioned sailor slang for a bed.

kling-kling, a small bird.

ma raqui, a shrub of the Arawak Indians, who occupied the islands
   before discovery by Christopher Columbus in 1494.

mark-seven bullets, bullets used by British Colonial police in ·303
   rifles, so called because of the marking -7.

Maroon, descendant of Spanish slaves (Africans) who fled into the mountains when the English under Admiral Penn and General Venables captured the island from their Spanish masters in 1655. From the mountain fastnesses they harried the English for one hundred and fifty years. From time to time they were hunted by large expeditions, including bloodhounds, Spanish chasseur mercenaries, and Indians from the Mosquito Coast, Nicaragua, brought in by the English. A treaty signed by the Maroons and the English governor finally brought peace. In the treaty the Maroons were given a section in the hinterland where they lived and hunted and paid no taxes. They had their own court of law, and until this day the Maroon settlement is the nearest approach to autonomy inside the Colonial Empire. There is now, of course, the "Jamaica Experiment", a partial self-government that began in 1944, when this story ends, and which is the "New Day".

met, meeting.

met-pots, large pots used in cooking for gatherings.

nanka, yellow snake.

Number Eleven, species of mango, so named because it was in the eleventh crate in Captain Bligh's *Bounty*.

ochroe, okra.

oonoo, dialect for "you".

orange quits, small, orange-coloured birds.

osnaburg, coarse cloth.

pancheleons, timber trees.

pickney (or *picaninny*), child.

pitcharrie, a small, very active bird.

renta, a yam; a root used for food.

skellion, scallion.

solitaire, a bird.

soosumber, cucumber.

springe, bamboo trap for catching birds.

supple-jack, a riding-whip.

tengre, a lance taken from a whip-ray fish (electric eel).

trash hat, jippi-jappa.

tweet-to-whit, same as john-to-whit.

water boatmen, swamp insects.

wayah, expression of wonder or fear.
yacca, wood capable of a high polish and very tough.
yubba, poor species of sugar cane.

A NOTE ON JAMAICAN DIALECT

The dialect spoken in Jamaica derives in part from the English of an earlier day and in part from Welsh. It is characterised by repetitions of words and by the use of forms that have gone out of fashion in England and the United States.

Instead of "walking", the Jamaican will "a-walk". This form with the prefix "a-" survives in such common English words as "aflame", and "afloat". Another Jamaican usage is that of repetition for purposes of emphasis and rhythm. "Is remember I remember one August month when rain was a-drown the earth." Here the repetition of "remember" is for emphasis and for rhythm, both of which give the dialect its uniquely poetic character. Another example of an easily understood dialect usage is that of saying that two people "make four eyes" instead of saying that they look at each other. Most of the other native usages are as easily understood and as persuasive in their context.

ABOUT THE AUTHOR

Victor Stafford Reid was born in Kingston Jamaica in 1913 into the relatively well-to-do family of a businessman. He credited his mother, a skilled story-teller, as a major influence on his writing. He worked as a farm overseer, journalist, newspaper editor and later in his life held several government posts.

He travelled widely, but never left Jamaica for long. His first novel, *New Day* (1949) was a landmark in Caribbean writing for its use of a poetic modification of Jamaican nation language as the language of fiction, and its broad historical sweep announced the Jamaican people's urge to sweep away colonialism. His second novel, *The Leopard* (1958), written before Reid had in fact visited Africa, was a major artistic statement of the Anglophone Caribbean's belated involvement with Africa. He wrote one further historical novel, *The Jamaicans* (1979) and four novels for children, *Sixty-Five*, *The Young Warriors*, *Peter of Mount Ephraim* and *Nanny-Town*.

He was awarded the silver (1950) and gold (1976) Musgrave Medals, the Order of Jamaica (1980) and the Norman Manley Award for Excellence in Literature in 1981.

He died in 1987.